ANTONIUS
SECOND IN COMMAND

ANTONIUS

SECOND IN COMMAND

BROOK ALLEN

 Published by Dawg House Books through
Ingram Spark Publishing

For information regarding rights & permission,
contact Brook Allen: 1brook.allen@gmail.com

ISBN 978-1-7329585-2-4 (paperback)
Printed in the USA

In memory of my Rome-loving friend, Mary Dove,
who shared my author dream but
never got to see it unfold. This one's for you.

REPUBLICAN ROME

CIRCA 71-50BC

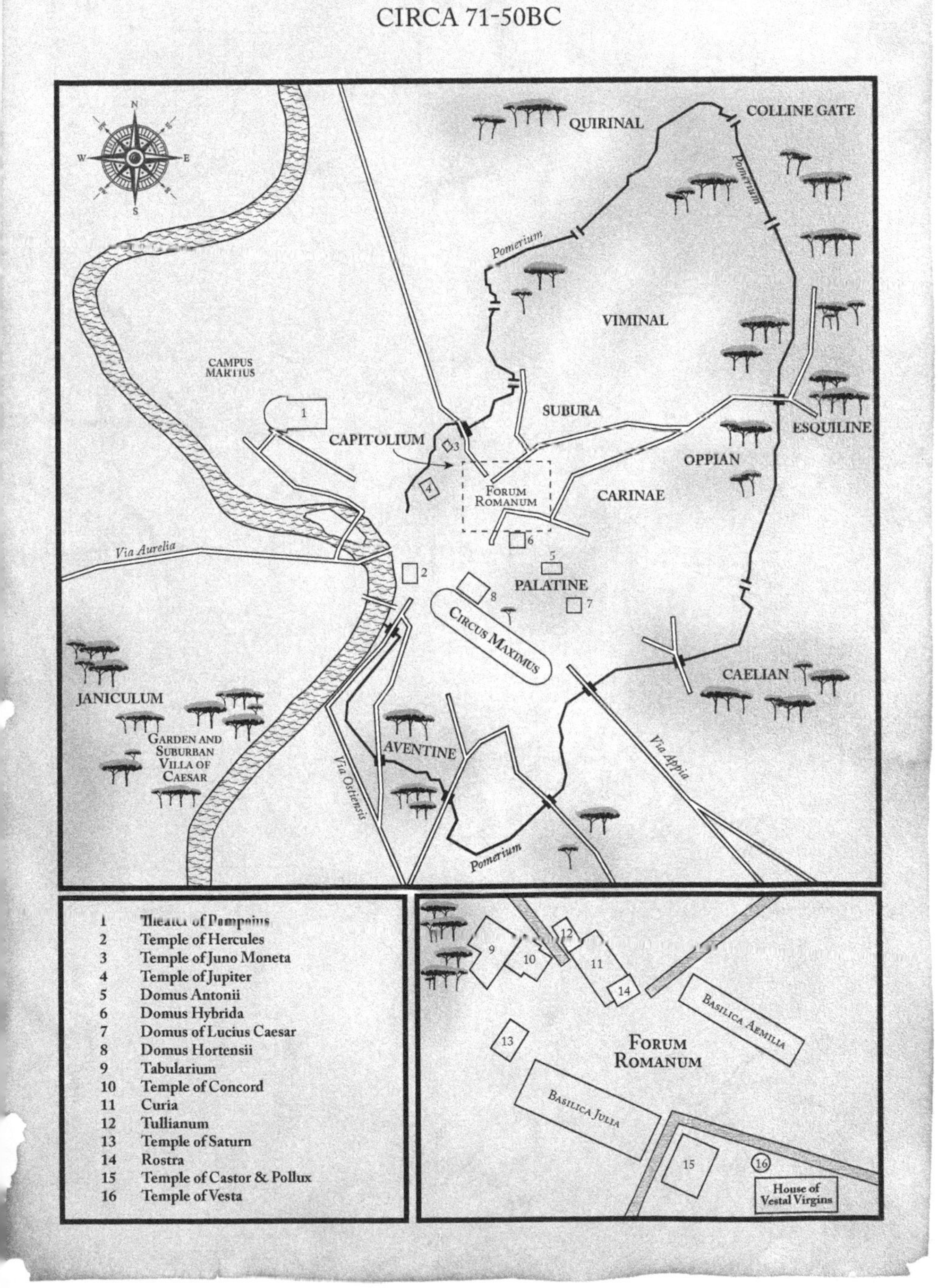

THE ROMAN WORLD
IN THE LATE REPUBLIC

BRITANNIA
PORTUS ITIUS
GALLIA COMATA
ALESIA
BIBRACTE
GALLIA CISALPINA
GERGOVIA
MASSILIA
NARBO
SPAIN
ILLYRICUM
ROME
MACEDONIA
PHILIPPI
NEAPOLIS
PHARSALUS
Pontus Euxinus
ASIA MINOR
ARMENIA
PHRAASPA
ATHENS
CORINTH
EPHESUS
METHONE
CARRHAE
PARTHIA
TARSUS
ANTIOCH
SYRIA
SICILIA
AFRICA
NUMIDIA
Mare Internum
CRETE
CYPRUS
JERUSALEM
ALEXANDRIA
PARAETONIUM
PELUSIUM
NABATAEA
EGYPT

1. Rome
2. Brundisium
3. Tarentum
4. Pompeii
5. Misenum
6. Baiae
7. Perusia
8. Arretium
9. Ariminum
10. Ravenna Classis
11. Bononia
12. Mutina
19. Dyrrachium
20. Apollonia
21. Actium
22. Leucas
23. Patrae

CHAPTER I

54 BC

MARCUS ANTONIUS WAS GOING TO BE A FATHER.

Such thrilling news jumbled his emotions as he walked through the pouring rain, chewing his lip distractedly.

A stray dog barked, chasing some geese and causing Marcus to detour, hopping over a puddle and then dodging a heaping pile of manure on the road. Tender scar tissue from a battle wound on his left calf constricted his quick movement, as it sometimes did. He grimaced, wiped water from his face, and kept moving.

Damned wound had taken forever to heal.

Outside Rome's walls, wagons sat idly in long queues along the Via Appia. Drenched drivers hunkered down under layered clothing, miserably awaiting sundown, when they'd finally gain entrance. Due to overcrowding, carts only had access at night. Several miles' worth sat in a stagnant line as far as the eye could see. Loaded with grain, amphorae, and reeking animal crates, their goods were piled precariously high.

Marcus kept to the footpath alongside the road as a string of chained slaves trudged by, barefoot in the mud. Packs of grubby-faced children scurried from the footpath and shimmied between stationary wagons. They lived among the tombs and lofty monuments lining the Via Appia. Whenever traffic was idle, they seized the opportunity to hawk cheap wine, sausages, and boiled eggs, but they were just as apt to steal. Considered pests by most, they were the progeny of lowborn prostitutes who sold themselves day and night along this stretch of the Via Appia.

Not much farther ahead was the Antonii tomb, where the urns of Marcus's father, grandfather, and other ancestors rested. He craned his neck around the traffic and adjusted the wineskin hanging from his shoulder.

A towering stand of pines separated the road from more monuments. He entered the woods and was promptly smacked in the face by two heavy branches, pelting him with more runoff. But now he was on a path he'd followed so often he could have walked it blind. Amid more tombs, it wound through a lovely grove where a modest stele marker stood.

He stopped stock-still, heart in his throat.

There it was.

Even after four years, each visit wrenched his heart. Tears were already stinging his eyes. Had she really been gone so long? It seemed only yesterday when he'd made love to her, kissing her and stroking her hair. Never had skin felt so soft, so supple—so *alive.*

Marcus stepped forward, reverently pulling his cloak over his head. His hand quivered slightly as he uncorked the wine.

He tilted the skin over the stele's offering holes, carefully pouring his libation. Emotion followed, as it always did. Tears he'd been holding back fell freely. Saturated and heavy, his hood slid off sideways, rain dripping down his face once more. His fingers skirted the rough edges of the stone, caressing it, wishing it were Fadia. He leaned forward until his forehead rested against its cold granite.

"I still love *you,*" he whispered to Fadia's shade. "I still miss you. Much has happened since I held you last. I'm to be a father. But it won't be the same. I wish it was *our* child growing up to bear your image or mine. I wish it with every breath."

Today was no different from other days spent at her stele. He'd pour his heart out to her and then leave feeling baffled and depressed. Four long years had passed. Marcus had remarried, which had been inevitable. Time moved on.

So why was he so miserable? Granted, it was rare when any man of his social status truly loved his wife. Yet many men still enjoyed themselves, making excellent husbands and fathers.

His wife and cousin, Antonia, was every bit as kind as Fadia had been. She was good to everyone with whom she came into contact, and her green eyes sparkled with love whenever he was near. Marcus recalled when he was little how Mother used to exclaim, "That Antonia! With her red hair and freckles, she looks like a Gallic chieftain's daughter."

Mother treasured her. She had even decided that, after all was said and done, Marcus had made a good match with Antonia. Household slaves adored her too. On their wedding day, they had taken extra time, festooning flower swags to make their new domina beam with shy smiles.

So why, oh why didn't Marcus *feel* anything for her? Whenever they were together, his heart was still as stone—not uncaring, but numb, as though it lay dead inside.

And poor Antonia. Ever timid, she lacked conversational skills. At a recent banquet, Marcus had been disappointed to discover she could barely answer their host's inquiries about her meal without turning as red as her hair. How would she act at dinners with distinguished political figures once he started realizing his ambitions? If she ventured into higher social circles, people might construe her as simple.

Marcus had confided this concern to his brother Gaius, who joked, "She's your spouse, not your best friend. Surely many men would be pleased to have a wife who rarely talks!"

Well, he did have a point there.

At least he'd done his duty by Antonia. She was pregnant and would hopefully produce an heir. Then Marcus would do what Roman husbands always did—take his desires elsewhere. But it was still a mess, for Antonia loved him. Marcus Antonius was many things, but he wasn't cruel. He was saddened that he'd never be able to return her sentiments.

Perhaps his heart was forever buried with Fadia, here—within her funerary stele. Fadia, the lovely slave he had freed and married, tragically killed because of his outrageous debt. He was as much at fault as the foul bastard who had brutally beaten her, bruising her innards, killing their baby, and finally, Fadia too.

That one truth haunted him more than any other mistake he'd ever made.

"My love," he whispered. "I'm still waiting to hear from Caesar. It's been over a month since I sent him Gabinius's recommendation from my service in Syria. You know how long I've wanted a position on his staff. Calpurnia thinks it will happen this time."

Marcus's mind overflowed with memories of Fadia touching his face, promising him that all would be well. But in reality, the only sound was more rain pelting down, replacing his tears. He had lost track of how long he had been there, embracing the sides of the stone monument. Memories of Fadia still consumed him.

One of his hands was asleep, and he felt the pricking of needles as he flexed his fingers. Slowly, Marcus raised his head from its granite cushion and stood up straight.

Yes, his heart was still here with the dead, but the rest of him had to return home to the living.

Gaius Julius Caesar, Proconsul Provinciae in Gallia Comata and General of the Northern Legions, to Commander Marcus Antonius in Rome:

Good health to you, Commander. I received an impressive commendation concerning your performance under Proconsul Aulus Gabinius. What an excellent referral. I'm most pleased that a kinsman of mine was decorated for valor on the field.

Obviously, Gabinius relied upon you greatly. This evidences your capabilities as a trustworthy officer.

As I write, I prepare to visit my winter camps. We continue ship-building for spring campaigns and a return to Britannia. Hopefully, the weather will permit more success there this year. Britons are aiding the Gauls, so they are also our enemies.

Please consider joining my staff as a legate. Should you accept, report personally to me at Portus Itius. Meanwhile, give warm regards to your mother and new wife.

After weeks of anticipation, planning, and charting his route north, Marcus stood in the atrium of the domus Antonii, saying his farewells to Mother and his brothers, Gaius, and Lucius.

"I still can't believe he signed you on as a *legate*!" Mother exclaimed. She'd been saying those same words ever since Caesar's life-altering message had arrived.

"My brother's a fine soldier, that's why," Gaius affirmed, next to Marcus. He clapped his brother hard on the shoulder.

Marcus grinned. He and Gaius had a special bond.

"But Marcus has never held office in the Senate," Mother reminded for the millionth time.

"That doesn't matter, Mother." This was from Lucius. "Whatever old Proconsul Gabinius said in that letter persuaded Caesar to give it to him anyway! He deserves it!"

"It'll matter to the conscript fathers," Mother insisted, still concerned. "You know how many senators declare Caesar's Gallic campaign to be illegal. They won't like him assigning such titles to staff members without senatorial consideration. Especially if the man in question hasn't even held office."

"Peace, Mother," Marcus intoned gently. "You worry far too

much." His words silenced her, and it didn't take any coaxing for her to walk into his arms.

Yes, Mother could be exasperating. She'd been raised by a traditional "Republican" father.

Marcus added, "Remember that Caesar can't always rely on the Senate. In Syria, I found out firsthand that it's often impossible for field commanders to consult superiors due to distance and time. Sometimes one must make decisions as best they can." He kissed the top of her head, then addressed his brothers. "Make her behave, won't you?"

They both laughed while she wriggled from his grasp and gave him a stern glare before kissing both his cheeks in farewell. "Be gentle when you give my cousin the news of Aurelia."

Caesar's mother had died shortly after Marcus's return from the East. She and Mother had been dear friends since he was a boy. "I've packed the scroll from Calpurnia on top of everything else in my bag. It will be the first thing he reads; I promise."

After trading good-byes with Gaius and Lucius, Marcus walked outside into the small courtyard. Antonia was waiting for him. Here they were alone, and words between them never flowed like wine.

She was silent, as usual, so he spoke first. "Watch over Mother for me. And see that Lucius stays away from pretty senators' daughters." That part came with a teasing smile. He winked at her and kissed her head gently. "And take care of yourself too. If you feel ill or anything, send for a physician. We want you strong and healthy for the birth."

She nodded, and he saw tears of emotion glisten in her eyes.

Antonia placed one hand protectively over her abdomen. "I'll take care of the baby. Just—please come home again and—"

"Shh," he said softly, reaching over embrace her. "What's this?" His coarse thumb brushed a tear from her cheek. "No more of these." She clung to him, and he indulged her for a moment. Finally, he whispered, "I really must go."

Like a coiled spring, Marcus swung on to his horse. The big, dark animal chomped at its bit, tossing its head impatiently. Eros, his slave boy, sat astride a pony in the street, followed by a mule cart loaded with armor, extra clothes, crates of correspondence for Caesar, and a few niceties from home. He twisted around, repositioning the saddlebags behind him.

Antonia took a step closer. Marcus saw her and raised his brows, gazing down at her. "What?"

"I'll sacrifice for you every day you're gone," she blurted. "I promise!"

He picked up the reins. "You're kind, Antonia. Mother always says so, and she's right."

"Gaul is a frightening place," she whispered, reaching up and putting a hand on his leg. It was the one with the scar on it, and she touched it lightly, knowing it often bothered him. "Don't risk yourself—come back." With that, she backed away, her face red and eyes wet.

Marcus didn't want a lecture, least of all from her. Still, she was right. Gaul was said to be a very dark place, especially now that it was engulfed in war. He had no clear picture at all of what he'd be riding into.

"I'll be careful." He clucked at his horse, leaving behind everything familiar.

CHAPTER II

MARCUS'S TRIP NORTH THROUGH CENTRAL GAUL WAS sheer misery.

Even before leaving Italia, harsh winds from upper elevations swept down to where his party traveled. Upon reaching Patavium, he purchased warmer garments for himself and his slaves. But farther north, freezing rain and snow pelted them mercilessly. Spring had not yet melted winter's frigid hold on the mountains. It was lonely, desolate, and unwelcoming.

Nor was Gallia Comata any traveler's paradise. The country was, at best, loosely occupied and insecure. Rarely was anybody found along the road except for starving villagers, forced to beg for food. They were wraith-like, materializing with thin hands outstretched in supplication. A sad lot, to be sure, but Marcus reminded himself that they were also the enemy. He and his men shied away from them, and the thought of these thin Gauls, hungry and begging, haunted his sleep at night. Were these not the same people who had sacked Rome three hundred years before? And Gallic warriors were known for their tenacity.

One afternoon a detachment of well-armed, mounted Gauls

galloped toward them at full tilt. Marcus braced himself. Their skillful riding shook him. Chances were scarce that he, Eros, and Morinus, the mule-drover, could fend off fourteen large, armed men. Luckily, the party was Aedui, a tribe known for its loyalty to Rome. To Marcus's relief, the warriors stopped and saluted, welcoming him to their land.

Twice, they encountered cohorts. The first defended heavy loads of grain and wool, heading for needy Roman encampments. Unfortunately, they were headed east. But the second was an infantry detachment, marching to Portus Itius. Relieved to join their numbers, Marcus relaxed somewhat. As he continued the journey with nearly five hundred armed men, he felt safer and allowed his mind to wander.

To earn honor, he needed a magistracy. That meant running for office—and winning. The very thought made him feel hopelessly inept. None of the Antonii had been hugely successful in politics since his grandfather, Antonius Orator. But Marcus pushed such thoughts out of his mind, for ahead loomed the fortified gates of Portus Itius on the northern coast of Gaul.

His horse trotted into camp at a brisk pace. Slate-gray skies hung suspended as cold, moist sea breezes blew off the channel. As his horse jogged through the camp's gates, mud sucked at its feet. The whole place smelled like fish. A single seagull hovered just above his head, drifting with the wind. It keened a bleak, haunting sound. When it attempted to land on a standard's outstretched eagle wing, the signifer on duty took a whack at it with his pilum.

Just ahead was Caesar's praetorium, center of Rome's legions in the untamed north. Marcus spurred his horse, cantering ahead of the others and spattering muck in all directions. Riding down the path designated as *cardo*, the north-south causeway through camp, he reined in before the command tent.

There was a flurry of activity. Legionaries scuttled about their business, several centurions exited the huge tent, and a large delegation of Gauls loitered outside. Under heavy guard, the natives were long-haired with beards and breeches. Their foreign tongues sounded guttural to Marcus's unaccustomed ear. He eyed them curiously, comparing their similarities to his memories of Vindelicus, a Germanic slave he'd once owned.

None were smiling, and their voices escalated. Something had angered them.

Away from the fuming natives, and protected from the rain under a pitched awning, sat a young man in legionary armor—a secretary of sorts. Effeminate and reedy, he hardly looked the sort to be toiling in a dank, soiled military camp. He rolled up some scrolls from where he sat at a small portable desk, safely dumping them into a thick wooden crate. Just in time too. A sheet of water poured off the praetorium tent as the wind kicked up. Hearing Marcus's approach, the fellow asked, "What may I do for you?"

Marcus shook excess water from his cloak. "I'm Marcus Antonius, newly arrived legate from Rome. Caesar expects me."

"Welcome, sir. I am Caesar's aide-de-camp, Mamurra of Formiae."

"Salve." Marcus gave him a curt nod.

"This way." Mamurra got up and lifted the tent flap.

Inside the praetorium, a consilium of officers was gathered. Marcus lingered in the back, dripping wet. A short, bullish man whose face resembled worn leather was speaking. His teeth were uneven, chipped and yellow. He'd probably been soldiering since exiting the womb.

"Just as you ordered, precision killing. Men surrounded him while still mounted. He'll trouble us no longer. It's the rest of the Aedui worrying me."

"Your thoughts on this, Atrius?" requested a quiet yet familiar and even-tempered voice hidden behind the other men.

"I do sense trouble, Caesar," answered another officer, leaning against a beam supporting the praetorium. "Dumnorix was well respected. His death will cause quite a stir. If the Aedui turn on us—"

"Listen to him, if you no longer give ear to me," the bullish one interrupted, his voice rising. "Dumnorix may have parted ways with us, but we can't afford losing the rest. If we do, we sit in a dangerous place even with you here. But with you away in Britannia—"

"*Enough*, Labienus." Caesar said, raising his voice in firm authority. "I hear your grievance. Dumnorix was a hotheaded fool, and his death will serve as a warning to the Aedui: behave or face dire consequences."

"If you would only *postpone* Britannia," Labienus pleaded. "Let's gain firmer footing here!"

Marcus cocked an eyebrow. Dissatisfaction among ranking officers was an ominous sign.

Atrius intervened with a gentler tone. "Caesar, remember the Aedui are our mainstay in this war. Labienus is justified in his concern. There are murmurings of unrest. It's said that—"

"Damn them to Dis Pater, all of them!" Labienus swore. "They'll rebel with you gone. We need all troops here where your real war is! I warn you, *do not leave*!"

Caesar arose suddenly from behind his desk, taller than the others, his face illuminated by lamplight. "There is no solid evidence that our present position is in danger."

Labienus and Atrius glanced at one another uncomfortably.

Caesar continued. "Your opinions are valued, and I'm aware of what a high cost it would be for our alliance with the Aedui to crumble. However, we maintain strongholds all over Gaul. Every tribe is dispersed, too contentious with one another to pose any real threat. Their disunity allows us to maintain an upper hand. Only if they join together could it cause real trouble."

"They may be awaiting your absence to do just that," Labienus suggested.

"Keep me informed, Labienus," Caesar said with a tight smile. "Remember, I'll only be across the channel, and you'll command here. We can return if need be, but I'll depart for Britannia as scheduled. Caesar *will* place his standard on that island's soil. Atrius, you're going with me. You've talent when it comes to ships. I need your help commanding the fleet."

Marcus still read dissatisfaction on Labienus's face.

Caesar addressed him again. "While I'm gone, reexamine spies within the Aedui, not to mention the Arverni, Bituriges, and Allobroges tribes. They all bear watching." Concluding the discussion, he spoke to everyone present, "You're all dismissed except for Labienus. I see someone I want him to meet." His cobalt-blue eyes met Marcus's.

The consilium ended, men conversing among themselves as they left. Some eyed Marcus, and he nodded at them amicably.

Emptied of men, Marcus took in Caesar's praetorium. Centered above a handsomely carved wooden desk inlaid with ivory, a shimmering banner hung, embroidered with a golden bull. It was the symbol of Caesar's legions. Rugs covered the ground. Worn and mud-caked from constant foot traffic, they still provided precious insulation from the cold. Twelve large, sturdy bronze lamps burned brightly on ornate stands. Caesar's central command space exuded an air of authority, privilege, and power.

"Antonius! What has it been? Five years? Welcome to Gaul." Caesar strode forth from his desk.

Marcus stepped up to meet him and they embraced, kissing each other in warm greeting.

"I want you to meet my bastion among the barbarians. This is Titus Labienus, second in command. Labienus, Antonius and I are cousins on his mother's side. He recently served in the East under Aulus Gabinius." He clapped Marcus on the back. "What an auspicious arrival. I didn't expect you until after I returned from Britannia, but now that you're here, I'll take you along."

Labienus offered Marcus his hand. "Salve, Antonius," he said tersely.

"I'm honored," Marcus returned.

"I wanted you two to meet. Antonius will hopefully become an integral part of our staff." With hardly a pause, he addressed Labienus directly. "Now before you go, one last thing. Allow the Aedui to bury Dumnorix according to custom. By doing so, it makes us appear pious, honoring him with a traditional burial. Tell your centurions to release the body to his men. No interference with their rituals unless violence erupts."

Labienus nodded. "Anything else, Caesar?"

"Not at present."

As Labienus exited the praetorium, Marcus remained silent, fingering the scroll canister on his belt, containing the news of Aurelia's death.

Caesar sighed. "He's hotheaded, but an expert at administering peace among so many different tribal groups. Just today a chieftain among our most influential allies, the Aedui, broke pact to foment rebellion. Labienus handled it nice and quiet. Blood spilled, but blood spilled cleanly—the way I like things done. With a little diplomacy and luck, I anticipate the Aedui to be deeply grieved at losing their chieftain but understanding of 'Caesar's circumstances.'" Caesar strolled over to a table laden with a red terra-cotta pitcher. "Wine?" he offered.

"Yes, gratias."

"You made excellent time." Caesar handed Marcus a full cup.

"I left as quickly as possible."

"How's married life? Are you settled into quiet domesticity now?"

Marcus took a sip of wine. "Marriage is duty, is it not?"

"I suppose. Helps when your wife is appealing. As I recall, Hybrida's daughter is pleasant and pleasing enough to the eye. Tell me, how did you find things in the East?"

Marcus snorted. "Rife with division, rebellion, and dissent. Too bad Alexander didn't achieve his dream of uniting all of those kingdoms. Somebody needs to tend to it."

Caesar cocked his head, gazing at Marcus thoughtfully. "True. And if it were a Roman, that unity could be joined to the west."

"Indeed," Marcus nodded. "Oh—and Ptolemy of Egypt is a nasty little piece of work."

"Yes. And I understand he was ready to line Gabinius's purse with more than just silk."

Marcus laughed. "Ten thousand talents worth! And only with

that creditor Rabirius's help in getting the Alexandrians to pay up. Right before I left Rome, Gabinius was recalled by the Senate. He'll be using every bronze piece he has, paying that creature Cicero for his trial. Our foray into Egypt wasn't exactly 'official.' And he never compensated me for it!"

Caesar nodded toward Marcus, shrewdly noting his armor. "Maybe not, but you must have had some financial gain. That cuirass is a masterpiece."

After swallowing more wine, Marcus patted his breastplate proudly. "From the house of Ptolemy. My efforts on the king's behalf were much appreciated."

"Such excellence in craftsmanship is rare." Caesar indicated a chair. "Please sit down."

As Marcus did so, the scroll canister he was carrying brushed his arm. Best to get it over with. "I'm afraid I bear unhappy news."

Caesar sipped his own wine, pausing and becoming grave. "Speak, then."

"Your mother—she has died."

The praetorium became still. Marcus watched Caesar solemnly, expecting grief. "This is from Calpurnia," he went on, offering his cousin the scroll. "It includes details. I have other correspondence addressed to you in my wagon, mostly political—letters from the Senate, colleagues of yours, that sort of thing. There are several crates' worth."

Caesar rubbed his chin idly, his brow furrowed. "Dead? She was so full of life when last I saw her."

Five years was a long time away from family. "If you'd like to be alone," Marcus offered, "I could meet with you tomorrow—"

"Did you see her?"

"Several weeks before, yes."

Caesar stared down at his cup. "Did she suffer?"

"Mother said she was tired—that she lived a full life and was prepared."

For a few moments, no words passed between them. Caesar nodded slowly, staring into his cup. In a flat, expressionless tone, he said, "Emotion—a luxury for which I've little time when there is much work to be done."

Marcus blinked in bewilderment, watching a metamorphosis take place, transfiguring Caesar's face into stony hardness.

Did he feel *nothing* for this loss? Marcus studied his cousin. Vainly combed forward, his hair was much thinner. Efforts at hiding encroaching baldness were less effective than before. He was like a marble bust before the artist chiseled character and human expression into the stone.

Caesar arose, placing his wine cup atop a table, and moved behind the big desk again. He sat, placing both hands on the chair arms in an air of authority, his tone turning imperious. "I have high expectations for my staff, Antonius. Firstly, we're never personal in this camp. You'll address me only as Caesar, and among legionaries, by my titles. Family you may be, but you must desist from calling me 'Cousin.' In public, we'll use every formality, showing discipline and decorum. And there's *no* public drunkenness allowed among my officers—no exceptions."

Marcus noted the extra stress he placed on that particular warning.

"Regarding women, there will be no whoring while on duty. When issuing orders, do so with one question in mind: What action would Caesar take? Failure to comply with orders or expectations will result in dismissal and humiliation. If you have slaves in camp, the same rules apply. For them, disobedience is punishable by death. I've no time for noncompliance from slaves, legionaries, or officers. During counsels of war within this tent, you're free to question my directives, as did Labienus. Feel at liberty to voice concerns about my strategies or objectives, but in so doing, offer feasible solutions to issues at hand. I'm used to disrespectful slurs and cadences from lowborn soldiers, but *never* question or insult my authority outside this tent in public. *Never.*"

Marcus sat stunned. Still clutching Calpurnia's letter in its cannister, he had expected Caesar to react like any other man upon receiving such tragic news. Gods, was he even human anymore?

"Mamurra will show you to a tent," Caesar said. "At dawn, return here with the shipment of correspondence you mentioned. At that time, you and I will sort through it. It's time you became familiar with the allies and enemies I have in the Senate. Such men are capable of hindering or aiding my successes. You'll accompany me to Britannia, but until then your assignments will be clerical. I urge you to emulate the rest of my staff. They're fine men. Most of them are older than you and highly experienced. Learn from them. That will be all. Rest until morning, and don't be late. Dismissed."

Within a week's time, Marcus was watching legionaries lower themselves from transports into the water to slog ashore. He stood with everyone else, still dripping from the beach landing when scouts returned with news of a Briton stronghold less than seven miles away.

Under cover of night, he followed Caesar as he led Legio VII to the site, ordering a ramp built to access the fortress. If they could take it, they'd have a defense that could serve as a base camp not too far from the ships. Built of soil and wood, it was indeed a daunting defense. Britons had deforested an entire hillside where it stood.

Marcus and Caesar sat astride their horses, listening to countless spades thudding against moist earth as legionaries began piling dirt. Once high enough to allow an easier entry, they'd mount the ramp and force their way in. Above them, one cohort maintained a canopy of shields locked in place—protection in case the Britons fired at them. But so far all was disconcertingly quiet, except for the digging and cursing of tired men.

Bored from doing nothing, Marcus dismounted and snatched a spare shovel from a supply cart. He hopped into the trench, relieving a soldier who had been toiling without letting up. Methodically hurling soil, his participation became encouragement to the others, who appreciated highborn Romans working like plebs.

After hours of digging, pitching dirt and hauling it from other locations under cover, Caesar ordered a fresh cohort onto the ramp, and the fort was easily breached. Most of the inhabitants had fled. Only a few elderly natives remained, either too feeble or ill to run away.

"They saw us land," Caesar muttered. "Ah, well. This will serve as our base camp for the rest of our forays deeper into the country."

Caesar ordered camp pitched and set squadrons of men to the task of felling surrounding trees to erect towers. Sentries stood on all perimeters as work commenced, everyone else stealing well-deserved rest in shifts.

Marcus sat outside his tent, finishing an evening meal, when Caesar rode up.

"Morale is good," he exclaimed, dismounting.

Marcus agreed. "Yes, and it'll improve more after everyone sleeps."

Caesar nodded. "I've a task for you at first light."

Marcus raised his eyebrows in curiosity.

"Take two cohorts of infantry, a detachment of cavalry, and see if you can find out where the people from this fort fled. If you locate them, find their leaders and take them hostage. I anticipate contact from one of their chieftains soon, and I'll need bargaining power."

"Good, I'm up for a game of chase." Marcus popped an olive into his mouth.

"I need success here, Antonius," Caesar remarked in a low voice. "Mamurra had a delicate time last year editing my commentaries. We must make an imprint here before leaving. Caesar must never allude to weakness."

"You're writing an account for the Senate, then?" Marcus queried.

"No, for the world. I will take Gaul, but I want recognition here in Britannia, if not their tribute too. Obviously, my enemies would prefer not to have it so."

Marcus snorted. "Who? Cicero?"

Caesar chuckled. "I swear you think Cicero is offspring of the Hydra! Let me assure you he has his uses. It's true that he and I make strange bedfellows, but Pompeius and Crassus are my greater concerns. Pompeius might be my son-in-law, but my trust in him is still limited. His marriage to my daughter Julia is the cement guaranteeing our alliance."

"At least you can keep your thumb on him that way."

"Ironically, it's a love match. My ancestress Venus blesses me. Otherwise I'd have less confidence in Pompeius than I do now."

"Who else worries you?"

"Crassus." Caesar sneered, "He desperately wanted the East, and when Gabinius was foolish enough to enter Egypt without the Senate's nod, he couldn't wait for his recall."

Marcus snorted. "He'll have his hands full in Syria. I know. I was there."

"That's only if he *stays* in Syria. His real ambition is conquering Parthia. He'll do anything he can to stir up that bee's nest just to have an excuse to attack."

"That probably wouldn't take much," Marcus said with a chuckle, stretching out his stiff, scarred leg. "Gabinius was always wary of them. He treated their dignitaries as though they were costly alabaster."

"Crassus won't do that. Oh, he'll make war with them, as surely as Britons paint themselves blue." He helped himself to a few pieces of dried fruit from a leather pouch Eros had left next to the fire. "I'll be watching how he fares," he said, chewing. "Much of my fortune rests in his victory or defeat."

The next morning, Marcus felt exhilarated, riding at the head of a column again. He was a legate on Caesar's staff; a position for which he'd dreamed. And Legio VII was a spirited force, disciplined and well-trained.

When they were only five miles or so out of camp, a lone rider galloped clear around the column. Marcus ordered a halt.

"Orders from Caesar, sir!" the courier called.

From Caesar? Already?

Opening the wax tablet, Marcus read the terse message in utter frustration:

Caesar to Antonius,
Return to camp immediately.

"Damn!" Marcus swore.

He studied the courier, a young, Romanized Gaul sporting a circular torque of gold around his neck. "Is this all?" he demanded. "Did he give you any details aside from this message?"

"That's all, sir." The Gaul's Latin was flawless.

Annoyed, Marcus called for his men to turn back and they returned to camp.

The place was in uproar. Men were everywhere. Some were loading carts; another unit was breaking down tents. Mamurra was manning his usual post in front of Caesar's praetorium. He stood, saluting crisply. Marcus completely ignored him, tossing back the tent flap and striding straight in.

Caesar was scribbling hurriedly on a wax tablet. "You made good time."

"What's happened?"

"Atrius wrote from where he awaits with the fleet. Last night, a storm stripped many of our ships from their moorings. Fortunately, Neptune sent some back to shore, but they're damaged. I must return there and see to repairs. They must be in ready condition if we need to make a hasty exit. I'll be gone for a week or so."

"What do you want me to do?"

"Command here." Caesar pressed his signet ring into wax on the tablet, handing it to a waiting legionary. "This message is going to Labienus across the channel. Upon its receipt, he's to send us any ships available. I'm taking skilled workers with me—about eight hundred men. They built a fortified camp here without incident, so now they'll be shipwrights. Hold our position until I get back. Those are your orders."

"And if we're attacked?"

Two slaves entered to lace Caesar into his cuirass. He arose, raising his arms for them. "Use good judgment. You're near the woods, not in them. Britons dislike pitched battle, from what I've seen, preferring skirmish warfare. I'd not be overly concerned."

Marcus caught his breath. Not overly concerned? Gods! He knew nothing about Britons! Caesar left within the hour, leaving him with most of Legio VII and the Gallic cavalry.

There was much to learn about these men. And first, he'd need to win them over.

CHAPTER III

MARCUS HAD ALWAYS HEARD THAT GAULS RESPECTED MEN who could hold a lot of wine. But above everything, they valued excellent horsemanship.

Few Romans ever took the art of riding seriously, so when horsemen from Caesar's Gallic cavalry saw Marcus ride, they stopped what they were doing and stared.

First, he joined them for daily exercises, taking part in mock charges and sparring drills. Training techniques and discipline he'd used in Syria with his cavalry had prepared him well for this challenge. He made daily excursions on horseback around camp, inviting Gallic cavalrymen to ride along. Actually German-born, not Gallic, they weren't used to an officer from Caesar's staff taking such detailed interest in their equestrian skills. Marcus went out of his way to make them aware of their value. He listened to their stories, laughed at their jokes, and even learned words and simple phrases in their dialects.

They called him "Antonius Roman-rider"—and did so respectfully.

One of the auxiliary officers was Bibrax, a tall, sinewy man who was half Gaul, half Germanic. Born in Germania among the Suebi people, he'd survived a tribal raid at the tender age of eight, and spent the rest of his youth in Gaul. Arrogant and coarse, he was a wealth of information, having accompanied Caesar on his first attempt at subduing Britannia.

Marcus liked his brassy boldness—it reminded him of himself.

"I've not seen many Britons yet. What are they like?" Marcus asked. "Caesar told me their skin's colored with some plant dye."

Bibrax nodded. "Yes, woad. But only in war. Many wear skins because they're not refined like Gauls. Their men wear no beards, only long mustaches."

Marcus smiled nostalgically. His old slave Vindelicus had worn similar facial hair.

On the fourth day after Caesar left, sentries saw movement in the woods around camp. At dawn on day five, a young tribune, Quintus Laberius Durus, awakened Marcus. Britons had been sighted on the forest's edge.

Marcus jogged alongside Durus in the dewy grass, panting up the wooden ladders inside a steep turret added to the original fortress gates. Once on top, he joined a cluster of legionaries pointing into the mist. Occasionally, a blue-stained body flitted amidst tall bushes.

Day six revealed even more activity. Now the visitors ventured within shooting distance, openly making their presence known. Marcus decided to keep peace. "Hold your fire," he ordered the tower's archers. "They don't appear hostile—at least not yet. Let them be nosy, but if they bare their teeth, they're done for."

On day seven, while Marcus judged two legionaries caught attacking an auxiliary Gaul over rations, Durus interrupted, whispering in his ear. "Sir, a delegation of Britons is at the gate."

Hastily postponing the tribunal, Marcus and Durus rushed up the tower again.

Outside the timber walls stood eight men and one woman. All were painted blue, dressed in earthen-colored woolen tunics and breeches adorned with skins—except for the woman. She wore a long sleeveless wool tunic, interwoven with greens and blues. Snugly at her waist was a red leather belt, and on her back, secure in its scabbard, hung a heavy long-sword. Marcus thought her surprisingly attractive in a barbaric sort of way, her dark hair braided into a single, thick plait. Large, expressive eyes peered from a blue-stained face, making her full lips appear rose-red.

"Let them in," Marcus ordered, clapping Durus on the back. "Have our men surround them, confiscate their weapons, and tell someone to serve up some tasty legionary porridge for our guests. Men are always happier to talk on full stomachs—women too, for that matter."

Soon, Marcus sat inside the praetorium, face to face with his nine "guests," noisily slurping from bowls under the supervision of Bibrax, Durus, and a handful of armed legionaries. The woman, as voracious an eater as the men, scooped up mush with her fingers, licking it off with her tongue.

Marcus made eye contact with Bibrax, motioning him over. "I want to question them. Can you translate?"

"I will try, sir. I heard the large one speaking some Treveri outside."

"Good. Start by asking why they're here."

Bibrax began an exchange and engaged the Briton a few more times before he turned to Marcus. "They want to know why we have returned. They know we war against Gaul, and they believe I'm a traitor since I serve you."

Marcus narrowed his eyes at his visitors. "Tell them you have our respect and friendship. Say you're a valued part of our legion. And remind them that Caesar knows they're aiding Gallic factions and that if they abet our enemies, they *are* our enemies."

Bibrax spoke the odd words again. It sounded like halting gibberish. Big Blond Hair's voice escalated, and he gesticulated with his hands. Bibrax turned back to Marcus with an explanation. "He says they never aided any Gauls and that you trespass on ancestral lands they mean to protect. They came to tell us that their chief orders us to leave."

Marcus shook his head, causing several of the guests to grumble loudly. Big Blond-Hair raised his hand to silence the others, awaiting Marcus's words.

"We will not leave," Marcus replied firmly. "Tell him who Caesar is and that he would like to know who his chief is, so they might speak together."

Once the translating ended, Bibrax reported, "He says because we have returned, their tribes have united. One high chief is now their leader. His name is Cassivellaunus."

"Cass-i-vell-au-nus," Marcus repeated, attempting correct pronunciation.

Tall, muscular Blond-Hair reacted to his attempt at pronunciation, raising his fist triumphantly and vocalizing with a throaty shout, "*Ah*-ha!"

Following his lead, the woman and other men nodded enthusiastically, getting up and shouting, "*Ah*-ha," and stamping their feet in vigorous approval.

It was hard not to smile at their antics. "Where does Cass-i-vell-au-nus live?"

Big Blond-Hair did more strange signals with both hands. At one point, the woman interrupted as though correcting him. Bibrax finally explained, "He is their high chief, so he is in his own lands, north of here."

"What did she say?" Marcus asked, nodding toward the female.

"She was speaking their own tongue, but I think she warned him not to say too much. They're probably afraid we'll head north in pursuit of him."

She was right about that. They had *very* good reason to be afraid. Still, the thought that the Briton tribes had united was sobering news.

Marcus decided to have a one-on-one chat with Big Blond-Hair later. If he plied him with enough posca, he was certain he could get the high chief's exact location—and only the gods knew what else.

Ten days after he'd left for the coast, Caesar returned. "Say that name again," he commanded.

"Cassivellaunus."

"He's their chieftain?"

"He's the high chief bringing unity to Britannia solely for making war on us."

"Understood. Where is he?"

"He remains in his own lands, a good way north across a river called the Tamesas. Blond-Hair said his company took six days arriving here on foot. I'd say the distance is near a hundred miles or more."

"Would this Blond-Hair be able to take us there?"

"Most likely."

"Where are the visitors now?"

"Hostages, Caesar. Treated well."

"Good." He nodded.

"How are things on the coast?" Marcus inquired, following his commander into the tent.

Caesar sighed, sitting down wearily behind a portable desk.

"Some ships were beyond repair. We probably lost forty. Labienus should have received my orders by now to send replacement vessels. Let's hope he does so quickly."

Marcus silently noted creases of concern on his commander's face.

Hoofbeats clattered outside and Caesar rose again, heading back to the entrance. "I brought Gaius Trebonius back with me. If the Britons engage us, I want him here."

Caesar had yet to see Marcus in action on the field. Naturally he wanted an experienced officer present, in case of trouble.

Moments later, Trebonius entered the praetorium. Tall and powerfully built, he had dark cropped hair and possessed a friendly face.

"Trebonius," Caesar called, "we have some good news. Antonius knows who we're fighting and discovered his approximate location. Tonight, we'll meet our hostages and afterward hold a consilium, discussing movement and route. Plan to depart in three days in search of Cassivellaunus."

Legio VII pressed well inland, through driving rains, damp nights, and dense fog. As they approached the Tamesas River, the forest became sparser and the landscape opened. Caesar kept them as close to the woods as possible, hesitant to expose his men. But they had to turn northeast—which meant more open terrain. There, trees grew in smaller clumps, punctuated only by areas of low thickets.

Marcus rode alongside Gaius Trebonius, with whom he now shared a tent. Trebonius had just commented on how wet the ground was when they heard legionaries on transports up ahead shouting and cursing. Supply carts and the heavily equipped war machines were stuck. Several centurions hurried back, warning that the ground was too soft and causing morale to fade.

Caesar himself galloped back to where they were upon hearing how his rear guard and cavalry were lagging behind. However, after dismounting and walking about on the spongy earth, he issued orders for the march to pause only until the wagons were freed. "We'll press onward as quickly as possible. Just up ahead there's firmer ground," he assured. "We'll be out of this in no time."

Marcus glanced about nervously as Trebonius ordered the cohort nearest them into a shield wall around the men frantically digging out wagons. These open plains raised everybody's hackles. Even the horses were nervous. Marcus's mount tensed its ears this way and that. If he were a Briton, this would be an ideal time for an attack. Every legionary was weighted down in a heavy marching pack. They'd have difficulty forming up and defending the rest of the column wearing their kits. It was unnerving, as he'd never considered how vulnerable they were while traveling.

He exchanged a troubled glance with Trebonius and sprang down from his horse, joining the legionaries who were digging and inserting long planks of wood in front of the cart wheels for better traction. Everyone felt the danger. It seemed to take forever to free those damned wheels!

Once they were rolling again, Marcus and Trebonius breathed a collective sigh of relief.

Then it happened.

Tribune Durus galloped up breathlessly. "Ambush!"

Marcus twisted around in his saddle.

At first, he saw nothing. Nor were there any battle sounds—swords clashing, screaming . . .

It took several moments for him to detect anything, and when he did the sound was only a distant rumbling off to his right. Pulled by stocky little ponies, a large cart-like chariot bounced swiftly into view. On it were at least ten Britons, if not more, balancing precariously and hanging on. Marcus had no time to count them since dozens of chariots materialized behind them, adding to the approaching grind of wheels churning over uneven earth. Following them came single riders, roaring and shrieking in their primitive tongue.

They crashed into Legio VII's rear. Just as Marcus had feared, legionaries there were rendered helpless in their kits, coupled with their armor. Several groups of Britons in chariots set upon them violently. It was horrifying seeing well-trained Roman soldiers fall with barely a fight, immobilized by their own equipment. In only a few blinks, the bastards would strike, then leap back into their chariot to retreat as more rolled in to replace them.

"Ride and inform Caesar!" Trebonius was ordering a nearby cavalryman. "Antonius and I will begin counteroffensives." Turning to Marcus, he barked, "Order the infantry to dig in and hold the column. I'll sweep the western side and rear. You take whatever's coming at us from the southeast."

Centurions along the line were already scrambling to shed excess gear and turn their shields outward to fend off incoming attacks.

Trebonius spurred hard toward the back cohort that was taking the worst hits at present. Marcus heard him shouting orders to men as he went.

"Form up!" Marcus called to the other cavalrymen.

For the first time in his field experience, he found himself acting more the part of a legate. Now his job was to survey, command, and win. But he didn't like it as much as he thought he would. Under Gabinius's command, he'd always been involved in combat. It simply wasn't in his nature to miss the intensity of a fight.

Britons were swarming everywhere. Single mounted warriors pressed close, their teeth yellowish under blue woad and bared like a dog's. Warriors literally sprang off their horses in their assault, then remounted before any Romans could effectively fight back.

Their chariot tactics were completely different from those used by the Egyptians Marcus had seen in the East. Briton chariots weren't light and made for speed, but built to haul and carry. Nor were their robust little horses sleek or long-legged like the animals of Arabic origin. They were bred with thick, muscular necks, and *damn*—they chewed up ground faster than a quadriga of Arabians at the races!

By now, Legio VII's rear ranks were panicking. Ambushers were fighting loosely in open areas while Roman defenders could only stand with their shields at the ready, awaiting another attack. They were completely on the defensive, and Marcus felt cold fear clench his heart. But jaw set, he wouldn't allow emotion to cloud his judgment.

"Forward!" he commanded, leading his cavalry in the direction of more incoming Britons. Hopefully, they'd intercept them before they reached the legion's beleaguered rear. As he cantered past a thicket, focusing on what was happening ahead of him, his horse shied at the sound of snapping branches. He could barely think before two Britons on foot erupted out of the dense green foliage.

Spooked and panicked, Marcus's horse squealed and feinted sideways, nearly pitching him into one of his enemy's arms.

Legs burning, he clamped his calves around his frightened animal to stay on. His right hand frantically grasped his horse's mane in an attempt to right himself. Simultaneously, his left arm pummeled his shield hard atop one of the Britons' heads, and the man's skull crunched. Still unsteady but recovering, he spurred his horse and looked back, breathing in relief when his other foe was taken from behind by another cavalryman.

Bibrax appeared adjacent to Marcus with a good fifty riders. The Gaul shook his arm in an obscene gesture toward the Britons.

"Bibrax," Marcus yelled breathlessly. "Go on and see how many you can take, but don't ride too far afield! They'll trap you!"

Bibrax responded by grinning arrogantly and shouting encouragement to his men.

Marcus cantered forward, scanning the field and chewing his lip. To the rear of the legion, Trebonius had the worst of it. Legio VII's southern flank was disintegrating. And there was still no sign of any reinforcements from Caesar.

Riding up a small hillock, Marcus stopped halfway, searching. Aha! There they were! At least two cohorts, if not three, were hastening to the legion's rear, toward the thick of Trebonius's battle. He nodded in satisfaction. Things would turn for the better now. Caesar was at work after all!

But looking back toward his own fight, his breath caught in his throat.

It was Durus, the young tribune. In what Marcus judged to be an attempt at maneuvering his men into a better position, Durus led them slightly away from the rest of the endangered rear column—forward with their shields in front. He was calling out something—Marcus wasn't sure what. Maybe he was shouting for more infantry to join in? Problem was the others either didn't hear or hadn't the nerve, and Durus led his men farther out than he probably intended. Now his contingent was separated from the rest.

From his vantage point on the hill, Marcus shook his head. Centurions closer to his own columns were keeping their men in defensive order to protect themselves and weren't budging. Incoming Britons were sure to separate Durus's unit from the rest of the legion.

Marcus looked up, hoping to signal Bibrax's horsemen to aid Durus's unit, but—*damn him*! He'd ridden his men out too far.

The Gaul was leading his cavalry toward another stand of thickets. It was perfect terrain for more ambushes. Still tight in formation, Bibrax's band was chasing a group of Britons who had turned in desperate retreat.

Marcus didn't like this. Not leading the men into the fight himself was making him crazy. He had to do something before Bibrax got half of the cavalry killed. With a harsh jerk, he wheeled his horse about, backtracking at full gallop until he located mounted tubicines. "Follow me and sound a cavalry retreat!" he cried.

Whirling his horse back again, he gave the animal its head as the instruments blasted behind him.

Listen to them, damn you! Listen before it's too late!

Ears ringing, he eyed the rise with anticipation and pulled up to watch. When the tubicines halted even with him, he ordered them to sound off again.

Bibrax's cavalry obeyed, turning in a furious retreat. And it was a good thing, for behind them was a sizeable group of Britons—three chariots worth and at least twelve riders.

Marcus chewed his lip.

Some of Bibrax's cavalry had become unhorsed and were running in panic. Not far away, Durus's infantry was preparing to face off with numerous Britons in a chariot.

He had to decide. Save Bibrax and his cavalrymen or Durus? He didn't have enough reserve riders for both.

Four more chariots bolted out of the trees behind Bibrax, and that made up Marcus's mind for him. He needed to save his largest number of men. In a heartbeat, he ordered the last of his cavalry toward Bibrax, furious at the Gaul for having risked so many lives. "Bring them back," he ordered, fury heating the command.

Marcus looked back toward Durus again. Well, since he *did* enjoy a good fight . . .

He spurred his horse hard, the animal bounding forward. Javelin raised high, Marcus aimed for the driver of the chariot racing toward Durus's men in front. What he'd do about more Britons rushing at Durus's unguarded rear, he had no idea. They were helplessly beyond the range of the legionary column now.

Marcus's javelin found its target, smacking into the chest of the Briton driving the incoming chariot. Back he fell, so hard that he knocked two men out of the conveyance before Durus's men successfully killed the others. Durus himself stumbled and fell, scrambling back to his feet in desperation.

One of his own men doomed him. The coward lost his nerve when he turned and saw more chariots coming up from behind. Instead of warning his unit to turn and stand firm, he bolted. Fear swept over the others as they all panicked. Out of formation they fled, scattering in all directions—easy prey for the Britons.

Durus alone stood his ground, and Marcus was just close enough to see fear and dismay on his face.

"Over here!" Marcus screamed, drawing his gladius and waving it wildly.

If Durus ran straight toward him, perhaps he could hold the enemy off long enough for the tribune to reach safety.

Durus saw him and charged his direction as though chased by evil spirits.

Then a lone Briton horseman cantered out to intersect him, laughing at Durus and taking his time.

Winded from running in full armor, Durus veered the other way, still keeping a good pace. However, the Briton was mounted and had the advantage. Now alongside his prey, the warrior raised his big broadsword, intentionally letting it fall clumsily and missing.

Britons who had paused to watch screamed with laughter at the scene, pointing.

Durus probably felt the whoosh of the weapon passing by his head, but still he ran on. Once more the Briton mocked him, all the while riding lazy circles around the ill-fated tribune. Durus was tiring now and ducked as the warrior thrust his sword about crazily. Unbalanced and dizzy from watching the Briton and fleeing for his life, Durus stumbled again.

And fell.

Marcus groaned aloud. The Briton warrior raised his sword again, but this time he slashed with deadly accuracy.

"Dis Pater," Marcus moaned, "He was a good soldier—"

Reopening his eyes, he saw the Briton leap down. When he arose, he lifted Durus's head, still strapped within its helmet, shaking it victoriously at his comrades.

At that very moment, Bibrax and his cavalry rode in safely along with the rest of Marcus's riders.

Some of Durus's exhausted legionaries returned to where Marcus sat astride his horse in sickened shock.

Bibrax exclaimed overzealously, "Let me pursue them, Antonius! Some are getting away!"

Marcus turned on him, enraged. "To the *rear*, Bibrax! That's the last time you *ever* disobey my orders!" Repulsed and furious, he gritted his teeth, leading everyone back to the safety of the legion.

This was *Bribrax's* fault! He'd sleep outside camp perimeters, eating nothing but barley mash for a month!

As Marcus trotted back to the column's formation, he had the satisfaction of seeing Caesar's reinforcing cohorts slicing through the last of the Britons. Still, the euphoric feeling of victory was missing now that Durus was dead.

"What did Caesar say about Durus?" Trebonius inquired, guiding his horse around a tree.

"He was sorry to have lost him," Marcus answered, following behind.

For a while they rode without talking. Both were exhausted. After yesterday's wild skirmish, in which Durus had died, Trebonius had joined Caesar to face more Britons in front of camp. Again, reserves had been needed before the enemy retreated.

Marcus missed that action. He was busy attending to Durus's funeral and cremation. It was a dismal, prolonged process, burning a man's remains and gathering the ashes to send to family. It wasn't the first time he'd held funeral rites for one of his men, but whenever it occurred, he dreaded it.

Today Caesar had sent Legio VII off foraging. Everyone was ready for some sort of embellishment to their simple diet. Soldier's porridge and beans were becoming tiresome. As the morning wore on, the men shot some pheasants and deer, and moments ago one of Marcus's cavalrymen had located a veritable mine of berries.

Trebonius moved on with his infantry, dismounting to lead his horse on foot. Marcus remained with his riders amid the berry bushes.

"These ones grow in Italia's north and in Gaul too," one of his men exclaimed.

"Sweet like nectar, they is!" his comrade replied in delight.

Marcus smiled, hopping down to try some for himself. They were blackberries—dark and bulbous. Sweet but full of tiny seeds that stuck in one's teeth. Aside from that drawback and the fact that they grew in sharp, thorny brambles, they tasted fabulous. When he looked up, two of the men nearest him had taken to filling their helmets with the little jewels.

"Use saddlebags, not your helmets," Marcus admonished, plopping two more into his mouth. Just as he offered one to his horse to sample, a bloodcurdling shriek sounded up ahead from the direction in which Trebonius had disappeared. Then came sounds of drawn swords, grunts, and the thud of shields being struck.

Since the action was so near, Marcus didn't need to gesture grandly to his men to mount up, only snapping his fingers to catch their attention. Everyone swiftly responded except for one luckless rider a stone's throw away, whose horse bolted at the screaming.

Marcus hissed at him, still trying to remain quiet. "Crawl through those brambles and find out what's happening." There was no way in Hades he'd lead his men beyond their present location unless he knew the situation.

The soldier had to fight his way through the thorns. It took so long Marcus nearly dismounted himself to go have a look. But presently the fellow returned, crawling back with a few trickles of blood on his cheek from the nasty burrs. "They're everywhere, sir! All over our infantry."

Marcus glanced about. It was probably these very brambles preventing the attacking Britons from coming their way. "What are they using? Chariots? Horse?"

"Sir, the Britons were all on foot."

This wouldn't be easy on horseback, as many trees as they'd have to contend with in this thick forest.

Marcus motioned his men to gather round.

"Leave your javelins. They'll be useless in such thick cover. We'll do better with just gladii. Use shields offensively. Let's go."

It wasn't much of a charge—more like an awkward foray at a jog, dodging branches and more thickets. But with all the shouting, banging, and pandemonium, the last thing the Britons were expecting was a host of horsemen descending upon them.

Small groups of infantrymen were huddled together all over the place behind their shields. Some crouched in what had been their column. Briton warriors, well-accustomed to forests, were hitting them hard.

Just as Marcus stabbed two in the back, one after another, he heard a cry off to his left. A lone Roman officer was fending off three warriors. Two had broadswords and the other a heavy axe. Once he turned his horse, Marcus gasped.

"Trebonius!"

Marcus spurred forward and aimed at the Britons' backs. As he neared them, the man with the axe whirled about to face him. Mad instinct took over, and Marcus launched himself out of his saddle, gladius bared and aiming to kill. The point caught the axe-wielding Briton deep in the throat, blood washing over Marcus's arm and torso. Trebonius managed to kill off one of his other two assailants, and Marcus stabbed the other straight through the back before he could even turn around.

Mars, it was a good thing he'd ordered his men to use gladii. He hadn't fought in such tight space since he'd killed Fadia's murderers years ago—and this was tighter still.

Winded, Trebonius shook his head, reaching out with a blood-smeared hand to grasp Marcus on the shoulder. "Antonius, *never* have I been as happy to see you!"

Marcus grinned and nodded, but he was still on his guard, immediately turning about to confirm they were out of danger. Trebonius was visibly shaken, and for a time the two men stood back-to-back, listening as the Britons gave up their attack and ran.

"You saved my life," Trebonius whispered huskily. "And my men . . . I thought we were done for—I really did."

"Well, I think we're finished foraging." Marcus snorted with a grim smile. "Let's get back to camp. You've had one shitty day."

"Why in Hades does he want this land anyway?" Trebonius grumbled, tossing the tent flap aside as they entered. "Everybody's all painted blue, it rains too much, and it's freezing cold at night. Here we are, and it's late spring. I can't even imagine winter."

Marcus sighed. "I'd like to imagine getting good and drunk right now."

Trebonius grunted in agreement, collapsing atop his cot.

Marcus followed suit. He hadn't slept well last night. All he saw again and again was an endless replay of Durus falling down and that bastard of a Briton lifting his severed head by the plume of his helmet. And once he had fallen asleep, he wished he hadn't. Ever since boyhood, he'd suffered nightmares after witnessing horrors from the Spartacan Revolt. Whenever he was worried or bothered by something, they visited with a vengeance.

Last night's dream had been especially disturbing. In it, he and Trebonius were arguing someplace. Then he ran into what he assumed to be Caesar's praetorium, only it wasn't the praetorium at all, but an extremely large chamber with ornate mosaic floors. There, he found Caesar sprawled on the ground, blood everywhere.

Well, bad dreams aside, at least Gaius Trebonius was excellent company. The two had become inseparable. Today's incident was testimony to the risks Marcus took to protect a fellow soldier—a man with whom he slept, drank, and joked.

Closer to Caesar's age, Trebonius stayed active and loved physical training, games, and swordplay. He had excellent rapport with legionaries, and his relaxed manner reminded Marcus of Lentulus, his stepfather, whom Cicero had executed without a trial.

Trebonius interrupted his thoughts. "Well, thanks to your cavalry today, Caesar thinks Cassivelaunus's men have given up their pursuit."

"We can hope."

"And he'll probably award you a corona civica for saving my life and those of my men."

Marcus joked, "Damn—another corona? I'd rather have a night with one of those raven-haired Briton women."

Trebonius cocked an eyebrow and chuckled, reaching over to pour both of them some posca. "What would the infamous, woman-loving Antonius know about them, hmm?"

Marcus grinned, rolling over onto his back. "Before leaving Rome, my brother Lucius said I'd have to 'put out my fires in hairy women.' I have to give him a fair report when I return, no?"

Trebonius laughed heartily, holding out a cup for Marcus. Then he quieted and shook his head. "Listen, Antonius. For once, I'm giving it to you straight—all joking aside. You're an incredible soldier, having proven yourself to all of us in the last few days. But when will you start working your way up the political ladder?

Caesar made you a legate, but he had no business doing so. You've never held office."

Marcus raised his head, eyeing Trebonius somewhat defensively. "I know what's expected of me."

Trebonius propped himself on an elbow, incredulous. "Don't you *want* to serve in the Senate?"

To truly return dignitas and imperium to the Antonii, Marcus knew the Senate was his fate. Mother, Antonia, and every other person in the family expected it of him. He'd sworn to achieve greatness when father died, and if he didn't he'd shame everyone—especially himself. Then life would be meaningless, as it was when Fadia died.

Well, if his expected child with Antonia survived, he wouldn't have it living in a shadow of indignity because of him. He would *not* be his father.

"I'll admit my life has lacked direction. Father losing face with the Senate, Uncle Hybrida in exile, my stepfather plotting against the state. Truth is, I despise the Senate. I have no respect for them."

"Your grandfather served dutifully. He was a great man. The *Senate* didn't kill him—Marius did. Orator was a man the people loved and respected. Follow in his steps."

"Pah! He's *forgotten*. The Republic is dead. Maybe it died when he did."

"Dead, you say?" Trebonius responded. "What if men restored it? Men like us."

Marcus scoffed, "Oh, now you sound like Cato—or worse—*Cicero*!"

"So what if I do? More than any other men alive, Cicero and Cato *want* what's best for Rome."

"You really believe that? I say not. Cicero's no different than any other influential man holding power in our nation. He wants his personal influence as the set precedent for every law and edict passed in the Senate. What did he start calling himself after executing my stepfather without a trial? Pater Patriae—Father of the Country!"

They both fell silent until Marcus finally answered Trebonius's question. "If you must know, I'm unsure I'd be as capable in the Senate as I am on the battlefield. I harbor that fear because of men in my family who have tried and failed."

Trebonius gave him a dark look. "That's open and candid of you, but refrain from advertising *that* to just anyone." He sighed, lying back on his cot. "The Senate can be dark as a battlefield sometimes. It's unwise allowing your enemies to know your weaknesses."

Marcus smiled and lay back down. "Then I needn't worry, Trebonius. We're friends."

"Yes, and you'll learn there are different types of friendships. Caesar and Pompeius embrace one another now, but only because of Julia Caesaris. I tell you, that girl is Rome's only peace. My guess is that you'll be wearing a toga again before the year is out. I can tell you have ambition, but you'd do well to remember that men with long lives never let their guards down—friendship or not."

Marcus frowned. Trebonius was right, of course. He must enter the Senate. He had to. Still, it was easier on the battlefield; things were so distinct. One simply had enemies and allies. It was becoming plain that political alliances would be ambiguous at best.

CHAPTER IV

JULIA ANTONIA TO HER SON MARCUS ANTONIUS, Legate with the Northern Legions in Gallia Comata:

I pray Fortuna has favored you. Part of me bursts with pride, imagining you at the head of a legion, but the mother in me merely prays for your safety.

First, I must share tragic news. Caesar is probably grieving as you read this. Julia Caesaris died in childbirth. She suffered dreadfully, dying as her mother did, bringing a child into the world. Only this poor babe did not survive.

Her funeral was the largest ever bestowed upon a woman in our history. Pompeius led the procession himself and is a broken man. He truly loved her. Poor Antonia was overwhelmed with grief too. She and Julia had formed a steadfast friendship since they were both to be mothers. Now Antonia fears her own labor. Marcus—she is terrified. I keep assuring her that she's of strong Antonii constitution and that all will be well.

Rome has been in a frenzy of exhilaration over the Britannia campaign. Your brothers long to hear tales of that land, for now they're talking of military careers for themselves. Gaius, who is as ill-at-ease with a gladius as your father was, now exercises at the baths. Lucius also trains, but with hired gladiators. This house will be desolate once all my sons are gone soldiering.

But in my heart, I know you, Marcus, are different than they. I believe your career will be illustrious and colorful. You've a talent for trouble, to be sure, but you also have a unique capacity for getting yourself out of it. How I miss you, yet I know you are where you must be.

Now for more news. Aulus Gabinius faces exile and an exorbitant fine. Ten thousand talents! It's the Senate's joke on him, ordering him to pay the same extravagant sum he expected of Ptolemy. I shall probably hear you laughing all the way from Gaul!

Lastly, Marcus Crassus has crossed the Euphrates, arriving in Parthia. Now Rome has campaigns in both East and West.

I sacrifice daily for your safety. Bring honor to those you love.

By late September, Legio VII had returned to Portus Itius. Marcus had to ask himself what Caesar had really accomplished in this second attempt to subdue Britannia. He was finding that his cousin wasn't always an easy man to understand.

While all five legions were ferried back to the mainland on limited numbers of ships in overcrowded conditions, Marcus found Caesar more concerned about whether Marcus Licinius Crassus would set foot in fabled Babylon. And Marcus knew firsthand that his cousin had worked hard ever since returning from Britannia to fend off derogatory letters from the Senate. Oh, Caesar worked extremely hard to assure that his weaknesses were never apparent. Yet what did he really have to prove any success with the Britons?

He certainly didn't have Cassivellaunus. The wily chieftain never even showed himself, instead sending envoys to negotiate. Due to the late season, Caesar had no choice but to propose acceptable terms in their lord's absence.

All Rome really gained from Britannia were a handful of hostages in Caesar's possession and a promise of tribute. And just how much wealth Britannia would really fork out remained questionable. Marcus doubted whether they'd even comply to the monetary demands. How would Caesar be able to enforce it while war still raged in Gallia Comata?

As autumn progressed, it proved to be a traumatic time for the Romans in Gaul. War had prevented the native Gallic people from cultivating successful harvests these past years, so food for legionaries was transported in—enough for tens of thousands of hungry men. Everyone remained on strict rations all winter, including officers. Stores had to be available in case of emergencies or in the terrible event a supply route was cut off. And after returning from Britannia, there was a constant struggle to keep that from happening.

To prepare for winter quartering, Caesar shifted his staff around. Trebonius took three legions into the troublesome Belgic territories. Young Marcus Crassus had been commanding there but left to serve with his father in Parthia. Caesar hated losing him. Besides, up until now, his presence had insured his father's loyalty. With him gone, a fresh rivalry with Marcus Licinius Crassus the elder would surely reopen. And the same could be said of Pompeius, now that Julia Caesaris was dead.

Cicero's younger brother, Quintus Tullius Cicero, took one legion into the Nervii lands. Two well-seasoned officers, Sabinus and Cotta, went to the Eburones with a detachment of some five cohorts, leaving Labienus with one legion among the Remi, neighbors of the troublesome Treveri.

Then came the disasters.

Problems began when Sabinus and Cotta devastatingly lost their entire force during a horrific attack. Germanic tribes allied with the Gauls, wasting their camp. Only a few stragglers escaped south to Labienus, living to tell the tale. Both Sabinus and Cotta died fighting while the rest of their men locked themselves inside camp, committing suicide together.

Shortly thereafter came a second setback.

Quintus Cicero's camp fell under siege until Caesar himself rode to the rescue, communicating with the younger Cicero through encoded letters in Greek. The end result was that the siege was broken.

To his chagrin, Caesar confined Marcus to clerical duties instead of taking him along to support Quintus Cicero. It was frustrating seeing his colleagues leaving to take influential posts and not getting one himself. Certainly, his performance in Britannia had been worthy enough to earn more than secretarial duties and counting cattle for quartermasters.

Once Caesar returned from rescuing Quintus Cicero, he summoned Marcus to his praetorium. As he paced toward Caesar's quarters, the first harsh weather of winter in central Gallia Comata wrapped its icy fingers around his feet—still bare in his military boots. He could see his own breath in the frigid air. Upon opening the tent flap, the chill accompanied him inside. A slave was stoking hot coals in a large brazier. Caesar had already gravitated toward the warmth, his hands over the red coals.

"You sent for me, Caesar?"

"Thaw yourself out and then be seated," Caesar said.

Once he'd warmed his blood, Marcus pulled up a folding chair, seating himself.

Caesar strode back to his desk, picked up a scroll, and tapped it against his palm. "Antonius, you're a gifted soldier and an excellent example to men serving under me. I've seen you pull more than your weight in responsibilities. Every Gallic horseman and Roman legionary looks at you with love and admiration in his eyes. However, you've absolutely no political experience whatsoever. I generously granted you the position of legate; therefore you must enter public life."

Marcus set his jaw. This was it. He'd be stepping into politics.

"What do you suggest?" he asked.

"I *suggest* you stand for quaestor," Caesar replied curtly. "It's time you enter the Senate, returning dignitas to your family. Whenever I look at you, I see a well-bred horse possessing speed, yet unbroken, unable to run a race effectively."

Marcus chewed his lip. "I long to serve, but I feel my talents are more on the field and—"

"You're *Roman*!" Caesar exclaimed loudly. "You must learn to master and command the Senate as well as the battlefield. They've accused me of starting an illegal war. I need men I can trust speaking for me in Rome and garnering support. I must have reliable reports keeping me abreast of current squabbles among my colleagues. You're truly one of the finest men I have. So I'll assist you in this endeavor, and you will succeed."

Marcus shifted uneasily—and damn, Caesar saw his discomfiture and probed deeper.

"Have you no desire to speak for your people in the Curia? Are you not eager to stand for my policies and decision-making in a public arena? *Join* me and take your stand as a Popularis. Be *for* the people! It's a powerful feeling, having plebs at your back."

Marcus was exasperated. "It's just that my talents are *military*. In a toga, I'll stand out like an ass-drawn chariot at the Circus!"

Caesar grinned, enjoying the analogy. "Nonsense! You're completely untried, that's all. I should think you'd have great interest in returning home. Aren't you about to become a father?"

"Yes," Marcus affirmed quietly.

Caesar paused, picked up a cup of wine on his desk, and took a deep swallow. He still never revealed personal feelings. He was as unreadable as a rock. This time, however, grief briefly shadowed his face, and he set his jaw. Losing both mother and daughter within a year's span had to be inexpressibly painful. Still, he never spoke of it—not to anyone.

"It's settled, then. You're going home." Caesar heaved a sigh, clapping his hands together and sitting down behind his desk. "What a relief it'll be having someone trustworthy enough to represent me. Word is the city's up in arms due to Publius Clodius. He's been causing violence and riots."

Marcus laughed at that. "Sounds like Clodius."

Caesar snorted. "I could forgive him his indiscretions with Pompeia years ago, as she was such an unworthy wife. However, he hardly deserves my help if he's forcing policies upon the Senate by implementing riots. Under my influence, the city must be kept at peace, however distant I may be."

"So while running for office, you'll want me to convince Clodius to use gentler means and make sure the plebs know you're the one sanctioning it?" Marcus assumed.

"Yes," Caesar nodded, smiling. "And I've asked someone with notoriety to familiarize you with senatorial protocol and introduce you to every man of influence in the city. He'll assist in your campaign and mentor you, being a support in the upcoming election. By Jupiter, Marcus Antonius! You'll slip into the office of quaestor as easily as my wife slides into her sandals." Caesar brandished the scroll with which he'd been toying. "Couriers brought me my man's reply from Rome today. Would you like to hear it?"

Assured guidance from a prominent senator? Marcus widened his eyes, intrigued and cautiously hopeful. "Certainly."

Caesar unrolled the document, reading aloud:

> *"You have my word, Caesar. I shall indeed speak to the Senate on behalf of your quaestorial candidate, Marcus Antonius. I shall look forward to meeting him again. Tell him he must call upon me after arriving*

in Rome so that I may brief him on the expectations of this office."

Marcus edged forward in his chair. It sounded like a choice opportunity, but who was this mystery senator? "Who is this 'kind patron'?" he asked in a low voice.

Caesar inhaled sharply. "You know him. He's a great Roman," he replied smugly.

"So—tell me his name."

"His name is Marcus Tullius Cicero!" Caesar crowed, eyes twinkling.

Marcus's jaw dropped. He looked to the side, speechless. His stomach heaved as though he'd just swallowed poison.

No. *No!*

Reaching up, he rubbed the space between his eyes, shaking his head. "I cannot—I *will* not do this."

"This isn't an option, Antonius, it's an *order*!" Caesar roared, slowly rising to his feet, his face like stone.

Marcus stood up too, raising his voice, "You *know* this man is my *enemy*! You were there the day he killed Lentulus without a trial. It nearly destroyed my family!" One of his fists clenched of its own volition and his voice broke with indignation.

Caesar's eyes narrowed, and he lowered his voice. "Let me tell you something. Pompeius and Crassus are *both* my enemies, and yet we've governed together now for years, peacefully. Do you think for one moment I loved Pompeius as a son because he married my daughter—may she dwell with the gods?"

"Caesar, there are some things I simply will not compromise—"

"Oh, *but you will*!" Caesar slammed the scroll onto the desk, causing a neat stack of correspondence to topple haphazardly to the ground. "You'll consider your career, putting it first, instead of holding grudges against Cicero with your long list of grievances. For when serving on my staff, you must realize how this temporary arrangement supports my cause. Nothing changes. Cicero's still your enemy. However, in this game of high stakes, policies, and conquests, Antonius, you keep your *true* goals hidden. You scratch one man's back in this world so he'll someday scratch yours, keeping your gladius keen and deadly should events require you use *it* instead of your fingernails! Cicero will be courteous, kind, and at your service. And in turn, you'll treat him courteously, kindly, and be at his. Set aside personal hatred long enough to enter public life and represent Caesar and his policies. *Dismissed!*"

Marcus ground his teeth, trembling with pent-up rage, his breathing ragged. This would be the toughest mission he'd ever faced, and it wouldn't even be on a battlefield.

CHAPTER V

53-52 BC

SPRING CAME EARLY UPON MARCUS'S RETURN TO ROME. However, there were too few days to lounge in the warm green gardens with his new daughter or visit lively taverns to catch up with his brothers. Today he was meeting Cicero—*again*—inside the Curia like an obedient dog. Granted, there was much to learn about senatorial deliberations, but sometimes Marcus wondered whether he was nothing more than a compliant servant instead of a legate.

Outside the Curia, in the crowded Forum Romanum, he pushed his way past public slaves distributing grain to the plebs. A man he hadn't seen in nearly a decade was leaning against the column of a nearby tavern.

"Clodius!"

"Ho!" Clodius gasped upon seeing Marcus. "You don't even look like the same person! And I heard you're entering politics!"

Marcus laughed, "Yes, standing for quaestor. You'll vote for me, won't you? If elected, I've heard the old-fashioned lottery they use to determine where I'll serve is now fixed."

Clodius nodded. "It's true. That's the state of our Republic. And if Caesar has anything to do with it, you'll be serving him in Gallia Comata, no questions asked. Everything's fixed these days . . . "

As Clodius's voice faded, there was a momentary awkwardness between them. They'd never been exceptionally close. Too many things in Marcus's youth had prevented that, but still—they'd always gravitated within similar social circles.

Years before, Clodius had championed Cicero's abuse of power in condemning Lentulus. At the time, Marcus thought it had permanently ended their friendship. However, Clodius himself had stepped forward to see justice served on that account. Upon running for tribune of the plebs, he had promised to take Cicero to task for overstepping legal boundaries. He'd passed a law in the Senate making it illegal for any man to sentence a citizen without trial. Because of Lentulus's death, it led to Cicero's exile.

That had been a joyous day for the domus Antonii.

Marcus owed Clodius a word of gratitude for that and clasped his hand. "Let me express my thanks that no other man will ever suffer what my stepfather went through."

Clodius pursed his lips and sighed. "Unfortunately, Cicero's exile didn't last nearly long enough. Barely a year—"

"I know," Marcus agreed, moving in closer to speak confidentially in Clodius's ear. "Why was he pardoned so soon?"

"That was Pompeius Magnus. He allied himself with my enemy, Titus Annius Milo. It made me so angry that at one point my constituents and I trapped old Magnus inside his domus for weeks on end. Ever since then, we've had serious clashes between our partisans."

"Your gladiators and thugs, you mean?" Marcus stated bluntly. He'd heard a bit about this and glanced around warily, wondering how many of Clodius's gang members were about.

Clodius grunted. "Politics isn't for the faint of heart, Antonius," he snapped. "You might be a soldier, but I tell you"—he pointed toward the Curia building— "there are battles in there that are bloody enough to scar men for life."

So Trebonius had said.

"So what happened? How did Cicero manage to wheedle his way back to Rome?" With a shrug of admission, Clodius answered, "Pompeius and Milo outmaneuvered me. After I reinstated the collegia, I thought all of those guildsmen would follow *me.* They should have. It was *my* agenda that provided more political clout for them—stonemasons, millers, fullers, and other workers of this city. That was when I found out Milo was out for my blood. Before I knew it, he and Pompeius had paid off some of the guilds, turning them against me. He's done everything he can to ruin me, prosecute me, destroy my dignitas—"

"I'm sure you know Cicero doesn't like your riots," Marcus whispered in warning. "He despises the use of gangs."

"Pah!" Clodius exploded, his voice escalating. "You think I give a shit about what that old weasel thinks? As though he really *cares* for the people! What he should really care about is how Pompeius *pays* Milo to incite riots for him. At least when I do it my motives are pure. I use my own men and do the dirty work of it myself."

"How noble of you," Marcus snorted.

"You know I kissed Cicero's cowardly ass once, when he executed Lentulus. That was my mistake, Antonius. I'll not make it again."

Marcus noticed several senatorial types glancing their way, eyebrows raised at Clodius's escalating tone. It was incredible how politics could turn about and change. "Shh. Calm yourself," he said under his breath. "People are staring. Look, you need to know something. There's someone else who doesn't like all your violence. Cicero's been writing to Caesar in Gallia Comata. Now Caesar likes you, Clodius. He agrees with your agenda and all you've done. But you know how Chickpea can twist words and change minds. Caesar's human and may start heeding him. Remember that. I'd hate to see your heavy-handedness be your downfall. That's all."

Lictors in front of the Curia loudly pounded the ends of their fasces onto the pavement, calling mingling senators into the building. Sessions would soon begin.

"I need to go," Clodius muttered.

"So do I. But take care," Marcus counseled.

As he watched Clodius move away, toward the steps leading to the Curia, he shook his head. Every single senator stood amid bunches of gladiators or tough-looking slaves, hired as bodyguards.

Street fighting between Clodius's and Milo's factions flared up unexpectedly and often, both day and night. Highborn politicians had all resorted to hiring bodyguards. Top senators of Cicero's ilk hired them by the dozen. One or two no longer sufficed. It took entire escorts of twenty or more armed men to ensure Chickpea's safety. Rome was languishing in suspended pandemonium.

Marcus took to wearing his gladius everywhere, concealed under the sinuses of his toga, tradition be damned. Selling four slaves he'd acquired from Britannia, he took Lucius's advice, hiring gladiators to guard the domus. First and foremost, he wanted his family safe. Now an imposing bastion of armed, muscular men were posted around the domus Antonii.

Truly, nobody served Rome, but rather themselves and their factions, pure and simple.

"Come, little girl. Come to Tata," Marcus coaxed playfully.

With wide eyes fastened to his, baby Tonia crawled forward, pushing up on wobbly arms and driving her chubby legs beneath her. Once she struggled half the distance, he swept her up, rolling onto his back laughing, buzzing her fat baby cheeks with his lips. She dangled above him, offering gurgles and giggles and smiling toothlessly, bare legs paddling. She was a joyful little thing. Marcus relished every moment spent in her presence.

Someone else, however, brought him no happiness whatsoever.

Cicero.

Their relationship was purely artificial and temporary. On one side was Pompeius and Milo, of the Optimate party. On the other was Caesar's preferred faction: the Populares. And of all the Populares, Clodius was the most zealous member.

And Cicero? Oh, Chickpea was Rome's most famous moderate, playing both sides. Marcus despised that too, and hated nothing more than having to lower his own standard to "study" senatorial politics under this man whom he reviled above all others.

For now, he juggled meetings with Cicero on one day and Clodius the next. Ill at ease in this game, only one pleasing element remained.

Sweet Tonia.

Lowering her onto his chest, he kept his hands about her, closing his eyes and relaxing in the warm sun.

Presently, a shadow disturbed his peace. "Dominus, you have a visitor."

"Who?"

Iophon, one of the family's most trusted slaves, leaned in closer, his voice dropping to a sobering whisper. "Marcus Tullius Cicero."

Marcus's eyes snapped open. "Here?"

"Yes, Dominus."

Cicero hadn't set foot inside the domus Antonii since Lentulus was arrested, years ago. *Damn.* So much for an enjoyable morning.

Owning gifts of oratory and political cleverness, Marcus Tullius Cicero was a prolific writer, ever enjoying the company of learned men. Like Caesar, he possessed foresight, but he sometimes lacked resolve. Everyone in Rome knew his brother, Quintus, had inherited all of the family's military ability—not Marcus Tullius. Instead, he had successfully navigated Rome's delicate political maze for years. Prone to be fretful, negative, and a candid talker, if ever there was gloom and doom, Cicero could uncover it easier than combing fleas off a street-mongrel.

Before Marcus could lift his daughter off the lawn, Cicero was already striding through the peristyle courtyard. Toga flowing, he lifted one hand in mock oratorical gesture upon seeing Tonia.

"Antonius! Is this enchanting creature the new addition to your household?"

"She is." Cradling Tonia in the crook of his arm, Marcus smiled proudly in spite of Cicero's presence, extending his right hand in civil courtesy.

Ignoring the gesture, Cicero reached for the baby instead. None too pleased that he was taking such interest in his child, Marcus ground his teeth as the statesman lifted her in scrutiny.

"I've never seen such flaming hair."

"She takes after her mother."

As Cicero raised Tonia up, her countenance changed now that she was no longer in her father's arms. She bawled like a bear.

Antonia and Nortia, the wet nurse, heard her cries and raced out to see what was wrong. Marcus laughed in smug satisfaction. Why, his daughter was already a fine judge of character!

"Is something wrong?" Antonia cried.

"She's hungry," Marcus answered, plucking Tonia from Cicero's hold. "Nortia, see to it." He expediently handed his daughter to the wet nurse.

"Salve, Marcus Tullius," Antonia shyly acknowledged before retreating back to the colonnade behind the nurse and babe.

"Your daughter is unaccustomed to strangers," Cicero testily called after her.

Marcus rolled his eyes. "What do you expect? She's not even through her first year."

Cicero murmured, "No matter. I daresay I miss days when my own were that young. Time never tarries."

"What brings you here?" Marcus inquired with far more brevity than intended.

Cicero regarded him coldly. "Firstly, our dinner with Pompeius the other night. I must ask you out of courtesy, when next we dine together, don't drink yourself into oblivion at table with me. We were honored guests."

"Drink myself into oblivion?" Marcus smirked. "Did I? I can't recall."

"Precisely. After all you consumed, your lack of memory is understandable."

"Forgive me. I tend to drink heaviest when dissatisfied with my circumstances." Marcus found one thing enjoyable with Cicero—pissing him off.

"Perhaps I should write Caesar concerning your 'dissatisfaction,'" Cicero threatened.

Crossing his arms, Marcus countered. "Do. And I could share all the criticism about him that you frequently voice with Pompeius."

Cicero set his jaw. "As always, we'll cool our quarrels. Next, I must inform you that this year's elections are to be delayed due to the city's violence."

"Pompeius certainly does little to improve matters. His demonstrations are no different than those of Clodius. If he posted his retired legionaries in problem areas and ceased his own uprisings, things would improve. Tell him to do so."

"Always the avid military man, aren't you? I've written to Caesar about Clodius swaying his mobs and how his forced legislation has led to disaster."

"Did you also tell him about the unrest caused by Pompeius and Milo? If not, then he hasn't heard an unbiased report."

"Caesar's concerns are solely focused on *Clodius*."

What a prattling, exasperating old ass was Cicero. "And he responded?"

"A courier arrived last evening. As you know, Caesar likes Clodius, but he feels a need to sever ties until he gentles his methods. We must handle this delicately. Clodius holds great sway with the people. Let's have a private dinner with him, just you and I, our wives, and my daughter's new husband. Dining always sends a message of goodwill."

"Why do you need me there?"

"Because you must be prepared to *renounce* Clodius. You are acting as Caesar's representative in Rome. He must see our unity as solid as iron."

Damned politics!

Three days later, Marcus reclined at Cicero's dinner. Conversation between courses of roast pheasant and stuffed kidneys centered on hopes that Parthia would soon be a new Roman territory. There was no news from Crassus yet, but everyone knew word of his progress was imminent.

After dinner, the women retired to the gardens. Cicero had yet to bring up the reason for Clodius's invitation. Instead, he initiated topics ranging from land for retired legionaries to beasts appearing in the most recent games. Idly awaiting him to introduce the subject, Marcus felt nature's call and excused himself for Cicero's latrines.

Once relieved, he detoured through the stately peristyle courtyard housing pieces of the politician's famed art collection. Mother had once told him of Cicero's stunning assortment of Greek sculptures. Marcus figured this was his chance to see it. Having had his former home destroyed by Clodius, Cicero's new domus was nearly as grandiose as Pompeius's.

Marcus took his time, looking about, hearing light laughter from the adjoining gardens, where the women were. Through dense shrubbery, he glimpsed Antonia as he passed, listening to Cicero's wife and daughter, Terentia and Tullia, chatting about hair dyes from Mauritania.

He stopped short in a space where the moonlight illuminated a lone statue. It was a magnificent Hercules that had once graced his own home, sold at auction right before Fadia's death. Evidently, it had escaped destruction when Clodius's mob razed Cicero's old residence while Marcus had been in the East.

Since he rarely strayed from Cicero's tablinum, where he endured lectures, greeted clients, or prepared official financial statements, he'd not seen it. There had never been reason to venture to this part of the domus.

Someday this statue would return to his family. Marcus stood right there and swore it to himself. He was so wrapped up in thought that when someone touched his arm, he nearly leapt out of his sandals.

"Surely it takes more than a woman's touch to frighten Caesar's bravest legate," a honeyed voice intoned.

Marcus's eyes widened. It was Clodius's wife, Fulvia. "Forgive me—I was lost in thought. I assumed all the ladies were enjoying the gardens."

"The 'ladies' are dreadful bores—all of them. Your wife barely talks, and Terentia's drivel never ends. Then there's silly Tullia, a brainless combination of the two." She leaned in toward his ear. Marcus smelled wine on her breath. "I'd rather be with you men, learning firsthand why Cicero invited us here." Her whisper tickled his ear suggestively. What man wasn't drawn to Fulvia Bambula?

Taller than most women, she possessed gazelle-like grace, striking looks, and charm, all often topics of male discussion at the baths. With large eyes—dark brown and mesmerizing—her cosmetics were tastefully applied. But the clear, creamy complexion paled in comparison to Fulvia's intelligence, ambition, and brazen, bold nature, which matched that of most men.

Marcus remembered Clodius bragging over a few too many cups of Chian once, "Fulvia harbors a whore's lust, the mind of Caesar, the courage of Pompeius, the looks of Venus—and the disposition of Medusa!"

Aware that both their spouses were nearby, Marcus answered her question bluntly. "Your husband's brutal mobbing is the reason we're here, Fulvia. The conscript fathers tire of his gangs."

Fulvia smiled and stepped forward again, closer to his face. Her warm breath caressed his cheek as she spoke. "These are troubled times. Ferocity is the standard now. Clodius isn't the only one using mob politics." Her scent was rose oil—soft, sweet, sensual.

"True. But powerful men consider it unwise."

She cocked her head. "I've heard you're unwise too," she whispered.

"In what way?" he asked, eyeing her and holding his ground.

"With women," Fulvia answered with a daring smile. "Clodius told me about the brothel you all enjoyed when you were young."

"You heard correctly."

Her hand slid up his chest, carelessly playing with threads in his tunic. Bangles on her wrists tinkled. "You're still unwise with women, aren't you?" Before he knew it, her other hand rested on his shoulder as she moved deftly, her lips suddenly covering his, moist and teasing.

He couldn't help but respond, reaching his hands about her waist. Soft, filmy silk from her stola hid a curvaceously inviting form beneath. Fulvia sighed, yielding into him.

That's when he heard soft footfalls hastily scurrying away from where they were. He released her abruptly, glancing about.

She smiled mischievously. "Don't worry. Slaves aren't reliable witnesses."

He shot her a look. "Let's hope it was just a slave." Venus! He sincerely hoped Clodius and Cicero were still talking about tigers and gladiators.

She laughed, reaching for his hand and lacing her fingers through his. "Don't worry!"

"Fulvia, we can't—I mean, this cannot be—not with you married to Clodius. Not now." He frowned, deeply regretting these last moments yet conscious of how much he'd enjoyed the little dalliance.

Since returning home, he had spent much time with his family and new daughter, and had been faithful to Antonia. Finding an occasional woman to lie with on campaign was much easier in the field. He'd settled for willing native women or one of the cleaner camp prostitutes. Unfortunately, this fleeting moment with Fulvia reminded him how little Antonia really satisfied him.

In fact, Fulvia's advances awakened a suppressed hunger. He'd need to sort this out, for life with Antonia meant nothing but boring, matronly sex. Marcus Antonius simply couldn't survive on that.

Fulvia reached out to him once more, meaning to caress the side of his face.

His hand intercepted hers. "*No.* You are remarkable, and we could pleasure ourselves well, but it would lead to nothing but trouble for us both. And you're right. I seldom practice discretion, but in this case, I take exception." He turned from her and forced himself to walk away, but he made the mistake of glancing back.

Fulvia was watching him, smiling wistfully.

Marcus hurried back to the triclinium, stunned at how just one kiss had roused his desire. Uneasy, he rejoined the other men. If the mood in the room was any indication, Cicero had finally addressed the evening's subject in his absence.

Clodius spoke to him immediately, sarcasm seeping through his voice. "Ah, Antonius. I've just been informed of Caesar's mind and that of our host. What does my *friend* say in my defense?"

Still distracted from his sultry encounter, Marcus gathered his wits. At least everyone was still in their places. With a sigh, he answered, "Clodius, though our city's never been safe enough to send bejeweled virgins into the streets at night, I returned from the north finding Rome more dangerous than Gaul. I must agree with Cicero. I've even considered sending Antonia and Mother to the south, removing them from all this madness. You make us Populares appear vicious and fanatical, embarrassing those of us who would otherwise assist you."

Clodius quipped in disgust, "My resolutions have pleased the Roman people. You can't argue how they love me for laws I've ushered through on their behalf."

"We merely insist your *methods* change," Cicero drawled impatiently.

"Think about this," Marcus suggested. "Populares in the Senate would welcome your proposals—once you stop inciting mobs to get things done."

"All of Rome longs for peace in the streets again, Clodius," Furius Crassipes, Tullia's husband, reminded gently. He'd spoken little during dinner, a man completely overshadowed by his father-in-law.

Cicero said, "Caesar receives word from Rome often. He's concerned about your actions."

"I *protect* myself, Cicero!" Clodius declared flatly, standing in outrage. "Have your puppets Pompeius and Milo set down *their* swords. Then you'll have your peace! Publius Clodius will continue speaking for the plebs and keeping their rights in the forefront. And if that means rioting for the people, then it shall be so." Looking directly at Marcus, he added, "And it sickens me, when 'friends' turn their backs!" Reaching up, he wiped away beads of sweat under his curling black hair, oiled to perfection. Followed by his body slave, he called loudly for Fulvia and made his exit.

Thankfully, the evening ended after that.

Marcus guided Antonia toward their litter. As he took her hand to help her in, she snatched it from his. Too preoccupied to care, he got in behind her, rapping for the slaves to depart.

"You must have enjoyed tonight as much as I," he remarked dryly, rubbing a dull ache from his eyes.

No response. Antonia's silence prompted him to look her way, wondering if she was ill. He was taken aback to see her glaring at him.

Finally, she spoke, her usual meekness replaced with seething offense. "Oh *yes*, I saw you enjoying yourself immensely."

Ho! This was a side of her he'd never seen. "What are you talking about?"

"Oh, *stop*. You know what I mean!"

Ah. Yes, he did. "What did you see?" he sighed.

Tears glistened in her eyes. Upper lip quivering, she looked away from him into the swaying curtains, struggling for composure.

"Antonia, let me explain—"

"Why bother? I walked into the peristyle finding you with your lips latched to hers! Such behavior merits but one explanation."

Marcus watched her for a moment. She just stared down at her lap, unwilling to meet his eyes. And her hands were shaking.

Weary of arguing, he surrendered. "Believe what you want, then. I can't control what you think. But kindly keep your tongue to yourself." Speaking softly but firmly, he added, "Don't make things worse than they already are."

Antonia remained silent, frosty as Gaul in December. Never had crossing one end of the Palatine to another taken so damned long.

CHAPTER VI

LATER THAT WEEK, MARCUS WANDERED INTO THE triclinium to find Mother playing her cithara. It had been too long since he'd heard her making music. He paused in the doorway, listening.

She must have sensed his presence, for she stopped and turned around. "Where's Antonia?" she asked, her cithara balanced on one knee.

"Octavia invited her to a play at Pompeius's theater," he answered, joining her in the chamber's cool shade.

"You're not going?"

Marcus shook his head, looking away. "I've been out too much lately, playing along as Cicero's menial subordinate and making others hate me for it. I'm in no mood to attend a play—especially a tragedy."

Mother smiled sadly. "Are you and Antonia—"

He held up one hand to stop her intrusion. "Don't—please. Might we just sit here quietly a while?" He reclined next to her, sinking onto the downy cushions of the dining couch. "Just play for me," he entreated.

With a tender smile, Mother lifted her cithara, repositioning it on her lap and holding it upright. She strummed something soft and melancholy, matching his mood. Marcus sighed deeply. He needed this, so he draped an arm over his eyes, listening and relaxing.

In the next section, Mother's fingers took flight, plucking a lighter melody, the tempo escalating until reaching an apex. It descended into gentle cascades of glissandi, the music resolving into its original form—mournful, slow, then fading, falling silent.

"That was beautiful, Mother," he breathed, eyes still closed.

"It's been a very long while since I've had you exclusively to myself."

Marcus smiled and opened his eyes, gazing up at her. "You know, only one other person has ever impressed me as much with their musical talent."

"Who?"

"Ptolemy, King of Egypt."

Mother laughed. "'Auletes'—the flute player. I had always imagined that title as derogatory, indicating lack of ability."

Marcus shook his head. "Not at all. When he played for me, it was mesmerizing."

"He performed for *you*?" she asked, fascinated.

"Yes. One night in the middle of the desert, he actually played me to sleep."

Mother chuckled. She reached over, lightly caressing his hair with her fingertips. After a time, she asked, "How's your time with Cicero been?"

Opening his eyes, he looked at her honestly, shaking his head. "On our first visit together, he informed me that he wouldn't oppose my quaestorial candidacy, but he declared he'd never have supported me except for Caesar. In turn, I reminded him I only accepted his assistance *because* of Caesar." Marcus shook his head. "I try, Mother, but I'm no good at this game. I hate politics because I detest duplicity."

"Oh, Marcus, for now, you must look beyond your present

circumstances. Perhaps someday you'll find you've learned from this experience."

"I've discovered one truth. People constantly debate whether or not the Republic is dead and gone—"

"You've an opinion on that?"

"It's over. Done. Rome needs new birth. She needs a firm hand, one wise enough to steer her into a new age. Too many men are scrambling about for absolute power. Today Clodius, Pompeius, and Cicero. Tomorrow . . ."

Mother remained still as his voice trailed off.

"Caesar might be the one," he declared suddenly, nodding in assurance.

Her eyes grew wide. "Caesar? *Alone?*"

Marcus smiled, crossing his arms behind his head. "That's the difficulty, isn't it? No man in the Senate would ever give him full rein. Nobody would admit needing a single ruler, but he's perfect for the role. He could do it, bringing peace, organization, and stability."

Mother shook her head. "Cicero would never support such a thing, and the Senate would be in uproar. Surely, Pompeius would resist as well. With Julia Caesaris's ashes growing colder daily, it'll take intercession from Jupiter Rex to prevent him and Caesar from squabbling. And there's Crassus to consider too. If he takes Parthia, Caesar shall be hard put equaling that."

"He'd find a way, Mother," Marcus declared with certainty. "Caesar would find a way."

Senatorial deliberations ended early the next day. Marcus was shouldering his way through thick crowds at the end of the Nova Via when he heard his name.

"Marcus Antonius!"

Glancing back toward the voice, he saw a woman parting the

curtains of an ornate litter not far away. Her litter-bearers placed their load down gently under a shade next to Vesta's Temple.

Grinning good-naturedly, Marcus exclaimed, "Calpurnia, how good to see you!"

"And you. Have you heard from my husband?"

"I'm afraid not."

"Nor have I." A fleeting look of disappointment crossed her face. They both had to speak louder than normal. Forum crowds were thick all around them. After a pause, she said, "You, your mother, and Antonia must visit. Come whenever it pleases you."

"We'd be honored."

"And bring little Tonia. I've only seen her a few times. Surely she must be growing."

Marcus wiped sweat off his face from the early summer heat, and nodded. "Soon we'll celebrate her first year. Since the elections are delayed, it seems I'll be here for the occasion."

"That should please everyone. Is Antonia well?"

Marcus opened his mouth to answer, hesitating just long enough for Calpurnia to detect his unease.

"You know, there's a peaceful walking path on the temple grounds. Would you care to take a stroll?"

"Let's go."

With the litter and press of humanity behind them, they retreated to the beautifully manicured gardens within the Temple of Vesta complex. Reflecting pools mirrored lazy clouds as they strolled. Marcus nodded courteously to two of the holy Vestals as they passed.

Calpurnia noted, "Wearing a toga gives you a most distinguished look, Legate."

He shook his head and laughed. "Whichever founding father designated this as the traditional vestige of senatorial office should've been sewn inside a sack with rats and tossed off the Tarpeian Rock!"

Calpurnia tilted her head back, laughing wholeheartedly.

They encountered three more Vestals in flowing robes,

reclining under an arbor. Just a little farther, and they were finally alone. The temple grounds were a peaceful island in the middle of the bustling city.

Marcus sensed he and Calpurnia both swam the same sea, and her next question confirmed it.

"Marriage has its difficulties, agreed?" she probed.

He nodded. "Suffice it to say I envy the plebs' simplicity in a lot of ways."

"True."

He asked the next question softly. "You regret being Caesar's wife?"

She shook her head thoughtfully. "No. He's an amazing man. Still, when marrying greatness, one sacrifices to that god daily, like it or not. Ours has been a very long separation. Will he even be the same once he returns?" She shook her head. "I don't know."

As Marcus considered her words, they sat down together upon a wide marble bench under welcoming fruit trees.

"Does he ever speak of me?" she queried.

Marcus chewed his lip, contemplating an acceptable response. "Honestly, he never brings up personal things."

Calpurnia pursed her lips and looked away. He nearly reached out to comfort her, but something stayed his hand. He settled for, "You must lead a lonely existence."

She nodded, eyeing him peripherally. Then she gave him a mischievous smile. "But you don't, do you?"

He blinked, puzzled. She was smirking.

"Everybody knows my reputation. But what makes you say that?"

"There's a certain rumor circulating."

Shaking his head, he encouraged her, "Do tell."

"Is Fulvia only a rumor?"

Marcus froze as if shot by a bolt. "What? Where did you hear that?"

She became serious. "Oh, please! You haven't heard? Marcus, it's all over Rome and has been for the past day or so."

"What's been said?" he gasped, incredulous.

"That the two of you are lovers, of course. Supposedly, Clodius is furious."

As well he would be!

Marcus swallowed painfully, his mouth suddenly dry as a desert. He hadn't seen Clodius since Cicero's dinner night before last. Gossip about an adulterous encounter with Fulvia could prove fatal to his present arrangement with Cicero, his already tenuous influence on Clodius, and even the eventual elections.

"Well, it's not true," he assured. "Nor would it please any of the men I support, including your husband. Though I won't deny she *tempted* me."

Calpurnia shrugged and touched his arm fondly. "If it's false, then of course I believe you. However, be warned—plebs love a good scandal. I wonder who would ignite such a tale?"

Marcus was grappling with the same question, and, infuriatingly, he kept coming up with only one answer.

Damn her!

Outraged, he hastily left Calpurnia among the Vestals, hastening up the Palatine Hill. Near the gate, he glanced irritably at some people laughing. They were staring at him. One pointed toward a wall on the side of a weaver's shop that always seemed to be the hub of Rome's graffiti.

Marcus halted. A hot flush of rage emanated outward from his core. Part of him wanted to launch himself at the guffawing group of plebs next to the road and beat them to pulp. But no—he'd save his anger.

For this was all *her* fault.

In typical caricature, the wall's graffiti was seared into his mind. An artist with extremely little talent had painted a crude picture of a man taking a woman from behind. Next to both figures, two names were scribbled: ANTONIVS ET FVLVIA.

"Antonia!"

Marcus was breathing hard as he came in, his heavy footfalls resounding throughout the domus.

Gaius and Lucius both looked up from where they were playing dice in the peristyle garden nearest the atrium.

Mother bolted out of her cubiculum. "What's wrong?"

Marcus ignored them, so intent was he on locating his wife. *Damn* her!

Antonia was at the other end of the garden.

As he approached, he could read the guilt on her face. At each breath, her breasts rose and fell. With eyes full of fear, she glanced down toward little Tonia at her feet, quickly snatching the child up and holding her close.

Tonia was drooling and gurgling infant sounds. She was cutting teeth and sucking on a shredded remnant of knotted silk that kitchen slaves always dipped in honey. Nortia stood up behind her, following her mistress' cue.

Furious, Marcus roared, "How *dare* you! I told you to keep it to yourself, and you disobeyed me!"

Gaius and Lucius stood nearby, mouths agape, having left their game to see what had happened. Mother had followed and stood off to one side.

Antonia managed, "You admit it, then?"

"I admit nothing," Marcus responded. "There's nothing to admit. Who did you tell, and what was said?"

"What's going on?" Gaius interjected cautiously.

Marcus circled Antonia like a lion closing in on prey. How could she have done this to him, when he told her to keep the incident quiet? Subconsciously, his fists kept opening and closing in angered frustration. He felt like strangling her.

All the while, she pressed Tonia close like a shield, glancing about, trying to watch his every move.

Marcus ignored Gaius's inquiry, barking at her, "Answer me! Who did you tell?"

Antonia responded, her voice only wavering at the last, "I sent a slave among Fulvia's to learn if it was true. They all came to the same conclusion. Everyone knows your reputation."

"You mean your information was based entirely on *assumption*? And from slaves not even in our household? That's just *insane*! What slave did you send?"

Mother spoke up next, her voice low. "Son, never punish a slave for obedience, regardless of what it entailed."

"Nortia, take my daughter to her cubiculum," Marcus commanded.

Antonia shielded Tonia's head with her hand. It made it impossible for Nortia to follow Marcus's order. "She's my daughter too," Antonia protested. "She's the only love I'll ever know!" Then she released an outpouring of tears, still staring at the ground.

"What drama," Lucius muttered, rolling his eyes.

Mother spoke calmly, "We all live in this domus, Marcus. We've a right to know what happened."

"I know what it is," Gaius deduced, nodding.

Marcus was conscious of Mother staring at her middle son as he continued stalking Antonia, who was now visibly shaking with sobs.

Gaius explained, "People were talking in the Forum today while I was out buying my new set of dice. It's Fulvia."

"It's what she *thinks* I did with Fulvia!" Marcus added. "But she has no proof! Her jealousy's gone so far she's probably shattered the already-fragile friendship I had with Clodius, and Cicero's probably heard about it too! How am I supposed to restore our honor when my own wife spreads lies about me?"

"Is it a lie?" Mother asked, one eyebrow cocked.

Marcus glared at her. "Fulvia tried seducing me at Cicero's the other night—that much is true. But I walked away. I tried explaining that to Antonia, but she wouldn't listen!"

Antonia sobbed. "I saw the way you held her and kissed her."

Marcus took her by surprise, moving as swiftly as he did on the battlefield, tearing his daughter away and plopping her into Nortia's arms.

Tonia started crying, and that made Antonia even more emotional.

"Antonia, you'll remove your belongings from our cubiculum and take residence in the guestroom."

"Marcus, don't be so hasty," Mother began.

But Antonia surprised everyone by countering back with uncharacteristic vehemence. "It'll be a relief not servicing you anymore like a broodmare in season! Because that's all I am to you!"

What? Marcus lost control. Less than a second later, his hand was tingling and Antonia lay sprawled in the grass from where he'd slapped her. "*That'll* teach you to spread lies about me!" he hissed. Breathless and too angry to feel remorse over the red mark on her face, he turned on his heel and paced out of the peristyle courtyard, Gaius and Lucius following closely behind.

Like a broodmare in season? That was unfair. He had done nothing to deserve this.

Marcus Antonius, legatus and quaestor-elect, to Publius Clodius:

Certainly, we have both suffered at the vicious rumors regarding Fulvia and myself. I want to assure you that both she and I are innocent of betraying you in any way. I hope you will believe me, as I have never had reason to lie to you. Let us hope that in the near future we might share a cup of wine together.

Marcus's work with Cicero went on—as non-conversationally as possible. His evenings were spent with Gaius and Lucius, away from the domus at taverns and brothels. He heard nothing from Clodius, nor did he see him.

If he was honest with himself, Fulvia had reignited a fire of sexual craving. Since he wouldn't be sleeping with Antonia anytime soon, he found himself glancing at other married women outside of his own circle and Cicero's.

Lucius immediately took action on his behalf, pointing out and suggesting promiscuous senators' wives who might be open to love affairs. Gaius, on the other hand, insisted they keep visiting high-end brothels instead. But Marcus was tired of whores, and wanted something special—something he'd be able to keep at arm's length yet was available whenever the need arose.

He wanted a mistress.

A couple of weeks after his confrontation with Antonia, Lucius eagerly invited, "There's a new mime in the Forum. Let's go!"

Marcus loved theater, and mime was his favorite genre since it was blunt, carefree, and rarely followed social mores. He, Lucius, and Gaius, bringing bread and wine to enjoy during the show, arrived early and found choice seats.

That's when Marcus saw her for the first time.

Volumnia Cytheris was a notoriously beautiful mime actress, and in this wicked little piece she was playing a prostitute. With her face painted like a doll's and her own hair covered with a large, ungainly wig, she was made to look comical—and she was. But what Marcus focused on was anything *but* ungainly. Shimmering golden skin, shapely breasts, and thighs that undulated beneath her nearly transparent garment.

Captivated, he couldn't take his eyes from her. And from the way men all around him were cheering and shouting suggestive drivel during the show, her popularity and reputation was renowned.

For two weeks afterward, Marcus attended the mime without his brothers, taking only bodyguards to avoid gang trouble in the streets. After each performance, he made a point of seeking Cytheris out and chatting with her. Usually, he stood nearby as she washed off her heavy cosmetics in a small bubbling fountain near the side of the Curia building. It gave him time to flirt with her and decide if he liked her well enough to make her an offer.

But there was one complication. Another man, Marcus Junius Brutus, had claimed her, and she was residing in one of his town houses.

Marcus remembered Brutus. They used to wrestle together at the baths, and he had been pathetically easy to beat. In fact, Brutus was more like Cicero or Marcus's Uncle Lucius Caesar. He was rich and had Patrician bloodlines, but was reserved, scholarly, and had no talent when it came to martial skills.

Tonight, when Marcus found Cytheris, her back was to him as she wiped water from her face.

Marcus murmured, "Oh, but you should wear only the finest silk on that skin of yours. Not ragged theatrical gowns."

Startled, she whirled about. Relieved it was someone familiar, she giggled. "Oh, it's you again!"

Marcus grinned. She looked genuinely happy to see him. "It's me," he affirmed. Venus, but he did want her. "Cytheris, we've been talking for some time now—"

She interrupted with a curt snort. "Take a guess at how many men 'talk' to me."

He cocked an eyebrow. "I imagine Brutus does, doesn't he, among other things?"

Cytheris surprised him by meeting his gaze and shaking her head. "That one. He may be rich, and his blood might flow straight from Romulus, but he's as dull and boring as this wig you hate so much."

Ha! This was the very opportunity for which he had waited. "Then I've an offer for you."

A slight tilt of her perfectly curved chin revealed curiosity. "An offer?"

Unfortunately, Cytheris's voice didn't match her exquisite face at all. It was brassy and hardened, with a course plebian accent, but at least her Latin was flawless. Only the subtlest hint of her native Greek bled through her speech.

Marcus leaned back against the Curia wall, ogling her. He'd enjoyed this dalliance and wanted her to yearn for him as much as he desired her. The problem was being sure she knew her place. She was far from being innocent, like Fadia had been, and with his rising status, he'd eventually have to remarry. There could be no strong emotions between them.

"You're about to receive the opportunity of a lifetime."

Cytheris's eyes widened with interest. "Oh, really? What?"

Common as a urine-stained dye slave, and as exquisite as Helen of Troy! Marcus stepped closer, his body brushing her diaphanous gown. "I want you, Cytheris. I think we'd be well-matched as lovers. And I'll house you and provide clothes, gifts, whatever you want."

"My manager, Eutrapelus, would want a cut of whatever you give me."

"Is he your pimp? He freed you, didn't he?"

"It's complicated," she admitted. "True, I was once his slave, but he still thinks I owe him, and he takes from me, whether I like it or not."

Marcus shrugged. "Well, with me you'll be under my protection from now on and needn't pay him anything. I'll even station bodyguards at your door to prevent him from harassing you."

"I'm not cheap," she reminded him. "I have my pride, and I'll want expensive things, like silk. Could you afford me? Brutus said you had to leave Rome once because of debt. And aren't you Fulvia's lover? What about her?"

Marcus laughed aloud. "You've heard a lot, girl. But there's nothing to worry about there. The rumor about Fulvia was just that—vicious gossip. As for my gambling? I like to roll dice once in a while. Next time I go, you could come too. You'll find I have no worries about coin now. I've already told you I'm Caesar's legate. We'll be conquerors before you know it, and I'll be drenched in gold."

"That means you're going back to Gaul. Married too, aren't you?"

He shrugged. "So is Brutus. But Antonia and I are estranged." Shit. She was a lot brighter about all this than he figured she'd be. He reached out, running a finger along the snagged silk of her much-worn costume. Her skin was hot to his touch. Abruptly, he dropped his hand. Women loved being touched. Best to lure her in to make her want him. "And if I do leave, you'd have a safe place to live in luxury. Maybe one of the renovated insulae on the Esquiline?"

She gazed up at him with eyes that were emerald-green pools of longing. No doubt, her life had been hard, beginning as old Eutrapelus's slave girl. How could that wrinkled, impotent old bag of bones bring such a girl any pleasure?

"Say yes," he murmured, leaning into her ear and grinning. In one swift motion, he caught her about the waist firmly with one hand, brushing his other gently across the clear skin on her face and letting it descend slowly, continuing downward to tantalize her jaw and neck. Lastly, it passed softly as a breeze over her left breast. She felt nice in his arms. Yes, he'd be quite satisfied with her.

Ragged with yearning, she breathed, "Yes."

"Lucky girl," he whispered. "You'll never have to return to the Subura or Marcus Junius Brutus's bed. I've no idea how that fool of a philosopher could possibly pleasure you."

In all his rowdy experience with whores, Marcus knew very well how his touch affected women. Aroused, he playfully bumped his forehead to hers. With a quick sideways dip of his head, he caught her off guard and kissed her full on the mouth, his right hand bracing her back. Pressed into her now, he felt womanly suppleness and yearned to feel her writhe beneath him.

As expected, Cytheris melted, her head falling back in surrender.

His mouth moved from her lips to her ear. Knotting his hand in her hair, he whispered huskily, "You'll be healthy, clean, comfortable, and most of all—content."

Then he stopped his overtures abruptly, taking a step back.

Cytheris stood there, speechless, wavering on her feet.

"But understand something," he warned. "Emotional love is not part of this arrangement. You'll have to accept that. We'll enjoy our time together, but it'll only be for sex." He paused, watching her. "So what do you say? Will you be Marcus Antonius's mistress?"

Breathless, she stood openmouthed, cheeks flushed. Her eyes burned wantonly, full breasts heaving under the thin, gauzy material. In her world, such an opportunity was welcome income, especially if the business was handsome and desirable.

At her nod, he swept her into his arms, laughing and leaning to kiss her as he carried her to his waiting litter.

CHAPTER VII

SEVERAL DAYS LATER, LIFE RETURNED TO REALITY AS Marcus hurried toward the Rostra.

Clodius was stirring up the masses again.

Of course, it was Cicero who ordered Marcus to face the dangerous mobs Clodius was inciting. Aware of the danger, he'd strapped on his gladius beneath his toga. His young slave Eros had begged him to take bodyguards, but what good would they be in a riot of thousands?

Within the swarming press, it was slow going. The entire time he mulled over what to say to Clodius. Undoubtedly, the scandal concerning Fulvia would undoubtedly raise its head. They hadn't spoken since Cicero's dinner party, and Marcus sensed Clodius's ire, as there had been no response to his written message. However, the glaring problem at hand was political upheaval—mobbing to pass legislature and threaten political figures. For calm to ensue today, Marcus would need to remain composed—something at which he wasn't always adept.

It took forever, shouldering his way through the sea of bodies. Some onlookers he judged to be Clodius's men, bearing daggers, pikes, and wooden clubs. He didn't much like the look of them. Marcus set his jaw, irritated. If only Caesar would call him back to Gallia Comata, where war with the Gauls seemed more peaceful than Rome's streets.

Clodius was striding back and forth atop the rostra, gesticulating and crying out his case before the people. Dressed immaculately in a perfectly draped toga, black hair curled over his wide brow.

"Caesar now joins Pompeius and Cicero, declaring my tactics to be nothing but violence. But, good people, what other language does Rome speak in our day and age? Our organized, civil Republic has crumbled, and now the only way to be heard by our obstinate conscript fathers is by pike and club. It's Milo—Pompeius's creature—who is causing the most harm, turning my honest attempts at restoring your collegia into nothing but his own mob."

Marcus roughly shoved plebs out of his way, trying to get closer so he could get Clodius's attention. He braced himself. This was going to be anything but pleasant.

"Here's *my* demand," Clodius went on, "for Pompeius to send Milo out of the city so he no longer causes division by bribing and turning collegia against one another. I will see our common workers *thriving*, not—"

"Clodius!" It came out as a roar.

He paused at Marcus's bellow, mild surprise on his face, then peered down at the multitude nearest the front of the platform. Once he locked eyes with Marcus, Clodius's face screwed into a scowl.

Pulse hammering, Marcus gestured to a host of ruffians nearby, cudgels barely concealed under their cloaks. "Get down! Let today pass without breaking any heads." Now at the foot of the Rostra's wooden steps, Marcus ascended, joining Clodius and addressing the crowd himself. "People of Rome, look about you and tell the men with weapons that they need not use them. Clodius and I are going to go share some wine. And I'm sure we'll find *something* to talk about!"

The plebs burst out hooting and laughing since everyone knew about the Fulvia scandal.

Clodius glanced over the crowd. "Have you lost your mind, Antonius?" he hissed under his breath.

Oh, he was thoroughly pissed. With a puff of his cheeks, Marcus firmly took him by the arm. "Come, friend," he said, still speaking loud enough for the people to hear. Then he addressed the populace once more. "Everyone, go—get back to work, earn yourselves an honest day's wage."

Clodius must have been stunned to the core, for Marcus had him all the way to the stairs before he jerked his arm away in rage. "Let go of me!"

"There's a fine tavern nearby," Marcus cajoled. "It's time we talked."

People were still watching, which worked to Marcus's advantage. As furious as Clodius was, he wouldn't let anyone see him ruffled.

As they passed through the crowds, people were already dispersing, several men clapping Clodius on the back, thanking him for his efforts on their behalf. Once at the tavern, Marcus chose a bench for himself, facing the Forum, enabling him to watch for any of Clodius's troublemakers who might still be nearby. Their table sat under a dilapidated awning providing shade. "You put on quite a show," he initiated.

"Seems you're the real showman—with *Fulvia*," Clodius spat.

Snapping his fingers at a server, Marcus civilly offered Clodius some wine. "Now listen, that was vicious gossip, nothing more. I'm angry about it too. Turns out my wife possesses a jealous nature. Stupid bitch started the whole scandal over nothing."

Clodius leaned forward, his voice edged with malice. "Curio had a jealous nature too," he reminisced. "He didn't want to lose you to all the girls, so he used to drug you all the time, taking you however he pleased. You must really miss it since you're turning cheap whores like Cytheris!"

Marcus was taken aback with this revelation about his dissipated youth. He knew Curio had drugged him and violated him once, but had there been other times? He swigged some more wine, forcing himself to plow ahead, distant memories of Curio sickening him. "Clodius, talk sense," he pleaded. "Why would I start something with Fulvia right under your nose when I'm standing for the quaestorship and Cicero keeps me leashed to his side?"

Clodius ignored him, swigging some wine and returning to his jabs. "Curio took you facedown so many times—I remember once he made you yelp like a pup. I *watched*! He was always the dominant!"

Marcus felt nauseous, and he struggled to keep composure. He inadvertently banged his wine cup down onto the table harder than intended. Red liquid sloshed out, spattering his toga. He growled through his teeth, "Cicero sent me down here to talk to you peaceably. Right now you see me as an enemy, but I'm trying to help you! Stop ruining your career by being hostile to the state."

Clodius crossed his arms defiantly.

Marcus tried once more. "Both Caesar and Cicero are more powerful than us! Ally yourself with them and they'll assist you against Milo's gang and Pompeius. If the violence ends, everyone benefits."

"For a soldier, you've certainly become soft, coddling Cicero like an old grandmother. And you think Caesar wants peace? He wants nothing more than Pompeius's imperium. He pulls your puppet strings all the way from Gaul. It credits you nothing, serving him like a pleasure-boy to a master!"

Marcus tried to close his mind to the building pressure of fury boiling inside. "Your insults are becoming tiresome," he warned in a low voice.

Clodius arose abruptly, his anger escalating. "Really? Yours is the *ultimate* insult: Taking my wife!"

Marcus got up too, a dominating presence over his shorter rival. "If Fulvia does pursue me, maybe she's unsatisfied in bed. Maybe height isn't your only *short* attribute!"

Wild with rage, Clodius hurled his wine cup at Marcus's face.

Marcus ducked lithely as it crashed into the tavern wall. It left a crimson trail across stones on the pavement, and more stains on his toga. Other patrons retreated, wary of what was coming.

Only the small wooden table separated them now. "How could a highborn lady like my wife possibly find sexual gratification in a homosexual playing submissive to 'Dominus' Cicero's tastes?" Clodius sneered.

Ho. *Submissive*? To Chickpea?

Nobody said that of Marcus Antonius!

Pushed beyond his limit, Marcus barely realized he'd drawn his gladius. Clodius reached for his pugio but changed his mind, wisely realizing it wouldn't suffice. Able to do little else, he shoved the table furiously against Marcus's knees, shedding his bulky toga as he bolted away.

Reacting instinctively, Marcus recovered and vaulted over the table, toga and all. He chased his prey across the busy Via Sacra, bumping into people and stumbling over his garment as he ran.

Clodius darted into a food stand, using an unfortunate seller as a shield. Marcus looked above them, whacking at hams strung over the counter. The owner cried out, fearful for his life and lost product, butts and shoulders of smoked meat pelting all three men. Clodius shoved the proprietor away like refuse, darting away again, a falling pork shank striking him heavily on one arm. He scrambled past other merchants and their produce, up four short stairs, and retreated into a scribe's shop, slamming the door behind him.

Marcus took his time approaching, glancing about cagily, ever leery of Clodius's devoted thugs, many of whom could still be around, watching.

Inside the shop, he heard Clodius shoving crates and furniture against the entrance. The owner, a small Greek, sounded horrified, protesting loudly at finding himself trapped inside his own shop with a desperate man.

Marcus pounded the thin, louvered barricade with the hilt of his gladius, hearing chairs and shelves rattling against it. Lifting his voice, he shouted, "Shameful you've only a pugio, Clodius! But I guess it's easy walking about safely surrounded by your thugs all the time. The rest of us have no such advantage. We're too busy protecting ourselves against your ruffians." He laughed, brandishing his sword in front of the small shop window.

Still chuckling, he turned to leave, feeling pleased with himself. He'd stopped a riot from happening and won the day. But when he looked up, he froze in astonishment. A huge horde had gathered, including togate senators. Some of Milo's and Clodius's brutes were intermingled too, weapons in hand. Thankfully, they were merely staring as spectators—for now.

Cautiously sheathing his sword, Marcus smiled, plenty grateful that an idea was already forming in his mind. He lifted his arms for the people's attention. Ha! He'd turn this business around and use plebs as protection to get home.

His booming voice echoed off buildings throughout the Forum Romanum. "Publius Clodius Pulcher just insulted my dear patron, Marcus Tullius Cicero, for the final time," he lied. "I assure you, good Romans, it will never happen again while Marcus Antonius is in this city!"

Damned politics!

As he descended the stairs, heart pounding, he was relieved to hear cheers and plebs shouting their approval of his standing up for Cicero. More joined in, so that despite the usual plebian love for Clodius, Marcus found them enamored of his courage on behalf of a supposed friend. Youths and even women were all about him. As he cautiously moved among them toward the Via Sacra, he waved and clasped their hands, grinning and thanking them for their kind support. As more joined in, he heard them shouting his name—some were even calling him quaestor! The Nova Via became his escape route away from any danger in the throng. He shouted thanks, inviting people to walk with him, using their presence to gain safe passage. All the way, Marcus let himself be buoyed, cheered, and encircled until he arrived, thankful and breathless, back to the domus Antonii.

That night at dinner, Eros brought him a note, delivered from Cicero, and he laughed until he cried:

> *Marcus Tullius Cicero, Pater Patriae to Marcus Antonius:*
>
> *I write with gratitude upon hearing how you defended my name so passionately today in the Forum. No doubt it was with utmost zeal, as several senators reported how Clodius's and Milo's thugs were amazed and impressed at your bearing and fearlessness. I'm moved and flattered that, at long last, you've become my noble and gallant friend. Though I commend your actions, I must insist you carry out your intentions peaceably.*

Marcus's escapades in the Forum granted him celebrity status. Plebs identified a spark of courage and affability in him that they adored.

The Clodius and Milo factions kept stalking the Forum in an unceasing impasse, ever straining Rome's frenetic daily pace. Of late, there had been a few skirmishes, but fortunately no major riots.

As always in late summer, humidity cloaked the city in a stagnant haze. Not a breeze stirred the air, and odious fumes from Rome's great sewage drain, the Cloaca Maxima, rose along with the temperature. Miserable, hot mugginess sent many a wealthy noble south to escape the discomfort and stench.

But Marcus Antonius stayed put. Old Chickpea kept his agenda full.

Today a special senatorial meeting had been called, so Marcus joined the other conscript fathers still in the city to brave the scorching Curia. Inside, it was an oven. Public slaves stood at strategic locations, waving large feathered fans to move the torpid air. Clodius was there, sitting at the other end of the chamber, sending Marcus occasional icy stares.

As usual, Cicero was late. He had an annoying habit of walking in once everyone else was seated to receive their acknowledgement as "Pater Patriae"—Father of the Country. It was especially sickening to Marcus since he had attained that very title as a result of putting Lentulus to death.

"What's all this about?" Marcus exacted impatiently as the elder statesman lowered himself into an adjacent seat.

"You'll soon find out," Cicero replied coolly. Judging by the look on his face, it wasn't good news.

The year's two consuls, Gnaeus Domitius Calvinus and Marcus Valerius Messala, took their seats. Lictors pounded the ends of their fasces on the floor, calling for order.

After a few minutes, Calvinus arose, one hand uplifted, bringing the chamber to silence. "Roman brothers, this august body has endured many tumultuous trials. We suffered humiliation when Gauls attacked our city three hundred years ago. In our own lifetimes, shame descended when a slave army threatened us. But today I must report a disaster just as horrible—and in a foreign place. My colleagues, we have been defeated—humiliated."

Nobody breathed.

Messala, the second consul held up a scroll. "I hold in my hand details on the defeat of Marcus Licinius Crassus, compiled here by his quaestor, Gaius Cassius Longinus." Clearing his throat, he began to read:

> *"Gaius Cassius Longinus, quaestor, to the Senatus Romanum:*
>
> *Salvete. Young Marcus Crassus fell first, the Parthians hiding the heart of their army out of sight. He rode with the cavalry and penetrated too deeply while chasing skirmishers. They cut him down."*

Marcus groaned aloud. The only reward for that mistake was a welcome to Hades by Cerberus, the three-headed dog.

Messala kept reading:

> *"Once the real battle started, Parthian horse archers surrounded our men, who huddled behind their shields, unable to maneuver. Parthian arrows can pierce their armored tunics, so long into evening they were forced to stay where they were, exhausted, mad with thirst, choking on the dust. By nightfall, the enemy finally disappeared, but many men couldn't walk for their wounds. There was disorder and fear that the Parthians might return, so rescue carts didn't dare venture out to relieve the wounded. Soon Crassus and his remaining force was under siege at Carrhae. Men in two contubernia believed the struggle to be hopeless. They awaited a moonless night and stole away. Unfortunately, only a small group of them survived to make it to the Syrian border, where my men found them. At this time, they remain under arrest for desertion and will be placed on trial."*

Marcus shook his head in horror and shifted in his chair. Only those with field experience understood how desperate this situation must have been.

"Next, Cassius describes what happened to Marcus Crassus the elder," Messala related. He read on:

> *"Seeing his army losing heart, and knowing Carrhae was surrounded, Crassus accepted an offer from Surenas the Parthian to discuss terms."*

An outburst of outrage and groans cut Messala off. Lictors pounded their fasces again, calling order back to the assembly. Once silence descended, he resumed.

> *"Surenas demanded Crassus meet him face-to-face. They came together between the two armies, escorted by equal numbers of men from both sides. While still at a distance, the barbarian offered Crassus*

a fine horse on which to ride out to meet him."

Marcus chewed his lip, fearing a grim ending. The chamber had fallen still as a tomb.

> *"Crassus was impressed with the gesture but hated leaving the safety of his own men. Still, he wished to bring an end to his army's suffering. Suddenly, the Parthians who brought him the horse sensed his indecision and seized him. That prompted the Roman escort to attack them. In the scuffle, the enemy stole Crassus away. They imprisoned him, treated him roughly, and before beheading him, pried his mouth open, pouring molten gold down his throat in mockery of his great wealth."*

Marcus swallowed hard. Rome had been disgraced, much less Crassus. By oath to Mars, no enemy would *ever* boast the satisfaction of taking Marcus Antonius alive and ending his life!

Never!

Summer was loath to end and fought hard before succumbing. And gray skies did nothing but accentuate an overall sense of gloom in Rome. Gangs belonging to both Clodius and Milo prowled, and the humid, heavy air foreshadowed danger.

Marcus spent most nights with Cytheris. This way he avoided Antonia, for whom he'd lost all desire. Last night was a delightfully wild celebration honoring the final performance of Cytheris's latest mime. Guests included every actor, costumer, and musician in Rome, all drinking like maenads and honored that one of Caesar's legates had attended. Marcus enjoyed them. Congenial and outgoing, they were entirely free to be themselves, unlike most company he was forced to keep these days.

He and Cytheris were asleep when a sudden pounding on the door roused them. Cytheris squealed and Marcus blinked, groaning and rubbing his head, thick from too much wine. Even a tiny, flickering lamplight at the bedside made him wince.

Then Eros was gently tapping his arm. "Dominus."

Raising one hand, Marcus waved him away. "Yes, yes—go open the door."

Eros obeyed, and in burst more eye-piercing light, along with a dash of chill air. Marcus rubbed his face miserably, jerking a tunic over his head as he ambled over, squinting.

Iophon was outside. "Dominus, there's trouble in the city."

"When is there not?" Marcus muttered, rubbing his grizzled chin.

"Cicero sent word to the domus—a special meeting has been called this morning. Senators are meeting at his house." Iophon hesitated, then added, "And, Dominus—Clodius is dead."

Marcus's jaw dropped. "What happened?"

"He was murdered."

"Eros, get my toga and help me dress."

Walking from the Esquiline to the Palatine took nearly two hours. Seas of agitated, questioning plebs clogged every nook and cranny of the Forum Romanum. Obviously, the news was now public knowledge.

Marcus walked briskly, Eros at his heels. Crowds were so thick that moving forward was a shoving match. He gripped his gladius beneath his toga's sinuses, shouldering people out of the way and occasionally snarling for them to step aside.

When they finally reached the Palatine Gate, Eros pointed out large hosts of patricians standing on an open precipice of the hill's cusp, gazing out over the Forum and the crowd. Forced to pause because of the gate's congestion, Marcus looked back. Morning's first sunlight was gleaming upon the Curia, its bronze doors shut and secure. Around it swarmed thousands, their disgruntled voices sounding like the threatening hum of agitated bees. A few ambitious bystanders had scaled the Temple of Vesta for a better view, perched on its round tile roof.

Not far away at Cicero's domus, Marcus left Eros outside and entered the atrium. Men of importance overflowed into the peristyle courtyard.

Soon the door to Cicero's tablinum opened. Consuls Calvinus and Messala filed out, flanked by Pompeius and Cicero.

Cicero motioned for silence. "Good senators, hear me. We've met this day to make important decisions in the wake of Publius Clodius's death. These next few days will be dangerous, keeping the city calm. We've all seen the thousands in the Forum. It would be disastrous if they turned on us."

An elderly senator in the atrium, not far from Marcus, called out, "Tell us, Cicero! How did Clodius die?"

Heads nodded and men murmured agreement, craving details.

Cicero spoke loudly so all could hear. "He was traveling with a small party of supporters on the Via Appia last night when a band of Milo's thugs appeared. During the ensuing fight, he was wounded, and his slaves carried him inside a small tavern. But Milo's men pursued, killing the innkeeper and dragging Clodius back to the road. There, he was stabbed repeatedly until dead." Finished with the facts, Cicero reached out, draping one arm across Pompeius Magnus's square shoulders. "Now that Clodius cruises with Charon, Pompeius has agreed to bring troops into the city. All rioting will cease."

Only now? This should have been done months ago! Had today's meeting all been arranged to make Pompeius look heroic? Marcus frowned, chewing his lip as his mind raced. Milo had performed the act, but who had his orders come from?

Cicero? Pompeius?

Pompeius added with gusto, "And since our streets will finally be safe, we'll hold elections!" Senators' heads nodded approval at that. "And I shall also act as sole consul since, at present, we face great challenges, repairing the city's order."

Sole consul? Ho—Pompeius was man of the hour now. This would interest Caesar.

Calvinus and Messala had been swatted aside like annoying

gnats. And all these deliberations took place behind closed doors in Chickpea's domus. Not in the Curia before the Senate!

Movement caught Marcus's eye. Tiro, Cicero's personal slave, burst into the atrium. Darting to Cicero's side, he whispered something to his dominus. Cicero strode toward the door breathlessly and opened it, motioning everyone to follow. Curious as anyone, Marcus fell into line. It had to be an odd sight, a huge white flock of togate men moving like a herd of sheep across the Palatine to gaze down onto the Forum.

Marcus left the senatorial droves and took a different path, down the road, just past the Palatine Gate. Here, he had a sweeping view across the Forum Romanum all the way to the Curia and Tabularium. On the east end of the Forum, there was much movement. More plebs were filing in, many flourishing knives, pikes, and clubs. But behind them, a handful bore something else. At first, Marcus couldn't tell what it was until he heard people below chanting Clodius's name.

Dis of the dead! It was Clodius's naked corpse! Slowly, the crowds below were giving way. They were porting Clodius to the Curia.

His eyes shifted to more movement at the other end of the Forum. Yet another large group was entering, carrying a rough-hewn battering ram made out of a beam, probably confiscated from a Tiber barge. Upon reaching the Curia, they began hammering its bronze doors. Each rhythmic crash was lost over the din of thousands upon thousands of voices screaming in unison: "Clodius, Clodius, Clodius!"

Marcus watched in grim fascination as the Curia's tall, stately doors were assaulted again and again. Finally bashed open upon their hinges, plebs operating the ram began forcing the rest of the crowd back, creating a path. The mob bearing Clodius's corpse followed it, carrying him straight into the building. Then more people scrambled inside, bearing scraps of wood and furniture.

Oh—*no* . . .

Marcus's heart hammered, realizing their purpose.

There was no stopping it. In no time, smoke poured from the doorways and high windows of Rome's Senate building. Those who had entered fled like rats from a burning warehouse.

From where he stood, Marcus watched, mesmerized and sickened, as Rome's seat of power imploded into flames; the Curia had become Clodius's funeral pyre.

Inexplicable sorrow gripped Marcus at Clodius's death. No, they hadn't been close; more times than not they were at odds. But here was a former acquaintance from his youth, and now he was dead. Life was so vulnerable.

Marcus sat at Lentulus's old desk, writing correspondence. First was a note of sympathy to Fulvia:

> *Marcus Antonius, Quaestor-elect, to Fulvia, widow of Publius Clodius Pulcher:*
>
> *Salve and peace to you. I wish to convey condolences upon the death of your husband. He was much-loved by the people. Be well so that I may be well.*

Next, he wrote a more urgent message:

> *Marcus Antonius, Legate, to Gaius Julius Caesar, Proconsul Provinciae of Gallia Cisalpina and General to the Legions of Gallia Comata:*
>
> *Salve, Caesar.*
>
> *Publius Clodius Pulcher was murdered on the Via Appia by Titus Annius Milo. Plebs cremated him in the Curia, so the Senate House now lies in ash.*
>
> *Pompeius has proclaimed himself sole consul. With this new imperium, he assures everyone that elections will finally take place. So hopefully I shall hold the quaestorship soon.*

Cicero fully supported Pompeius in taking the curule chair alone. Pompeius is clearly establishing a power base here in Rome. And Cicero will be defending Milo in his upcoming trial. Now you know where his real alliance is—with Pompeius.

May Mars keep you, for if you are well, then I am well.

Gaius Julius Caesar, Proconsul Provinciae of Gallia Cisalpina and General to the Legions of Gallia Comata, to Marcus Antonius, Legate and Quaestor-elect in Rome:

I dictate this letter as I ride. Central Gaul is in uproar. Labienus is meeting me, and together we're marching on any fortress in which the enemy will likely take refuge.

Fortuna will be loyal, as I am Venus's chosen son. However, the days ahead will be full of bronze and blood. Come quickly, elections or not. I need every trusted officer by my side, for the unthinkable has happened.

The Gauls have united under a single man's leadership.

They've a new king, a man from the Arverni tribe. His name is Vercingetorix, and he's a powerful leader who knows our weaknesses. Labienus writes how our men in the north hunger, for this new king of theirs even subjects his own people to starvation and hardship so that we also suffer. Mark my words, he means to destroy me. What a cunning and worthy opponent the gods have chosen for me to vanquish.

CHAPTER VIII

"SHIELDS UP AND HOLD!" MARCUS YELLED, HIS HORSE nervously prancing back and forth.

A mounted centurion galloped back to the cohort's rear, where trouble had first begun. Hastily regrouping, the legionaries held formation, their shields a solid line of defense on both sides of the road.

Gallic villagers were attacking to steal provision wagons carrying grain, oil, wine, and a limited supply of smoked meat. They were poor, starving wretches desperate for food, but if they were able to kill Romans in the effort, then so much the better.

"They're very thin, Dominus," Eros noted.

"They're not real warriors." Marcus's eyes were still scanning both sides of the road.

Eros was lucky to have ridden with the vanguard today of all days. "Then who are they?"

"Ordinary citizens—farmers? Who knows? Starving people do anything for food. That, I suppose, even means attacking a well-armed cohort!" He spat to one side, hoping it would be nothing but a brief scuffle.

"Look!" Eros cried, pointing to the rear.

A few more Gauls dashed out of the woods, wielding knives and axes. Whistles sounded from a centurion, and after only a few maneuvers, it was over. Four more Gauls fell, and two bolted back to the woods for cover.

None of Marcus's men were injured, but these ambushers were desperate, taking such high risks. Like skinny mongrels, they darted away through the woods with their clubs, knives, and other crude weaponry.

Glancing back at the troops, Eros murmured, "It's good Pompeius sent this cohort. What if we were alone?"

Marcus didn't answer. What the boy didn't realize was that their numbers would never keep them "safe." In truth, Pompeius's "gift" of a cohort was nothing more than an insult to Caesar. Not if a really large army of Gauls materialized. Their limited company equaled just over four hundred and fifty men. That was nothing compared to the Gallic hosts he'd heard about.

Marcus was stressed. Though they'd traveled far, it was impossible to tell exactly where Caesar was located. To protect his men the best he could, he forebade campfires at night and desperately tried to maintain a low profile as he marched such a miniscule force northward. Mile after mile, scorched fields and smoke on the horizon became common sights. Were they Caesar's fires—or those of Vercingetorix?

He fumbled through his saddlebag, finding the crude, well-worn map he'd used to keep track of their location. He had to find Caesar's main force before a larger number of Gauls found his. Their very survival depended on it. If attacked again, the enemy wasn't likely to be weak-hearted, starving scavengers, but an enemy army at full strength. The last official word was that Caesar had confronted Vercingetorix outside a hill fort called Gergovia. But as of yet the outcome was unknown.

Hearing hoof beats, Marcus looked up.

A single scout breathlessly reined in, kicking up dust. "Sir! A large contingent is crossing a hillside several miles ahead."

"Gauls?"

"No, sir. Romans!"

Marcus closed his eyes in relief. "We found them." Turning to his cohort, he shouted, "We sleep safe tonight!" Everyone cheered as word swept through the ranks. Once within sight of the large force, he ordered several tubicines to sound off.

Marcus cantered ahead, the Romans on the hillside altering their course to meet him. They consisted of several cohorts—mostly infantry, battle-weary and exhausted. Some bore minor wounds with soiled bandages wrapped around appendages.

Their leader was a tall, dignified sort. He parted from the unit, riding down to greet Marcus.

"Salve!" Marcus called, coming to a stop with a crisp salute. As the officer approached, Marcus's eyes widened in recognition. *Uncle Lucius?* Gods infernal! He would have preferred Vercingetorix!

"If you were leading your men to Gergovia, don't bother," Uncle Lucius called. "Join us instead. You'll be much needed at Alesia. Are you new to—" He stopped abruptly, recognition dawning. "Nephew? Is that you?"

"It is," Marcus answered flatly. His uncle rode closer and extended his hand. Marcus leaned over, clasping it reluctantly and suppressing bitter words. Anger and humiliation from past encounters was still unforgotten and unforgiven. Ever since an unpleasant morning so long ago in Uncle Lucius's tablinum, when he had all but condemned Lentulus, he and Marcus had found little love for one another. However, these men meant added protection, and he'd embrace that, if not Uncle himself.

Marcus scrapped about for something to say. "Mother mentioned you were in Germania, recruiting."

"Yes. I returned several weeks ago."

Marcus nodded. He had nothing to say to this man who had always held him in contempt. But things had changed. Marcus was no longer the wasted youth that Uncle Lucius always believed him to be. Nor did it matter than he'd once been consul and held a priesthood. Marcus now shared the same rank as he did.

Lucius Julius seemed to read his mind. "You're much changed, Marcus."

"My time in the East made a soldier out of me," he replied. "And then Caesar offered me a position worth my while."

The older man smiled slightly. "He has a way of doing that."

"Yes. He needs good men, especially now."

Uncle Lucius's next words were sobering, "Let's hope he'll have enough good men."

Marcus frowned. "What do you mean?"

"We lost Gergovia."

"Lost?" Marcus signaled a tubicen to call his troops. Meanwhile, he and Uncle Lucius rode together up the rise toward the waiting cohorts.

Uncle Lucius wearily shook his head. "This Vercingetorix is an enigma. He knows our style of warfare, and the tribes trust him. Fortunately, Caesar redeemed himself during a fight after the loss. It scattered the Gallic factions. They fled northeast to Alesia, where Vercingetorix is now holed-in with sixty thousand men. Caesar's there now, organizing a siege. It's where I was headed before intercepting you."

Marcus remained silent, digesting the news.

"They say Vercingetorix means 'Great King of One-Hundred Battles,'" Uncle continued. "A Gaul in our company says we Romans are sure to beat him now because now we know the meaning of his name. Gauls believe that if the meaning of someone's name is revealed, their power is forever lost." He chuckled softly, shaking his head at the thought. "Fascinating."

"Sounds as though Alesia will be the final battle."

"Everyone hopes so. Our men are battle-weary. They just want to go home." After a moment, he added, "Fortunately, Caesar still maintains respect and support. Legionaries call him 'imperator' now, despite Gergovia."

That raised Marcus's eyebrows. "An honor, to be sure." The title of imperator was the highest accolade legionaries could bestow upon a commander.

"How are you faring?" Lucius Julius queried after a pause. "Your Mother wrote how you're standing for quaestor."

"Yes. Elections are supposed to take place soon."

"And your marriage to Hybrida's Antonia?"

"I've a daughter. Sweet little thing."

"Ah, the delights of marriage! My sweet Aelia has always been a lamb. Returning to her is never a burden, but a sweet homecoming. Perhaps we may all go home once this business at Alesia ends."

Marcus smiled tightly to himself at the irony. Scholarly Uncle Lucius would be much relieved to be home again. But he, on the other hand, was more than pleased to return to the field.

Marcus and Uncle Lucius led their men through rough-hewn timber gates on the plain beneath Alesia. Large groups of soldiers were laboring. September had been mild, and legionaries were stripped to their waists in the warm sun. Teams of oxen hauled logs, drovers behind each set of animals, smacking rumps with leather strips to keep them moving. The place was an anthill of activity. Free men and slaves worked doggedly side by side at multiple tasks.

And rising above them all was Alesia.

Marcus finally parted ways with Uncle Lucius and rode straight to Caesar's praetorium. When he entered, Caesar was with his engineering staff, discussing various defenses he was building around the hill fort.

When Marcus appeared, the imperator glanced back from the map they were studying. "Antonius! Come in." Turning back to his engineers, he ended the consultation. "Now you understand where the towers should be. Express my orders to the centurions that we'll need work rotations day and night to finish quickly. Let's plan on meeting again in three days to see where we stand. Dismissed."

As they filed out, Marcus embraced his cousin.

"How's your dear friend Cicero?" Caesar jested.

Marcus didn't smile. "Incorrigible. And he's Pompeius's man, through and through. Be advised of that."

"Yes. Your letter said as much. Who do you think was *really* behind Clodius's murder?"

With a shrug, Marcus responded, "Pompeius, Cicero—maybe both. Milo didn't act alone. I've never met him, but everyone would agree that he is better at following orders than giving them himself."

Caesar shook his head. "It's a shame. I could have used Clodius—especially now that you're here. It's difficult knowing who to trust."

"Well, I'm *not* confident that Clodius would have been the right choice. He was too set in his ways and unwilling to change."

Caesar changed subjects and Marcus knew why. He never liked being proved wrong. "Was your journey safe?"

"By the grace of Fortuna. Pompeius sent you an entire cohort."

Caesar raised his brows. "Hmph. He disappoints."

Marcus studied him, certain Caesar was feeling a lot more than disappointment. Provocation, maybe?

"And Crassus failed," Caesar added thoughtfully.

"Young Marcus Crassus too. I hated hearing that. He was a good man."

"I hated seeing him leave us, knowing he'd wind up in Parthia."

"You didn't think his tata had a chance?"

Caesar shook his head, leaning on his desk. "I was his tribune in the Spartacan Revolt, remember? He took forever sorting that mess out and created chaos afterward by decimating so many men. I doubted him from the beginning."

Marcus paused, wondering how to ask, but his curiosity won out and his question was blunt. "I rode in here with Uncle Lucius. He said you lost Gergovia. What happened?"

"Damned error in communication. I was calling for a retreat as a means to bring Vercingetorix down off of the oppidum to face me. There was some sort of confusion with the message, and instead my men *engaged* the Gauls. They were routed by the heart of

Vercingetorix's army before I could intervene. It was a bloodbath—terrible. We were sorely beaten. It will *not* happen again."

"Surely not." Marcus frowned in concern.

"I'll starve them out if I must since that high chief of theirs refuses to meet me on the field. Hear me now—I *will* take Gallia Comata, Antonius. It will be *ours*. Rome needs new fields for her veterans, lands that will make her purses fat and heavy with gold."

"Let's make it so," Marcus said, smiling. "It's good to be back with you."

Caesar gave a curt nod. "You seemed to get on well with Trebonius. He knows you're coming, so you'll share a tent again. I'm off to ride the perimeters to see how our lazy girls are doing building my wall. Dine with me tonight—and bring Trebonius."

Marcus followed Caesar outside and watched him mount. Then his gaze shifted to the oppidum itself.

Built on lofty heights, the majestic hill fort deterred any approach from below. Wispy fingers of smoke from countless cooking fires formed a haze above the stronghold. Native homeplace of the Mandubii tribe, it was now the beating heart of Gallic resistance. Somewhere behind its walls was the iron-fisted king who had united all of Gallia Comata: Vercingetorix.

Marcus blinked, unrolling yet another scroll. His eyes burned from too much reading. Shadows were long, and the lamp's wick was burning down.

By day, he trained cavalry units, managed legionary accounts, and inspected fortifications. Now, in the wee hours, he lagged behind in his additional work. Since he'd arrived, most letters from the Senate and Caesar's personal acquaintances now crossed his desk. It was his personal judgment whether a message was worthy of the imperator's immediate attention or not.

This position was an honor of which he was keenly aware. Caesar had placed him in his most intimate circle. Being trusted with correspondence from political enemies and allies demanded loyalty.

Trebonius had said that even Titus Labienus grumbled that he hadn't warranted such confidence. As Caesar's second, Labienus was an able, gifted general, but Caesar suspected he courted Pompeius. Marcus recalled how Clodius had declared what he thought was Caesar's real goal—seizing Pompeius's imperium. Clodius had been right. Even all the way out here in Gallia Comata, civil war was brewing.

At Marcus's fingertips rested a delicate letter concerning Octavia, one of Antonia's friends who was also Caesar's great niece. Caesar had recently offered her to Pompeius to replace Julia Caesaris as his wife. This was done covertly, for it would've taken some maneuvering. Octavia was already married to the notorious Optimate Marcellus.

In a recent letter, Pompeius had not only rejected the offer by selecting another woman to marry, but declined a second proposal, Caesar's suggestion that *he* marry Pompeius's daughter! Both refusals carried one message—a chasm between the world's two most powerful men.

Marcus pitied poor Calpurnia. So far from Gaul, she seldom received word from her husband. And now here was proof that Caesar loved her very little if he was so willing to divorce her for Pompeius's young daughter.

Caesar's own responses to Pompeius's previous slights had been curt but courteous. Now he'd have to respond to two snubbed offers of marital alliance. All good Romans would be saddened since the marriage between Julia Caesaris and Pompeius had brought such agreeable peace and goodwill.

No, this wouldn't be pretty.

Rolling the letters back into scroll form, Marcus heard wheels grind to a stop outside his tent. It was Eros, who had been delivering water all day to thirsty legionaries building the defense wall.

Marcus arose, opening the tent flap to find the slave whispering urgently to a sentry.

"At ease," Marcus assured the soldier. To Eros, he invited, "I'm awake. Come in."

The boy entered, flushed and out of breath. "I was filling jugs in the river, Dominus. I heard voices."

Marcus cocked one eyebrow. "Gauls?"

Eros nodded. "I crept closer, but it was too dark, and I don't know their words. I heard horses moving within a stone's throw in the woods. Up ahead of where I was, they rode into the river to escape."

The river ran free between the walls and two watchtowers. Theoretically, if sentries weren't watching closely, it would be easy for someone from the oppidum to slosh or ride their way to freedom there.

A rustling in the back of the tent caused both Marcus and Eros to glance back. It was Trebonius. Asleep on his cot, he had awakened and overheard them. Intense concern creased his face.

"What's this?" he asked, arising to join them.

"Eros overheard Gauls escaping Alesia." Marcus turned back to the boy. "Could you tell how many got out?"

Eros shrugged. "Fifteen—twenty, maybe. It was hard to tell. I know they took the river because I heard the horses splashing."

"Damn. Right under our noses," Trebonius swore, shaking his head with a sigh. "Our sentries should've seen them—or *heard* them."

"Did any watches respond? Could you tell?" Marcus queried.

"I don't know. I came straight to you," Eros replied.

"Caesar must be told," Trebonius advised.

Marcus nodded. "Yes. But first I'm sending out a cavalry pursuit. Maybe they'll intercept them."

"Good idea," Trebonius said. "In the meantime, I'll visit watchtowers and ask if anyone saw anything."

Marcus turned back to Eros, ruffling his hair "You did well, boy."

As they stepped out of the tent together and into the darkness,

Trebonius placed a hand on Marcus's arm. He whispered in a troubled voice, "You do know what this means?"

"We might have a relief army headed our way," Marcus answered, voice low.

"Only the gods know how many might respond."

Marcus nodded. There were a lot more Gauls *outside* than inside Alesia. And every single one swore allegiance to Vercingetorix.

Crisp air and new danger awakened Marcus's senses as he strode to Caesar's praetorium. As expected, a soft glow from a lamp burned inside. Two sentries snapped to attention.

"Inform the imperator I have vital information."

Before the sentry could respond, Caesar himself came to the front of the tent, flipping back the flap. "Come in."

Marcus took a deep breath. "My slave heard something down by the river."

"What?"

"Fifteen, maybe twenty Gallic cavalry escaped Alesia tonight." There was silence a moment before he went on. "I took the liberty of ordering a cavalry pursuit. Hopefully, we can run some of them down and question them."

Caesar nodded. "Good."

"If they do get away, they'll seek relief, won't they? How many do you think would respond?"

Caesar sat down at his desk, pondering the question. "Gaul is a large country. Who knows how many thousands are out there, ready to hearken to their king? I'm afraid I cannot say. Hopefully, by tomorrow your cavalry will have prisoners. After hearing them out, I'll meet with staff, so we're ready for them if they do come."

Marcus stared at him, incredulous. "*Ready* for them? Shouldn't we break siege and make a tactical retreat?"

Caesar rose, lifting his chin. "Indeed not! I'm here to *win* this war. I'm taking that long-haired bastard to Rome in chains!"

Marcus reasoned, shaking his head. "Even as strong as your seasoned veterans are, they couldn't last a day pressed between two large Gallic armies."

Caesar lifted one hand and rubbed the late-night stubble on his chin. "You're right. There's really only one option, isn't there? A second ring of fortifications will be necessary."

Marcus exhaled slowly, taking a step backward in shock. Had he heard Caesar correctly? "Our legionaries are exhausted, completing nearly eleven miles of walls and traps in just a few weeks," he reminded, voice low. "We'd be fighting a war on two fronts!"

"You're correct. Would I have your support, Marcus Antonius? I'll need it when I go before the skeptics, like Labienus. In the past, you've always been a gambler." Caesar smiled, eyes twinkling. "You're a risk-taker. Will you wager all with me?"

Dis Pater! They might end up like Crassus's army!

"Caesar awaits response." His voice had gone cold.

Marcus's pulse raced. The Gauls would either wipe out the entire Roman force or make Caesar the greatest general since Alexander the Great. This man was family and had supported him when he was in need and had nearly self-destructed after Fadia died. And Caesar's only major defeat had been Gergovia.

Marcus licked his lips, his voice hoarse but firm. "I'll wager all. I'm with you." Extending his hand, he clasped that of his kinsman, Caesar's gaze burning in a deadly lock with his.

Marcus eyed the men of war around him in wonder from where he stood in the back corner of the praetorium.

First, his eyes settled on Labienus.

The brawny general had been a mainstay for Caesar since the beginning of the Gallic campaign. Of provincial birth, like Pompeius, he'd never held great sway in the Senate. Much like Marcus, he'd found his place on the battlefield. However, he had taken to his own counsel more and more, questioning Caesar constantly. Now Caesar relied more on other men, including Marcus. Did Labienus belong to Pompeius? It was something to ponder.

Then there was Uncle Lucius. Trebonius said he'd done well at recruiting, but that wasn't real soldiering. Tribunes, lower-ranking officers, and centurions were present. Caesar always invited them to consilia. He'd have to convince lowborn soldiers and high-rankers alike to remain loyal; stay and fight.

Quintus Cicero, Chickpea's younger brother, was whispering with others around him. Now *here* was a Cicero with military talent. Marcus was impressed with his organization, courage, and self-confidence. His brother, Marcus Tullius, certainly had none of it.

Marcus Junius Brutus sat alone, refusing to even make eye contact with Marcus, probably because of Cytheris. Marcus grinned at the thought. Ah, well—the better man had won!

He was a quiet, saturnine sort, and Marcus hardly knew him. Like everyone in Rome, he knew that Caesar and Brutus's mother, Servilia, had been lovers. He figured the imperator's adoration for the son stemmed from that, for he had about as much skill with a gladius as baby Antonia. Unfortunately, Brutus's politics were not exactly in line with Caesar's interests. The extremely conservative statesman Cato was like a father to him. Yet despite such differences, Caesar never ceased in his generosity and favor toward his former lover's son.

Opening his arms in welcome, Caesar began. "Let us commence with the consilium."

Talk in the praetorium ceased.

"Before dawn this morning, a detachment of cavalry sent out by Antonius intercepted nine Gauls on horseback attempting to escape Alesia."

The tent filled with murmurs.

Caesar ignored them. "After interrogations," he explained, raising his voice to be heard, "it was discovered they were sent out by Vercingetorix to rally a relief army. Five succeeded in escaping, so we must assume they're carrying out orders. We also spoke with a deserter from the oppidum, captured two days past. He confirmed the riders' accounts. Therefore I must determine our next phase of the campaign. Do any of you wish to offer up opinions on the situation?"

A primus pilus centurion said, "We already face impressive numbers inside the oppidum. Is there any way to coerce battle before relief arrives?"

Caesar pursed his lips, shaking his head. "Vercingetorix will await reinforcements, even if his conditions worsen. Things up there must be critical now. Their stores can't last forever. He'll wait. I would, under the same circumstances."

"As long as the arriving opposition contains undisciplined forces, we should beat them," said Quintus Cicero. "However, we'll need to engage as soon as they arrive. We can't afford to let them organize."

"Yes, and while we're busy fighting the relief, here comes Vercingetorix charging down the hill, aiming for our backs!"

That was Labienus.

Caesar scooted a heavy bronze lamp stand closer to a map he had drawn of the area. "Colleagues: my proposal is to double our investments by building a second ring of fortifications. Here's where I wish to place them." Taking a lump of charred wood from a nearby brazier, he drew a great circle around the present ring. "Contravallation. There it is. We'll construct a series of walls and watchtowers, similar to those in the first encirclement, but facing *out* toward our anticipated enemy."

"It might work," said a young tribune standing near the entrance. "Especially if the oppidum's warriors are wasting thin."

"But take care, Caesar," Brutus cautioned. "The Senate would construe this action as too perilous. Anyone here can see what great risk is involved."

As if on cue, Labienus stepped forth next, his burly frame casting grotesque shadows on sides of the tent. "Exactly what gives you the right to put our trusting men in such a position?"

Caesar leaned back on his desk, his mouth set in a rigid smile. He always allowed his men to vent their views. Labienus would be no exception.

Still, Marcus cocked an eyebrow as the man continued.

"We've barely completed our *first* ring of fortifications, yet now you propose a *second*, with us ensnared in the middle? We'd be a tortoise inside the maws of a ravenous crocodile. For a time, the reptile waits, undaunted. Poor, doomed tortoise sitting at ease, thinking it'll escape at leisure, when suddenly—*crack*!" Labienus slapped his hands together dramatically, accentuating the illustration. "Those monstrous jaws snap tight with such force the tortoise barely feels death when it comes!"

Marcus chuckled, along with everyone else. For all of Labienus's gruff, irritating nature, he was quite the colorful orator when he so chose. Maybe he'd find a place in the Senate after all.

Uncle Lucius called out, "Caesar, though my time with you has been brief, I've seen nothing but clumsy, ill-organized movement by the enemy. You scattered them easily after Gergovia. I say do it again, and I'll stand by you. You have my word. Then this Gallic War will be over and the Senate will have to keep their peace."

"Honorable words, Lucius Caesar," Labienus sneered. "However, you've been too busy manning your farms with slaves down in Italia and haven't endured eight long years of unending conflict with these filthy barbarians. You don't know Atrebates from Aedui any more than you can recognize the difference between a turnip and a melon!"

Marcus stifled laughter by feigning a cough. Others laughed at the slur too.

Labienus pressed onward in his attack. "You mention defeating them so easily after Gergovia, but do you forget what happened *at* Gergovia? We *lost*, you fool!"

Caesar interjected softly but firmly. "Titus Labienus, be reminded that every man in this praetorium is entitled to *his* opinion, not just yours. Also remember I consider personal slights to be unprofessional behavior." To Uncle Lucius, he said, "Rest assured your opinion is highly valued."

Attempts at reining Labienus in only raised his hackles all the more. "Look here, all of you," the aging soldier snarled, striding all the way to the front of the praetorium and, momentarily, eclipsing Caesar. "Our noble boys are exhausted—ho! Everyone's wearing thin! A contravallation will fray us at the seams, depleting what little food reserves we have left. All of us will starve like the Gauls. We nearly already are!"

"His words are sure, Caesar." Quintus Cicero stood to speak. "I mentioned engaging a relief army quickly, but what really troubles me most is how the Gauls have started mimicking our style of warfare. If we choose not to retreat, with numbers on their side, they could beat us at our own game. Now that's the worst-case scenario, of course," he allowed.

"Of course," Caesar agreed.

Brutus said, "Our men are homesick. Would it be fair after all these years in Gaul to doom them here, much like Crassus's army?"

Marcus found himself stepping forward, nodding to Labienus respectfully as he made his way to the front. He was no longer Caesar's new and untried legate. Now he was standing for political office, and held a history of courage on the field.

Every eye rested upon him with curious regard.

"Brothers, I was at the Senate the day we learned of Crassus's fate. I heard of his defeat in all its horror. There were mistakes—disorganization—in that campaign. But here in Gallia Comata, we rarely face such oversights. We have an imperator who strives for safety, taking necessary steps to keep us beyond the enemy's grasp. Titus Labienus just reminded us that Gergovia was lost, and that is truth. But let us remember instead how many battles Caesar has *won*. What can the Gauls do that we cannot? Ambush us?" Marcus snorted. "They can't surprise us here. They'll be forced to fight openly. And should they use our tactics, then we'll rely on our superior weapons and armor, not to mention how we Romans always have the advantage of discipline when pressed."

Marcus jabbed his forefinger downward for effect. "Here on this ground, we can end a bloody campaign lasting nearly a decade. Or we can burn these fortifications our men have toiled over, retreating at the first thought of a relief army. I'll tell you something—that latter plan hasn't the nerve of Romans *I* care to drink with."

Lots of men laughed aloud at that. Marcus raised his hand for silence, grinning unabashedly at himself. "For myself, I shall remain here. Let's build the second ring and whatever numbers they send—*finish* them."

Caesar nodded in obvious appreciation. He closed the meeting by saying, "Danger, my friends? Of course. Peril? Absolutely. However, contravallation is achievable. If there's any man in this tent who cannot stomach this venture, speak now."

Silence.

Caesar waited, turning his back and studying the map. The black charcoal circle stood out clearly against the leather's faded sketches.

Uncle Lucius finally stood. "I'm with you, Imperator."

"I speak for all of us, Caesar," voiced the primus pilus of Legio X Equestris. "It's a serious risk, but we've faced others. We stand with you."

"Good," Caesar said.

Trebonius, who had been silent up until now, spoke quietly, "I don't agree, but I'd never shame my father's shade by leaving a post I was ordered to defend. I'll stay and fight—die here, if I must."

Marcus was surprised at his response but relieved that he'd voiced approval, albeit begrudgingly.

"Gratias, friend," Caesar acknowledged.

"I share Trebonius's sentiment," Quintus Cicero declared. "But you rescued me and my army two years ago. In return, I give you my all."

"Your honesty is valued. Now, dear Brutus . . ." Caesar prompted.

"Dear Caesar," Brutus returned with a placid smile. "I've

listened to reasonable debate, and I think you're doing what must be done to win this war. As always, I'm at your service."

Caesar lifted both arms. "Then I conclude this consilium, recommending everyone get a fair night's sleep. We'll start building new fortifications at dawn. I'll send engineering detachments to each legion with orders to centurions on which units will be building what. For now, be dismissed. However, Marcus Antonius and Titus Labienus—attend me."

As everyone funneled out, Marcus made his way to Caesar's desk and stood next to Labienus.

Caesar sat down with an air of imperious control, staring hard at Labienus. His jaw was set, and Marcus sensed that what was coming wasn't going to be pleasant.

Caesar waited until everyone had exited. "I'll say this only once," he intoned softly. "And Antonius is here as my witness. At times, Labienus, your choice of words could be construed by some as . . . mutinous. Care to respond?"

Labienus didn't hesitate. "You've always encouraged open opinions during consilia. You know me personally. I've no spit and polish, like patricians."

Caesar responded with a wry smile. "Agreed. But see to it that your 'opinions' don't stir or inflame men serving under you. Be reminded that when there is no way out, men fight *harder*."

"In return, I respectfully ask that you not slight me because of my humble birth. I've handed you victory after victory, yet I've received little accolade. There are others in this camp who seem to receive more esteem—undeservedly, perhaps."

Marcus felt Labienus's stare. It was the first time the man had voiced dislike toward him.

"Labienus, when have either you or I been present in the Senate these past eight years to demand or receive commendation?" Caesar said. "As you are most certainly aware, instead of praise, I endure constant accusations. Also, don't presume to dictate to me what I may owe you. You've become as rich off the wealth of Gaul as any man here. Antonius, whom I believe you just insinuated, happens to be loyal, a trait I consider admirable. By your words this night, have I sensed the same sentiment from you? You hold the position of second in command—at present. Be wise you don't earn my displeasure or distrust. Confidence is only awarded to those one *holds* in confidence."

Labienus scoffed in contempt. Stepping close, he rested both fists on the heavy wooden desk, leaning in as he spoke. "Soon we'll be surrounded from within and without. We'll be lucky if one man returns alive to Rome to tell our tale. So before I die fighting for you, I want to know one thing. Why is it that you can never admit defeat?"

Marcus's eyes widened. Gods, he'd done it now! Labienus had earned both Caesar's displeasure and mistrust with that one question.

Gaius Julius Caesar stood up slowly to his full and intimidating height, hovering over the squat, rugged general, eyes glittering with rage. "I don't admit defeat because I've not been defeated. *Dismissed!*"

CHAPTER IX

MARCUS ANTONIUS, LEGATE IN GALLIA Comata, to his brother Gaius Antonius in Rome:

Salve.

I write this with grave uncertainty. While fighting in the East with Gabinius, I sometimes encountered danger, but this upcoming conflict is similar to those of gladiators. Placed in an arena with nowhere to go, they never know what sort of beast they'll fight. None of us knows how many Gauls will respond to Vercingetorix's call for aid. Caesar is a superb commander, and it's a privilege to serve him, to call him my kinsman. However, this battle, when it comes, will be the bloodiest I've ever experienced.

If I die, instruct Mother and Antonia to raise my daughter as befits a woman of Rome. Please tell her stories about me so she'll know who I was. Also, encourage my wife to remarry for happiness, as would suit her. If the slave Eros survives me, free him and give him a bag of aureii in my name. Because of his youth, welcome him within the family until he's secure in an occupation for himself.

I'm sending you my signet ring. It's yours if I don't return, so in that event, wear it well. I'd prefer it on your hand than for it to fall into those of barbarians.

Be assured I won't cause our family any shame. If the upcoming battle goes awry, I'll either fall fighting or take the course Father could not.

Give my love to Mother, Tonia, and Lucius. Tell Antonia I wish her health and happiness.

Stay well so that I may be well.

Every man wrote similar letters to wives, brothers, fathers, mothers, or friends in case Caesar's luck ended at Alesia.

An air of anxiety descended upon the legionary camp. Construction on the new contravallation walls had started. If and when the Gallic army arrived, there'd be no more messages to or from the Roman fortifications.

There was something Marcus needed to do—something he'd put off.

No longer.

He lifted the tent flap and hailed Eros, who was harnessing his pony for another day of hauling water to thirsty soldiers. "Eros, inside." Turning his back to the entrance, he strode to his cot, placing the letter to Gaius to one side and drawing his gladius from its sheath with a hiss.

Eros paused at the entrance, waiting expectantly for instructions. "Dominus?"

"Over here."

Padding over, Eros stood before him, willing, as always, to serve.

Marcus rested the deadly blade comfortably atop one palm. "I need to show you something." He offered it to the slave. "Go on, take it."

Eros grasped the hilt firmly.

Marcus smiled. "Heavy?"

"Yes, Dominus."

"Know how to use it?"

Eros moistened his lips nervously, shaking his head.

"It's time you learned."

With eyes round as agate gaming pieces, Eros stared at him.

"If I were your enemy," Marcus asked, "where would you strike me?"

"I'd stab at your vitals. Maybe slash at your legs if luck allowed. That's what legionaries do."

"Very good!" Marcus praised. But it was awkward introducing the subject nagging at him.

Eros lowered the sword.

"Eros, if we're defeated, if things don't end well, I'll need help," Marcus began. Extending one hand for his sword, he reclaimed the weapon, holding it out and studying it. "As one of Caesar's legates, it would be extremely dishonorable to be taken prisoner. Gauls are brutal to us Romans when captured. If I'm not killed in battle, I'd need to end my life. Ever since I was young I've dealt with dishonor within my family, and I'll have no more of that."

"Dominus . . ." Eros breathed, shaking his head slowly.

"Now listen." Marcus's eyes and voice turned hard. He placed one hand firmly on the boy's shoulder. "I think the best way to do it would be for me to kneel." He lifted the sword's point, placing it between his left shoulder blade and neck, where a pulse beat. "You're still rather small, so you'd need to hold it firmly with both hands, not just one. Aim and thrust straight down, ramming the blade into me as hard as possible. If you do it right, I'll be dead before hitting the ground. If and when the time comes, I'll coach you through it."

Eros looked horrified. "I—I could never—"

Marcus interrupted. "If required to do it, there will be no

arguing. Once done, you could try escaping or choose to kill yourself as well. If captured, you'd probably be enslaved and mistreated. I take no pleasure in discussing this, but it's war. You begged to be at my side, did you not?"

Eros was fighting tears and nodding at the same time.

"Very well. In serving a soldier, you must have courage yourself. We'll leave the subject behind, but understand that this battle will be bloody. If I give such an order, you must do what's required."

Marcus picked up the cylinder with Gaius's letter. "Now take this to one of the couriers leaving for Rome. Have them deliver it directly to my brother Gaius Antonius, and no other. Understood?"

"Yes, Dominus." Eros's eyes were still troubled.

Marcus smiled at him. "Gratias."

Rations were now strictly enforced. Any officer, legionary, or slave caught stealing food faced immediate execution. Everyone was much thinner, and Eros had to lace Marcus's Alexandrian cuirass as tightly as possible.

Still, Roman hunger was nothing in comparison to the pitiful Gauls up in Alesia. Caesar had been correct in assuming that starvation raged inside the oppidum.

While the contravallation walls were still in their earliest stages, Marcus was out with Caesar, observing the progress, when legionaries manning towers adjacent to the hill fort sounded an alarm.

"Mars!" Caesar gasped. "They're opening their gates."

Everyone watched wordlessly. Did Vercingetorix mean to offer battle? As they waited and watched, out straggled an exodus of people—elderly, women, children. They were all Mandubii, the native inhabitants of Alesia.

"He's expelling them," Marcus thought aloud.

Caesar nodded. "Yes. Starvation up there must be at its worst.

Vercingetorix is choosing his men over the oppidum's native people."

A virtual multitude streamed forth. Old men limping along with canes, small boys clinging to mothers, babies screaming in hunger, and girls weeping with fear. Slaves of the Mandubii and presumably of Vercingetorix's army were also ejected. They carried nothing, not even blankets. Once all were out, the entrance was closed and bolted, shutting out their pleas. Healthier ones turned, pounding at the gates, crying for mercy.

For a few days after, the Mandubii were the talk of camp and legionaries couldn't help but line the watchtowers, watching the poor, displaced Gauls wander. A huge territory surrounded Alesia up to Caesar's fortification walls, so they had plenty of space, yet nowhere to go. Nearly all the area's game had been hunted down and even fish in the river were gone, cleared out by both Romans and Gauls looking for extra meals.

Finally, a Mandubii delegation of old women and girls appeared at the Roman gates. As a last resort, they knelt and begged to be taken as slaves and whores so they wouldn't starve.

Caesar refused. "No enemies of Rome will receive food needed by my own men, already suffering slim rations."

So the desperate Mandubii plodded about in their empty no-man zone, someplace between madness and death, void of hope. At night, they wailed, calling out to their gods. It took weeks for them to die.

Naturally, the horror of it affected the Roman camp. Marcus and Trebonius stuffed their ears with scraps of wool from their tunics before sleeping, muting the mournful cries.

"It's like trying to sleep in Hades," Trebonius grumbled.

During the day, Caesar had bucinatores and tubicines drilling signals throughout camp to drown out the suffering. It worked to extinguish the cries, but nobody remained unaffected by the slow, piteous deaths of old men, women, and children, regardless of race or status. The area surrounding the oppidum was filled with the stench of rotting corpses, the odor permeating the Roman encampment.

On a brilliant fall day, Marcus Antonius rode to the top of a hill outside the contravallations, breathing fresh air at last. But as he looked up into what should have been a glorious blue sky, he was greeted instead by soaring carrion birds. How sickeningly strange that their flight was so graceful and weightless, fed as they were on bodies of Mandubii girls and boys. Marcus sucked in the air, wishing to get drunk on it. The reek of death had brought back terrible nightmares of long ago—along the Via Appia, when he'd witnessed the crucifixions of Spartacus's defeated slave army. Caesar had been there too. He'd told Marcus that he'd need to get used to the smell.

A brisk autumn breeze carried voices up the hill. Legionaries were chanting a cadence about Caesar:

Old Baldy's tough as tough can be
His cloak crimson, for dignity
To starving soldiers, he feeds nil
But he still arms us, dressed to kill!

Their grim humor made him smile despite the present circumstances.

Moments later, he heard a rider approach. A single horseman was cantering uphill, obviously intent on joining him.

It was Uncle Lucius. Marcus had been able to mostly avoid him since arriving at Alesia, having nothing pleasant to say to him.

"Salve, Nephew," Uncle called, lifting a hand in greeting.

Damn. No way out of it now.

Marcus chewed his lip. Truth be told, he liked Uncle Lucius no more now than he had the day he turned his back on the Antonii family, refusing to speak on Lentulus's behalf.

Uncle made it up the hill and reined in beside him, spirits high. "A splendid day, isn't it? The weather's changing!"

"It's only splendid if you're not Mandubii," Marcus muttered.

Uncle Lucius nodded and even laughed drily. Then he became serious. "Marcus, I've waited, seeking opportunity to approach you. I know because of past circumstances things remain unsettled between us."

Marcus regarded this man who had never been kindred to him except in name.

"Please," Uncle implored, "let's put the past away. You have an entire lifetime, but I'm not getting any younger. I want to enjoy my family. And your mother would be so pleased to hear that we're reconciled."

"You were never concerned about pleasing her when it counted," Marcus pointed out. "You should have thought of that when you let Lentulus die without a trial. What could you possibly gain from my friendship now?"

"Simply to be done with the awkwardness around one another since we share blood. We certainly *fight* for the same purpose, do we not?"

Marcus said nothing, turning his head back toward camp and wishing Uncle Lucius would simply go away.

"You've done well for yourself," Uncle cajoled. "Your mother is proud of you. She's told me so often."

There was still nothing to say.

"Some say Caesar looks upon you as a son."

Marcus whipped his head around, glaring at Uncle Lucius. The implication was now as clear as blown glass. "Ah! *Now* I see! Whatever good standing I happen to have with Caesar you hope to profit from?"

"Not at all—"

"Enough!" Marcus spat in disgust. "Mother might have found some incomprehensible reason to forgive you, but I have not."

He dug his heels into his horse's sides, and it started, loping back toward camp. Uncle Lucius was left alone beneath circling vultures. Even the stench of dead Mandubii was preferable to his company.

Two weeks later, Marcus climbed up a newly completed contravallation watchtower.

For a while, he stood gazing up at Alesia. There was no more smoke from cooking fires to be seen. Vercingetorix's men simply had nothing to eat. Now any thin wisps of smoke threading into the air probably indicated that the Gauls were boiling scraps of leather to chew—or consuming their dead.

Sickened at the thought, he turned his back on the oppidum and stared out into the open countryside. There had been a light frost on the ground this morning, and when the wind kicked up, he shivered.

Sentries on the tower were playing a familiar game, each man taking turns fantasizing about what their favorite meal would be. Gauls inside Alesia weren't the only ones hungry.

Marcus grinned and chuckled at the soldier taking his turn.

"Thirty hot loaves drizzled with herbs and oil. Then some of those li'l shrimps lightly cooked over a fire. And then some cheese that my grandfather's famous for making. It crumbles a bit over the bread . . ."

An excellent meal, to be sure!

Another sentry on duty interrupted, tapping Marcus on the shoulder and pointing toward the horizon. What he saw turned his blood cold.

A massive army had crested the far hill in eerie silence. No blasting carnyx horn heralded their arrival. Myriads of Gauls—too many to count—were on the move, as far as he could see.

Next to him, the sentry whispered, "Sir, how many do you figure there are?"

Marcus blinked in bewilderment, trying to make a rough estimate in his mind. He simply shook his head, cold sweat beading his brow. "Tens of thousands, thousands upon thousands."

The Gallic relief force attacked head-on.

Stark-naked men streamed toward the Roman camp, brandishing swords. They rushed madly, screaming and gnashing their teeth like manifestations of the Furies. Headlong on foot and horseback too—none of them even slowed, crashing into the contravallation walls so hard that the earth and timbers shook. Somchow a few found footing, scrambling all the way to the tops of the walls like rats. One toppled two sentries, all three falling to their deaths.

Their attack wasn't successful, but gods, were they ever intimidating. Caesar ordered scorpions to send out a rain of bolts, but it took some time to reposition the machinery to an angle closer to the very front of the encampment. Marcus's orders were to support the centurions whose squadrons were working the machinery. Once set in place, they were wickedly effective, blowing right through the Gallic front lines. Barbs pierced defenseless flesh, and most of the Gauls leading the initial charge died instantly.

But that was only the first line.

Behind were armored warriors, some astride muscular horses with long manes and tails. Their ranks stretched clear to the horizon. Wealthy noblemen, probably personal friends of Vercingetorix, sported polished bronze helmets and bore enormous shields brightly painted with ornate animal designs. Silver or gold trinkets dangled over their heavy mail.

Vercingetorix chose this moment to lead his army out of Alesia, straight to the interior walls. In a daring move, Caesar intercepted them, leading cavalry beyond the walls, straight into their midst to drive them away. When armed Gauls started scaling the walls again, Marcus joined Trebonius and led their company over to repel any making it inside.

But Vercingetorix had a nasty surprise. The king used a small band of archers to rain hell down onto Marcus's infantry, who, along with Trebonius's men, were reinforcing that sector. Only by locking shields above their heads in a stationary testudo formation could they maintain ground. Marcus and Trebonius had to call in their own archers to pick off Gauls scaling the walls.

It wasn't until after sunset that both sides withdrew and the camp dropped into an unnerving calm.

The sheer numbers of the resistance had everyone shaken up. Caesar had Mamurra calculate on his abacus how many there were. His estimate was nearly two hundred thousand, and that was just the relief army. Inside Alesia was Vercingetorix's army.

At dawn the next day, everything was far too quiet, and there was no sign of the enemy.

Marcus sat on his cot, finishing one last bit of soggy grain in his bowl's recesses. Again, and again, he swept one finger around the edges, cleaning up every trace of porridge he could find. Disgusted, he tossed the bowl away, lying back unsatisfied, his stomach rumbling in complaint.

The tent flap snapped and Trebonius entered. "Quintus Cicero said our scouts barely made it back. Bastards were firing at them from the forest."

"Did they find out anything?"

He shrugged. "They're building something. Siege engines—battering rams? Who knows? He said it was too dark for anyone to tell. They heard hammering, though."

Marcus shook his head, staring at his feet. "Now we're the besieged."

"Exactly, and we have no more food than Vercingetorix."

"What day is it?"

Trebonius scratched his head, trying to remember. "The kalends of October," he replied, voice hoarse and fatigued.

"This has been the longest autumn of my life."

Trebonius shook his head, sighing. "I can't see us coming out of this one. Caesar's notorious good luck is spent." Marcus didn't argue, and after a pause Trebonius queried, "Do you know what troubles me in all this?"

"What?"

"When our fathers fought for Rome, they fought to bring victory and glory to *her*, bringing *her* more lands, enlarging *her* territories. Now we're fighting for a single man instead of Rome. It's unsettling, don't you think?"

Marcus got up. He was too tired to consider political views right now. "Honestly, at this moment I really don't *care* who I'm fighting for. I'd gladly dress as a woman and fight for an army of Amazons if only we could have something substantial to eat. I'd trade this tent and everything in it for a platter of steaming pork, honeyed figs, and an amphora of Chian taller than the Pharos Lighthouse."

He left the tent, visiting cavalry camps in his sector and tents full of injured men from the day before, trying to bolster their spirits. To see them smile when he approached their cots moved him. He sat down, speaking and joking with them. Several would probably never stand again, much less ride.

Marcus Antonius kept those thoughts to himself.

That night, Marcus's sleep was interrupted when bucinatores sounded a call to arms, awaking him, Trebonius, and their slaves. Moments later, a sentry was outside shrieking, "We're under attack! Man your sectors!"

"This is it," Trebonius muttered under his breath.

"Maybe, but they won't take me down without bleeding along with me," Marcus responded, his voice gravelly from sleep. He had slept in his armor, so he hoisted his gladius over his shoulder and fastened it. "Eros, Lyco," he directed their slaves, who were frozen in fear on their cots, "go to the streambed and haul in extra water for the horses. They'll need every drop. And no lamps or torches. If you're seen, you're a target."

After that, it was pandemonium.

It was difficult to tell what was happening in the dark. Marcus heard the whoosh of scorpions being fired from someplace nearby. But there was no order, no discipline. If this continued, the men would panic.

Hearing shouts from behind, Marcus whirled his horse about. "Trebonius, look!"

"What is it?" With eyes not as young as Marcus's, he simply couldn't see.

"Those were ladders they were building yesterday! They're up our walls and moving in! Some are already coming down over there. I'll take what men we've got and begin a defense."

It went on all night.

Marcus led both infantry and cavalry against Gauls descending in droves from the contravallation wall. Fatigue was rife within his ranks, yet they fought like madmen. Skirmish after skirmish, squads of cavalry pursued any enemy warriors infiltrating past the infantry. Engage, withdraw, engage, withdraw—again and again.

Less than a watch into the fight, a centurion reported that Gauls outside the walls were using a ram. There was so much noise Marcus had to borrow an infantryman's shield and rush up the nearest tower to confirm the report.

It was true. Crude though it was, the Gauls were manning long, sturdy logs they'd cut—probably the day before. Five men on each side were cradling the great timber in a rough-hewn rope harness and charging the wall. Behind them were ten more Gauls with yet another log, awaiting their turn.

Marcus screamed at the centurion, "I want archers up here! Let's see how many they can bring down!"

He feared it was too late; those makeshift rams were vicious, and the hairy brutes were startlingly well-organized with them. Reports from legionaries fighting nearest the wall on the Roman side were that timbers there were starting to split.

Marcus had barely descended the tower again when a portion of the wall caved.

An entire cohort nearest the break turned tail, ready to bolt, but he saw them and screamed, "Turn your asses around and fight like Romans! Take another step toward me and I'll see you flogged to death after this battle!"

Confronted with his rage—and their centurions' staves—they slowly turned back. From where he joined them, Marcus heard a mighty roar of bellowing as more of the Roman wall gave way. Now more Gauls were getting in than ever.

Soon, there were so many dead from both sides that Marcus commanded slaves and low-ranking infantry to haul corpses out of the way just to clear a space for those fighting. In the darkness, he couldn't risk his men or horses tripping over the dead.

Trebonius was commanding in the neighboring sector, and they needed to communicate. If they were to keep this part of camp from falling, they needed reinforcements.

He barked at a young tribune who had been fighting courageously alongside the men, "Take command until I return. I'll try to bring back more units."

When Marcus found Trebonius, his arms were smeared red, and a wound in his neck was draining blood. He looked desperate.

"Antonius, we need relief! My infantry is buckling! Go—and quickly!" he cried. "Take one of my men with you so that if one of you falls, the other can finish the task!"

He signaled a single cavalryman over to Marcus, and, without even knowing one another's names, they barreled off, galloping side by side.

Through the blackness, Marcus's tiring horse grunted at every stride. He cursed himself for not changing mounts. Eyes burning, he hoped the animal could see through the night as he passed two sections of wall crackling in flames. At one point, he was close enough to the outer wall in another sector to see a large number of Gauls shimmying up. Marcus's comrade veered off to deal with an advancing Gaul who was too close for comfort. Alert to the danger, Marcus spurred hard, leaning forward over his mount's neck, giving it full rein.

Smoke from burning pitch choked him as he rode at breakneck speed, glancing about. His gut was telling him that he wasn't far from Labienus's sector. *Mars, let it be so!* If anyone had men in reserve, he would.

Then out of nowhere a hard jolt sent Marcus flying. Relentlessly, the earth arose, jarring him, air to his lungs passing into oblivion. For uncounted heartbeats, he tumbled uncontrollably. Gasping to catch the breath knocked from his body, he grappled at the ground, chest heaving.

Fingers locating his gladius, they snaked around the hilt, and he used the weapon to drag himself to his knees, wary of Gauls. Shaken but safe, he looked back to see his horse lying crumpled with its neck extended. Once a gift from Eros's father, it now lay still as stone, an arrow deeply imbedded through its chest.

Marcus's eyes widened as he looked just past his horse. Trebonius's cavalryman, who'd been riding with him, was in sorry condition too. As his horse circled about nervously, the soldier was trying to push himself up in vain. He writhed, paddling his legs and groaning, a bolt protruding from his gut. He was beyond help, but Marcus needed his horse!

Forward . . .

Wary of archers, head swiveling this way and that, Marcus forced his legs to move. Within a few bounds, he snatched the dying soldier's terrified mount by the bridle. He murmured soft words to calm the animal, sliding his hands down the reins as it pranced and rolled its front legs. Right hand gripping the saddle, he sprang upward, swinging on while the horse was half rearing in fright. Moments later, he gained control and galloped straight toward Labienus's sector.

Chill night air blew his hair back from his sweating forehead. His helmet was lost—but there was no going back now.

Relief rushed over him as he saw that, only feet away, a centurion was snapping orders at legionaries, who were rolling a creaking scorpion into place. This sector was strangely intact. Marcus didn't sense desperation the way he had in his own.

"Where's Labienus?" he demanded loudly.

The centurion waved him on. "Over there, sir!"

Marcus barely heard his last words, digging his heels into the horse's sides. "Titus Labienus!" he screamed. Hopefully, someone would hear and direct him.

Indeed, several men responded as he rode by. And at last Marcus saw Labienus himself, on foot and ordering detachments to his walls, where Gauls were trying to ascend by ladder. Hundreds of auxiliary archers were hard at work, picking off the enemy as they continued to appear over the Roman barricade.

"Trebonius and I need reinforcements," Marcus yelled. "We're overrun!"

"And you think I can spare men?"

Marcus rode in closer, temper flaring. "You've more than we do! Our sector will fall if we don't have immediate help."

"I can't spare—"

"How would Caesar react when he learns his second refused help to legates nearest him—men defending walls that have been rammed wide open?" Marcus snarled. "If we fall, those bastards will be inside and coming up behind *you*! We'll lose this battle!"

Labienus glared at him, but Marcus saw him reconsider.

"Burrus! I'm transferring your cohort and Ennius's to Antonius. Form up your men! Now!" Then he turned back to Marcus, snapping, "Satisfied?"

Marcus answered by whirling his horse away, not even bothering to respond.

The new units were mustering. Never had he been so relieved to see ranks of infantry falling in before him. Their drawn gladii shone in the torchlight.

One cohort for me, and one for Trebonius. It will have to be enough.

He reached out to a signifer and lifted the unit's eagle high, shouting, "My division and that of Gaius Trebonius is nearly lost.

It's up to *you* to see this battle snatched from the hands of the Gauls! If they scale the walls, pull them *down*! If they break through in front of you, smash their faces with your shields. Decide to win, and I'll lead you to victory! *Follow me!*"

A deafening roar of Roman spirit rose from the soldiers now under Marcus's command. They jogged at the double behind him.

As they passed through the sector where he'd lost his horse, he ordered their shields raised against any missiles. One of the centurions started an invigorating cadence, and it was the most heartening sound Marcus had heard all night. The vibrant voices of his men chanted in rhythm about Caesar's indiscretions with women, and it made him grin unabashedly.

As soon as Gauls near the collapsed wall saw four hundred fresh legionaries marching in, they began to waver.

"Push forward!" Marcus yelled over the din. It was true that sex thrilled him as few things did, but this night of nights, surrounded by danger and death, his five senses were heightened like never before.

Sights.

It was nearly impossible to see all of the action around him, even now with his eyes accustomed to the night. Torches held aloft by slaves and smoldering pitch-fed fires were the only sources of light available. It was too risky to hurl javelins for fear of hitting one another instead of Gauls. He kept reminding his cavalry, "Trust your horses' eyes in the dark!"

Sounds.

Men screaming, unnerved horses blowing snorts, and hooves drumming the ground. Metal clanging on metal. Someplace in the darkness some damnable Gaul was blasting a carnyx trumpet every ten beats of Marcus's racing heart. Now and then an arrow hissed past his ear. If one took him by chance, there'd be nothing to do but fall and die. Tonight death was as random as a Venus in dice.

Smells.

Beneath the broken walls, billowing smoke nearly choked everyone. The stink of burning flesh and hair, mixed with feces from men who'd taken gut wounds, hung low on the battleground. Intermingled in the tightest knots of desperately fighting men was the odor of unwashed bodies reeking from weeks of work and hard labor.

Touch.

Beneath him, Marcus's horse quivered. Sometimes it stumbled, probably on a corpse shrouded in the night. Marcus's left hand ached from the weight of his shield; his neck twitched with tension. He kept his gladius drawn, using its shining length to guide his men.

Taste.

Thick smoke from torches and pitch, coupled with burning oil, made him gag. Marcus could actually taste the acrid soot. Once, his horse spooked, and he bit his tongue, drawing blood, a warm, metallic trickle inside his dry mouth. After one engagement, he reached for the wineskin on his saddle, relishing the watered grape, a temporary relief for his parched throat.

Bellows of cheering men, glints of polished weapons, and quick-tramping infantry were what Marcus Antonius remembered about the night he and Trebonius worked together to turn a near defeat into Caesar's greatest triumph.

Alesia was won!

CHAPTER X
51-50 BC

LEGATE MARCUS ANTONIUS IN BIBRACTE, Gallia Comata, to his family in Rome:

Salve. Good fortune to us all. By now, you've heard of our victory at Alesia. Now we watch carefully, never completely turning our backs. Our eyes are also on Rome, watching Pompeius and the Senate. There's little love between him and Caesar these days.

The fight at Alesia was the most desperate in which I've ever engaged. Death was everywhere. I lost my cherished horse, but at least everyone claimed a fair share of booty and slaves, enriching us all.

A handful of my captured Gauls could serve Lucius well in the arena. I'm sending him ten worthy Gallic warriors just for that purpose. May he enjoy himself in the next games, winning coin instead of losing it!

Mother, your gift is three useful slaves who will please you. Two are skilled at farming, knowing plants as Castor does. The other is an artist who can brighten our domus walls.

Gaius, I found you a beautiful Parisi woman, skilled in the arts of love. Be assured she'll entertain you well. She comes with a girl-child who is shy and mild-mannered. We might consider her as a companion for Tonia. If Antonia likes her, have Iophon teach her to read and hire someone to give her music lessons. Henceforth, I want every personal slave at our domus to be literate and cultured. Everyone in Rome must see that I'm now a prominent member of Caesar's inner circle.

Antonia, I'm sending you a golden torque from the neck of a Gallic chieftain who once served Vercingetorix. Take it to the markets and have it melted down and worked into something dazzling for you, Mother, and Tonia.

Lastly, I would like our home to have a new, enlarged triclinium. Upon mentioning this idea to Caesar, he suggested I consult his highly favored engineer Marcus Vitruvius Pollio, who may be able to give us a stunning ceiling that would be unique on the Palatine. Mother, a Hercules mosaic must appear central to the design. It's my gift to us all, in honor of our victory.

Caesar is dealing with uprisings occurring in other regions and has sent me to Bibracte to oversee the Aedui. I think he gave me a well-deserved birthday gift for my thirty-second year. I'm now commanding Legio XII.

May the gods grant health to you all, for if you are well, then I am well.

Marcus slid the ball of an abacus to one side, staring blankly at statistics he'd scribbled in wax. His mind wandered.

After Alesia, active Gallic factions spurred rebellions all over the countryside. There was no rest, no conclusion. Caesar's legions were in constant motion, relocating, quelling opposition, building encampment after encampment.

"It's always been common practice to postpone wars during winter," Caesar observed during a post-Alesia consilium. "What a wasteful use of time!" he argued. "Year-round military exercises are logical and cathartic. I find them strategically necessary." True to his philosophy, he kept everyone active throughout Gaul year-round.

Shortly after Alesia, Marcus received word from Rome that he had been elected as Caesar's quaestor. That honor was now coupled with his new orders as legate in central Gallia Comata, a role Labienus would usually fulfill. Legion XII's nickname was "Fulminata"—the Thunderbolts. Their shields bore brightly painted lightning insignia with bolts crisscrossing in the middle.

At long last, he felt as though he was actively restoring his family's reputation. And it gave him great pride.

Bibracte was a large oppidum in central Gaul—an important hub in which commerce could begin again and strategically vital for supplies bolstering Caesar's forces. It was impressive, constructed of sturdy logs and earthen walls. Channels conveniently provided clean water from building to building; cisterns caught rainwater for fresh supply.

Renewed industry here promised better times for the Gauls, a stubborn, resilient people. Hammers clanged and skilled metal workers tinkered in shops. Their noise echoed through the streets. Diligent and hardworking, weavers busily toiled at looms, creating colorful woolen fabrics. There was even an old man and his servant who delicately blew hot glass, producing dainty, decorative rings for jewelry. Such finery promised an upward swing in the devastated Gallic economy.

Most of the population in Bibracte accepted Roman rule now.

Yet as spring and summer came, Marcus became aware of resentful undercurrents resounding in a single name: Commius.

Once loyal to Rome, Commius had switched sides, becoming one of Vercingetorix's top men and fighting in the relief army at Alesia. But unlike his king, he had escaped.

Earlier in the year, Caesar had sent an industrious cavalry officer, Gaius Volusenus Quadratus, to trick and kill the dissenter with a proposed meeting. However, the ruse failed and Commius escaped a second time, bloodied and furious. He swore oaths never to meet peaceably with another Roman. Ever more elusive, his attacks on legionary transports and detachments made travel, commerce, and supply routes in central Gaul unsafe.

Volusenus remained in Bibracte and was near Marcus's own age. Strikingly handsome, he could best most legionaries at arms and was popular with whores. Marcus liked him. He reminded him of himself. Respected by the men as a seasoned veteran, Volusenus had been with Caesar since the Fulminata's formation, and was deeply attached to the "Bolts." He was also excellent company, and he and Marcus often went riding together. They were an unusual breed in Rome's legions since they were both expert horsemen.

But today Marcus placed enjoyable pastimes on hold to deal with pressing administrative matters. Caesar was inordinately particular when it came to money, always sending trustworthy slaves to audit his camps. For Marcus, financial drivel was one part of field command that he detested. A necessary evil.

Eros entered, wordlessly placing a cup of wine on his master's cluttered desk. He carried an armful of Marcus's correspondence back into his personal quarters, sorting and packing it all neatly away. In Bibracte, Eros had begun light secretarial work. Marcus was proud of the boy. He'd mastered Latin, and his reading and writing skills were impressive.

Before Marcus could tabulate numbers of livestock presently stabled in Bibracte, he heard a sentry enter. "Excuse me, sir, but injured men have arrived asking to see you."

"Romans, Gauls?"

"Romans, sir. They were escorting grain transports."

Marcus groaned. Transports? Damn. He was expecting that shipment for winter stores. "Send them in."

Sentries escorted the worn travelers, all of whom were legionaries. Their mail was unoiled, cloaks tattered, each looking grimy, exhausted, and roughed-up. The tallest of the six bore an open, bleeding wound on one arm. Upon closer inspection, several others were bloodied too, their hands, feet, and knees wrapped in soiled, makeshift bandages.

"Legate," the tall spokesman began, "we traveled all the way from Massilia with grain for your legion. We had ten huge ox-carts' worth. About twenty miles or so south of here, barbarians ambushed us. Most of our party was killed, and we thought we'd die too. One attacker, a brassy sort, charged forward and tossed me this sack."

Reaching inside, the soldier withdrew an exquisite Roman gladius in its scabbard, obviously property of an officer. Marcus accepted the weapon, inspecting it, and finding the well-forged blade inscribed with three letters: GVQ.

Motioning to one of the sentries, Marcus smiled wryly. "Send for Volusenus."

When his friend finally arrived, Marcus held the sword aloft. "Look familiar?"

Volusenus's face registered amazement, ignoring the newcomers. "My gladius!" He stepped forward, eagerly reclaiming his property. "I lost it wounding Commius in the fight after Alesia. How did you find it?"

Marcus gestured to his wounded guests. "Thank these unfortunates, attacked while transporting our grain supply. They arrived on foot since their wagons were confiscated. One of their assailants gave them this weapon, I'm sure knowing they'd come here. Someone in particular knows you're with the Fulminata, Volusenus."

"It's that cocksucker Commius," Volusenus swore with a scowl.

"Want to use it on him again? I assume this was a personal challenge."

Volusenus nodded assuredly. "Oh yes." The young commander's eyes were aflame. "And I'll take him, this time!" he declared.

"Good," Marcus replied. "Leave tonight. These men can guide you to the area of their attack. From there, seek campfires and maneuver in the dark. Let's play by their rules for once. Try setting up ambushes and take *them* unawares."

During the next several days, reports filtered back to Bibracte concerning Volusenus's efforts. Most sounded hopeful. Apparently, he was whittling down Commius's party bit by bit. However, the Gaul was infuriatingly slippery. Marcus privately feared the young officer would become too rash and desperate in his tactics.

And, indeed, Marcus was correct.

Several days later, a handful of riders burst through Bibracte's gates. Two bore prisoners riding spare horses in tow, their hands bound and mouths gagged. But a more disturbing sight brought up the rear. Lying on a makeshift pallet, Volusenus was borne between two horsemen, semiconscious.

Marcus hurried down. "Quickly! Bring him to the praetorium and send for our physician!"

Volusenus was bleeding hard, still clutching his grandfather's sword. As legionaries hauled him in, Marcus swept loose articles off his desk to make room. "Eros, fetch some unwatered wine," he ordered. To Volusenus, he urged, "Stay down. The physician is coming. We'll fill you with wine to make it easier."

Blood oozed steadily from a gash in his thigh, dripping onto the floor. It was the sort of wound from which a man could gradually weaken and die. Marcus stripped his own cot of linens to staunch the flow before the legionary physician and his assistant arrived. Perched atop his desk, he relinquished all medical responsibilities but kept Volusenus occupied. "What happened? Focus on me—it'll keep your mind busy."

Volusenus set his teeth, skin pale with agony. "We engaged in several skirmishes, picking off Commius's men like ticks off a cur. Coward never even showed himself. We knew he was near—probably up a tree somewhere—but not far."

He paused, accepting wine from Eros, who appeared near his head bearing a full cup. The cavalryman grimaced at the wine's undiluted potency. Trying to shift upward, he gasped in misery.

"Stay down," Marcus ordered. "Now go on— talk—and keep drinking."

"This morning, before dawn, we had a fierce skirmish, and I saw him." Volusenus took another gulp as the physician's assistant pinched his shredded skin together. Now the sewing would commence.

Eros kept the wine coming, and Volusenus gulped another mouthful, sputtering. He cried out when the physician's assistant began suturing. Marcus pressed down on his shoulders, holding him in place.

Finally, Volusenus breathed deep, continuing. "I ordered a handful of men after him. They rode off, and I continued fighting where I was. Then suddenly, as if out of nowhere, I heard a savage shout. Commius was charging me!"

He groaned and tensed. The physician was working lower on another spot, picking out splintered wood from a Gallic spear.

Marcus wondered if he'd ever walk again. The laceration went clear to the bone. "Were you able to kill him?"

"He rode at me so hard he knocked my horse down, along with two others of his own men! I fell so hard the only thing I had in hand was my javelin. Before I could recover, he lanced me." Eyes squeezing shut, he grunted, "Oh—I think it went clear through."

Marcus shook his head, puzzled. "He had you at his mercy and could've killed you, but chose not to. I wonder why?"

Gauls were odd. Their tactics of attacking, wounding, and then running often made no sense.

Marcus breathed through his nose, making a hissing sound. "So he escaped again?"

"Yes." Volusenus growled in pain as the stitching continued.

Marcus sighed, patting the wounded man's shoulder before

leaving him with the physician. Outside, sunshine bathed his face, and he inhaled clear air no longer tainted with the coppery smell of blood. Losing a major supply route would spell disaster. With such a serious problem afoot, it would take more than the day's pleasant weather to improve his humor.

This Commius was no different from the Hasmoneans he'd faced during his Syrian assignment—able to materialize out of nowhere and disappear just as quickly.

That night, Eros interrupted his sleep with urgency. "Dominus—Dominus—"

Marcus stirred, his arm still draped across a voluptuous Gallic prostitute with whom he'd spent the night. They lay entangled on the simple soldier's cot he preferred. He'd been concerned over Commius's attacks, and it was upsetting to have lost Volusenus's service to such a grave wound. Sometimes the solace a woman brought helped disperse nightmares and calm his spirit.

When he opened his eyes, Eros stood above him, holding a small, poorly rolled scroll like a trophy, along with a flickering lamp.

"It's from Commius!"

Marcus sat upright, blinking sleep from his eyes.

Since Volusenus's attack, there had been no news of the Gaul. Until now, that is.

"Brianag, get up. It's time to go," Marcus said, giving the woman a gentle prodding.

Across the room, Eros reached into a satchel filled with coin. He handed over a reasonable sum, and Marcus placed the denarii on Brianag's discarded clothing next to the cot.

Marcus winked at Eros, who was ogling Brianag's naked form hungrily. Eros was almost fifteen now, older than Marcus was when he first sacrificed to Venus. He'd grown up these past several years. Though small, he'd developed a lean, healthy frame. He kept his straight, dark hair well-trimmed in Roman military fashion and wore cast-off legionary tunics and caligae boots. Had the youth even taken a girl yet? Sometime soon, Marcus decided, he'd have to give Eros a little surprise in feminine form.

Brianag arose sleepily and reached for her tunic and coins.

Once she was gone, Eros suggested, "Perhaps Commius will meet with you." Still grasping the lamp, he held it near so Marcus could read.

"Pah! He declares he's now regained his repute, wounding Volusenus as he'd been wounded. He offers hostages, vowing to retire to Britannia and not trouble us any longer."

Eros's eyes grew large. "That's all?"

Marcus chuckled. "No. As further 'concession' to his leaving, he requests not to be in the presence of any Roman."

"So send another detachment before he gets away. One more attempt could do the trick. And you might retrieve the grain shipment."

"What?" Marcus shook his head. "Eros, that load has probably already filled the bellies of Gauls right here in Bibracte under my very nose. No, I'll take no hasty action." He sat down on the sleeping couch again, brows together.

Eros left the lamp on a nearby stand and picked up a flask of oil, busily adding it to flickering lamps around the chamber.

The light brightened the shadows, and Marcus held the scroll near one of the flames, rereading. "I mustn't botch this," he murmured quietly. "Caesar constantly observes me, preparing me for higher honors."

"You've served him with courage, Dominus."

Marcus thought aloud, "If I keep pursuing Commius, it makes us look desperate to take him."

"But capturing him would be so impressive," the slave reasoned, reaching his hand out to catch oil that had overflowed down the side of a lamp.

"That's exactly what Caesar and I thought when we tried outrunning that other rebel, Ambiorix earlier this year. He evaded us too. These chieftains—they're like that oil there, able to run straight through our hands. We feel their presence but can never grasp them."

"Except for Vercingetorix. At least you have him."

"True," Marcus conceded. He talked to himself, considering the scenario. "Caesar let Ambiorix escape. He had other things to accomplish, and so do I. My immediate objective must be storing enough grain to feed the Bolts through winter. Chasing phantom Gauls and endangering my men unnecessarily wastes time and energy, as much as I'd like to heave a javelin through Commius's back."

"Why do you doubt yourself?" Eros asked, turning around. His question was sincere.

Marcus looked down, once more feeling the nagging shame that always dogged him. "Because I'm Antonii—haunted by failure. My father failed the Senate, my stepfather was seized and executed by the State, and my Uncle Hybrida was shamed and sent into exile."

There were few things Marcus withheld from Eros these days. Here in Gaul, life had been unpredictable, dangerous, and frightening. In many ways, he and Eros depended on one another for safety, sustenance, and companionship. The boy had earned more and more of his trust.

Marcus looked up to see his slave studying him.

"Share your thoughts."

"Dominus, it's times like this when I am thankful to be only a slave. To have to prove yourself constantly when everyone—your mother, wife, daughter, brothers, legion—all depend on you to be successful. It's a great relief being only Eros!"

Marcus smiled at him. "Then take pity on me and hear me out. Two efforts have already been made to destroy Commius. The first failed and men were lost. The second has failed, and one of my finest officers was nearly killed. Now the enemy offers to leave peaceably, going to the end of civilization." His eyes widened, and he shook his head in amazement. "Really, the way I see it, that bastard has solved my problem for me!"

"And if he stirs the Britons against us?"

Marcus chuckled. "Ho, I spared you Caesar's Britannia adventure! Neptune smiled on us twice, once safely making it over to that ghastly island and the second time bringing us back. It's a perilous journey—one no Briton is equipped to make."

"Yes, but natives helped build Caesar's ships. What if Commius discovers how to make them too? He could employ Britons as shipbuilders to do the job, recruiting both Britons and Gauls to fight for him."

Marcus wagged his head. "The year's already half-past. Such an endeavor would take time and coin. He might have time, but no coin. Even if some Briton supported his cause, it'd be a year at least before he could launch an invasion, probably longer. We're well-fortified enough here on the mainland to maintain positions. I think Commius's very departure concedes an honest defeat."

"Then you'll accept his offer?"

Marcus stood up, pacing a bit and debating in his own mind. At last returning to his sleeping couch, he retrieved the message, rereading it aloud.

"My only request is that you never again require me to be in the presence of any Roman. The betrayal of trust by Caesar's men often haunts me. I deeply fear 'peaceful' negotiations face-to-face with your countrymen."

Marcus pitched the scroll like rubbish across the praetorium's space, barking, "Commius has every reason to *fear* being in Roman presence!" He made his decision. "Write him back, Eros. Tell him I'll accept his hostages, but he'd best get his wily, Gallic ass swiftly to Britannia or he *will* visit another Roman face-to-face—me!"

Julia Antonia in Rome to her son, Legate and Quaestor Marcus Antonius in Bibracte, Gallia Comata:

We rejoiced to hear of your great victory! Your Grandfather Orator would have been most proud.

At a recent dinner party, I learned from Aelia that your Uncle Lucius also fought at Alesia. I hope the two of you have reconciled. Please tell me it is so.

A new triclinium would be most welcome! Tell the engineer Vitruvius we'll receive him and provide whatever materials are needed. And many thanks for the new slaves. Unfortunately, the girl you sent for Tonia was not to Antonia's liking. She took her to the slave markets the very next day. That child was a lively little thing and well-behaved. It was a mistake selling her.

Now I must be candid. Antonia has changed. She has become sullen and sulky, rarely spending time with me anymore. Admittedly, I'm hurt to the heart because of it. She has been no less than a daughter to me. I desperately miss our closeness, but her sweet and kind spirit has darkened. I long for what she once was.

I shall move on to political news. Your former "friend" Curio now leads a life among great and powerful men. Though an Optimate, some think he is leaning toward the Caesarian cause. Recently, he exposed Pompeius's unwillingness to give up his own military power. He suggested that both he and Caesar lay down arms. You can well imagine how Pompeius Magnus received that!

Now for news from across the Great Sea. Old Ptolemy Auletes died, passing his throne on to his eldest son, Ptolemy, and daughter, Cleopatra. I remember that you disliked the old tata. I wonder how his offspring shall rule?

Dear Marcus, Gaius is far too proud to ask this of you himself. Therefore I'll inquire on his behalf. If you think him worthy of anything at all, ask Caesar to consider him for a staff position.

Please write when you're able. Your letters are few and far between. I long for the time when you are home safe once more.

At last, Gaul journeyed toward peace.

Fewer skirmishes arose, and everyone cautiously hoped the land would remain settled, allowing farming and trade to resume.

Mounted and ready to leave Bibracte for Rome, Marcus paused, seeing a sizeable contingent of horsemen clattering his way.

"Antonius! How goes it?"

A broad grin of recognition spread across Marcus's face. "Trebonius! Good to see you."

"And you! I'm here to receive new orders. And I bear good news. Labienus and I believe the Belgic tribes are finally subdued. Starvation brings any man to his knees, doesn't it? I think Gaul has finally found peace, as well."

"We can hope."

"And I suppose you've heard—Labienus landed a promotion."

"Ah, yes—as governor."

Trebonius cocked his head. "Indeed, but without consent of the Senate. Then again, Caesar is all-powerful." Pausing after studying Marcus a moment, he pried, "Are you envious?"

Marcus shrugged, sensing his friend was questioning Caesar's wisdom. "Yes and no," he responded honestly. "As for Caesar's decision, it may be contested, but not by me. Labienus is a wise choice. He understands the Gauls, and he's an expert at recruiting since he's been doing it at Caesar's side for a decade. True, my preference would be to remain here, but Caesar has other plans for me. At least I'm going home. Then again, you know how much I enjoy politics." He winked knowingly.

Trebonius snickered and his horse stamped. He waved his

entourage of riders ahead. "Yes, well, never mind any contentment Labienus may have. He's already grumbling how Caesar's appointment only prevents him receiving senatorial accolades by waylaying him here."

"That cantankerous ass would complain if Venus herself descended to offer him a kiss! He gets to stay in familiar territory—*in the field*! If he returned to Rome, he'd suffer the same abuse Caesar does."

"You're leaving now, then?"

"I am. Another foray into magistracy."

Trebonius laughed heartily. "Yes—word is out! Antonius, selected by Caesar to stand as tribune—and augur too!"

"Well, I'm not looking forward to the augur part. A priest? In temples? Watching damned flocks of birds?" Marcus shook his head. "That's not me, Trebonius."

"It's an honor. Caesar is rewarding your successes. I heard how you handled that Commius affair. You show yourself more than capable of making sound decisions. I tell you; fortune runs in your veins like it does your cousin's. A safe and speedy passage to you, friend."

"Gratias."

Glancing about cautiously, Trebonius edged his horse closer to speak in private. "Before you go—tell me something. Labienus and I heard troubling talk. The late Gaius Scribonius the elder managed to fashion his son, Curio, into a well-heeled politician. Calpurnius Piso even applauds him as—"

"Old Scribonius died?" Marcus interrupted, cocking an eyebrow. "I hadn't heard."

"I think it happened around the time of your quaestorship. I'm surprised you didn't hear, as I'm well aware you and Curio were once . . . close."

"I've not seen or heard from him in a decade. Nor have I missed his company," Marcus said defensively. Vicious gossip never died, regardless of time having past. Even Mother probably still believed that he and Curio had once been lovers.

Trebonius did his best to smooth over any insinuation, "Ah, well, according to gossip, Caesar might have piddled about King Nicomedes's Bithynian bedside in his younger years!"

"So it's said. Now what 'troubling talk' were you concerned about?"

"Ah, that! Is it true that Caesar is *bribing* Curio and his clients away from Pompeius's side?"

Marcus studied Trebonius thoughtfully. "That sort of thing happens all the time. You know that. You also know what Caesar's up against. Those Optimate senators are ready to tear him apart. Never has a man been treated so unfairly for doing such courageous and successful acts for his people."

"Yes, and that's precisely the center of my fear. For *his* people, not necessarily for Rome. Laying down arms maintains peace, but buying a man's loyalty only leads to contention. The way things are going, it—"

"—would end Caesar's career to give up his command." Marcus raised his voice pointedly. "Is that really what you want? He's treated both you and Labienus with the utmost fairness and generosity. You *owe* him loyalty, Trebonius. Every staff officer down to the lowest latrine-digging grunt owes allegiance to him."

"I honor and admire my commander, but he's only a *man*," Trebonius emphasized. "Ultimately, I serve the *Republic*, not him."

Oh. The Republic? Trebonius harbored far too many unrealistic ideals. Especially about that. Marcus wanted to maintain patience with this friend who'd always been a dependable soldier and comrade. He sighed in exasperation. "Caesar has conquered Gaul—a feat bringing calm, prosperity, and protection to Rome's northern borders. Pompeius and the Senate are denouncing a general who has succeeded against all odds. They accuse him of war crimes, wanting him to disband his legions—*our* legions. Furthermore, do you want to answer to a Senate full of Optimates giving Pompeius full control over the state treasury? Why, he even holds sway over the grain supply. It's fact, you know. Single-man rule's already in place. It merely hides beneath toga-clad decorum. Your precious

Republic has been on its funeral bier for years, slowly but steadily carried toward cremation. Maybe you should simply reevaluate *who* you want for single-man rule. Did you know Caesar intercepted letters from Pompeian Senators to rebels here in Gaul, *urging* the tribes to hold out against us and not give up? Some of our own countrymen were cheering for our downfall."

Those words silenced Trebonius, so Marcus added, "I, for one, will not let punitive men like Pompeius dictate how my imperator is treated or in what manner my city's wealth is kept. I'll go to Rome as Caesar's representative, and the conquerors of Gaul won't be forsaken lightly."

"Forgive me, Antonius," Trebonius said, his voice filled with emotion. He appeared visibly moved, offering his hand for Marcus to clasp. "You shame me. You're younger than I, yet you see things I've failed to consider. Mercury give you wings, and Jupiter himself protect you. Now go—follow your orders."

Clasping Trebonius's hand briefly in friendship, Marcus began the journey back to Italia, resigned to pursue politics, like it or not. Eros and the baggage wagons followed, grinding their way out of Bibracte.

Turning back once, Marcus raised a hand to Trebonius in farewell. Uncertain times lay ahead. He didn't want to lose this man's friendship. He needed friends, for he'd be making more enemies soon enough.

CHAPTER XI

MARCUS STEPPED OVER THE NEW TRICLINIUM FOUNDATION, lifting his toga, careful not to soil it or the new senatorial boots he wore. Ho, how he longed to forget these last three days!

He hadn't realized how little land his domus rested upon. The new dining space wound up hedged against his neighbor's wall, resulting in a more limited plan for the renovation.

But it wasn't just the new triclinium's issues bothering him. Ever since he'd returned to Rome, Mother kept harping about his need to sire an heir. It was a daily ritual. "A man without sons has no assurance his line will continue," she insisted.

Damn it all, she was right. At thirty-three, he'd reached maturity.

But certain things could not change—at least not now. Antonia was still his wife despite their mostly avoiding one another. And now was no time to seek new marriage prospects. He was too busy with his election and political business. Afterward, perhaps.

To keep domestic peace, he had relented to Mother's pleas, temporarily giving up evenings with Cytheris to attempt siring another child. And what a bizarre, distasteful task *that* was.

Granted, there had been few tender words between them since Antonia had opened her mouth and started the scandal concerning Fulvia. Still, sex was the most enjoyable of pastimes— that is until these last several nights, which Marcus could only describe as misery. Antonia, unresponsive as a corpse, refused to speak or even look into his face during the act. If he kissed her, she locked her jaw, turning away from him as though he sickened her.

Being sexually unsuccessful was something entirely new to Marcus Antonius. Women usually benefited greatly from the experience—as did he. Having Antonia stiff and uninterested during lovemaking nearly prevented him from performing at all.

And to top things off, this morning Gaius Scribonius Curio was paying a visit. Years ago, he had dishonored Marcus in the worst of ways. Even after all this time, his very presence could dredge up nasty memories. Yes, the week had been dreadful, and today's agenda didn't promise to be any better.

Vaguely, Marcus became aware of a voice interrupting his thoughts.

". . . and hopefully by this afternoon my contracted artisans will install the perimeter mosaics."

"Good, good," Marcus replied absently. "I want the Hercules available for my guests to view two nights from now."

"Most of that should be completed," Vitruvius assured him.

Marcus Vitruvius Pollio, Caesar's gifted engineer, had become a frequent visitor, coming and going daily. Near Marcus's own age, polite, and businesslike, he was a man of few words, always toting a plumb line and libra for leveling. Humble and earthy, he'd made a name for himself in the legions by designing bridges and useful military machines. Bevies of slaves followed him bearing tool boxes, lugging masonry bricks, and sweeping away excess dust.

"Dominus!"

Marcus glanced over his shoulder, smirking to himself as Eros approached bearing a wax tablet. Now here was someone who deserved some teasing. "Lonely in your bed, boy?" Marcus probed.

"No, Dominus," Eros answered forthrightly.

Shortly before leaving Gaul, Marcus had generously given the youth a Gallic slave girl of his own, one nearly as lovely as the one he'd given Gaius. Eros kept her for a month or so, then abruptly sold her upon returning to Rome. With all his marital issues, it baffled Marcus, auctioning off such a ripe, seductive little vixen.

He shook his head. "How could you do it? She was exquisite." The mere *thought* of Eros's girl brought more satisfaction than his past two nights with Antonia put together.

"She talked too much and argued," Eros replied.

Grinning, Marcus shook his head. "A shrew? Be more of a dominus, then! Next time I'll help you."

The youth shifted his feet, glancing at the engineer uneasily. "She brought a good price, and I'm more the practical sort," he said softly.

Marcus burst out laughing. "Yes, that would be you—safe and sensible Eros!"

The boy always brought a smile to his face, regardless of mood. Leaving Vitruvius to his project, Marcus eyed the wax tablet in Eros's hands. "Now mark this down. Tell the cooks I want the same olive relish they served at my toga ceremony years ago. That stuff was the highlight of the evening, and everyone wanted more."

Eros nodded. "That should go nicely with the main course—exotic shrimp and shellfish, all caught in waters near your villa."

Nothing had made Mother smile like the moment Marcus had handed her legal documents to Grandfather Orator's Misenum villa, Antonian property once more.

Clapping Eros on the shoulder, he mused, "Once things settle, we need a new cook, someone with training and experience to prepare sumptuous meals for high-ranking society. Be sure to send a note of thanks to Calpurnia for letting us borrow hers."

"Anything more, Dominus?"

"Today a theatrical friend of Cytheris's is visiting. Watch his routine, and if you think it's good, hire him for the dinner party. We could always use more entertainment. And before I forget again, remind me next time I write Caesar to request a position for Gaius."

"I'll remind you."

"Gratias." Marcus shook his head and sighed. "This house will burst at the seams with the numbers Gaius and Lucius invited. I'm thinking I'll need a larger place soon . . ."

Eros asked, "Is that all, Dominus?"

Marcus nodded. "For now."

"The Tribune Gaius Scribonius Curio has arrived. Your brother is with him."

"Gaius or Lucius?"

"Gaius, Dominus."

Marcus ruffled Eros's hair fondly, pausing only to straighten a sinus of his toga before striding back to the main wing of the domus.

Approaching the sun-drenched impluvium, he spied a familiar golden head gleaming in oiled curls from across the atrium.

At his footfalls, Curio turned away from conversing with Gaius. Marcus noticed immediately that he'd aged considerably in the past decade. His once boyishly handsome face bore fine lines, transforming him into a humorless senatorial sort. Truth be told, it was a pleasing life-moment, for Marcus realized he'd surpassed Curio in both looks and physique.

Still, his rehearsal of cordial greetings for this reunion had done no good. It was impossible to feign enthusiasm upon seeing Gaius Scribonius Curio. "Salve, Curio," he managed.

"Antonius! How long has it been? Over a decade?"

"Not long enough," he quipped. Ho, that was awful.

Gaius shot him a corrective glare. "Well, Marcus, since you two are so well-met, I'll go." As he passed, he leaned in, whispering into Marcus's ear, "Don't forget yourself."

As his brother disappeared, Marcus said, "I only recently heard of your father's death. My condolences."

Curio nodded, genuine sorrow in his expression. "He made a real Roman of me. I miss him."

"Undoubtedly." He changed subjects. "Caesar thinks highly of you."

"Does he? Excellent. I intend to be more vocal on his behalf."

"I should hope so," Marcus stated flatly. "He's paying dearly to lure you from Pompeius."

Curio answered that remark with a smug smile of satisfaction. "He can well afford it."

"Then you'd best make his investment worth its while."

"Absolutely. I'll combine my zeal with Quintus Longinus. He's staunchly Caesarian."

"Really? I've never met him, but I'll invite him to the banquet. We'll have a crowd, but there's always space for a friend of Caesar."

"He'll appreciate that. It's a Caesarians-only event, I presume?"

"Nearly. Cicero seems set on driving both chariots for now, as does one of my uncles. I've included them because Caesar would have it so."

Curio veered away from politics. "How's your family?"

"Very well."

"Let me see, you married—"

"My cousin, Antonia. I've a daughter—Tonia. Mother's mad for her."

"Wonderful! Does she look like you?"

"Not at all. She favors her mother. Same red hair and green eyes."

Curio grinned in amusement. "Red hair?"

Marcus ignored him, "So how does marriage suit you?"

"Extremely well, actually. Fulvia's a pleasing wife."

"Good for you," Marcus voiced, none too convincingly. He chewed at his lip again.

Fulvia hadn't waited long in remarrying after Clodius's murder. Certainly, Curio had heard about the scandal. Did he believe it? To be sure, he was eyeing Marcus strangely, tilting his chin back in calculating coolness.

"Our union was proposed to me by my mother. She knows my tastes, believing Fulvia to be the perfect choice."

"She was right. Fulvia's quite a handful, to be enjoyed immensely." Gods, what have I said?

Curio's eyes turned hard as rock, boring into his. "I've heard you enjoyed her *too* much," was the icy response.

"Not so," Marcus assured him hastily. "Cicero feasted Clodius often the year before his murder. I saw her at those occasions only. Ask her yourself. She'll speak truthfully. Rome often ignites fires of gossip unjustly. Of all people, you and I know that." He forced himself to swallow every shred of distaste at his own hypocrisy, adding, "I congratulate you, Curio. Fulvia's beautiful and innocent of any slander you've heard."

"Stay away from her," Curio hissed. "Leave her be, and you'll have my full support and friendship."

Marcus remained calm. "I assure you it was *only* gossip. Now I need your help with my campaign."

Curio stepped back, analyzing him. "Let me guess—you wish you were still in the field."

Marcus snorted, eyebrows raised. "I hope the Senate never reads me as easily as you just did."

"We're opposites, Antonius. My mind is political, and yours is soldierly. But if I must, I'll succeed on the field. And if necessary, you'll survive in the Senate."

"Well put."

Curio sighed. "Let me speak plainly. Caesar wants you as augur and tribune. No easy feat, especially for the priesthood. Lucius Domitius Ahenobarbus wants that seat, and he once held the curule chair."

"Yes, an ex-consul." Marcus puffed out his cheeks in concern. "Have I any chance at all?"

Curio grinned, and Marcus noted a fleeting glimmer of the raffish youth from the past. "Ah yes, but not without a little mischief. A little rioting will lift your name far above Ahenobarbus's. I'll handle that end of it. I enjoy working crowds as much as Clodius did."

"What about tribune?"

"You'll succeed me once my term ends. At least, that's how we'll play it to the populace. As much as they love Caesar and me, they'll love you and vote accordingly. You'll be their hero from Gaul, soldierly and noble. They'll want you in since you won the war at Caesar's side."

Feeling more at ease, Marcus stood up, head held high. "Then I have but one more bit of business."

Curio smiled. "Name it."

Marcus lowered his voice. "Caesar left Labienus in Gaul on purpose. He won't be second in command much longer."

Curio's smile faded. "Your point?"

"*I'll* soon be second in command. That, Curio, is only the first of three points I wish to make. Here are the others. Number two: never put me off or disgrace me again. Three: you once owed me coin and refused payment. Such must never occur again for us to be civil to one another. You dishonored me before your father and all of Rome. Rumors from that day still dog me."

Crossing his arms, Curio shrugged with a dry laugh. "A little scandal is natural and indispensable if you want to succeed and be remembered. If you expect me to humble myself over an incident a decade past, you'll wallow in disappointment. I never apologize; I simply move on. Be wise. We'll advance together, and I'll treat you honorably. Accept my word on that. Can we agree?"

Swallowing the past like bile, Marcus clenched his teeth, answering only with a nod.

Curio snickered. With a wicked smile, he grasped Marcus's hand, leaning in and whispering in his ear, "In case you're wondering, I no longer lust for you." A tone of remorse accompanied the comment. "Pity—you've finally lost that youthful look I prefer in boys."

Marcus withdrew his hand in revulsion, face red with anger.

Laughing again, Curio slapped him on the shoulder. "Thicken your skin. We're about to do battle, and wars in the Senate are exceptionally brutal!"

Marcus strolled past couches of togate senators with jewel-bedecked wives.

He marveled that this celebration honored his part in a major conquest. Ever since he'd come home, he'd ascended to hero-status. In the Forum, plebs would stop, call his name, and wave. Wherever he went, he took along Gallic bodyguards. Not only were they imposing, but it only made him more popular, seeing him protected by former enemies. Marcus Antonius was famous in Rome now and known for his courage, tenacity, and closeness to Caesar. Common people loved his easy manner; Marcus didn't mind drinking with actors or senators alike.

But tonight he drank with Rome's elite.

Everyone flattered him, but Marcus was guarded at their well-wishing. There were men in his domus tonight who would prefer seeing him fail—or for that matter, even die.

Torches flickered as he made his way down the peristyle colonnade. Reedy music from tibicines on their double flutes rose wildly on welcome breezes. Gaius had hired expensive Syrian girls who had quickly discarded the little clothing they wore and were now romping naked in the glowing light to feral beat patterns resembling Bacchante rhythms.

Marcus paused to watch, a yearning in his loins. He needed a break from Antonia and would return to Cytheris soon, heir or not.

Cytheris . . . common as any pleb, but she was *free*. She never had to worry about being respectable or rising up social ladders. Ever liberated to be herself entirely, she could make of her life whatever she chose. Though highborn and privileged, Marcus didn't have that liberty. Life was all expectation and duty. Cytheris would be his escape—along with her theatrical friends, wine, and wild, unabashed parties. Nor did it hurt that she was still considered the most beautiful woman in Rome aside from Clodia.

Most everyone was enjoying the entertainment, brazenly tossing coins at the Syrian girls. Younger male guests were gesturing obscenely and calling out lewd comments. Poor Mother! She sat at the head table, looking utterly shocked.

Curio reclined at the honorary trio of tables, deep in his cups. His friend Longinus was beside him, along with Longinus's wife. Antonia had already left her place. She had to share her couch with Fulvia, and throughout the banquet they'd glumly stared at one another with no more affinity than two rival gladiators.

But overall the evening was a huge success. Marcus needed to impress the senatorial elite with his increased duty to Caesar. Yes—even Cicero was here. Caesar would have expected his inclusion.

The Syrian girls finished their routine, and he resumed his way between couches of guests. Several reached out, catching his hand, raining compliments on the meal, the decorations, and the Hercules mosaic in the new dining wing. He smiled warmly, answering each with personal accolade.

"Antonius! A moment of your time!"

Marcus winced, recognizing *that* familiar voice. Marcus Tullius Cicero was gesturing to him, his wife, Terentia, at his side.

Once beside Cicero's couch, Marcus found not only he and Terentia, but Cicero's daughter, Tullia, and several others contentedly munching spiced honey cakes, all smiling at the eleventh-hour comic friend of Cytheris's that Eros had added to the entertainment.

"Compliments on the seafood," Cicero began. "I've never tasted such excellent prawns! Lucius Caesar told me you lost the villa in Misenum where they were harvested."

"I recently repurchased it. It's well-staffed and thriving." *Just like me,* Marcus thought.

Cicero lithely changed topics away from Antonian success. "The Senate eagerly awaits the priestly elections. You've quite a challenge in Ahenobarbus."

"Ah, but I share Caesar's luck," Marcus reminded, forcing a hospitable smile. "The people know it, for I earned their respect at Alesia."

"Alesia? A desperate and viciously fought bloodbath," Cicero opined, shaking his head. "Caesar showed little courage in bullying the Gauls into this war to begin with."

Arrogant toad, Marcus thought. He paraded himself as Pater Patriae yet had barely ever lifted a gladius. How *dare* he judge Caesar or any of the men who bravely fought at Alesia. Leaning in, Marcus hissed, "Tell me, Cicero. Exactly how much *courage* did it take to escort Lentulus to his strangulation?"

Before Cicero could reply, Terentia intervened. "Husband, introduce Antonius to our new son."

Cicero recovered himself. "Ah—yes." He swallowed, turning about and then frowning. "Tullia," he questioned his daughter. "Where's your husband?"

"Viewing the new mosaic, Father."

"Ah, well—another time." He shrugged. "Antonius, I like the mosaic. It's impressive, although I've never cared personally for Herculean depictions. I prefer traditional Homeric themes."

"Really?" Marcus replied. "Strange, then, how you've given my family's Hercules such a prominent position in your peristyle courtyard."

Cicero wasn't usually bereft of words, but his jaw hung open speechlessly.

"Well, it was kind of you to accept an invitation to honor my success. A pleasant night to you," Marcus said, dismissively.

Since his hot head needed cooling, he proceeded beyond the peaceful peristyle gardens toward the new triclinium. Once completed, maybe he'd celebrate with another party. And after that, a newer, larger property might be in store.

Abruptly turning into a serene glade, he stopped in his tracks. Antonia nearly ran into him head-on, accompanied by a swarthy bull of a man.

She deftly unlinked her arm from the stranger's. "Marcus!" Obviously equally stunned, her words exploded forth in a gasp. After that, her tongue was as tied as Dirce to the bull. "Publius Dolabella here, he—he—he wished to see our new baths," she stuttered.

Dolabella smiled, his brutish face displaying an astonishingly boyish grin and perfect teeth beneath a tiny scar above his lip.

"Your wife has just given me a perfect retelling of the Twelve Labors of Hercules."

"Antonia reciting myths? When exactly did you become a poet?" Marcus asked, genuinely surprised and cocking an eyebrow.

"The mosaics are brilliant, I tell you," Dolabella praised.

Dolabella—Dolabella? He remembered the name from the guest list, but to which family was he linked? No matter. Marcus responded, "Gratias for the compliment." Then, looking directly at Antonia, he said firmly, "I should think Tonia requires your attention. See to her needs."

Antonia swallowed hard. "Marcus—"

"*Now*, Antonia. Go to her."

Antonia glanced fleetingly at Dolabella, then turned without a word and disappeared into the colonnade. Marcus followed her with his eyes, and when he turned back, Dolabella was gone.

That was when it hit. Suddenly he remembered exactly who that man was. Publius Cornelius Dolabella was husband to Tullia, the daughter of Marcus Tullius Cicero!

Calming himself, Marcus rationalized his suspicions away. Was she carrying on with Dolabella and welcoming his advances? Cicero's *son-in-law*? Surely, Antonia wouldn't be *that* stupid.

CHAPTER XII
50 BC

MARCUS ANTONIUS, AUGUR IN ROME, TO GAIUS Julius Caesar, Imperator in Ravenna Classis:

Salve. I write to inform you that I'm now an augur. Curio and I are busy with my campaign for tribune.

Unfortunately, the Senate remains adamant. Now that your tenure of governance as proconsul has ended, they demand you to lay down your command. They're also outraged that you have moved legions to Ravenna Classis, closer to Rome.

Before I close, one other matter comes to mind. Just this week, my brother Lucius departed for Asia to fulfill his quaestorship. Gaius, who is still at home, needs military experience and requests your consideration for a post. I can assure you there is no more loyal man in all of Rome. He'd readily die for your cause.

Be well, Caesar, so I may be well.

Gaius Julius Caesar, Imperator and Proconsul Provinciae Gallicum in Ravenna Classis, to Marcus Antonius, Augur in Rome:

Congratulations on achieving the priesthood. It also pleases me that your campaign for tribune progresses. Hopefully, you'll soon be serving in that capacity. In the meantime, I've sent a letter to Curio, which he is to read aloud in the Senate. It will clearly define my terms and intentions in regard to Pompeius's demands that I lay down arms. You are my delegate in Rome, so do not hesitate to speak on my behalf. Assure them I will lay down arms, but Pompeius must do the same.

Tell your brother I'm pleased to offer him a junior post. Meanwhile, may Fortuna grant you the office of tribune.

Marcus sat still as stone, frowning. Palpable unease dampened every man's mood inside the meeting hall attached to Pompeius's theater.

Since the old Curia building had burned around Clodius's corpse, Rome's senators had nowhere to convene. No new building yet replaced the charred ruins. So Pompeius had offered a solution by welcoming the Senate into his theater's smaller curia space with open arms. Each time they met, they sat encircled by his generosity, wealth, and success—reminders of his imperium and influence. Located not far from the Forum, it served its purpose well.

This year Pompeius stepped aside in favor of a co-consulship between two Optimates. Politically, it made no difference since the two men were both his lackeys and exclusively promoted his agenda. One of them, Lucius Cornelius Crus, rose from his curule chair to address the large assembly about Caesar's encampment at Ravenna Classis, not far from Rome's official borders.

"Peace, Brothers!" Crus called over the many loud discussions. Once things quieted, he continued, "We proclaim that Pompeius's two legions outside the city are necessary for our protection in these uncertain times. Protection, that is, from the possibility of an attack by Caesar, whose present position can only be taken as a threat to Rome."

When defiant Caesarian backers behind Marcus stood, reacting in outrage at that remark, Crus lifted his hand. Lictors pounded their fasces, noise from the bound axes reverberating through the chamber.

Crus continued, "If Gnaeus Pompeius Magnus brings legionaries to our aid, why complain? I say this assembly should welcome that protection, for Caesar threatens the very tenets of our Republic!"

Marcus snorted, shaking his head. He had to be patient—a virtue with which he had little familiarity—before he had a go at them. He had just been elected as tribune of the plebs and fully expected that he might have to use his right of veto should they take hasty action and threaten Caesar.

Crus moved to the center of the floor. He was not a large man, and his voice faded beneath Curio's agitated whispers to Caesarian supporters. Frustrated by the commotion and wanting to hear every word, Marcus gathered up the folds of his toga, scooting forward on the smooth, stone seat, listening.

"Let us waste no more words concerning Caesar," Consul Crus rambled on. "He claims to have 'prevented war' by striking Gaul first. Did any Gauls threaten your households? Were there mutterings of war prior to his acquisition of the province? Now, after raping and pillaging a country that will forever hold us in contempt, he insists his war has ended." Mockingly, the Consul cupped his hands to his mouth, turning north and shouting, "Well,

Caesar! If so, respond to our demand! Disband your army and return to Rome a civilian. Your war is *over*!"

Optimates all over the chamber chuckled, nodding in approval at the consul's performance. In closure, Crus glared straight at Marcus and his band of Caesarian Populares. "So," he blathered, "to prevent another *Sulla* marching against our sacred pomerium, I call upon Gnaeus Pompeius Magnus to declare Gaius Julius Caesar a public enemy. He should be denied fire, food, and water, and those loyal to him should take care for their lives!"

Marcus immediately rose and descended to the floor, wearing his stark-white tribunal toga. It was time to put these Pompeian asses in their place. He took his time, pacing over floral acanthus mosaics, one hand raised to demand silence. Once he stood at the center of the pattern, where an eagle grasped at leafy foliage, he inhaled deeply. "Conscript Fathers!" His powerful voice caught everyone's attention, and the chamber hushed. "When Marius governed Rome, my own grandfather Antonius Orator was sacrificed. But unlike Marius or Sulla, Caesar has no intention of attacking you or lopping off heads, as did they. He simply wishes to serve Rome in peace. Yet you give him no opportunity to prove himself. Allow me, as the new tribune of the plebs—*all* of whom love Caesar—to repeat his requests. He promises to lay down arms and dissemble his legions, fully meeting your demands. However, he requires the same of Pompeius. That is all—and that is fair."

Turmoil sounded again as Optimates loyal to Pompeius lifted fists in opposition.

With both hands raised for silence, Marcus paused, fasces drumming on his behalf, the din causing sonorous vibrations beneath his feet, blending with the clamor of surrounding arguments. Ever so slowly the noise faded, and Marcus strolled casually toward Pompeius, who sat with the consuls, each in ivory curule chairs.

"Pompeius Magnus," he began, "with your permission, allow me to remind this assembly why they follow, trust, and respect you."

Pompeius eyed Marcus guardedly but nodded assent.

This was it. It was *the* moment to declare in Caesar's favor. If he failed, civil war would probably break out. Still, in the back of his mind a troubling thought darkened his defense of Caesar—that his cousin *wanted* civil war, that Caesar was certain Pompeius would abandon peace . . .

Save murder, wasn't it the only way Caesar could attain sole power?

"Brothers," Marcus plowed ahead, regardless, "no wonder the aristocracy places such high regard upon Pompeius. After all, is he not a Roman of noble birth?" Hesitating, Marcus shook his head, pretending to correct himself. "Why, no—not exactly. I forgot! He hails from the country town of Picenum, I believe. Oh, but certainly the birthplace of Pompeius is *far* worthier than Rome, where all of us were born and raised."

He paced slowly, back and forth in front of Caesar's aging rival, guffaws from the Caesarian section escalating tension in the hall. Curio's fist was balled and raised, cheering him on. Other Caesarian Populares nodded and applauded.

Marcus's heart hammered. An unpleasant fact dawned on him that he wasn't just Caesar's man now. Right now—at this very moment—he was his *game piece.*

"It must be his *father's* credentials drawing you to Pompeius," he mocked anyway. "Yet, if my memory serves, old Strabo wasn't part of any ancient or worthy family either." He sighed, shaking his head. "Odd. Still, the name Pompeius can gather more Optimates together in one place than a hot, steaming pile of shit attracts flies!"

Populares burst into laughter. Across the room, Cicero cleared his throat and crossed his arms defiantly, setting his jaw into a scowl.

Marcus grinned good-naturedly at his audience, pacing back to where Pompeius sat and clapping him on the back. Beneath his beaming face, he was hoping Caesar would be worth a war because his words might begin one today. "Forgive me, Pompeius," he apologized. "As everyone knows, I'm first and foremost a soldier and often forget how crude I am."

Optimates nodded in agreement, several shouting for him to sit down.

But Marcus lifted his eyes back to the Senate, voice raised again. "Let's consider the time early on in Pompeius's career when he was prosecuted for misappropriation of coin. Lucky for him, *his* loyal Senate, full of *Pompeian* champions, acquitted him. Some in my family were not as fortunate in past years, though they were no guiltier than he."

Several senators called out in displeasure, Cicero among them.

"This is an outrage!" bellowed Marcus Porcius Cato, leaping up from his seat near the front. Known for his extremist views, he staunchly backed Pompeius in everything. His keen, raven-black eyes snapped with fury.

"An outrage? I think not," Marcus countered with a shrug, keeping his tone steady. "After all, I'm only reminding you why you follow him. Let's see—Pompeius was a Sullan supporter. Now here you must exercise patience," he said, rubbing his chin, as though perplexed. "Being new at this sort of thing, I pause momentarily just to reason things out. If Pompeius fought for Sulla, then he supported the very *first* Roman to march against our city with legions. And yet here you sit, worried Caesar will storm your gates, when *Pompeius*, the man you now trust to *rescue* Rome, championed the very general who first took her by force!"

Pandemonium erupted, lictors banging fasces, voices of senators from the Populares party chanting, "Caesar, Caesar, Caesar!"

On the other side, Pompeian Optimates hurled objections, both factions yelling, faces red and contorted with ardor.

Marcus held up both hands again, waiting until the din settled enough for his voice to carry. "Thus, in my estimation, if Pompeius supported the very man who first stormed Rome, then *he* should be the *real* enemy of the state, *not Caesar*!"

And indeed—that message carried.

Before more rumbles of agitation could cause another outburst, he proceeded doggedly. "Sometime after his association with Sulla, Pompeius was given the cognomen 'Magnus.' I'm not entirely sure when that took place. Maybe during his triumph, when he planned to have an elephant lead the parade. Only the creature couldn't fit through the arch he'd designed. You see, Brothers, Pompeius has always wanted a little too much glory—the 'elephantine' type, which he can't quite pull off. I worry this is the real reason he can't stomach Caesar's return. Finally, someone has done something grander than he! After all, how many men here can say they won a war on two fronts with sixty thousand pitted against over two hundred thousand strong?"

At this, Pompeius arose, his face red with rage. "Preposterous, this! You shame nobody but yourself, Marcus Antonius!"

"Do I?" Marcus shook his head. "I think instead you shame yourself by repressing Caesar's rights and refusing to allow him to prove his good word." Turning his back on Pompeius, he finished on the way back to his seat, commenting, "Yes, I can see why Optimates hold you in such *high* regard."

With that, he sat down.

Immediately, Cato stood, crying vehemently, "Now give him your reply, Magnus!"

Pompeius stood up in accord, eyes burning into Marcus's with loathing. "Good members of this Senate," he called out. "Why listen to a penniless gambler who's nothing but Caesar's straw scarecrow? Ignore 'Antonius the Nobody,' the son of a cowardly failure! Instead, let's concentrate on legions Caesar has moved to Ravenna Classis—*strategically* closer than ever to Rome."

No. There was no reason to concede this one to Pompeius. Not this easily. Marcus got back up quickly, shaking his head in defiance. "Stop belittling me and *act*! First, reposition the two legions encamped outside this city over to Syria, where they might serve Rome better by keeping Parthians at bay. You think Caesar's a ruthless warmonger? You're the one stationing legions right outside Rome's gates, ready to give battle. And everyone in this chamber knows you're raising more troops to add to your numbers!"

At that, other Caesarians arose, supporting Marcus with encouraging cries, nodding their approval.

Curio took this opportunity to step forward bearing the scroll from Caesar. "Senators! We have Caesar's intentions right here, *in writing*," he cried, brandishing the scroll before the crowd. "Listen to his own words—"

Cato moved like Jupiter's bolt, descending in time to snatch the scroll from Curio's hands, thrusting it aside so hard it nearly hit one of Pompeius's lictors. "We've nothing further to hear from any of you," he growled, his voice hoarse.

Marcus was down on the Senate floor again in a heartbeat, retrieving the scroll. "Then let the tribune of the plebs make it public! For nobody here will dare touch me!" He spoke truth since the office of tribune of the plebs had always been sacrosanct—at least until now. It would be unlawful for any man to lay a hand upon him.

Hurriedly, Marcus broke the scroll's seal, reading aloud:

> *"Gaius Julius Caesar, Imperator and Proconsul of Gaul, to the Conscript Fathers:*
>
> *For a decade I have honored my word, securing Rome's borders from a fear Rome has dealt with for three centuries and enlarging our possessions and lands for veterans. Now you inform me that my work has ended, ordering me to lay down my arms and dissemble my legions.*
>
> *I shall agree to do so, provided that Gnaeus Pompeius Magnus does the same."*

There were no surprises in Caesar's letter, but the Senate's response sent the chamber into chaos again. Lictors hurried forward to surround Pompeius protectively as both factions exploded into hundreds of arguments. And when Marcus raised his voice to repeat Caesar's proposal suggesting both sides give up arms, nobody was listening.

Cato motioned to Cicero, who joined him at Pompeius's elbow on the floor alongside the fanatical Optimates at Pompeius's side. Together, they held a momentary discourse.

Finally, Pompeius rose. "Brothers," he began in a somber tone. "I propose Senatus consultum ultimum—absolute power to the consul—and I move that *I* shall administer that power. If the majority votes accordingly, I will declare Caesar a public enemy!"

Marcus set his jaw as Curio grasped his arm in a viselike grip, whispering desperately, "Just wait. Let them vote."

"To what end? They're not going to concede—"

"If the vote's against us," Longinus interrupted, "then Pompeius will be the one having to deal with the pressure of the populace. You've tried to *prevent* a war today."

Marcus chewed his lip, deep down seeing the bitter truth. *Both* Caesar and Pompeius wanted war. There would only be one man left standing.

Curio murmured with urgency, "Remember, Antonius, you're tribune of the plebs. You have power of veto."

Gods above—*this* was what Caesar wanted. He wanted the Senate to be seen as the aggressors.

The vote was a simple process. Consul Crus ordered any senator in agreement with Pompeius's proclamation to move to the floor near where he stood. Those against it would remain in their seats.

It didn't take long. Practically all of the Senate moved forward, filling empty space on the floor. Marcus, Curio, and Longinus moved back to their seats, indicating their vote, along with the sparser crowd of Caesarians.

Crus stepped forward, speaking in his bland voice. "This body proclaims Senatus consultum ultimum in favor of Gnaeus Pompeius Magnus."

Pompeius arose, arms lifted high in fervent declaration. "Gaius

Julius Caesar is now an enemy of the state, denied fire, food, and water!"

Marcus stepped forward boldly, one hand clutching the sinus of his toga. Loudly, he raised his voice. "I, Marcus Antonius, tribune of the plebs, *veto* this motion!"

Pompeius shouted back at him over the ensuing disorder. "Then let you and all of Caesar's constituents be warned; your safety in Rome is *forfeit*!"

You have your war, Caesar.

As if in response to Pompeius' words, one of his lictors bolted forward in the heat of the moment, taking a swing at Marcus with his fasces. The axe-crowned bundle of rods symbolizing magisterial power caught him in the back of his right shoulder, knocking him to his knees on the floor. When he opened his eyes in shock, blood had speckled the black-and-white mosaics around him. That damned axe within the bundle of rods had sliced through his toga and gouged his shoulder blade. Both Curio and Longinus sprinted over, helping him up. He felt warmth oozing down his back.

"You'd best look to your well-being," Pompeius warned. "You've no friends here. Many a man in this chamber would smile at mention of your death!"

"By striking me—a tribune of the plebs—you just lit the cremation fires of the Republic!" Marcus roared back.

He turned to where he thought Longinus and Curio had been standing. Instead, they'd moved back toward the Caesarian faction, and before he could move to join them, another of Pompeius's lictors struck him with his fasces, this time in the jaw. At least the iron axe blade missed him. Still, the tightly bound wooden rods caused Marcus's teeth to rattle. He wondered if his jaw was cracked. His mouth filled with blood, and the entire side of his face smarted.

On impulse, he snatched the lictor by the front of his tunic, ready to pummel the man to death. Someone jerked him away.

It was Curio.

By now the entire Senate was descending into mayhem, men

yelling, the Caesarians loudly chanting Caesar's name in rhythm, and Cato screaming at the top of his lungs for someone to grab that Antonian bastard!

Heart hammering, Marcus turned to Curio and Longinus. He heard Curio mutter, "Come—quickly. Stay together and follow me."

As they hurried to exit the chamber, senators and slaves alike pelted them with scrolls, fruit pits, pebbles, and any other rubbish they could find.

Optimates jeered them, and this time Marcus saw Pompeius signal his lictors, the men shoving senators aside to pursue them.

Outside, Curio motioned his litter and those of Marcus and Longinus to leave, creating a temporary false trail.

"This way!" Marcus shouted, red saliva spattering from his bleeding mouth. He led the three of them in the other direction, dodging merchant stalls in the crowded streets. Once they were behind some insulae and out of sight, he paused to spit out a mouthful of blood. His tongue felt thick and slurred his speech. "Let's think a moment. Where—where are we going?"

Longinus looked desperate. "Curio, have you a plan? "No, I was just hoping our litters would lead them the wrong way."

It had been a good idea, but Marcus already heard the cries from lictors searching not far away. He spat more blood onto the pavement. "Follow me!"

Marcus led them up the Esquiline behind more insulae, taking a circuitous route on purpose, trying to lose their pursuers. He rounded a turn, bringing them onto the main road. It was dangerous, but he was exactly where he wanted to be.

When Marcus pounded on the door, Cytheris opened, wide-eyed.

Sweaty and bloody, with his face swollen, Marcus hastily ushered the others in. Longinus swiftly bolted the door.

"What's happened?" Cytheris's voice was low with fear. She reached for Marcus's battered face, her hands trembling.

"Tell her, Antonius," Curio grumbled, removing his toga and tossing it aside. "She's involved now, for good or ill."

Marcus explained with his thickening tongue. "Today the Senate bestowed full power to Pompeius. Caesar was proclaimed an enemy of the state. As tribune, I vetoed, but it changed nothing. If Pompeius's men find us, they'll kill us."

Cytheris paled. She was no fool. "Civil war," she whispered shakily. She opened a small sewing box, pulling out clean strips of fabric. "Open your mouth."

Marcus let her apply a strip with pressure inside his mouth.

"We must get out of the city," Curio growled as he paced. Longinus closed the shutters of the insula's several windows.

"Patience!" Marcus snapped through Cytheris's ministrations. He ripped the bloodstained cotton out of his mouth. "First, we must see to our families. I'll not leave without knowing they're safe." He turned to Cytheris. "I need your help." With a twist, he removed his signet ring, which Gaius had returned to him. "Go to my domus and show this to Iophon at the door. Ask for Gaius and tell him what's happened. He needs to dress the family as plebs and bring them here. Then go to Longinus's and Curio's homes too. Repeat the message and tell them to take precautions."

"My family's visiting relatives in the south," Longinus said. "Save your time and just go to Curio's." Then he added, "But if Pompeius's men visit your homes looking for us, your families had best have the same story."

He was right.

Marcus nodded, thinking quickly. "Tell someone in each household this: that we dressed as slaves and left the city by cart. If they all say the same thing, people will believe it."

"And tell Fulvia this is as safe a place as any," Curio added.

Cytheris nodded, snatching her cloak from a peg on the wall and unbolting the latch. She looked back and Marcus caught her hand, pulling her to him and kissing her full on the mouth. Then she opened the door and let herself out. He hastily replaced the bolt.

"What now?" Longinus fretted.

"We wait," Marcus answered.

"Our families might be safe, but we can't stay at your lover's insula while civil war breaks out around us!" Curio argued.

Marcus growled. "Until dark, it's too risky to go anywhere. Not every centurion will believe the cart story. Pompeius will have legionaries combing the streets for us, and every gate to the city will be under surveillance."

It seemed eons until Cytheris returned. Marcus only opened the door when she swore nobody else was near.

"Your brother has his message," she assured them. "So does Fulvia. She's bringing Clodius's children with her."

Marcus grasped her by the shoulders. "What did Gaius say?"

She shook her head. "Not much. He hurried back into your household, calling for your mother."

"And you told him what to tell the slaves—about our alleged escape by cart?"

"Yes."

"Good."

Cytheris pursed her lips in concern. "Legionaries are everywhere." Kneeling at her sleeping couch, she peered beneath it. "I have old costumes you can put on. You won't get far wearing fine togas."

Marcus agreed. "I'll wager there's a hefty price on our heads by now."

"They'll still recognize us," Curio fretted, shaking his head in apprehension.

Marcus shook his head. "Our odds will be best at night. And there's safety in numbers, so we need to stay together. I once took down four men alone, so three of us plus Gaius could be formidable, if it comes to that."

Longinus held out his hands. "But we're unarmed!"

"Wrong," Marcus said with a smile. "Cytheris, show them what you've got. My actress has a fine collection of weapon props. They may be old, but they are sharp enough to maim."

Cytheris opened a chest next to her bed, pulling out five gladii. "Let's pray to the gods your family makes it here," she murmured. "The streets are getting dangerous."

Her concern touched Marcus. She was a surprising creature, to be sure. "Nobody will recognize them," he assured her. "They'll look like slaves or plebs." Gods, let it be so. *Minerva protect them and give them wisdom,* he prayed despite his usual doubts in the pantheon.

Cytheris began picking up clutter from the insula's living space. "I don't want your mother thinking I'm a pig as well as a whore."

Marcus laughed at her. "Come here, girl." He snatched her hand, and his reward was the feel of her hips meeting his as he drew her close. He didn't care if Curio and Longinus were present. He kissed her deeply—sore jaw be damned—aware that both men were watching and probably envying him. His hands traveled through her long hair, down her back and buttocks. Moving his mouth to her ear, he whispered, "Play the perfect hostess—I simply can't risk leaving them at the domus. And go put on your best silk. Tonight you'll be dressed finer than Antonia!"

The next hours were silent and tense until the stillness ended with a soft scraping on the door. Marcus was there first, peering through the peephole. Satisfied all was well, he opened the door to Gaius, Mother, Antonia, and several female slaves, one bearing Tonia.

As the little group filled the insula, Cytheris stepped forward, attired like a goddess. "You may find my insula small and its wall-paintings beneath your tastes," she said, "but you are welcome."

Fulvia finally arrived with her children and two slaves. Immediately, she took control over Curio's costume, thinking it was too rich-looking. She ripped the fabric of his hood, making it appear worn.

Marcus eyed her. Loosely swept back, her neat hair made her doe-eyes appear as luminous and alluring as ever. But she was a woman on a mission, determined not to allow her husband's face to be seen.

Antonia rested on cushions against a dark wall, miserable and cross. Here she was, forced to share the same space with both Cytheris *and* Fulvia.

Ah, well. There were times in life when practicality had to replace pride. Mobs had burned Cicero's house to the ground when the Senate declared him an outlaw. As deep as his association with Caesar now was, Marcus wouldn't risk his family to that.

Cytheris mixed what wine she had, placing soft cushions in corners of her small flat. Once Tonia and Fulvia's children had warm blankets, she poured oil in a bowl with herbs, breaking bread and serving refreshment to everyone in her now-packed space. She even insisted that Mother use her bed. Marcus shook his head, laughing to himself at this twist of fate. Mother would sleep in his mistress's bed, and he was thankful for it.

Once darkness fell, he knelt down to Mother, Gaius close behind. "I'll send word when I can. Stay here. Cytheris will see to your needs and keep you all safely hidden. Be mindful: Cicero knows we have lands in Misenum. Don't go there."

Gaius added, "We don't know whether Pompeius will destroy our domus, but Marcus and I have peace knowing you're out of harm's way. Iophon knows you're here. He or Eros will deliver provisions and come for you when it's safe. Do *not* leave until then."

"All will be well if you do as we say," Marcus assured her.

Mother touched his bruised, swollen face with a courageous smile. "Well played, Marcus. This is the last place they would look for us."

He nodded and leaned in to kiss her. "I hoped you'd see it that way."

Marcus drifted toward the back wall, fondling his daughter's bronze hair where she slept. He glanced Antonia's way, but wasted no words on her. Then he headed for the door, followed by the rest, where Apollo had yielded to a moonless night.

"Be safe, my sons. Come back to me," Mother whispered.

CHAPTER XIII

MARCUS KEPT A BRISK PACE AS HE LED HIS FRIENDS AND brother through the darkness, taking back streets through the Esquiline district and heading downhill toward the Subura. They'd barely entered the slums when they encountered their first trouble.

"Stop in the name of Pompeius Magnus!"

Legionaries. Marcus halted in his tracks.

"Cover me," Marcus whispered to Gaius. "If they try anything, stick them like swine." Hand hovering close to his concealed gladius, Marcus hailed the soldiers in a jovial voice, striding forward. "Salvete! Too dark to linger in these streets, agreed?"

One bore a torch. He came up close, holding it high to see their faces. It was blinding. "Where are you off to?" he demanded.

Gaius answered, striding up even with Marcus. "Up the Via Flaminia. There's good coin in working cattle and goats up that way."

Marcus's jaw dropped in spite of himself. His idiot brother had just told them exactly where they were headed!

Suspicious, one of the eight soldiers circled behind them.

Longinus was edgy. "We mean no harm, just want work, as he says . . ."

The torch-bearing legionary cocked his head. "Well, not many men in the Subura this time of night speak genteel like you. And how'd your face get roughed up?" he demanded of Marcus.

He chewed his lip. Bloody legionary was smarter than Gaius!

"Careful, they might be armed," warned another guard.

Torch-Man didn't care. He brandished his fire close enough to Marcus's pained face so that it nearly seared his eyelashes. "You! I've seen you before. You're the new tribune, Antonius, yes?"

Nerves frayed, Marcus lost patience. "Now!"

Gladius singing from its scabbard, he plunged it into the soldier's throat. The other legionaries shouted, rushing to their dying comrade's aid. Curio stumbled forward in the dark, swearing and off balance, yet dispatching another unfortunate man.

Now there were six.

Gaius cried out, dark blood staining his tunic. Marcus barreled forward, followed by Longinus. His brother's attacker was easily run through, but now the other five were calling for reinforcements. One retreated, disappearing into the night, seeking his commander, no doubt.

Longinus took one man, Curio another. Lamplights appeared in nearby windows as people heard the clash of blades in the street. Bit by bit, a crowd was gathering.

Marcus fought frantically, defending Gaius, who had slumped against a building. Anxiety for his brother clouded his concentration. The soldier before him was using his shield offensively. He managed to strike Marcus with it, solidly pounding his already injured jaw. Grunting from the blow, he felt blood trickle down his neck. Curio appeared at his side, having dealt a death blow to his man.

At last, Marcus trapped both attackers against a wall, kicking the one without a shield. As the soldier recoiled, the point of Curio's gladius slid through his shoulder. Master of the Shield tried his trick once more, lunging forward, but this time it didn't work. Savagely grabbing the shield with his left hand, Marcus jerked both it and the soldier forward and off balance. Now he took control, stabbing him efficiently in the gut.

Without pause, he dropped the shield and hauled Gaius up, jerking layers of clothing loose to inspect his wound. Fortunately, it was only a bloody slash.

"I can make it," he said, though his voice was full of fear.

"Good. Because you'll have to." Marcus let him be, staggering backward himself a little and seeing stars from the newest bash to his head. Disillusioned at Gaius's poor efforts and unsure how to respond, he ordered gruffly, "*I'll* do the talking from now on." His voice sounded like gravel and was nearly unintelligible. It hurt to move his mouth, so he hoped he wouldn't have to say much.

Down the narrow street where the legionary had escaped came the distinct sound of nail-shod boots. Reinforcements . . .

"Now where?" Longinus whispered, panicked.

"I say we hold our ground," Curio exclaimed, face flushed and sweating in the flickering torchlight. "We finished the first ones." Gesturing to the growing crowd, he reasoned, "Surely, most of these people are Caesarians. We could start a riot to our advantage!"

Marcus shook his head. "No. Gaius is wounded, so we're down a man. It's too risky."

"Let's leave while we can," Gaius urged, wincing at his injury and eyeing the gawking plebs.

"Come on," Marcus directed, heading southwest. "Stay in the shadows."

"Wrong way, Antonius," Curio exclaimed. "The Via Flaminia is northeast."

"I know."

"Then where are we going?"

"These streets are too dangerous." Marcus winced again, trying to talk coherently. His tongue throbbed, and his whole head hurt. "I have an idea. But let's hurry before more soldiers get here because one of these plebs is bound to point them our direction."

With the Subura behind them, they threaded through winding alleys to the remains of the gutted Curia building. Glancing behind,

Marcus gestured to the others in urgency. Legionaries could appear at any time.

And from the sound of the tramping feet echoing through the narrow streets, they were near. Together, the four men squeezed behind a charred brick wall of the burned building, crouching down into the shadows. "Be quiet and still," Marcus breathed, squinting in pain.

A contubernium of armed men exploded from the Subura, this time led by a centurion. It was a huge relief when he halted his soldiers just short of the ruins.

The centurion thought he was a brainy sort. "If it really was Antonius," he reasoned aloud to his men, "why would he flee to the Forum? He'd try the Flaminia and run to Caesar. And if he does that, we'll catch him. We're wasting time. Back to the Subura—all of you. They're likely hiding in the maze of streets."

Calmed at the soldiers' retreat, Marcus tentatively lifted one hand, touching his face. It pulsed with dull, unending agony. Careful not to make things worse, he manipulated his lower jaw, running his split tongue over his upper incisors. Miraculously, his teeth were intact.

Curio was first to speak. "So," he whispered, "we're trapped in the Forum. There are always people about, no matter the time. Somebody will recognize us."

Glancing about, Marcus slipped out into the open. "We won't be here long," he mumbled. "Come on."

This time he ran, leading them through the shadows. It was only a short jaunt to the Basilica Aemilia. Rome's beggars and thieves were about, but at least the place wasn't teeming with people. Warily, Marcus led them past three men on a corner huddling around a brazier. Homeless urchins and drunkards lay in doorways and against buildings. Several plebs scurried by. Thank the gods it was dark. Past several money-changer stalls, they entered the confines of the Basilica.

Just south of the western corner, Marcus halted. There was their escape. Nearly as high as a large plinth was an iron grate fastened to a stone mount. Beneath lay a stinking abyss and sounds of running water—the very bowels of Rome. He pressed one foot against the masonry, gripping the iron bars firmly. It didn't budge.

Curio balked like a mule. "*This* is your solution? The sewer?"

Testily, Gaius sided with Marcus. "It'll get us out of the city, Curio."

Longinus glanced about, pacing and acting jittery, weighing other options. "We could try the Via Appia, then circle north."

Still tugging at the grid, Marcus was in no mood to argue. "Shut up and help me!"

Longinus sighed and stepped forward, joining in the effort, and the drain finally yielded with a rasping sound, its gaping mouth an inky cavern.

"I agree with Longinus," argued Curio. "I say we try the Via Appia."

"Feel free," Marcus snapped. "But we already encountered Pompeius's troops twice, and the city exits will be swarming with men looking for us! Besides, Cytheris already spread the lie that we'd exit Rome by cart. I guarantee there'll be legionaries looking for us at the city entrances. But *nobody* will look for us down here!"

"*Whfff!* Not with that smell!" Longinus admitted.

"Look," Marcus reasoned, "we may swim in shit a while, but at the end, there's a nice, icy river we can all bathe in. And I intend to be alive to feel it. Come on, Gaius."

Distressed, Longinus hesitated, turning back briefly to the nearby shrine of Venus Cloacina, protectress of the sewers. Marcus looked over one shoulder and snorted with amusement, catching Longinus caress the small deity's statue and kiss the top of its head.

As he eased himself down into the sewer's stinking labyrinth, Marcus's stomach turned. One thing was certain. A single misstep would find him landing in a gooey slime of urine, excrement, and refuse. Slick algae claimed most of the narrow walkways, and as he slowly felt his way along, he chafed his hands, grasping for balance against rough-hewn stones in the blackness. Somewhere ahead, a rat chattered, disturbed by the intruders.

Gaius breathed raggedly behind him. His brother's wound was not deep, but it obviously pained him.

Curio kept swearing, especially when he finally lost footing and fell in. He yelped as the brutally cold cesspool claimed him. Marcus would have laughed, but he dismally realized at the same time that the passage was narrowing. Now they had no choice. While Curio tried without success to struggle back onto the narrow ledge, Marcus squatted, slowly lowering himself into the frigid muck of Januarius. He gasped at the chill, remarking sarcastically, "I hope that kiss you gave the goddess back there satisfied her, Longinus!"

For what seemed an eternity, Curio damned Marcus to Hades nearly a hundred times, Gaius vomited twice, and Longinus uttered not a word. It was a joyous moment when they finally heard the Tiber's steady currents ahead.

Half walking, half swimming, and sometimes sloughing their way through uneven stonework, the passage opened up. Glorious, rushing currents of the river's flow rumbled a sweeter melody than that of Mother's cithara.

The arrival at Caesar's camp was memorable.

After a debriefing, Caesar mounted Marcus, Gaius, Curio, and Longinus onto a baggage cart to display—filthy, stinking, and battered—before the entire assembly.

"Pompeius," Caesar began, riding his big warhorse back and forth before his troops. "A man I thought of as a brother. But this Roman I once trusted has denied Tribune Antonius his legal right to veto and *attacked* him in the Senate! Moreover, the conscript fathers in all of their wisdom declared *me*—Gaius Julius Caesar—*an enemy of the state*!"

As the legionaries roared their displeasure, the noise's vibrations made Marcus's aching face throb. Still, it was unforgettable hearing a simultaneous roar of rage from thousands of men, all banging shields in unison.

Caesar lifted his arms for silence. As things quieted, he walked his horse slowly around the cart where Marcus and the others stood. Caesar pointed first to Gaius's bloody tunic, then at Marcus's face. "Look at them. Their only crime was representing me in the Senate. Should that be a crime? They were struck with refuse and fasces, stripped of their dignitas, and forced to escape like criminals."

Again, the din—gladii banging atop shields.

Caesar lifted his hand. "If Pompeius and the Optimates have denied me fire, water, and shelter, it means you too must endure my shame! You, who have won Gaul and opened the north to our people. Mars Almighty, that I should live to see my victorious soldiers banned from their own city! What would you have me do about this attack on my person and our tribune, Marcus Antonius? How should I respond when my own men are unwelcome as heroes in Rome? Shall I keep forgiving Pompeius's insults and casual disregard of Roman law?"

Pandemonium ensued.

Marcus marveled at Caesar. So cool, calm, and shrewd. He could read men's intentions, knew their minds and foibles. He'd planned this all along, using Marcus and allowing the power-hungry Optimates to demand blood for blood.

At sunrise, Marcus mounted a borrowed horse in the frigid predawn air and turned down the cardo. Caesar's camp was located just southwest of Ravenna Classis.

Since his nose was battered and swollen with dark, purplish bruising, it was easier breathing out of his mouth. A medic had stitched and cleansed his shoulder, but today it felt feverish to the touch.

He spurred the mare, cantering past ranks of marching men, his lungs filling with smoky, cold camp air. With every stride of his horse, his face pulsed with pain—agonizing reminders of the Senate's "justice."

"We honor you, Tribune, no matter what Rome does!" one legionary called out loudly.

"Shame upon Pompeius!" another shouted.

Marcus reined in, reaching down to clasp their hands and thank them. After greeting the soldiers, he headed downhill, joining Caesar for the day's march.

For a good six hours, they headed due south until Caesar halted the column and disengaged from the rest of his men. Marcus watched him ride down a short distance to a narrow riverbed, where he stopped.

Unimpressive. That's what Marcus was thinking as he stared at the stream. Slow-moving, narrow, and shallow in most areas, the Rubicon River got its name from its red clay that, in some lighting, gave it auburn hues. It was the official boundary separating Italia from Gallia Cisalpina.

Everything depended on what Caesar did right now. Much weighed in the balance. By crossing that river, he'd start a civil war.

Finally, Marcus cantered up to join him. "This is it?" he quipped, nodding toward the insignificant stream.

"Yes."

"I was expecting something broader—at least as wide as the Tiber."

"It's merely a geographical boundary, Antonius, not the Great Pyramid."

Marcus shrugged. "A river's a river, I suppose. What have you decided?"

He didn't even pause. "That you'll take two thousand infantry and my Gallic cavalry, who love you. Head overland to Arretium. Secure that city for me, and it'll protect my flank as we head south. We can't risk any northward movement by Pompeius. We'll need to move faster than he does. Grant clemency to every city on your way yielding to Caesar. And since my former colleague has been busy recruiting, let's do the same thing. We need men."

"So it's really war?"

It was though Caesar didn't hear him. He continued planning.

"I'll move due south, securing Etruria as I go." Then, studying Marcus momentarily, he queried, "You're a gambling man, aren't you?"

Marcus nodded. "What of it?"

Caesar's mouth turned up slightly into a grim smile, eyes sparking with vindictive intent, like those of a falcon about to take a bird in flight. "We have risky gaming ahead, and I don't intend losing." With a noisy smack on his horse's rear, he shouted loudly so men behind him heard every word, "Follow me and *throw the dice*!"

With cheering legions at their backs, Marcus followed, and at Caesar's side he splashed across a diminutive river called the Rubicon.

Eight days later, Marcus was sore and fatigued from riding fourteen hours. He and his men hadn't spent more than a single night at any encampment in the past week. The return trip had been a whirlwind tour of Etruria to meet Caesar in distant Ancona on Italia's eastern shores.

A nearby legionary took Marcus's reins as he swung down from his mount. His welcome wasn't warm.

"I expected you two days ago," Caesar complained curtly. "What took so damned long?" Seated outside his praetorium, haughty impatience replaced Caesar's usual calm, Julian demeanor. His fingers pulsed upon a portable writing table.

Marcus clenched his jaw at the chilly reception. "It's Januarius," he reminded him. "Mountain passes are snowy this time of year. There were places where we had to dig our way through." Sensing no empathy, he added, "However, I bear good news. Arretium is yours, and I recruited as ordered. Our numbers are swelling."

"So are Pompeius's," Caesar snapped in disgust.

Marcus raised his eyebrows at his cousin's tone. "By the gods, you're foul-tempered. Who pissed in your porridge?"

"Labienus."

Oh, what had that man gone and done now? Before he could inquire, Caesar answered his question.

"He defected to Pompeius."

"So he's headed south with him?"

"Ah. You already know."

"We intercepted a courier headed north yesterday. Pompeius has quit Rome and is engaging in a tactical retreat."

Tight-lipped, Caesar nodded. "He'll cross over to Greece. He has plenty of loyal legions there."

Marcus sighed, puffing his cheeks out. Right now he didn't give a whore's tit what Pompeius was up to. He just wanted to rest.

"I know you're weary. Go get some sleep," Caesar muttered brusquely. "Tomorrow morning you'll ride with Longinus to Rome and set up camp. I need someone to assure the people of my goodwill, keep the peace, and call the Senate to convene once I return."

Marcus frowned at his cousin's unusually pale and fatigued countenance. His behavior was that of a hard taskmaster—a grumpy, exacting old bastard! Was he just tired, or had Caesar changed since Alesia?

Ah, well. If Pompeius had retreated, being first into Rome meant browsing the best properties vacated by the cowards before anyone else laid claim.

No more swimming in sewers for Marcus Antonius.

CHAPTER XIV

49-48 BC

MARCUS AND LONGINUS FOUND ROME AS SILENT AS A tomb. Pompeius and his allies had fled safely across the Adriatic.

Mother and the rest of the family were safe and back at home, much to Marcus's relief. They had spent only a few days at Cytheris's insula before Pompeius became occupied with his own dilemma—Caesar's advance.

And while awaiting the imperator's arrival, Marcus had plans of his own. Caesar had attained the priesthood of pontifex maximus years ago, and he valued that honor almost as much as his new status as conqueror. He would have no desire to leave the grand public domus that housed Rome's chief priest to claim one of Pompeius's properties.

So Marcus stood in Gnaeus Pompeius Magnus's impressive atrium, greeting slaves. "Please rise; there's no need to be afraid," he assured, smiling grandly.

Pompeius's apprehensive household slaves knelt before him subserviently, their hands outstretched in supplication, dreading the unknown. Iophon and Eros greeted each one, gathering personal information and determining each slave's age and skills.

"Those of you wishing to return to Pompeius may do so," Marcus said in a voice all could hear. "I'll even pay for your transport to Greece. However, if you commit yourself to staying here as part of my household, I'll be generous. Whatever incentives were once granted you for hard work and loyalty will continue. You'll see that my slaves bear no marks of cruelty."

Most chose to remain, eager to ingratiate themselves to anyone controlling the city in such uncertain times. To the older ones, Marcus bestowed reassuring hand clasps, smiles, and words of encouragement. Decency dictated that these seniors receive their freedom, after which they'd be his clients, out of gratitude.

Some of the young female slaves eyed him, one even pressing close as he passed, licking full lips, and discreetly touching his thigh. Slaves of the domus Antonii on the Palatine had never been as numerous, desirable, or exquisite as these—aside from Fadia, of course.

As Iophon and Eros led them away, Marcus moved leisurely about the spacious atrium, enjoying unusually warm, winter sunshine streaming into the open space. A graceful bronze Venus posed between columns that supported the compluvium. "That Venus is lovely," Marcus commented. "I'll send it to Caesar as a gift once he returns. Venus is his patroness, after all."

"This isn't right," Mother stated in a low voice, interrupting his reverie. Her stamp of disapproval had been obvious at his first mention of the property. "I rather doubt Caesar sent you ahead of him to confiscate others people's homes."

"He sent me ahead because he trusts me to secure the city. And what do you mean, 'not right'?" Marcus demanded. "Caesar's wealth is beyond belief now. I doubt he'd want his enemy's domus, especially when he could build a monumental new one if he wanted. Pompeius left the entire city to us. All his lands and properties will be confiscated and sold cheaply, so why shouldn't I help myself?"

"At least Pompeius was merciful. Our domus still stands."

"True. But your *son* wouldn't be standing if he'd had his way. He meant to *kill* me, Mother."

She pursed her lips, looking around at the imposing surroundings. "It's ill-mannered to just 'take' another man's home like this."

Marcus laughed. "Remember how crowded our domus was when I came home after Alesia? It's far too small to host the sort of dinners I'm expected to have now. I need more space. Caesar will be pleased for me to have it."

"You're being presumptive. Here you are in Rome, basking in victory, when others, including your own brothers, are off fighting. If Caesar pursues peaceful relations—"

"Please stop," Marcus begged, walking over to her and taking her hands. "Enjoy the fruits of my labors for once. I've endured starvation, deprivation, hardship, injuries, dangers of every kind. Now I intend to enjoy life a bit."

"Think hard before doing this," she insisted. "How might this 'occupancy' of Pompeius's domus be perceived by the people? He still has sympathizers in the city."

Marcus snorted. "You know I care little what others think. Didn't you hear the plebs cheering our litter all the way here? How many times must I remind you? I'm Caesar's second in command now—a military hero. Gone are the days when we Antonii scrabbled about as inferior nobles. Once prices plummet, of course I'll purchase the place outright. In the meantime, enjoy our bounty!"

She shook her head adamantly. "I won't live here. It's far too ostentatious for my tastes. I prefer my life as it is."

"Suit yourself. Our domus on the Palatine shall be yours—with Antonia. But I'm moving here to the Carinae. It's stately up here near the old Temple of Tellus, and it's got a fabulous view of the Forum and Palatine. It suits me, I think." He grinned. What was wrong with feeling pleased with himself for once?

"Just look at these mosaics!" he declared, turning around and strolling over a favorite depicting Alexander at the Battle of Issus. "These tesserae are smaller than my littlest toenails!" While treading over the vivid art, he studied the compluvium's roof, with small decorative motifs atop each rainwater drain.

"What else have you 'claimed,' Marcus?"

Only mildly irritated at her apprehension, he answered with unusual patience. "A new gilt litter, two more Pompeian properties—one's a lovely little town house in which I'll place Cytheris. She deserves it after taking such fine care of all of you. The other's a spacious villa outside Rome."

Mother shook her head, aghast. "Gilt litters? Two more Pompeian properties? Such excess!" she exclaimed under her breath, shaking her head. "Either you'll be bankrupt again or the gods will strike you down for hubris!"

He ignored her, leaning back on a column and breathing in the fresh air. Eyes closed, he listened to cries of a songbird in the peristyle courtyard. Caesar's Gallic War had ended and another was beginning. Indeed, he'd celebrate before death and peril camped at his door again.

And what a party he intended to have!

As soon as Caesar arrived, Marcus led a contingent of senators to the Campus Martius, intent upon discussing the imperator's objectives.

Able to satisfy their initial concerns, Caesar downplayed his return to Rome. He could have entered like Sulla, with legions at his back and tubicines trumpeting. However, he came on foot, at night, hooded and escorted only by Marcus, Longinus, and a few carefully chosen guards. For the first time in a decade, he set foot inside his city's sacred boundaries.

His visit would be brief as he prepared to deal with numerous far-flung Pompeian armies. Beyond Italia, the war was well underway. Caesarian forces were facing dire challenges in Spain and North Africa. Curio departed for Numidia to lead the fight against King Juba, a dynastic despot declaring for Pompeius. Caesar aimed for Spain first to seize the upper hand from Pompeian lieutenants there. Marcus's orders were to remain in Rome, functioning as Caesar's lieutenant.

Again he was frustrated. It was one thing to have Caesar's trust, but disappointing not to be in the field.

Before leaving, Caesar hosted an intimate banquet. Cicero came, along with Terentia. Also in attendance was Caesar's niece Atia and her Optimate husband, Lucius Marcius Philippus.

As they dined, Marcus observed one of his cousin's most admirable traits—something he lacked. Caesar could casually entertain people he disliked or distrusted—Cicero and Philippus, in this case—turning the evening into effortless entertainment. It never mattered whether he esteemed someone, their views, or their comments. Intentions and personal opinions were always masked, turning effrontery into wit and criticism into humor. Caesar liked his enemies nearby, under a watchful eye.

Tapping a finger on his silver wine cup, Marcus was forced to listen to Cicero. As slaves removed the final courses, Chickpea was referring to his many writings. Thank Bacchus some slaves appeared with honeyed wine. It helped dull the boredom. Shutting his mind to tedious details on music of the spheres, Marcus sipped the numbing, sweet drink, only returning to the present when Cicero mentioned his name.

"—in front of Marcus Antonius."

"Pardon?" Marcus looked up, instantly attentive.

Cicero nodded toward a gold platter bearing fruits and cheeses. "That platter next to you—I assume it's of Gallic workmanship?"

"Actually, it's from Pontus," Caesar answered. "A gift from the remaining Pontic clan upon my Gallic victory."

"A kind gesture," Cicero remarked. "Now tell me, Caesar, for many of us are wondering. Where shall the conqueror of Gaul take up residence?"

Caesar pushed aside his small plate and wiped both hands politely on a cloth offered by a slave. "I've no intention of relocating. Whatever gave you that impression?"

"Cicero's referring to Antonius's procurement of Pompeius's domus," Philippus interjected, his eyes narrowing at Marcus in distaste.

Marcus cocked an eyebrow at him. What a peculiar man. For some time, he'd been riding the fence between the Optimates and Populares. However, he'd recently settled in the Optimate camp and was staunchly *against* Caesar despite his close affiliation to the Julii through Atia.

"Everybody's wondering where Caesar, the great imperator, could find a grander house?" Philippus went on. "Surely, Rome's hero should have a finer residence than our tribune here?"

Marcus scowled, turning his head away.

Fortunately, Caesar smiled, stroking his chin. "I believe there's far more to a home than riches. If it's splendor Antonius covets, this time I'll indulge him. He's been indispensably supportive in my efforts to add Gaul to our provinces."

Marcus cleared his throat, adding, "Caesar, if Pompeius returns to claim his house, I assure you I'd vacate the property. How dreadful I'd feel putting him out of his own home, especially when the last time we were together, he tried to *kill* me."

Cicero ignored Marcus's remark. "Caesar, why not invite Pompeius back, along with Cato, Labienus, and the rest? If you wish to show magnanimity, do so by extending peace instead of the sword. Stop this violence already raging outside Italia."

Calpurnia spoke up, "I won't hear my husband blamed for violence Pompeius has instigated."

Caesar smiled, shaking his head dismissively. "My gentle wife needn't defend me, but pray tell, when *did* I offer violence to Pompeius? Antonius presented my intentions clearly, and, as he just said, Pompeius offered him nothing but hostility. I would've laid aside both authority and legions had he done the same."

While Cicero contemplated a reply, Marcus noticed Eros approaching bearing a scroll. He raised up to see what it was about.

Eros whispered in his ear. "Iophon just brought this from home. He thought it might be important since it's from Gaius," he said, presenting the scroll.

Glancing at the seal, Marcus frowned with concern. Gaius was posted across the Adriatic in wild, untamed Illyricum.

Gaius Antonius, Legate in Illyricum, to his brother, Tribune and Augur Marcus Antonius in Rome:

Salve, Brother. Publius Dolabella is also serving with me here in Illyricum. Though we're holding our own, fighting here has been fiercer than expected. Dolabella worries our supply lines could be jeopardized. And Pompeius is building up his navy in our area, so we might not be able to send communications as easily.

Next, there's a private and personal matter I must address. When my colleague Publius Dolabella drinks, he often entertains with stories about his sexual exploits. In fact, he tells about women he's had, from lowborn trollops in the Subura to his own wife, Cicero's daughter, Tullia.

Recently, a soldier loyal to me related how Dolabella bragged about a red-haired lady he "enjoyed" in Rome named Antonia. At first, I was skeptical, but because I'm your brother, I confronted him. When asked who the red-headed matrona was, he admitted, "Antonius's wife, of course! Since Calpurnia's too virtuous, why not sample Rome's second lady?" After that, he added, "With your brother's reputation, I'm surprised she requires servicing! Perhaps he's a lesser man than everyone thinks!"

I told Dolabella in no uncertain terms how you'd receive this news. Undoubtedly, divorce will follow if this affair is genuine. I regret having to inform you. However, better it comes from me than someone else.

A few more pleasantries ended the letter, but Marcus stopped reading and chewed his lip furiously. Quips over his new residence and Caesar's present actions toward Pompeius all dimmed. Angry as he was about the infidelity, he felt no jealousy. There was so little invested in his marriage now that the only emotion left to wound was pride. No man had rights to his wife.

Dolabella had trespassed. And oh—he *would* pay.

Never had Marcus deceived Antonia concerning his emotions. She knew his marriage to Fadia had been a love match and it had been violently torn from him. It was outrageous that she was betraying him just because he couldn't love her the way *she* wanted. That time he'd run into her with Dolabella in the peristyle gardens—had they been making love somewhere in the back of the domus under his very nose? But worst of all was the family to which Dolabella now belonged.

Marcus ground his teeth, reminding himself of one positive. Now he had a worthy excuse for divorcing Antonia.

Liquid sloshed over the sides of his wine cup as he plopped it down and rose. Without a courteous excuse to anyone, he stalked to the end of the couch, where Antonia was dining silently in the place of least importance. Heads turned as he snatched his wife's arm, viselike, hauling her up. Clumsily, she staggered behind him. Marcus led her all the way to Caesar's stately atrium, away from everyone. There, he thrust her toward the door so hard that she staggered, surrounded by the enameled, staring eyes of Julian ancestral busts.

Raggedly breathing, before he could say anything, a familiar voice spoke from behind him. "What's happened, Marcus? Are Gaius and Lucius safe?"

Not only Mother, but Calpurnia had followed them, their faces full of concern.

By Venus, he'd tell all, and by dawn Antonia would be out of his life. "Gaius sent a newsy letter. Read it." He tossed Mother the scroll and paced like a lion, eager to see her response.

Antonia stood still and ashen as a corpse. Marcus eyed her in disgust, sneering, "Caught like a rabbit in a snare, aren't you?"

She lowered guilty eyes, lips trembling.

Time seemed to slow as Mother read. Calpurnia remained

hushed and still next to the farthest column in the atrium, politely keeping distance. Marcus's footfalls were the only sound as he paced.

Without warning, Mother hurled the scroll clear across the room. It made everyone jump, Marcus included. He stopped and stared, amazed as she marched forward, confronting Antonia, her breasts heaving between agitated breaths. "When did this start?"

Marcus's eyes widened. He hadn't seen Mother this angry since the day his scandal with Curio broke.

Antonia opened her mouth to speak, but nothing came out.

"Answer me!" Mother hissed in fury.

Eyes lowered, Antonia quivered, her words barely audible. "I'm miserable in this loveless marriage."

"What naive stupidity!" Mother spat. "You think you're the only lonely woman in the world? You think it's a *requirement* for a husband to love you? Is it ever a man's duty to *love* his wife? It's *duty* we women are about, girl! *Duty!* Nothing more than duty to family, to your children, and most of all, to your *husband*, to whom you're bound."

Antonia burst out, "There's nothing wrong with desiring love!"

Marcus's eyes widened. Ho! Mother was losing control, her face going red and her fists clenching open, shut, then open again. Funny! That was often the way he reacted when angry!

"Shame upon you! Love or not, you should've thought of your daughter! Whatever will she hear of you when she comes of age?" In unexpected vehemence, Mother struck Antonia hard across the face, the smack cracking like a whip.

Marcus's jaw dropped. Was this Mother or a feral cat? He half expected her to jump on Antonia and pin her to the mosaic floor like a wrestler at the baths.

Antonia stumbled backward, sinking into a deplorable, sobbing pile under the statue of Venus Genetrix that Marcus had recently given Caesar.

Indeed, Mother did pursue her. "For years, your father has endured his own humiliation in exile with the utmost dignity, never once begging to return. Marcus nearly starved in Gaul, fighting to bring you and the rest of us honor! When he ran for quaestor, were you at his side, standing proudly in the Forum Romanum as a faithful wife should? No! Instead, you sulked and accused him of sleeping with another magistrate's wife, beginning a scandal that haunts him to this day! You're not worthy to call yourself Antonii!"

Tears streaked down Antonia's face. She turned miserably to Marcus, groping for his hand.

He snatched it away. "You've lost your mind. Playing whore to *Cicero's* son-in-law? Of all the men in Rome for you to open your legs to, it had to be Dolabella? How much fuel will that add to Cicero's list of reasons why I'm ill-fit to be Caesar's second? Oh, and make no mistake, when opportunity presents itself, Dolabella will *beg* me for mercy!"

Antonia shook her head, overcome. "Please, no violence! None of this was his fault! Only tell me where I should go and what I must do."

"I know exactly what must be done," Mother advised, hard as iron. "Divorce her quietly and immediately," she instructed Marcus. "Once the war ends, seek a highborn woman to marry—one who's trustworthy and capable of honoring you with sons."

Between sobs, Antonia managed the most tragic of all questions. "What about Tonia? Give me my daughter! She's all I have, Marcus!"

Marcus started pacing around her again, but now he took his time, thinking. Antonia had no more family in Rome. Where could she go? He'd send her to Hybrida—in his exile. That's where she'd go. But Tonia? No, he wouldn't send his daughter away. Even if it meant separating her from Antonia. She'd have to do without the girl until Hybrida was pardoned and returned to Rome.

"My, my." Marcus shook his head. She really did look pathetic. "You should've thought of Tonia instead of throwing yourself into Dolabella's arms. Do you think I *intentionally* hurt you?" he demanded. "Mother first gave you shelter when the Senate exiled your father. When we married, did I ever lie to you about my feelings in the beginning? Did I? In return, you've given me bitterness, deceit, and now disloyalty. So hear me now. I *divorce* you, Antonia. Take Nortia and the rest of your personal slaves. Leave my family home on the Palatine and join your father. I'll write to him explaining exactly what's happened. It saddens me to add to his humiliation. Tonia will remain here with us."

Wiping away tears, Antonia shook her head frantically. "No! No, please, Marcus—let me see her before I leave. Grant me that!"

He snorted. "Why should you see her now when you could've been with her the whole time instead of offering yourself to Dolabella like some sacrificial goat?"

Antonia dropped to the floor, reduced to begging. "Husband, please! I must see my child—"

"You did more than merely betray me. You chose a man in Cicero's family, a man I hate above *all* others!"

Desperate, Antonia got up again, turning to Calpurnia, who still stood behind Mother in the shadows. "Calpurnia, you've always been kind to me, and you're Caesar's wife. I implore you, convince Marcus to let me see Tonia."

Calpurnia replied softly but with cool demeanor, "It seems you no longer have a husband for me to convince. Go now. You're Roman. Show some mettle."

Antonia pleaded with Mother again, her voice softer. "Aunt Julia, please—we've always been close."

Julia lifted a hand, stopping her cold. "I took you in as my own daughter, and you've turned my trust into a charade. For shame, Antonia. For *shame*!" With that, she turned her back, Calpurnia following her into the triclinium.

Antonia wiped her face, visibly trembling. She took another tentative step toward Marcus.

Shaking his head, he showed her his back. This business saddened him terribly. But it had more to do with Tonia losing her mother than his marriage ending so untidily. As he strode out, Antonia's sobs echoed through the capacious atrium.

CHAPTER XV

IMMEDIATELY FOLLOWING MARCUS'S DIVORCE, ONE PERSON benefited more than anyone.

Cytheris became a frequent guest in the domus commandeered from Pompeius. For several months now, she'd hosted scandalous parties, inviting all of her actor friends, and Marcus didn't care. Yes, they were earthy, course, and ribald. But they were *free.* He envied them, and they adored him in return.

Then a sobering reminder of mortality struck.

Curio died.

When the news arrived in Rome, Marcus spent the next several evenings in Cytheris's arms. Usually, her company and that of her friends lifted his spirits. But the suddenness of his colleague's demise jolted him to his very core. Now both Curio and Clodius were shades. They had been his companions in that stormy time of youth when Marcus burst into manhood with as much force and energy as a spirited horse in the Circus—and with just as many brains!

Curio.

The man who had haunted him ever since he was fourteen,

introducing him to adulthood—sex, gambling, and betrayal. Either demanding Marcus pay larger and larger shares in their joint brothel club or drugging him for sex, Curio was ever at the core of Marcus's adolescent problems.

While making his daily rounds in Caesar's legionary camp out in the Field of Mars, Marcus had spoken personally to a courier who had brought the word. Curio had died honorably in Africa.

Strange as it all was, Marcus was relieved. He was comforted that in death Curio had managed to exhibit stalwart courage and not shame himself as he had so often in life.

Once he'd left for the African province of Numidia, Fortuna had deserted him. Numidia's puppet-king, Juba, loyal to Pompeius, had overwhelmed him in a savage attack. Surrounded by his dying men and realizing there was no hope, he had taken his own life.

"We're opposites, Antonius," Curio had once said. "If I must, I'll succeed on the field. If you must, you'll survive in the Senate."

Well, in the end, Curio had failed in the field.

What did that mean for Marcus and politics? It was bizarre how much this death plagued him. Tonight, while sleeping next to Cytheris, a bleeding Curio limped into Marcus's dreams. One of the apparition's hands groped his bloodstained tunic, covering his self-inflicted wound.

Naturally, Marcus arose to greet him, but Curio only shook his head. "I'm dead, so don't touch me and defile yourself."

Marcus obeyed and just listened.

"It's the loneliest thing I've ever known, Antonius—losing all hope. In the end, there was much blood and pain, but it kept my honor. I died Roman."

Marcus awakened with a jerk, feeling as though he were falling from some high precipice, only to find himself in Cytheris's arms, sweating and shaken.

"What's wrong?" she kept asking him, over and over.

As always, discussing his nightmares never came easy. It was simpler to drink them away, blurring the reverie into a befuddled haze. Marcus left, spending the rest of the night drinking at a cheap shithole in the Subura he couldn't even remember later.

Never a good idea.

Eventually, he made his way home, but just in time, staggering over to the atrium fountain. Without hesitating, he stuck his head under the water's rush, allowing the deluge to ease his throbbing head and roiling stomach. His skull felt as brittle as blown glass. An oddly conflicted sort of grief wrenched his spirit, and his torso shook as he began to weep.

Wet and dripping from his douse in the fountain, he closed his eyes and leaned against a veined marble column. Water mixed with tears coursed down his face, and glittery stars danced in his vision. He whispered a silent petition to Dis of the dead. "From this time forth, may Curio's ghost rest in Elysium and leave me be."

Gaius Julius Caesar, Imperator in Spain, to Marcus Antonius, Tribune and Augur in Rome:

I had to wrestle Massilia away from Pompeian forces. Therefore, three of my six legions must remain there, securing my back. Send me Legions VIII, XII, and XIII to Spain immediately as reinforcements.

Also, spies have reported that Cicero has left Rome for his lands in the south. I need you to find him and prevent his leaving Italia to join Pompeius. He holds far too much sway among Optimates despite his insistence that he's moderate. If he stays in Rome, I may yet earn his loyalty.

There was no problem dispatching legions. That only took a few weeks' time, and Marcus had ample experience moving troops.

It was the second order with which he struggled. Cicero had

fled south to a favorite villa near Cumae. Marcus dreaded dealing with him.

"I know you don't want to go, so take me and my friends. Our company will provide cheer in the middle of your trial," Cytheris suggested. "We'll make you laugh again!"

Eros discovered a spacious villa near Cumae, nearly on top of Cicero's, that Marcus promptly rented. He invited Mother to come too. She was raising Tonia now and deserved a holiday.

Since the nightmare about Curio, Marcus struggled to sleep. So along came Cytheris, with her entire company of mimes, musicians, comics, and lowborn artists. On the journey down, Marcus alternated between sharing her litter and Mother's. He was astounded at how well the two women got along. Ever since his mistress had opened her insula, providing safe harbor for the Antonii, the two had developed a sort of unspoken mutual respect.

Indeed, it was refreshing having the distraction because playing watchdog over Cicero wasn't Marcus's idea of a good time.

Once at the villa, he sent Cicero notice of his arrival, encouraging him to remain in Italia and trying to sound cordial. Cicero sent back a hasty note criticizing Marcus's "wild and scandalous behavior" since he'd brought along "harlots and ignoble nobodies."

"Visit him personally," Mother urged. "You'll accomplish more if you meet face-to-face."

"Why? I explained Caesar's concerns in the letter, and it bore my seal. Instead of a civil reply, he insults me, as usual. He's not my personal censor, authorized to monitor my life. Who I consort with is none of his damned business!"

"Then post legionaries at his villa to keep him there until Caesar returns."

"If I did that, he'd complain to Caesar. As moody as Caesar's been lately, he'd probably berate me for physically restraining him. No, I won't go that far."

She sighed and shook her head. "Oh, Marcus. I've warned you before to mind your lifestyle," she warned gently. "I know it's an 'escape' for you, but prominent men in the Senate believe such behavior is improper."

"And you agree with them."

Mother smiled. "Actually, I rather like Cytheris's spirit and zest for life, but neither of us can change the facts. She *is* lowborn, and so are her friends. Senators look down upon you for fraternizing with any of them."

"Cytheris could provide me a substantial list of upstanding senators she slept with before she was mine," Marcus exclaimed. "They're all hypocrites!"

Gods, how he hated politics. And how frustrated he was here instead of commanding alongside Caesar in Spain.

The next morning he wrote a second letter to Cicero, dictating it to Eros. In flowery speech, he tried to sound friendly and cajoling. Cicero loved flattery, so hopefully it would be enough to persuade him to follow Caesar's wishes.

After a full month in Cumae, Marcus headed north again. His large entourage of litters, baggage carts, horses, and a small contingency of legionaries—not to mention Cytheris's company—stopped for a midday meal.

Marcus and Cytheris reclined together on a woolen coverlet in the grass, sipping wine and eating nuts. Sultry strains of tibia music sounded from Sergius, Cytheris's friend who was a gifted actor and musician. A few other troupe members laughed gaily nearby, sharing wineskins.

Marcus relaxed his head in Cytheris's lap, eyes closed. The wine was sweetened with honey and had calmed him.

"More, Tribune?" This from Hippias, a comedian Marcus enjoyed for his clever jocularity. Adorned with kindheartedness, he ambled over, offering a swollen wineskin.

Marcus reopened his eyes but declined. "No. I'm afraid I'm returning to reality and responsibility. Therefore, my head must be clear."

The comic smiled warmly. "It matters little what anyone else thinks. We're most pleased to call you friend."

"Gratias. You people are blessed with a simple life," Marcus replied. He was proud of his common touch, knowing it was one characteristic neither Cicero or Caesar possessed. These ordinary people adored him because he got down on *their* level.

But unfortunately, Mother was all too correct. Such a gift never swayed the Senate or commanded armies.

Someone else was coming over. Marcus glanced up, shielding his eyes from the sun. It was Mother, carrying her cithara. Hippias bowed elegantly, gesturing to her instrument. "What fame you could earn by playing in our mimes, lady," he laughed.

She returned his smile. "Yes, and what scandal that would cause. I could earn you several talents every night. Every senator and highborn lady would pay well to hear Marcus Antonius's mother play in public!"

"By sharing your talents, everyone would see where your son gets his generous heart," assured Hippias.

Marcus and Cytheris made room for Mother to sit down.

She was a good woman. Why, she actually *enjoyed* being with these people. She saw how his affiliation with members of Cytheris's troupe eased his own unhappiness. Uncomfortable in the Senate, constantly worried about political duties for which he had no natural gift, Cytheris's folk made him feel like a king.

Hoofbeats sounded on the road, and dust rose as a rider approached. Glancing at Mother, he read the concern in her eyes. Both Gaius and Lucius now held military positions abroad. Lucius had written not long ago from his post in Asia Minor. He served a Pompeian governor who had ordered him to recruit for Caesar's enemy. Though disturbed by the letter, Marcus could offer him no help. He could only respond, urging Lucius to carry out his orders, protecting his own interests. It wasn't the answer he wanted to give, but it was the only advice that would safeguard his brother.

As the messenger drew near, Marcus arose and left the others under the pines to greet the rider. He was from Cicero's household, delivering a wax tablet.

"Is it serious?" Mother was on his heels.

"I should have posted a guard, as you suggested," Marcus muttered in disgust.

"Why? Did he leave?"

"Straight to Greece to join Pompeius." He shook his head, staring down the road. Cicero! He'd been a burr in Marcus's flesh since the Catilina conspiracy. "Someday, I swear he'll die at my order," he vowed. "I swear it on Mars the Avenger!"

Not long after arriving back in Rome, life took another sobering turn.

Publius Cornelius Dolabella, Antonia's lover and Gaius's associate in Illyria, wrote to Marcus begging for reinforcements. He also reported that Gaius had been captured by the Pompeian fleet while defending the island of Curicta. Dolabella knew nothing of his whereabouts or even whether he was still alive.

Because of Marcus's personal grievance with Antonia's former lover, he admittedly took his time responding. Too long, actually.

Today he was paying for it.

Caesar had returned. As their horses jogged toward Brundisium, Rome's main port city, his reprimand cut with a biting edge.

"It matters very little to me how you *feel* about Dolabella," he blasted, uncaring whether legionaries behind them heard. "If a fellow officer requires aid, dispatch it immediately or go *yourself.* I can turn a blind eye to your drinking, womanizing, and even your profligate acquisitions of properties not yet for sale. However, I'll hold you accountable for future errors in judgment or lack of action. Is that clear?"

"Yes, Caesar." Marcus forced himself to breathe evenly.

"Need I mention you should've *detained* Cicero—physically preventing his leaving?"

Marcus said nothing. Caesar had always been so tolerant toward Chickpea. He figured this was a situation that would have damned him either way—with or without any physical restraint.

"You served me well in Gaul and proved yourself reliable in the field," Caesar rattled on, "but I will *not* tolerate any more lapses in decision-making."

"Yes, Caesar," Marcus repeated, minding his tone. Best to stay calm, quiet, and accept the reprimand.

"It had best be '*Yes*, Caesar,' or I'll modify my chain of command again. There are legions of men groveling for my favor, Marcus Antonius."

Marcus chewed his lip, eyes plastered on the road ahead. Perhaps he deserved today's lecture, but he wished it had been a private tongue-lashing instead of Caesar berating him in front of marching legionaries. Yes, he'd performed poorly, but there were times when Caesar had too. What about his arrogance in wanting to take Britannia and failing both times? He had left officers in Gallia Comata to fend for themselves, even as alliances were falling apart.

Over exuding self-confidence, Caesar often acted beyond mortal these days. Lately, his personality, which had been so charismatic and charming, had turned colder.

A sentry galloped up. "Details on the Brundisium garrison you requested, Imperator."

They veered off to one side of the road as the legion marched on. Caesar was fortifying Brundisium as his base for the launch to Greece against Pompeius.

Caesar read speedily, as always. "This should amuse you."

"What?" Marcus studied him warily. So far today hadn't been much fun.

"A former exile is commanding at Brundisium. Take a guess who."

Marcus shrugged. "My Uncle Hybrida?"

Caesar shook his head, smiling tightly. "Try again."

Knotting his reins, Marcus reached up, removed his helmet, and rubbed at a residual hangover between his eyes. "Drop me a clue, at least."

"How about *ten thousand talents* worth of clues?"

Marcus's jaw dropped, his head snapping around at Caesar. "*Aulus Gabinius?*"

"None other."

Gabinius had been his commanding officer when he had reinstated Ptolemy on the Egyptian throne. The man was supposed to have paid Marcus two thousand of those ten, but that never happened. Gabinius was recalled from his proconsulship and found guilty of treason and extortion. The Senate eventually charged him to pay ten-thousand talents.

Marcus snorted. "Pompeius must be desperate, recalling that old shit."

Caesar glared at him. "It wasn't *Pompeius* who recalled the 'old shit.'"

Marcus stared at him incredulously. "*You* did?"

Caesar nodded, a crooked smile showing yellowing teeth. "Yes. Men like Gabinius will be appreciative of my mercies, and I imagine you'll now relish being his equal."

Marcus chuckled, grinning at the thought. Equal? No. Today's discipline behind him, he was Caesar's second in command. Just let Gabinius deal with that!

"Be wise," Caesar reminded him, as though reading his thoughts. "Remember I expect only the best from you."

With that, Caesar Imperator whipped his horse's head about, whacked its backside, and cantered back toward the head of the column.

Weather be damned! Caesar needed his reinforcements, and Marcus had to act. Any more wasted time spelled disaster.

Low on ships, Caesar took seven legions over to Greece in cramped conditions. His usual speed coupled with an early winter crossing took Pompeius by surprise. However, when Caesar's ships attempted to return to Brundisium to transport more men, they faced Pompeius's admiral Bibulus, a lifelong enemy of Caesar's.

Only a limited number trickled back to Brundisium, each captain sharing nightmarish tales of Caesar's desperate position.

Marcus was expected to ferry over another four legions. However, winter was a raging bitch this year. Strings of violent storms made the passage across the Adriatic perilous. Constant winds, violent squalls, and frothing seas turned the crossing into an impossibility for weeks on end. Adding to nature's relentless attacks, Bibulus's naval blockade just beyond the mouth of Brundisium's harbor was like a granite wall.

Marcus called for a consilium. How would they break the enemy barricade and get through, especially faced with such forbidding elements? He had no idea. Something had to come to him. It simply *had* to.

He marched into the hastily called meeting of officers and slapped a leather map of Italia and Greece onto a low wooden table for all to see. Everyone gathered around, and Marcus unrolled it with a flick of his wrist.

Indeed, familiar faces had been waiting when he and Caesar arrived in Brundisium. Marcus reunited with his former commander from Syria, Aulus Gabinius, who had recently defected from Pompeius. Still in Gabinius's company was Marcus's friend and fellow officer from his Syrian days, Publius Canidius Crassus, with whom he had served a decade earlier.

"The waters are still too rough," Gabinius groused, head wagging.

Everyone agreed. But Caesar needed reinforcements now.

Unsurprised at how things were starting, Marcus said tersely, "Caesar made it to Greece and it's winter—call it his undeniable luck or the love of Venus. However, his luck and lady love will desert him if we can't figure out a way to cross over. Gabinius, I've heeded your caution up until now, but we've wasted too much time. We *must* act."

Gabinius lowered himself into a leather chair, still frowning and shaking his balding head. "It's too hazardous. There are thousands of men to transport, and there's the blockade. If we place all hope in our small fleet and fail, this war is lost."

The man had no nerve at all, but he was right about one element. Pompeius's crack admiral, Bibulus, had masterminded numerous attacks and blockades against the Populares. He was also the commander who had defeated and imprisoned Gaius Antonius at Curicta. However, news arrived yesterday that spurred Marcus to act.

Admiral Bibulus had suddenly died.

Marcus addressed Gabinius, his voice tinged with impatience. "This is *war*, and we're dealt with stormy seas! I'm not here to lament the weather with you. I'm here to transport an army. Caesar would have us work together and *succeed*."

"Then do so by going the long way around on land," Gabinius argued. "That way, the men will be sure to survive."

"True. They might. But will Caesar? I think not. We'd arrive too late, and the war could be lost."

"Crossing in these conditions is *suicide*," Gabinius emphasized. Stubbornly, he rested his case, sitting down, his face frozen in a defiant scowl.

Murmurs of disagreement on the issue erupted from the other officers.

Canidius voiced an idea. "It's said a man called Libo has replaced Bibulus, correct? Since the master is gone, is there a way to tap into Libo's inexperience? He probably doesn't have Bibulus's sharp instincts."

"A fine idea," Marcus agreed, pacing across the room to fetch a cup of wine. "Let me think. You might have something here. What would Libo do in a pinch? Only one way to find out, really. We must tempt him with some sort of challenge—a diversion to weaken the blockade just long enough to break through."

"We could offer battle with what boats we have," Canidius offered.

Gabinius countered, "Impossible! This morning Libo sent skirmishers to pick off our watches along the coast. He's already done damage without Bibulus. By engaging him, we'd lose every ship we have."

Another officer spoke up, "We need a ruse, not a full-scale attack."

Deep in thought, Marcus nodded, and a smile curled his lips as an idea formed. "In our present position, Libo knows we're no threat. We need to do something out of the ordinary and use it to our advantage." He snickered, a scheme taking hold. "Tonight let's load the ships with men, stock, and as many provisions as possible, ready to leave for Greece. Pack the sails and hide them out of sight. We'll use oarsmen to feign battle intent." He began to pace as he spoke, his plan igniting. "We can detach about sixty rowboats from our main ships and hide them along the coast, filled with archers. Two of our finest ships will act as decoys to perform ordinary drills first thing in the morning, as we usually do. Only we'll allow those decoys to approach Libo and his blockade a little too closely. We'll tempt him with our arrogance, and hopefully he'll give chase. Once he does, the two bait-ships will withdraw."

"A lot of good that'll do!" Gabinius contended with a disgusted snort.

Marcus ignored him. "Canidius, I'll signal the fleet to depart through the opening in his lines, and your rowboats and the two decoys will hound the enemy on all sides. It'll create a flea-sized skirmish he'll never forget and should be enough of a distraction to allow me to break through with the rest of the fleet. And if luck holds, I'll land the rest of the army in Greece."

Canidius looked up from the map, his long, lean face widening into a bright smile. "It might work, especially if my archers use fire and cause real damage!"

Marcus tilted his head back, laughing aloud and smacking him on the back. "I think so! Now who wants to join me in drinking to success?"

As predawn preparations were being made for the next morning's subterfuge, a single battered ship attempted entry into the harbor. Libo's men attacked and burned it, but not before a single freedman, acting as a courier, survived to swim and scramble onto the rocky coast of Brundisium. Now he sat shivering next to a brazier in Marcus's quarters drinking warmed wine, his mission accomplished.

Gaius Julius Caesar Imperator to Marcus Antonius:

I will be brief. If you don't embark for Greece immediately, all will be lost. Bring at least three legions, cavalry, and supplies.

CHAPTER XVI

MARCUS AGREED WITH GABINIUS ABOUT ONE THING. Sailing conditions were dreadful.

Prior to departure, sacrifices were performed, but the priests couldn't locate a liver in one of the birds. That did nothing to boost morale.

Marcus stood on the prow of the lead galley, his face spattered by sea-spray as stiff sirocco winds whipped up from the south. Once they reached high seas, miles from shore, they'd increase even more and be key in escaping pursuit.

Marcus even muttered a prayer to Neptune that it would be so.

Each ship in the small flotilla was crammed with men. He selected three legions composed of Gallic War veterans. A fourth was full of new recruits, soldiers who'd gain experience soon—if they landed safely. In the largest triremes were hobbled eight hundred horse and cavalrymen, an invaluable asset on a campaign involving distance. Unfortunately, it was supplies and food stores which Marcus had to limit, allotting space enough for living beings.

Neptune was honored, because Libo gave chase to the decoys.

Archers on Canidius's rowboats acted fast, surrounding the enemy ships and firing flaming arrows mercilessly.

Now!

Marcus ordered the rowers into action and felt the ship rock forward, followed by the others. Muscles of sweating, grunting men pressed into their oars to break the fleet into open water. Leaning out over the rail, Marcus looked back. Canidius disengaged, as planned, trying to save his men. Only too late did Libo realize what was happening, sacrificing his configuration and one ship to fire.

It *worked*!

What a thrill to pass safely by the enemy fleet, as it rested securely at anchor even now. From where Marcus stood, he saw legionaries on board Libo's ships shouting to one another and scurrying to their posts. Some of his own men began laughing and gesturing obscenely to the Pompeians.

Determined to outrun any pursuit, Marcus paced aft, descending into the belly of the boat. He shouted encouragement, weaving among the rowers. The tight press of bodies filled the cabin with an acrid smell of unwashed flesh. These men were hard—straining, every arm taut, veins pulsing with each heave. Several moaned and one audibly cried out, gnashing teeth to keep the strict rhythm of the hortator, who beat his leather drum in hollow, rapid thumps.

Satisfied at their performance, Marcus returned to the deck, and called to the captain, "Hoist the sails."

"Legate," the captain warned, "we risk missiles and torching, for the enemy's still within range."

Marcus shook his head stubbornly. "Our rowers are spent. Sound the command!"

A loud snap from flapping canvas signaled a swinging boom, and the whole boat heaved as south winds took control. Cold rain pelted Marcus's face, his crimson cloak whipping like a miniature sail in the wind behind him. His other ships followed, faint voices of sailors drifting from vessel to vessel.

Libo's blockade became more distant with each swell. Still, Marcus knew his flotilla was far from safe. Slate-gray skies ahead offered no hope of improved weather and they had over a full day of sailing ahead. A lone gull voiced complaint, its cries a lamentation over the wind's eerie song.

All day and night, they tracked northerly, then finally bore east, where the rocky shores of Greece appeared with yet another menace. Northwest of the coastline, another fleet lay at anchor. Masts of these towering triremes dwarfed any of Libo's boats.

"Who in Hades is that?" Marcus shouted to the captain.

"Pompeius has a Rhodian fleet patrolling these parts. It must be them."

"Gods—if we can see them, they see *us*!"

Marcus's heart pounded. This would be no unseasoned admiral like Libo, easily tricked into blunder. This commander would have one thing in mind—total destruction of any Caesarian reinforcements.

Then another terrifying reality unfolded. Rocky shoals along the coastline in this region made a direct landing impossible. Pompeians were familiar with the lay of the land, and already the ships were moving toward them. As they closed in, their plan became apparent. They meant to drive Marcus's boats into the deathtrap of the coast. Waters surrounding the shoreline churned to froth. Any shipwreck survivors there would drown or die a bloody death on jagged rocks.

As they neared land, two small, swift biremes broke from the rest of the Pompeian fleet, forcing two of Marcus's legionary transports into an especially hazardous area of sheer cliffs and rocks.

Marcus watched helplessly. They'd shred like straw.

One of the two imperiled crafts lifted its oars in unison, preferring surrender to being smashed to pieces. Immediately, the nearest Pompeian bireme captured the vessel, dropping its corvus atop the beleaguered ship. The heavy boarding plank sank onto the prow with a sonorous crunch, drawing it closer for easy boarding.

Marcus watched with a sinking heart. If it was mercy they expected in surrender, they'd be mistaken. Powerless to intercede, he paced furiously, watching from afar. Enemy soldiers boarded the ship, swords drawn. Over the raging sea came the panicked screams of dying men.

The captured boat's sister continued to drift. Ever unrelenting, the wind carried Marcus the splitting sounds of its doom as it foundered on the rocks. It was eerie and bizarre hearing the ship's death throes and not those of the men. As legionaries yielded to the wild waters, howling gales silenced them forever.

Then, as quickly as tragedy struck, Fortuna changed her capricious mind again. Marcus's cloak abruptly snapped behind him, tugging on the two fibulae that clasped it in place.

The winds—they were changing!

The captain rejoiced. "The gregales! They'll save us!"

Northeasterly gales strained the ship's riggings, giving the fleet a sudden advantage despite pellet-sized hail battering the crew, who sought to maneuver the boom.

Now it was the Pompeians who were in peril.

Tossed and assaulted by the winds, the enemy fleet began to collide into each other. A nautical suicide played out as the ships crunched, screeched, and groaned in an inadvertent frenzy. Even a worse fate loomed as they desperately tried to disentangle themselves. Soon *they* would be the ones running aground.

Still holding fast to the rigging, Marcus felt himself in thin air as the ship dropped into a low wake. His feet slammed into the deck as it arose again, and he groped for balance, his boat veering south along the coast, seeking better harbor, followed by the rest of his ships.

"Find us calmer waters and a place to land this wreck!" he yelled at the captain. Sailors on board scrambled to steady themselves at their posts, keeping both course and footing while harnessing the miraculous winds that seemingly came from nowhere.

Marcus glanced at his hands. All of his knuckles were white as lilies, his heart pumping crazily as he hung on like a wet cat.

Ho, he *hated* boats and the sea!

Marcus and his legions tendered ashore to find their bearings, only to witness Pompeian scouts on horseback galloping away. The enemy had observed their landing, so the newly landed troops would soon have plenty of company.

There was nothing to do but dig entrenchments as quickly as possible into the shoreline where they had disembarked. It was difficult. Men were seasick, and the ground was too rocky to dig easily.

Marcus sent out some of his own scouts who returned by dusk to announce that Pompeius himself was riding north from Dyrrachium, accompanied by a good-sized force.

But Fortuna, fickle as always, sent a blessing. The relief arrived in the form of a tribune galloping in with excellent news. "Caesar sent me to tell you that he's coming. He's got two of his four legions and will soon have Pompeius trapped between your army and his."

Outmaneuvered, Pompeius gave up in a hurry, leading his men the long way home and giving Caesar and Marcus Antonius plenty of space.

Marcus arrived at Caesar's camp as he did at Alesia—in the middle of serious fortification-building: a series of walls, over seventeen miles long, that pinned Pompeius's army against the sea. The way he saw it, Caesar had three advantages: war-hardened men, water, and his luck, which never failed. And if they could capture Pompeius's water source, the war would be over. Only one dark shadow stalked both sides like a curse.

Starvation.

Word in camp was that Pompeius's men were feeding on draft animals to spare their cavalry. Sometimes soldiers on both sides broke through barricades, robbing one another's minimal supplies. Foraging parties were often attacked whenever they'd located food. Nourishment of any kind was diminishing to almost nothing.

Marcus was especially bothered about the lack of supplies.

He had been personally responsible for sacrificing provisions in favor of men on the crossing to Greece. Since his landing, no other supply vessels had arrived. It drove home a dismal fact: Caesar did not control the seas, Pompeius did. If Brundisium was sending provisions, they were filling Pompeian bellies.

While on a routine infantry drill, Marcus saw a lizard nibbling a root. Hungry like everyone else, he stopped, shooed the creature away, and bit off a piece. It was hard and slightly bitter, but it didn't sicken him. At his suggestion, Eros took a turn at experimenting with more samples. After boiling and baking several specimens, the slave brought over a small platter for Marcus to try.

"They're still tough," Marcus complained as he chewed.

Eros replied somewhat irritably, "If it disgusts you, don't look at what you're eating! It'll fill bellies."

He was right.

Poor Eros. He and the other legionary slaves were the thinnest of all. As conditions worsened, Caesar ordered them down to quarter-rations. The youth stubbornly swore he wouldn't go to his funeral pyre with an empty belly. Together, he and Marcus dug up more roots. Soon other men joined in.

Hot and tough after roasting over coals, Marcus nearly broke a tooth on a stiff, blistering lump of root failing to soften. He wound up sucking on it until it was chewable. Really, it was awful—everyone agreed. But they fed hungry, working soldiers. Nothing would be wasted.

Pompeius's legionaries heard of the new supplement and hurled insults at Caesar's army, declaring them to be "animals, not men" for surviving on barbaric food.

The stalemate between the two hungry armies lasted for months until two deserters from Caesar's camp fled to Pompeius, seeking asylum. Details on the weakest part of Caesar's chain of walls motivated Pompeius to attack in earnest along the camp's fragile southern extremity.

Marcus's sector.

Dawn broke on a searing summer's day, and so did the unsteady calm.

At first, Marcus found himself leading a fight that was consistently two-to-one—sometimes three against one. And Pompeius had managed to land a fresh army on the beach. They just kept coming. By now, he estimated that for every one of his men, there were ten Pompeians.

If there was anything positive in the situation, it was that Pompeians were landing in an area surrounded by rocky shoals. Caesar finally arrived, and he and Marcus pressed their men forward, trying to prevent any of the enemy from outflanking them.

Truly, a clash between Titans couldn't be much different from civil war between two Roman armies. Each side used identical weaponry, armor, and tactics. Sometimes it was difficult or even impossible to distinguish friend from foe. Fighting was an intimidating, one-on-one brawl, the winner often being the side with the stronger, larger men and better training, or better swordsmen and marksmen.

"Antonius!"

To encourage his men, Marcus had dismounted and joined in the fray. Hearing Caesar calling, he shoved his shield forward mercilessly, dumping a Pompeian legionary flat into the man to his rear. With furtive glances each direction, Marcus backed away, disengaging as another legionary took his place.

Lines of tramping soldiers were incoming toward the action. Marcus had to weave his way to Caesar like a fish headed upstream. Winded, he paused, leaning over to rest his hands on his knees, gulping air. Caesar reached into his saddlebag, producing a leather map of Greece. One end he handed down to Marcus, and they looked at it together. Caesar jabbed at Macedonia with his forefinger. "We'll go here. It's far, I know, but I have loyal legions to the east. Provided luck holds and the men can march inland, we can win another day."

Marcus nodded west toward shore. "The farther we are from his reinforcements, the better. Let's hope he doesn't chase us down."

Caesar agreed with a grim smile. "Yes, if he does, we may have to turn and fight. Pompeius also has loyal legions east of here. Look . . ." Caesar moved his finger slowly over the cracked leather until it reached the plains of Thessaly. "What do you think? Can we make it?"

Marcus puffed out his cheeks, wearily smearing someone's blood from his forehead. "We have to. We can't win here. Either we try or everything ends on this cursed coast." Moving closer to see better, he queried, "Where will we end up?"

"I'm guessing we'll be near a town called . . . Pharsalus."

"Then I'll order retreat. Let's move before any more ships arrive. We're hopelessly outnumbered."

Caesar gave Marcus an approving nod. Still, his face was creased in concern. "I wonder if he even knows he's beaten me?" Caesar smacked his horse's rump, yelling for tubicines to call his troops back.

Well, he had a plan now. Marcus knew he'd move like lightning. Pompeius would think he was chasing Jupiter's bolts!

Covered in dust and grime, Marcus Antonius sat in Caesar's camp in southern Thessaly, slurping bone-filled fish soup. It was as oily and murky as the lazy Enipeus River it had come from, but there was nothing more to eat except Eros's starchy root-bread. And only a few roots were left. They didn't grow in this region. In this heat, hardly anything did.

Suddenly, Eros tossed aside the tent flap, his eyes wide with excitement. "Dominus! Scouts have returned. Pompeius is camped to the east of us."

"*East?* How—"

Eros shook his head, just as confused. "I don't know. Somehow, in the past month they outflanked us. They've got the high ground too."

Marcus shoved the half empty bowl of soup toward his slave. "Well, you've lucked into extra breakfast."

Eros's eyes widened as he hungrily grabbed the bowl.

As Marcus strode briskly toward the praetorium, a messenger intercepted him. "Sir, I was just coming for you. Caesar has called for a consilium."

One thing Marcus had learned about war: always expect the unexpected.

The whole encampment was on edge, so it didn't take long for officers and centurions to gather. Mamurra was busily raising up a map of the area so everyone could see.

Caesar began, "This morning at dawn, scouts returned from the acropolis of Pharsalus, which you've all seen to our south. Villagers from surrounding towns have been sacked for food. They claimed Pompeius's men looted their stores and stole their animals. Just over an hour ago, another scout rode in, and he's seen Pompeius's camp. It's located east of here, just beyond that big rocky promontory."

Marcus stopped him with a winning grin. "Sorry, Caesar. But how did they manage that?"

Caesar smiled back wryly. "It appears that Pompeius was fortunate enough to have found a different route, *faster* than Caesar's!"

Everyone laughed.

"Gentlemen, let me assure you—Pompeius might outrun me, but he will *never* outwit me."

That drew shouts of approval.

Caesar nodded, getting back to business and raising his hand for silence. "Pompeius is forming a line. So that's what we'll be doing shortly. My intent is to outflank *him* this time." He used charcoal to sketch on the hide map for all to see. "Publius Sulla and I will take the right wing, planting the better portion of our cavalry on the end of it. Just behind will be more infantry; let's keep them at a bit of an angle. That will allow for a better rotation as they engage. Sulla, I have a feeling Pompeius will send his cavalry straight at us. Keep those men on the angle in reserve, prepared to swing wide and intercept enemy horse. Then you can pick them off at close range. And tell your men to aim at their officers as well as the horses. Most are young, inexperienced Patricians who will probably duck and run at anything that might scar their pretty faces."

"Yes, Caesar," Sulla responded, chuckling along with Marcus and a few others.

"Antonius, you and Calvinus have the taxing job of holding everyone else together. At Dyrrhachium, you bonded well with Legio IX. Stay with them and Legio VIII, holding position next to the river. They're undermanned, but they're battle-hardened. Tell them I believe they'll perform honorably. Now listen carefully, all of you. Pompeius knows our men have seen the most action these last years. Therefore he'll be very cautious about facing his infantry against us. He'll most likely rely on cavalry. Let's hope that doesn't change before confrontation time. His numbers are superior, and disabling our horse will be his all-important task. If my plan works and his cavalry breaks, I'll outflank his left with our cavalry and infantry together. Antonius, if you and Calvinus keep pressuring his front and hold your men tight, it should work."

The consilium ended abruptly, and after the priests took auspices, Marcus sent every centurion packing to prepare the men. He ordered the storage of heavy gear and medical transports to the legions' rear.

Soon he was positioned and waiting next to the river. It was a cloudy little stream that probably didn't have much current except in thunderstorms. Looking to his right, he gazed appraisingly over his men. Both these legions had sustained hard hits in Gaul and most recently at Dyrrhachium. Together, Legions VIII and IX barely numbered one full-strength unit. And today they'd fight against full-strength forces outnumbering them again at least two-to-one. That wasn't as grave a concern when fighting barbarians, but this was different.

Roman legions were fighting each other.

Recent reports assured Caesar that Pompeius's army was assembled several miles away beyond the rocky hill on which they'd camped. Pharsalus's huge plain was long and broad, making distance deceptive to the naked eye. It was unnerving not being able to see an opponent's exact position.

Marcus cantered his horse before his men and Calvinus's, addressing them.

"Brothers," he shouted, "today you're the professionals on this field, and Caesar has told me he *believes* in you! Your task is to remain in position at all times. I really don't care if Pompeius's men descend on you like locusts. *Expect* it! They have the numbers. However, Caesar reminded me today that you're more proficient. Pompeius's armies haven't defeated Vercingetorix and proven to Rome their superiority. *You* have! Nor have they had a decade's experience fighting in Gaul. Only *you* have that. Mark my words!"

Several thousand voices rose in approval, the sound of which made a chill break out under Marcus's cuirass despite the heat. Determined voices of legionaries ready for battle never ceased to stir his emotion.

He went on, guiding his horse down through their ranks. "Now hear me. Once engaged, we're only moving forward. I want no retreating and no fast advances where positions could be lost. To win, we remain together as one and keep pressure on their front. We'll break Pompeius and his Optimate asses and watch them running with tails between their legs! Understood?"

He grinned, drawing his gladius and lifting it high in the air, brandishing it with flourish. A deafening response was what he expected, and they didn't disappoint. Marcus spurred his horse into a canter and laughed in pride, sword arm raised and nimbly twirling his weapon as he rode. Gladii pummeled onto shields, legionary thunder roaring through the plain. Yes, they were hungry and weary, but they'd give him their best. Of that, he was confident.

A courier reported that Caesar had decided to make the first move.

Together, twenty-three thousand men and horse marched forward onto Pharsalus field. For the first mile, drums beat a reasonable, steady walking pace. However, once they were in sight of Pompeius's lines, the tempo increased. Each legionary and horse broke into a jog.

Marcus glanced frequently down the line, concerned his men would fade under Apollo's rays. Already the morning was heating up. In front of the marching ranks, he sent a messenger riding to Caesar, suggesting a halt to regroup, breathe easy, and intimidate.

Caesar agreed, and in a short time tubicines sounded. The advance stopped abruptly, and centurions whistled for the lines to change, bringing up soldiers from the rear that hadn't moved as fast. After the crisp change of guard, they presented themselves as a motionless, deadly mass. Caesar's army stood at attention close enough to Pompeius's front lines that Marcus heard enemy cavalry stamping on the opposite end of the field.

He loved this. Let them *see* Caesar's disciplined troops. They'd piss themselves!

Briefly, Marcus left his position, cantering in front of the lines, to meet up with Calvinus, Caesar, and Sulla. While they spoke, they didn't look at one another, but their eyes were ever on the enemy, a wall of men, shields, and javelins arrayed before them.

"Good idea, Antonius," Caesar said, nodding. "By stopping like this, it displays our disciplined order. Now remember to hold strong along that river. Sulla and I will handle the rest. Let's begin!"

Mental games over, the next two hours were tense as the battle began. Marcus positioned himself alongside the Enipeus, shouting encouragement as his men engaged. At Alesia, there had been so much movement and noise—even in the darkness. Here at Pharsalus, it was a slower business, gladius on gladius, shoving with shields, and a lot of grunting and crashing. Both sides' matching weapons made it difficult for one or the other to gain an advantage.

Clumps of sparse trees became landmarks for assessing whether his men lost or gained ground. If Pompeius's soldiers pushed too hard, he barked at his own to press forward. Several times Marcus dismounted, entering the fray himself and relieving men when he could by taking a turn on the front.

Three hours into the fight, he was hoarse from shouting. Heat was taking its toll on both sides. Many times, soldiers were actually gripping, shoving, or smashing one another's shields in the press. Marcus ordered centurions to change the lines more frequently, and he called in slaves to port in water to relieve rankers.

He was heartened when Calvinus reported that the Caesarian reinforcements were finally outflanking Pompeius's legions. Despite the battle noise, Marcus rode back and forth shouting the good news in his dry, grating voice. He saw the vibrant strengthening of confidence on his legionaries' faces despite their fatigue.

When Pompeius's army broke and started retreating back toward his camp, Caesar sent orders for Marcus to command the cavalry in pursuit of stragglers.

It was time to ride!

"Look, sir!"

Marcus followed the cavalryman's finger, spying a high-ranking Pompeian officer flanked by three enemy cavalrymen, whipping his horse in a desperate retreat.

Marcus spurred his own weary animal to give chase, signaling his other riders to back him up and take them out, if possible. The fleeing officer glanced back. His helmet was lost and his head was matted with blood. With such an ornate cuirass, he had to be one of Pompeius's top generals. Once Marcus got closer, he saw flaming red hair and recognized him. It was Lucius Domitius Ahenobarbus, a powerful senator and born soldier. In fact, he was the very man who had run for the priestly office of augur against Marcus—and lost.

"Surrender to Caesar's mercy," Marcus called.

Ahenobarbus did stop, but far from surrendering, he spurred hard toward Marcus, gladius drawn. For several awkward moments, they traded blows. Marcus cursed, fighting defensively to deflect Ahenobarbus's mad blows. If only he'd yield. The ring of blades sounded above the hoofbeats and calls of the other men as they caught up, surrounding them.

Damn, Ahenobarbus was a fierce swordsman for a man his age! Marcus had no choice but to press forward more aggressively, hoping he'd tire. "It's over! Just surrender," he cried.

However, Ahenobarbus was no coward. He was ready to die for the Optimate cause. Vaguely, Marcus recalled Caesar pardoning him once already.

Abruptly, Ahenobarbus dropped his arms and raised his eyes toward the blue skies. Marcus was already in mid-blow, his blade biting deep into Ahenobarbus's neck and shoulder, severing flesh and artery. There was a momentary fountain of blood before he arced sideways, falling heavily to the ground, his horse backing up, wild-eyed and snorting.

"Why did he do that?" one of the horsemen behind Marcus exclaimed, not comprehending.

Marcus swung a leg over his saddle horn, hopping down. He snatched Ahenobarbus's horse by the bridle. None of these fools behind him understood, but Marcus had a great deal of respect for a man who died for his cause, though it was lost.

Caesar met Marcus as he entered the praetorium, clapping his cousin on the back. "Not a bad day!" he laughed. "And only two hundred of our men lost compared to fifteen *thousand* of theirs!"

"Really?" Marcus grinned, shaking his head in amazement and

accepting the proffered cup of wine. With a sigh, he dropped down on a makeshift dining couch. "You had Pompeius's every movement figured out and countered them all. Incredible—especially since we were *so* outnumbered."

"One thing about my legions," Caesar switched to a serious tone, "they fight their best when outmanned. Our men's discipline saved them. It does every time. And congratulations on taking Ahenobarbus. He always despised me."

Marcus shook his head and shrugged. "I offered surrender, in case you're wondering. He chose honor over mercy. Any word on Pompeius's whereabouts?"

"Not yet. Unless he chooses death like Ahenobarbus, I'll have to pursue him."

"He still has plenty of allies."

Caesar nodded. Though pleased at his victory, he looked worn and pale. For a time, their conversation died and they both nibbled on brown bread and honey.

"Pompeius wasn't the only one to escape, you know," Marcus said at last. "Other senators who defected to his camp and followed him, Cicero included, evaded capture."

Caesar smirked. "I can well imagine how Cicero's escape would disappoint you! How exactly would you kill him if I gave you leave? Strangulation? Like Lentulus?"

Marcus considered. "Maybe." He gulped some wine down and signaled a serving slave for more. "It'd be a just reward for the grief he's brought me and my family. But knowing you, he'll be pardoned."

"You're learning!" Caesar chuckled. "Having men indebted for their lives is no bad thing. Besides, mercy enhances my popularity with the people. It forms my character."

Caesar's character? Marcus laughed drily and took another swig. Exactly what *was* Caesar's character? He never allowed anyone close enough to find out. "I'm not sure I agree with your methodology, but you'll do as you wish. Seeing as I'm back in your good graces, I have two requests, if you'll hear me out."

"Speak freely."

"First, as you well know, my brother Gaius was captured in Illyricum. I want him located as soon as possible. I pray they didn't harm him."

"Because of you, he's a high-profile prisoner. We'll find him."

"I hope so. The other thing is my exiled uncle, Antonius Hybrida. I may have divorced his daughter, but he's always been close to my family. I was hoping you'd pardon him."

"Of course, but first I must be unequivocally in control of Rome. Let me assure you of his return, but it must wait until the war's completely over."

"Fair enough."

"Now let's discuss the upcoming months. I need you to go to Rome and keep order there until I return."

Marcus tried best he could to hide his disappointment. "How long will that be?"

Caesar sighed, pursing his lips. "I don't know. If Pompeius has escaped, it's bound to take time. My greatest fear is that troops loyal to him in North Africa embrace his arrival with open arms. That would prove dangerous."

"Then I should be with you. I'm far more valuable in the field—"

"No. I want you back home in the Senate to secure a dictatorship for me. Since I'm away tending to the defeat of rebels, tell the Senate it's necessary that I be appointed in absentia. I know it's an irregular request, but I've got the upper hand. They should acquiesce."

"Isn't a dictatorship only valid for six months?" Marcus countered. "You may be fast, but there's no way you'd be finished with the war by then."

Caesar smiled brightly. "Then constitute my appointment for a year. That may not be enough time either, but we'll extend my term if need be."

Marcus was still contemplating the looming dictatorship when Caesar forged ahead. "There's also the matter of colonization. You get on well with my Gallic legions. Take them, along with

Pompeius's surrendered army, and settle them in Campania until I return. Assure them they'll receive lands and bonuses."

"Gods, that'll require boatloads of gold. They'll want their pay."

"Tell them they'll have it in full once the war ends. For now, they must trust Caesar. Italian soil is at a premium these days, so march them into Campania to camp temporarily until I'm able to assign them lands. Someday, after the war, I intend to—"

A sentry interrupted, flipping back the tent flap. "Imperator, I have news. Marcus Junius Brutus has surrendered. He revealed where Pompeius is headed."

"Where?"

"South—with plans to sail for Egypt."

Caesar's brows lifted, mildly surprised. "Egypt? Very well. Inform me of any other developments. Once Brutus arrives, I'll receive him here."

The sentry nodded and disappeared.

Marcus frowned, shaking his head. "Why would he go to Egypt? Gabinius left at least one legion in Alexandria, but by now it's probably an undisciplined lot. If I were him, I'd head straight to North Africa."

Caesar leaned back, stretching. "I'd nearly forgotten. You know Egypt, don't you?"

Marcus shrugged. "I wasn't there long. But I know it was in as much disarray and revolt as the rest of the East."

"It sounds as though you have an opinion of how Eastern provinces should be run."

Marcus smiled. "Actually, yes. What we need out that way are organized client kingdoms that we choose and trust."

Caesar nodded, impressed. "And that would probably work."

"Are you positive you want me in Rome?" Marcus asked. If only Caesar would change his mind.

"Absolutely certain. Did you ever meet Ptolemy, this boy-king of Egypt?"

Marcus sighed and shook his head. "No, I knew his father—

one sorry piece of work. Never met the son. He must've been very young when I was there."

"A shame. I was hoping for details."

"Well, here's one for you. I met his sister, the princess who is now queen. Cleopatra is amazing. She was barely a woman then, but very impressive. She had Gabinius and her own father pegged for exactly what they were. She'd be worth dealing with."

A ghost of a smile played upon Caesar's lips. "Then deal with her, I shall," he murmured. Eyes narrowing, he lifted his silver cup in toast. "Here's to great victories, sole power, and charming queens!"

Marcus grinned unabashedly, sipping his own wine. It had been a very long while since he'd thought of the gifted young woman who now sat on Egypt's throne. Even now, memory of her lotus perfume triggered pleasant thoughts.

Caesar had defeated Vercingetorix and Pompeius, but his most worthy adversary might just be waiting in Alexandria. How Marcus wished he could go. Seeing Cleopatra again would be far more enjoyable than the unruliness of Rome.

CHAPTER XVII

48-47BC

IT WAS A HERO'S WELCOME.

Marcus draped an arm over Gaius's shoulders, leading him down the gangplank of the galley toward waiting crowds in Brundisium. Caesar had made good on his word, locating his brother promptly. Gaius and his few remaining soldiers were thin, but unharmed.

When Marcus asked his brother whether Dolabella's actions had in some way led to his capture, Gaius had frowned uncertainly. "It would be convenient to blame him, but I won't fault any one man. I was simply outnumbered."

Marcus kept his own counsel. Gaius was less skilled in war than a woman. But at least he was safe. Still, there remained the nagging issue of repaying Publius Cornelius Dolabella for his insult with Antonia.

But for today, people cheered with voice and heart. Trumpets and flutes sounded in honor. Bedecked in full military regalia, the Antonii brothers strode toward two uniformed officers: Aulus Gabinius and Publius Canidius Crassus.

As they all clasped hands, Marcus felt his brother nudge him.

Following Gaius's nod, he saw Mother, standing proudly behind Gabinius and his delegation.

Emotion glistened in her eyes. With three sons at war, worry had likely been her constant companion during these past months. Marcus felt inexpressible joy and peace at the sight of her.

He made his way to her, kissing her cheeks and hands. While his mouth was near her ear, he whispered, "Lucius is safe. He'll return once his tenure in the East ends."

Her whole body sighed, and he settled one arm around her protectively, lifting her hand, kissing it and holding it aloft. This prompted more response from the citizenry. Mother responded with a brilliant smile, nodding at the crowd in modest dignity.

Gabinius stepped up to Marcus's elbow. "A delegation of senators awaits," he advised. "They're anxious to hear Caesar's intentions. And I'm prepared to assign cohorts to travel with the returning troops that are to be temporarily settled in Campania."

Marcus grumbled in reply, "This returning army is an ill-tempered lot, having endured much for no pay as of yet. As for the senators, I'll greet my friends first." He had toiled hard in Greece with Caesar. Let there be some joy before duty!

His eyes swept over the waiting bunch of toga-clad men, and he nodded at them curtly. Dealing with them was bound to make a fun-filled afternoon! But just beyond them—Marcus glanced twice and blinked in amazement.

Cytheris was standing beside her gaudily painted litter. Some of her company had come too—Sergius, Hippias, and a few others. How kind of them to travel such distance. Mother and that flock of senators could afford such luxury, but not poor actors. Their efforts to honor him had been a true sacrifice on his behalf.

Deeply touched, Marcus walked swiftly into the crowd, at first moving toward the senators, who all vainly assumed he meant to greet them. Several hailed him hopefully, extending hands his way, but he passed them by without a word, catching Cytheris by both hands and calling out greetings to her company.

Her rich brown hair was bound loosely; her full lips painted to perfection. She wore exotic-looking eastern jewelry and a Greek-style chiton cut low at the breast, tied on each shoulder.

Pulling her toward him, Marcus engulfed her mouth hungrily, his body igniting like kindling upon feeling her softness. Her company of actors and performers cheered and applauded the reunion. However, crowds at his back fell suddenly silent at the unexpected public display. Ending the kiss, he breathed hungrily in her ear, "Venus—I've not had a woman since Corinth! Find us a stable, a shop, anyplace!"

In the sudden silence of the crowd, Cytheris's titillating laughter filled the square.

Sex.

Wine.

Jubilant receptions of every kind.

That first month after returning to Rome, Marcus's life was blurred by strings of distractions. First was his formal welcome into Rome. Then Mother insisted on a lavish party to honor the return of her hero sons, followed by Calpurnia's feast celebrating officers winning at Pharsalus. Punctuating these events were appearances at senators' homes to support Caesar's dictatorship, which was quickly approved. Marcus also had himself appointed as equitum magister—master of the horse to the dictator, Caesar's official lieutenant.

When Cytheris's new play opened, she and the cast asked Marcus to introduce the show, something no man of his status had ever done. He was surprised and disappointed at the plebian response after his short preface. Why, they fell completely silent, staring at him in shock. What was the matter with them? Of all people in Rome, shouldn't the *common* people appreciate his *common* touch?

Of course, Mother had the answer. She always did. "Up until now, you've been their military hero. But by introducing a risqué mime, you weren't displaying gravitas—the solemn manner they expect from a Roman."

Marcus stared at her, speechless. None of these people had starved or had to kill fellow countrymen, eaten amid barbarians, or fought Neptune's seas to achieve what he had. Damn them all! He was his *own* man and would *not* follow ridiculous social conventions.

Toward the end of the same month, Cytheris's friend, Hippias the comedian, took a wife and humbly invited Marcus to the wedding. Not only agreeing, he surprised the lowborn comic by paying for the wedding feast. It was a night worth remembering.

But not the day after.

Truth be told, it wasn't the wine, though Marcus had guzzled his fair share. Oysters were on the menu, and Marcus ate some bad ones.

Up at dawn, he had scheduled an oration for the plebs. Stomach churning from the previous night's indulgences, he let Eros assist with his toga before meandering into the triclinium. Canidius had accompanied him back to Rome and was thoroughly enjoying his friend's hospitality in Pompeius's former domus, casually breakfasting on warm wheat bread and honey.

"That was quite a party last evening. The look on Hippias's face was priceless when you surprised him! Beautiful, willing women too. Did you arrange them as well? I tell you, I thoroughly enjoyed myself. What a shame people of our status never see what happiness a simple plebian life offers."

"Yes, a pity," Marcus muttered, miserably staring at the bread and fruit on the table. Both the sight and smell sickened him.

Canidius chuckled at his friend. "Hungover?"

Marcus shook his head dazedly. "I feel ill, but not from wine."

"I warned you about eating oysters purchased in the Subura."

"Next time I'll listen."

"What's your agenda this morning?"

Marcus waved a platter of cheeses away, offered him by serving slaves. "Dolabella's trying to pass some law forgiving debtors and renters their back-payments. Most of it sounds worthy of Caesar's approval, but he's instigating mobs like Clodius once did and using plebs in collegia to stir up violence. It appears my job is to scold them back into order and keep the peace."

Canidius, ever the affable sort, said, "Then I'll don my toga, go with you, and look official. At lease that way it will be a lot more bearable."

Marcus Antonius, Canidius, and Eros, followed by numerous clients, made their way to the Rostra, led by the six lictors serving in accordance with Marcus's new imperium as magister equitum.

Ever able to read his dominus, Eros remained at Marcus's elbow. "You're white as your toga," he whispered worriedly, keeping pace with his long strides.

Marcus didn't answer. His teeth were chattering, and his hands had turned clammy. Nor did the crowds look content. Everywhere he looked, plebs' faces were cross and sullen, nothing like the cheering throng he'd enjoyed in Brundisium.

"Antonius, you could postpone—" Canidius attempted discreetly.

"No." Marcus shook his head. "It was publicly announced I'd address the crowds this morning. I'll keep my word."

He mounted the wooden stairs of the Rostra, legs as heavy as lead. Head spinning, he sucked in air. Could the multitude before him tell how dreadful he felt?

"Good people—citizens of Rome—I appeal to you." Words halting, Marcus was just not himself. Shivering despite the warm day, he felt light-headed and his stomach churned like chariot wheels in the Circus. "Listen to reason," he attempted. "There's been far too much violence in our streets. Caesar has not—"

The platform seemed to lurch. He blinked, feeling faint.

He started again, but his voice sounded hollow in his own ears.

"Caesar has not taken Gaul and fought for you at Pharsalus so that you may embrace anarchy. I'm aware of your many needs . . ."

Voice trailing again, his extremities tingled in cold sweat, gall rising to his throat, heralding his stomach's rebellion.

"Drink too much at Hippias's wedding?" someone in the crowd yelled.

Hundreds snickered with laughter.

Another voice cried out harshly, "We want Caesar back! If he *really* conquered Pompeius, he'd be here!"

Able to do nothing but what his body demanded, Marcus turned his back to the populace as best he could. Canidius scrambled up the stairs to help, but Marcus retched into the sinuses of his toga. Unstable and miserable, he knew his audience was lost, along with a hefty portion of dignitas—not to mention last night's oysters.

But the crowd turned threatening as people started hurling things onto the platform. Nutshells, pieces of rotting fruit, even rocks . . .

Gripping Canidius's arm, he let his friend guide him down the stairs, where Eros and the lictors surrounded him protectively. He was used to facing insults of senators, not plebs. Usually, they loved him.

Even Eros scolded him, whispering, "Oh, Dominus—you're a stubborn man."

Scowling, and with a sour taste in his mouth from vomiting, Marcus hated himself. His slave was right.

Ripping off his soiled toga, he wadded and hurled it behind the platform, wearing only his tunic. But it wasn't enough to be sick and humiliated before all of Rome. No, fate had more mischief in store, for as he headed home, Dolabella's litter swayed past.

The latter stuck his burly head out of the curtains, grinning wickedly at Marcus's misery. "Too bad your wine doesn't agree with you today, Antonius!"

Then the bastard laughed.

After that, Marcus had no respite.

He wrote to Caesar in Alexandria, informing him of his newly appointed dictatorship, but also requesting coin and further orders about land grants for the returned legions encamped in Campania. They were making a lot of noise about not being paid like good, honest soldiers should be.

And Marcus agreed with them.

Caesar didn't reply. And news from Alexandria was grim. Caesar had landed, only to find that Pompeius had been beheaded upon arriving by order of the boy-king Ptolemy. Apparently, he and Cleopatra were at serious odds, and an Egyptian civil war had broken out with Caesar in the middle of it all.

News stopped entirely after that.

Street violence all over Rome was escalating, so Marcus began using his own growing collection of bodyguards to police the city.

Then the veterans and unpaid legionaries in the Campanian camps threatened to march on Rome. Marcus promptly sent orders for them to march to Sicily instead. There, they could await Caesar and be farther from Rome and central Italia. Most importantly, they'd be on the move, *doing* something besides sitting idle.

Not receiving a reply, Marcus then sent a military tribune to verify the command's receipt. The man fled for his life, reporting that the Campanian troops had mutinied.

It was all horrible timing with Dolabella organizing more political riots. That problem alone demanded all of Marcus's attention. The Campanians would have to wait. But frequent messages trickled in, one after the other containing threats and demands. Even worse were reports of rapes and pillaging from small towns in the surrounding countryside. No longer could they be ignored.

Sitting in his private bath, steam rising, Marcus unleashed his predicament aloud to Canidius.

"What in the name of the gods is Caesar doing? He hasn't responded to any of my letters, and so far, I don't even have tangible proof he's *in* Egypt—only reports coming from trade ships. The man gave me absolutely *nothing* to offer these men but empty promises. For all I know, Ptolemy cut off Caesar's head after he stepped off his boat, just like he did to Pompeius! Sounds like he's exactly like his tata. One nasty little shit!"

"Dominus—"

Marcus groaned. Whenever Eros used that tone, it always meant more complications or tragic news.

"Cicero writes from Brundisium, where he's returned from mainland Greece," Eros announced, his voice resonating against the marble walls.

Marcus muttered, "Go ahead, Eros. Read it."

> *"Marcus Tullius Cicero, Pater Patriae in Brundisium, to Marcus Antonius, Legate in Rome:*
>
> *Salve. By now you have surely had adequate time to relax and prepare for business after feting yourself these past months. Certainly, you're aware of popular opinion. My sources tell me that even plebs complain how 'Antonius never ceases his merry-making.'*
>
> *Your private life along with its rapacious appetites doesn't concern me unless it involves Rome. Placing precedence on your cheap actress over men of quality—your country's senators—brings me terrible unease.*
>
> *Several of these men who were prepared to support you wholeheartedly have written how you requisitioned funds from them. They may have 'Pompeian tendencies,' true enough, but you show your quality by using their gold on your own frivolous gaming and women."*

"I never did that!" Marcus exclaimed, his fist slamming into the water. "Well, I requisitioned coin from them—they're the enemy—we're still at war with them! But I swear I never used it when gaming. And women? What does he think Cytheris is for?"

Eros continued.

> *"I was also informed that you claimed the office of magister equitum, a position that only the dictator himself bestows upon a worthy man. I shall ask Caesar if he really appointed you. You may dress up and 'play' conqueror, Antonius, but you're cast from a lesser mold."*

Marcus sat in the water, a trickle of sweat dripping down and stinging one eye. Helplessness wasn't something to which he was accustomed.

Canidius spoke up, "I was present when you suggested to the Senate that they bestow magister equitum upon you. Caesar himself placed you here to lead during his absence. Surely, he expected you to carry that title since he's now dictator."

Marcus shook his head in disgust. "As if Cicero hasn't ever paid for pleasure with a bribe? I swear, he'd accuse me of raping my own mother if he thought people would believe it. The most urgent matter is to get gold from *someplace* and pay off these damned legions! Caesar isn't here and is certainly not answering my messages. Nor is coin falling from the skies. Even with what I scraped from the senators, there's not enough to placate this many men. Almost forty thousand demand compensation and refuse to obey orders. If they *did* march on Rome . . ."

Eros's wide blue eyes sparkled in alarm.

Marcus saw him and laughed. "No fear, boy! We're not dead yet." With a heavy sigh, he arose from the water, naked and dripping, snatching a clean linen cloth and tying it about his waist.

"Not yet, but soon, Dominus," Eros responded gloomily. "I'm afraid I've got more news."

"What *else*?" Canidius queried.

"Another dispatch from Campania. The leaders say they'll wait no longer for Caesar. They want their pay or they'll march on Rome."

Marcus blew air out of his mouth. "They'd take us too. We've only one legion here. Anything more?"

"Dolabella demands an answer. Will you join him, publicly supporting debt-cancellation?"

Marcus chewed his lip. "I know Caesar would love championing such a plebian cause, but I can't risk pulling the country down further economically." He shook his head, unsure.

The debt-cancellation argument was the most heated debate in the Forum. Plebs were near revolt with euphoria about Dolabella's promises of canceled debts and overdue rents. Marcus had to admit he'd vacillated from one side to the other.

Would Caesar want him to risk more economic hardship and support the people with Dolabella or be more conservative in this matter?

"Inform him he does *not* have my support." There. A decision was made. "What else?"

"Your mother's here. She has someone in mind to keep Rome under control if and when you leave for Campania."

Marcus snorted. "She should volunteer herself! As tenacious as she is, she'd keep the Senate satisfied better than I!"

Marcus reined in, eyeing a thin haze of smoke smudged upon the Campanian horizon. Thousands of cooking fires were difficult to miss.

In an act of boldness, he ordered his accompanying delegation of soldiers to remain behind. A mere cohort would be no help against ten hardened legions anyway.

Coming to them alone and unguarded would either prove his goodwill or get him killed. Only Canidius and another fellow officer from Brundisium's garrison, Gnaeus Tuccius, remained with him.

They slowed their horses, passing hovels and tents. A poorly maintained legionary eagle leaned against one side of the crudely built praetorium.

Marcus's horse was jumpy as swarms of soldiers pressed close, surrounding him along the narrow cardo leading through the settlement.

"Give us pay!"

"Where's Caesar? Why isn't he with you?"

"We want our coin!"

"We want lands and rich earth for planting!"

"Give us our due, or else!"

Undisciplined curs needed a centurion's staff to knock patience into their heads! Their lean, greasy faces evidenced hard living, and many bore physical scars from past campaigns. Many a neck bore a bronze or iron torque looted from Gaul.

Two officers emerged from the praetorium, flanked by centurions and more legionaries crowding in, watching.

Marcus reined in and swung down. An unsettling silence prevailed as he removed his helmet and strode forward, offering his hand to each tribune. "Salve, Gaius Avienus, and good health to you, Aulus Fonteius."

"Antonius," Avienus said, stiffly grasping Marcus's hand. "Come, we have posca." Avienus led the way into the rough-hewn wooden structure.

Despite the circumstances, Marcus still felt he was in his element—among soldiers. Offered the one chair facing both men, he sat down. Canidius and Tuccius stood, flanking him on either side.

The mutineers' leaders were very different men, from what Marcus had learned prior to arriving. Fonteius was burly and muscular, wearing a permanent scowl, with overfull, moist lips and a flushed face. Avienus was a quiet sort of plebian birth who had worked his way up through the ranks to tribune. Gray threaded through his wiry hair, which was receding, displaying a prominent forehead.

"What do you hear from Caesar?" Fonteius began, the dictator's name turning his mouth to a sneer.

Marcus bristled at his animosity. "He's in Egypt, fighting a war to secure rulers designated by the Senate."

Avienus clarified, "What Fonteius means, is have you heard from him personally?"

Avienus struck him as direct, and Marcus decided he was the one to win over. "He's not written to me personally," he admitted. There was no point lying.

The tribunes glanced at one another. Avienus cocked a graying eyebrow. "Is there proof he's even alive? Some of our men believe he's dead."

"Merchant ships from Alexandria attest to his safety."

Fonteius scoffed, "Safe as Pompeius was in Egypt, is he?"

Avienus ignored his colleague's acidic humor, aptly pointing out, "Caesar already has one war and yet starts another?"

"Wars are seldom sought after. Tribunes, you should know by now that our imperator is trustworthy and an expert strategist. Caesar knows his business and has assured me you'll receive pay and land allotments once the war is won. Fortuna granted us victory at Pharsalus. Caesar simply needs time enough to finish the campaign, one on several continents. You must be patient."

Fonteius tilted his head, gulping down a mouthful of posca. Swallowing, his voice rose, and his face reddened. "We followed you in good faith back across the sea, then were led here by officers not even attached to our legions . . ."

Avienus reached over, placing a hand on his comrade's arm to steady him. He kept his voice level, even as Fonteius's nostrils flared like a stallion's. "Careful. Antonius has always been one of us."

Marcus nodded. "You know that I am."

Canidius added, "The magister equitum traveled a good distance to prove his honorable intentions. Antonius is a man on whom you may rely, even if you've lost trust in Caesar."

Tiring of niceties, Marcus tilted his head back, warning them,

"Though I am one of you, as you say, so was my tribune, whom you chased back to Rome on threat of his life. I sent you orders to travel south to await Caesar's pleasure. He won't be pleased hearing you ignored them. Nor am *I* pleased. Blatant disregard of command usually ends in disgrace and *death* for those involved."

Avienus ignored him, sitting up taller, his voice becoming hard. "How many legions are in Rome, hmmm? One? Two at the most? Look here. We're ten to your one or two. If we wanted, we could take Rome and cleanse the Senate of all her lies and corruption. You and your highborn friends would be dead, and it'd be us 'welcoming Caesar' home, if he ever comes back."

Marcus stiffened, a chill running up his spine. "Careful, soldier," he whispered in a low voice. "Do nothing rash. I want your word that you'll remain here peaceably until Caesar returns. No more looting of towns, no more raping of women. You're soldiers of Rome who can expect land grants and rewards, *if* you maintain peace."

Fonteius spat to the side, disgusted. Scooting forward on his bench, he licked both lips, his breathing accelerating as he spoke. "Let me tell you why we're angry since you and your ilk have forgotten what soldiering's about. Our legions faced hardships of every kind in Greece, never receiving pay. These past ten years, we've been sent everywhere against barbarians and even our own brothers, without food—and for *nothing*! We've no interest in fighting for Caesar. He broke oath with us."

Avienus nodded. "He speaks truth, Antonius. As for our looting—it was to supplement our stores. Grain is as scant as it was in Greece, but there are no roots here for eating." He shrugged. "If we take an occasional woman—"

Fonteius interrupted, "One thing we hate is how Caesar spares those filthy Pompeian bastards. Why does he *pardon* them?"

"Our imperator breaks bread with the likes of *Cicero*!" Avienus agreed, lifting his hands hopelessly. "I heard he even wept at Pompeius's murder. If that's true, he may as well spit upon us, his men who have given him our very lives, turning him into a conqueror! Our own commander consorts with the men he designated as our enemies!"

Marcus nodded in wholehearted agreement. "In this, you're justified. Caesar should hear you out, and I assure you I'll convey these sentiments to him."

Fonteius added, "And what about good plunder, eh? Damned Pompeians were freed, protected from us as though we had no right to them. We've had nothing since Gaul."

"Pompeians are *Romans*," Marcus reminded them, raising his finger to make his point, "therefore above plundering. Soon we'll be past civil wars, so there will be opportunities for other campaigns in foreign lands."

Fonteius smacked his hand atop the table, causing Tuccius to flinch involuntarily. "Another empty promise. We demand payment. Feed us and grant us lands."

"You'll have what you seek," Marcus reassured again, as calmly as possible. "But you're also obligated to obey orders."

"Stop your talk!" Fonteius shouted. "We have swords here, *demanding* pay!"

Out of the corner of his eye, Marcus saw Canidius's hand shift to the hilt of his sheathed gladius.

Avienus stood. Face grim, he said, "We will mutiny if our requests are not met, Antonius."

Marcus's pulse quickened, and he arose, confronting Avienus man to man. This was the most serious threat Rome had faced since Spartacus. "Your many messages to me have stated your intent," he said coolly. "But do you really think you'd get what you want by marching on Rome? You could kill the three of us here. Now. But let me ask this: Would the plebs love you for plundering *their* nearly depleted food stores? Kill us, march on the city, and you'd be as beloved as Hannibal or Spartacus. But today you have opportunity to show *character* as soldiers. I want your word as *Romans*—not as mutineers—that you'll maintain your position here. I promise Caesar will hear your grievances, but you're not to storm the city. Every god in Olympus will curse you if you do."

"Sulla did it," Fonteius barked insolently. "He marched on Rome!"

Marcus held Avienus's steely gaze, all the while answering Fonteius, "Yes, and he paid for it ever after. To this day his memory is held in infamy." He paused, taking measure of both men. "Both of you best remember that, as of now, you're heroes. Cherish that reputation to pass on to your sons. Yes, these are difficult days for us all, but keep peace. If you do, your blatant disregard of my orders will be forgiven and you'll receive your ample due from Caesar, as promised. I'll even send stores of barley and spelt from granaries in Rome to fill your bellies. Agreed?" Marcus knew he couldn't convince them to muster south for Caesar, but this might preserve the city and buy him more time.

Fonteius spat on the floor, but Avienus extended his hand. "We'll await Caesar," he answered, "but only until the year is done. If he doesn't meet our demands by then, Rome is ours."

CHAPTER XVIII

A MILITARY MESSENGER MET MARCUS AS SOON AS ROME was within sight. He bore a terse message from Gaius. The news wasn't good.

> *Gaius Antonius to his brother, Magister Equitum Marcus Antonius:*
>
> *Today Mother was attacked in her litter by a mob. All the bearers were killed, including Iophon. He died protecting her.*

Horrified, he blinked, rereading the message twice more before managing, "Is she alright?"

The courier nodded, "Yes, sir. I hear she was the fortunate one."

Indeed. Poor Iophon certainly wasn't.

Before Marcus left, Mother had pleaded with him to name Uncle Lucius city prefect in his absence. He had humored her, agreeing, albeit with hesitation. Now he'd pay for it. Uncle had failed miserably at preventing Dolabella's riots touting debt-cancellation. Rome's streets were in such anarchy that even the Vestal Virgins feared for their lives. For the first time in history, they left, taking along their holy treasures and deserting the eternal flame.

Ho—that wasn't good.

It occurred to Marcus that the Campanian legions didn't need to destroy Rome. It was perfectly capable of destroying itself from the inside out.

He snapped a quick order to the messenger before sending him back into the city. "Announce that I'll meet with the Senate in Pompeius's theater tonight. We need to discuss measures to maintain order and stop this violence."

Later, as torchlight flickered, Marcus sat in a curule chair to the right of a larger, empty one meant for the dictator.

One of the consuls was speaking vehemently, "Our inept city prefect, appointed by Antonius, has lost all respect. Rioters laugh and mock him as being old and incompetent!"

Marcus glared at Uncle Lucius scornfully.

He sat alone in the front row but now arose, hesitant. "We've little choice but to appoint the magister equitum to exercise force since it's the only deterrent these miscreants will understand."

The Senate approved, though with hesitation. Even Pompeians in the back of the chamber acquiesced.

Marcus stood to accept, but the decision sent his emotions into turmoil. Mars knew he had no problem shedding blood, but would he really be any different than the mutineers in Campania, leading armed legionaries within boundaries of the pomerium? Certainly, his critics would say he was no different than Sulla.

But then again, he'd have the chance to take Dolabella down.

He lifted his hand solemnly for silence, acknowledging his duty. "As called upon to take action against Publius Dolabella and his rabble, I accept your endorsement."

Legionaries assigned to the task were ecstatic. Weary and bored of camping in the increasingly crowded Campus Martius, they craved a good fight. None of them gave a fig that it meant spilling the very lifeblood of Rome.

Publius Dolabella to Marcus Antonius:
Be advised: tomorrow the people and I will enact forced legislation. Plebian debts will be no more!

Marcus's mood was as dismal as dawn's gray light. In a misty Forum Romanum, he sat astride his horse, commanding over four thousand legionaries, all of whom surrounded the Forum's perimeters.

Dolabella and his gangs were already there. They had built hasty barricades of old wooden crates, broken-down carts, and even discarded amphorae, all hauled in from Rome's enormous garbage heap next to the river. Political placards hung on monuments heralding the promises of the debt relief intended to become law. Mobs of plebs, armed with clubs and cudgels, could already be heard chanting raucously down by the Rostra.

It was the shopkeepers Marcus pitied most. They would be the ones who would innocently die for no reason—men, women, and children who had no care for the political scene and simply wanted to rake in enough coin to survive another day.

And it was they who were first to see Marcus's legionaries. They panicked at the sight of armed men inside the city boundaries. Some left immediately, repacking their wares, escaping while they could. Others remained, either hopeful bloodshed could be avoided or unworried that legionaries would harm civilians.

Though it was a senatorial decree, Marcus knew his reputation would suffer from this. Most of his soldiers were war-hardened, overzealous with bloodlust. Women and children would be lost despite his command to the contrary.

Yet something had to be done.

"Tighten the noose," he ordered coldly. "Remember, my orders are to go after the mobs *only*. Women and children are to be spared."

But once it started, his fears were confirmed. Plebian cries for mercy were largely ignored. Sounds of tramping soldiers' feet comingled with sobs of the innocent. When the fog slowly lifted, a blood-spattered daybreak was revealed. Bodies of unfortunates caught in the middle of the violence lay everywhere.

Tuccius rode up to report. "Some ringleaders held out. We took them prisoner, but Dolabella escaped."

Well, damn it *all*! Marcus clenched his jaw so hard his teeth ached.

When he didn't immediately reply, Tuccius asked, "Shall we lock the holdouts in the Tullianum?"

"Yes," Marcus growled.

But Tuccius's orders were for nothing. Some centurions were out for blood too, taking their own action. They hauled the prisoners atop the Tarpeian Rock and cast them down, one by one. At least anyone watching knew that riots would no longer be tolerated.

Furious and in a dark temperament, Marcus hissed a curse, "May their blood be upon *Dolabella*!"

Marcus hadn't had opportunity to see Mother since returning from Campania.

Her brush with danger amid Dolabella's mobs and Iophon's untimely death had become common knowledge all over the city. Poor Iophon. The slave had fought six or seven men off of her litter, enabling her to scramble out and run away. He really had traded his life for hers. At least there was some good in the world.

Marcus found her in the peristyle courtyard, cutting a rose for her guest, Calpurnia. Mother's face still bore bruising and a cut from her harrowing scrape.

Naturally, the two women were talking about what everyone else in Rome was tittering about: Marcus Antonius's brutal massacre. The tragedy was nothing of which to pride himself. Specific commands had been given—and many men didn't follow them . . .

"Oh, Marcus! Over eight hundred dead," Mother exclaimed, aghast. "How will you ever get past this?"

"The rioting had to stop," he sighed. He was weary and settled himself on a cushion next to Calpurnia. "Think of what happened to you—and to Iophon. It was only getting worse. I gave orders not to harm women and children, but things happen during violence that can't always be controlled." Still, it brought no honor to the Antonii.

"I'd love to travel south to Misenum and escape all this, but I'm afraid to leave the Palatine now," Mother said.

"Marcus acted on a senatorial ultimatum," Calpurnia reminded gently, examining the delicate rose. "He did his duty, and if only the plebs were wiser, they'd realize that."

"Unless you're a pleb who lost a loved one that day," Marcus said. He'd had nightmares ever since the bloodbath, with dead bodies of ordinary plebians pointing fingers at him and hissing curses. Surely it was the stuff of demons.

Mother touched the small sore near her temple that remained from her near-death experience. "I almost died," she murmured. "It's a wonder the gods protected me."

"I'm just thankful you're safe," Marcus told her softly.

Mother frowned at him. "Marcus, you *must* end your high and scandalous living. If the plebs dislike you, then it's time to stop scorning your critics and take heed. Your parties with Cytheris's friends, driving chariots pulled by lions—"

"I heard about that!" Calpurnia exclaimed, unable to hide a smile despite the staid conversation.

Marcus smiled sadly at her. He had always liked Calpurnia. It had been a long time since he'd seen her. "How are you faring?" he asked. "Any word from Caesar?" He doubted it, but why not ask?

She shook her head, but her smile instantly vanished, a great sadness replacing the sparkle in her hazel eyes. "But I did receive news. And there's no point keeping it to myself. Soon all of Rome will know."

"Know what?" Mother asked, moving over to her and sitting down.

Calpurnia picked at the rose's leaves, looking down as she spoke. "A loyal and reliable slave who's been in Egypt with my husband sent me a private letter. As you've heard, war broke out in Alexandria between the factions of King Ptolemy and his sister, Cleopatra. This young queen is said to be intelligent and wise beyond her years. Somehow she smuggled herself into the palace complex and convinced Julius that she should be sole ruler."

Marcus grinned and nodded. "She has spirit. I'm not surprised."

Calpurnia gave him a troubled glance. "Well, Julius won the war but risked much on her behalf. Young King Ptolemy died, and Cleopatra was restored to her throne. To honor Julius, she's giving him a trip on her royal barque down the Nile." With a flick of her fingers, she discarded the rose onto the ground. Looking up again, her eyes brimmed with tears and hurt.

Mother saw the truth in Calpurnia's words before Marcus. Women were always so insightful.

"No!" she inhaled, taking Calpurnia into her arms.

Marcus averted his eyes as a peacock's cries pierced the silence, punctuated only by Calpurnia's weeping. Surely, she had to know that Caesar, of all men, had never been faithful to her.

She regained her composure, wiping her eyes. "His entire staff believes that he and the queen have shared a bed since her return to the palace."

Had Caesar demanded Cleopatra's affections? Marcus stared at a fly buzzing. Oddly, the thought of Caesar sleeping with her annoyed him.

"Oh, dear one," Mother whispered to Calpurnia in comfort, "I've no words . . . I'm so sorry."

Calpurnia took a breath before continuing. "There's more. Cleopatra will bear his child sometime this winter."

"But the child may not be his!" Mother blurted out.

Calpurnia smiled bravely, shaking her head. "As a queen, Cleopatra would have everything to lose by throwing herself at just any man. There is every reason to believe Julius is the father, don't you think, Marcus?"

"I do," he admitted.

"You met Cleopatra when you were in Egypt, didn't you?" Mother asked.

"Yes."

His answer piqued Calpurnia's interest. "Is she beautiful?"

Marcus moistened his lips, considering how to answer. "She has a pleasing personality." He settled for that, though he could have added a lot more . . .

And she speaks seven languages, knows my thoughts before I even share them, and her voice is like sweet music—

"But is she beautiful?" Calpurnia persisted.

"Not overly so, no." Not like Fadia was, or Cytheris.

But her eyes are molten gold, her perfume captivates, and her skin is translucent as alabaster.

"Calpurnia," Mother redirected, to Marcus's relief. "Through your grief, remember one thing. *You* are his wife. Whatever offspring this easterner produces cannot be legitimate." Mother placed her hands on each side of Calpurnia's face, her voice gentle but sure. "Cleopatra is not Roman, therefore Caesar's relationship with her will never be accepted here. *You* are his reality. Never forget that."

Struggling emotionally, Calpurnia shook her head in tragic surrender. "His legal wife I may be, but Cleopatra may do that which I have never been able—she could give him a son!"

"You're still young," Marcus offered. "You could still conceive when the war's done and he returns. He's hardly been home with you long enough to give you a child."

Calpurnia shook her head, sighing sorrowfully. "No. He's not even visited my bed but once since returning from Gaul. He's my husband only in name."

Those final words betrayed a bitterness Marcus had never seen in her before.

Nor could he imagine Cleopatra's twinkling eyes and coquettish dimples beaming at Caesar, who was old enough to be her father.

No, he couldn't picture that at all.

"Dominus—it's urgent."

Marcus exhaled, stirring from sleep, and opened his eyes to find Eros holding a lamp above his head. He squinted at the flame as Cytheris moved beside him, her hair wild, breasts uncovered.

"Caesar's back," Eros whispered.

"And we must all rise before the cock crows to welcome him?" Cytheris grumbled irritably, turning over and covering her head with a pillow.

"I'll visit him first thing in the morning," Marcus assured the slave dismissively, drawing Cytheris close with one arm.

"Dominus, a slave from Caesar's house just came to me."

"What slave?" Marcus groused, peering at Eros over his shoulder. He knew of more than a few of Caesar's household staff . . .

Eros hesitated before admitting, "A girl I've taken as a lover. She works in his kitchens."

"Good for you. Go on."

"She said there was a scuffle at Caesar's tonight. A stranger entered under cover of darkness. He was armed with a pugio—an assassin!"

Cytheris rose up on one elbow. "Is it those cursed mutineers again, causing trouble?"

Eros shook his head fearfully, and his explanation silenced the room. "Dominus, the assassin claimed *you* hired him to kill Caesar!"

Dumbly, Marcus shook his head in disbelief. "Wha-What?"

Rolling out of bed in one fluid motion, he grasped Eros by the shoulders, eyes wide in alarm.

"The assassin's dead, Dominus," Eros explained. "They tortured him for the truth, and he died."

"What will you do?" Cytheris gasped. "You could be arrested, exiled—or worse!"

Marcus's mind was reeling. "I'll go to Caesar personally."

"*Go* to him?" she cried out. "No! Wait for him to summon you, or better yet, leave Rome until it blows over."

"She's right, Dominus," Eros said, his face pale with urgency in the lamplight.

"I'm not *running* from Caesar! He's my cousin, and I've been nothing but loyal!"

Cytheris launched herself across the bed, frantically snatching Marcus's arm. "For once, listen to me, Antonius. My heart tells me this will not end well—don't go to him!"

Prying her off, Marcus showed her his back, holding both wrists out as Eros clamped on his armillae. Next came a clean tunic from a strongbox in one corner. He jerked it over his head, slipping his feet into his sandals. Eros knelt down, working the laces.

Cytheris stumbled from the bed onto the floor at his feet, pleading for him not to go.

Marcus ignored her. Jupiter Magnus, he was many things, but *not* an assassin!

Ushered into Caesar's tablinum with haste, Marcus's palms were sweating and he gnawed on his lip. Caesar gestured his bodyguards outside and sat down at his large desk, brows furrowed.

Left standing, Marcus shrugged helplessly. "I came to assure you—whoever sent that monster last night, it was *not* me. I swear on the Vestals' holy flames!"

"Exactly how would you do that, Antonius?" Caesar questioned coldly, his eyes narrowing. "The Vestals had to flee the city."

"Oh—th-that?" he stammered. "I was away, dealing with the Campanian legions, and my uncle is a fool who can't control the masses—"

"Nor can you," Caesar snapped, "unless you kill them, that is. Over eight hundred? You can't lead people if they hate you."

Marcus paused, staring at him defensively. "I acted on a senatorial ultimatum. I ordered all women and children to be spared, but the men went savage—you *know* that happens!"

"And my legions in Campania?" Caesar challenged. "They're no longer described to me as soldiers, but mutineers."

"I met with them personally, bargaining for time and persuading them to await your return. Ho! They could have taken the city, and I prevented that from happening!"

Caesar retorted, "I told you to give them my *word*."

Angry now, Marcus exploded. "Your *word*? You think it's really all-powerful, reaching across the sea from Egypt? They wanted *coin*, and I had none to give! No lands, no word from you, no *orders*! Lastly, they're angry you pardoned Pompeius's swine. And for that, I don't blame them. In fact, I *agree* with them! You only added numbers to his army by pardoning so many!"

Caesar narrowed his eyes, his words a low growl, "Don't cross me, Antonius."

"It's the truth! And better you hear it from me than someone else, don't you think?"

Caesar paused momentarily before asking, "What of Dolabella? Where is he?"

"How should I know? He bolted like the cowardly wretch he is."

"Well, I'll find him and hear him out on debt-cancellation. You chose the wrong side this time. The Plebs supported him, as will I."

Marcus felt as though he'd just been shot by a bolt. "What?"

"I trusted you to manage this city. You failed. And one more thing," Caesar informed him, calmly, "you are no longer magister equitum."

Dropping his jaw, Marcus swallowed, shaking his head. "I see.

Then what am I to do? Join my uncle in exile? Turn my sword upon myself? Surely, you don't believe I hired someone to kill you! You're my cousin—my beloved kinsman."

Caesar smiled smoothly. "I promised to return Hybrida to Rome, and Caesar keeps his word. As for harming yourself, you've everything to live for, I assure you."

"This is absurd! I *swear* to you I knew nothing about this attempt on your life. I beg you to reconsider."

"Cicero wrote to me about your consorting with Cytheris and her troupe openly. Your profligate parties added to everyone's complaints. So I've other plans for you that will hopefully restore the people's respect for you. You're going to remarry."

Marcus blinked, another shock rocking his world.

Caesar laughed aloud. "Yes! You're going to marry Fulvia Bambula, get sons on her, and become respectable. You'll cease consorting with actors and their whores, driving lion-drawn chariots, and taking others' properties without paying. And you still owe for Pompeius's domus. Pay for it before the month is out."

Marcus sat frozen, aghast. He shook his head in disbelief. "I know of many men's debts you've overlooked and canceled, including those of Pompeian *enemies*! I've risked my very life for you *so* many times, always showing allegiance—"

"Silence!" Caesar roared, shutting Marcus up in mid-sentence. Casually heading toward the door, he scoffed. "Your allegiance, you say? Of that I'm unsure since I lost sleep last evening due to a certain unexpected houseguest." Pausing, he looked back at Marcus's desperation. "You'll need to prove yourself, Antonius. And in the meantime, pay for your domus. You'll need an impressive threshold over which to carry such a bride."

Marcus shook his head sadly, his next words coming as a whisper. "I rode at your side across the Rubicon, nearly died defending your lines in Dyrrachium, and risked my life trying to protect Rome from legionary mutinies and riots. Why would you believe I sent someone to *kill* you? Do my former acts prove nothing?"

Ignoring his plea, Caesar repeated, "You owe for your domus. And if Cicero is right and your gambling debts have increased again, rest assured. Fulvia has an abundant dowry."

Left alone in the tablinum, a cold sweat broke out on Marcus's brow and his heart sank. He found himself trembling and breathing hard. The point of distrust had been driven home as brutally as the tip of a gladius.

Those serving Caesar had to remain above suspicion.

CHAPTER XIX

46-45BC

WHEN THE MUTINOUS CAMPANIAN LEGIONS MARCHED TO Rome and presented their demands to Caesar, he pulled off a daring, courageous act, facing them alone and on foot. Brash as it was, he spewed forth a fiery oration, reducing some of the men to such shame that they begged for reenlistment.

Caesar dealt with his legions.

Marcus dealt with his bride-to-be. But Fulvia made one non-negotiable demand that bothered him more than he wanted to admit. It was her one stipulation on their upcoming marriage, and she would have it no other way.

He had to cast Cytheris aside, along with any other women.

It was a tall order from a bride, demanding that her future husband remain faithful. However, Caesar's wishes, Fulvia's wealth, and her notoriety dictated how little choice he had in the matter—especially after losing all imperium.

Sunlight filtered through decorative iron florets high in the walls of Marcus's domus. Anxiously, he paced the mosaic floor of his spacious atrium. As of this week, the house of Pompeius was truly his. The final payment had nearly emptied his coffers.

Another reason he had to marry Fulvia. Her dowry was as much as he'd won in Gaul!

But today's agenda?

Cytheris.

She wasn't any ordinary mistress; that much was certain. She'd been dependable, someone to whom he'd entrusted his family when escaping Pompeius's wrath. Her kindness, playfulness, and free, unfettered living made him regret parting with her company.

And Fulvia wanted to know up front whether he loved the actress.

Actually, there were moments when he wondered himself. Certainly, Cytheris had always met his sexual cravings, taken his mind off politics, and supported him through good times and bad. Her peculiar courage, when she summoned it, matched his own, and her natural humor had always soothed him whenever he needed laughter. And what hospitality she had shown, sharing her insula with Mother, Antonia, Fulvia, and the rest.

Yet parts of himself he'd kept hidden from her. Personal fears, his nightmares, and admissions of weakness were things he'd never confided to anyone, save Fadia or Eros, upon occasion. Surely, a woman he deeply loved would eventually know those things.

Fadia had. She had known him like no other.

Word of Marcus's upcoming wedding swept across Rome overnight, so Cytheris had to know what was coming. Eros said plebs were chattering about it in the Forum, declaring Fulvia to be the one woman capable of "taming Antonius once and for all."

So today was the day. And hearing footsteps outside, he knew Cytheris's litter had arrived.

She entered the tablinum alone. Dressed more conservatively than usual, her hair was swept back modestly with ribbons woven between neat plaits. If he hadn't known her, Marcus would've mistaken her for a respectable senator's wife.

Strange how they stood in awkward silence before Lentulus's old desk, surrounded by wax busts of his ancestors. They both were hesitant to speak; they both knew what was coming.

Finally, Marcus went first. "It was not my idea. If I had chosen to marry again, I'd never willingly cast you off."

"I warned you not to go to Caesar," she breathed, tears filling her eyes despite her efforts to hold them back.

He shook his head. "Even if I'd left Rome, he would've arranged it when I returned."

No response.

He forged ahead. "Well, I'm giving you five talents of gold as severance. It's the last of my Gallic booty. Even a princess could live decently with that much for the rest of her life."

Unsurprisingly, she turned proudly indignant. "Keep your coin. Since I'm no longer your whore, I won't be treated as such."

At that, the awkward hush between them descended again. It had never been like this with them before. Marcus heard nothing but the atrium fountain, which, at that particular moment, sounded more like a waterfall. He stepped toward her, reaching for her hand, but she clasped them, making contact impossible.

Perhaps she was right. A human touch would make things more difficult now. "Cytheris, I release you. But I offer you wealth and my sincerest hope that you'll find happiness. I'll deeply miss you."

There was another excruciating pause before she confessed, "Once, you warned me never to love you, but I always have and always will. There may come a day when you need help, even from a lowborn woman like me. I'll be waiting, Antonius. Remember that."

Those words touched him more than she could ever know. "Then consider the gold as a gift—not a payment. Castor will see it safely to the banker of your choice. And keep the insula. Esquiline elegance suits you far better than the Subura. You have been and will always be a dear, dear friend." At least he'd succeeded in elevating her living conditions. That was something. And his last words brought a hint of a smile to her face.

Cytheris had pride, that much was sure.

Using admirable self-control, she spoke with only a slight

emotional tremor in her voice. "Sex with Fulvia should bring you much pleasure. You always did want her." Stiffly, she turned away, crossing to the door. Pausing for a moment, she looked back sorrowfully before walking out of his life.

Oh, how he'd miss their escapes, for he was as much a slave to Rome as any captive from Gaul.

There were two benefits to marriage with Fulvia Bambula. Financial comfort and intense sexual gratification. Cytheris had been correct about that part.

"You'll never need another woman," Fulvia pledged as they lay abed their first night, legs entangled and breathing hard. "I'll satisfy you like no prostitute ever could."

Sweet Venus! She upheld that promise, experimenting nightly to determine his preferences and offering herself to him in the triclinium while slaves were present, several times in the gardens, and even once on Lentulus's desk in the tablinum. Marcus obliged with relish. Some nights she pleasured him with her mouth or straddled him as though riding a horse. Like Cytheris, her libido matched his own. And she was right. There was *no* need to bother with slave girls or prostitutes.

Still, Marcus found his feelings for Fulvia tangled and confused.

Abed, she was a hot-blooded temptress, and that was more than enjoyable. But she had few friends and wasn't well-received among highborn women. Her personality was perplexing. Strong-willed and obstinate, Fulvia rarely took "no" for an answer. On the other hand, she was ever supportive. An expert manipulator, she was social for purely personal and political reasons, planning frequent dinner parties with high-ranking Caesarian senators.

But Marcus decided that he had little reason to complain, for within a month of their wedding, Fulvia was with child. She certainly knew what was expected of her. Perhaps at last he'd have a son.

While the Antonii awaited the birth, Caesar conquered a host of enemies in North Africa at Thapsus. However, Pompeius's two sons managed to escape, slipping through the lines and sailing to Spain. The overzealous Optimate Cato took his own life rather than submit to Caesar, who then pursued Pompeius's sons, preparing to face them on the plains of Munda. A note from Calpurnia informed Marcus about the battle's outcome:

> *Calpurnia to Marcus Antonius:*
>
> *Salve, my friend. I've just received word that my husband was victorious. The war has ended at last, and once Spain is secure, he'll return to Rome. My sincerest hope is that the two of you will be reconciled. I never believed you were behind the attempt on his life.*

Fulvia's time arrived in late spring, and it wasn't long before cries of a newborn echoed through the domus. Mother brought out a small bundle into the sun-dappled gardens, where Marcus waited with his friends Canidius and Tuccius. Upon her approach, he sprang to his feet.

"You have an heir, my son!" she announced, proudly placing the swaddled infant down on the tender grass before him in traditional Roman fashion.

Marcus knelt down immediately, raising the baby up to claim paternity according to Roman custom. He held him aloft for the others to admire. Red and wrinkled, the child opened and closed his mouth repeatedly, like a tiny fish sucking in air.

"Look, he's already hungry!" Marcus laughed.

"He was born with his tata's many appetites," Tuccius chided suggestively.

"How's Fulvia?" Marcus inquired.

Mother beamed. "Sleeping soundly. I declare it was the easiest birth I've ever attended. Only two hours laboring and the babe popped out like a cork from an overripe wineskin!"

The three men laughed, Canidius slapping Marcus on the back with affection.

"Will he be another Marcus Antonius, then?" Tuccius asked.

"Oh yes," Marcus confirmed, nodding enthusiastically and offering his little finger for the baby to suckle. It made him laugh, the tiny tongue curling neatly around his appendage. Suddenly, the tiny new Marcus, tugged an arm free and reached up toward his Tata's face.

Marcus chuckled in glee.

"Look at those arm muscles—already bulging!" Tuccius jested.

"Like those of an archer," agreed Canidius.

With a broad grin, Marcus nodded. "Then we'll call him 'Antyllus'—so as not to confuse him with me."

Antyllus. The archer.

Marcus lifted his child closer, kissing the little head already covered with thick, dark hair, just like his. Both thankful and in awe of this new life given, he murmured next to the baby's ear, "Marcus Antonius Antyllus, my firstborn son and heir."

After Antyllus's birth, Marcus quickly learned that Fulvia considered childrearing the curse of womankind. She preferred political games to coddling her young. Still, he tried to encourage her in maternal interests. She'd borne children in each of her marriages, after all. Clodius had seeded her with two, and Curio's one whelp kept their house slaves ever busy. Marcus welcomed the brood into his domus, of course, each child followed closely by dependable slave companions.

In the wake of disfavor from Caesar, he had to admit that Fulvia did her part to repair his reputation among the plebs. Antyllus's healthy, jovial countenance was a useful tool, restoring people's faith in Caesar's former "lieutenant." Fulvia purposefully took her little son to the Forum Romanum daily, lifting him high for all to see and gaining approval from the people. Antyllus was robust, a strapping, growing bundle, ever laughing and full of fun, just like his father.

Wanting to reward her for her efforts, Marcus surprised Fulvia with plans to attend a play at Pompeius's theater. Menander's *The Difficult Man* was to be the evening's entertainment.

"I heard none of the other leading magistrates are coming tonight," Fulvia commented as they quit their litter. "That means you could sit where Caesar or the consuls normally preside." She nodded toward the most prestigious men's seats. "Go on—everyone will see you in a seat of power. Look! I see Canidius waving at you."

Marcus gallantly kissed her hand to keep her happy but had no intention of starting any contentious talk by assuming Caesar's place in the audience. Her intentions were good, but that would be far too presumptive. Instead, he'd sit to the right of it. That could send just as favorable a message.

Before he left her at the women's seats, she caught a sinus of his toga, pressing her lips to his ear. "Save yourself for what I've planned once we return to bed tonight."

"Ho! Will I have stamina enough for it?" Marcus joked, his brows raised in curiosity.

"You always do."

Marcus joined him in the men's section. Once they had seated themselves, there was a tittering through the audience and shouts of, "Look! Over there!"

Bare-chested African men wearing pleated white kilts and bearing ostrich-plumed fans were entering the theater. Each was bald, wearing a single solid-gold armband. Behind them followed a parade of exotically attired dignitaries in colorful silks. Marcus grinned brilliantly, knowing full well where he'd seen such finery before.

Cleopatra of Egypt had recently arrived in Rome at Caesar's invitation. Though he wasn't yet back from Spain, the imperator's staff had opened his grandiose estate across the Tiber just for her.

What had rocked the city was the baby boy she'd brought with her: Caesar's son, whom she had named Ptolemy Caesar—Caesarion. Perhaps the queen saw nothing wrong with this, but to Romans it was an affront for her to have named a bastard after his father, as though he were Caesar's legitimate heir.

Marcus couldn't help but smile. She'd been in Rome for over a month now, but he hadn't seen her since he'd been in Alexandria. Due to his falling out with Caesar, he had been removed from most guest lists.

A small litter was borne behind the African bodyguards. Glimmering, it was gilt in both gold and silver plate, its edges encrusted by jewels. Borne by more enormous men the color of night, two women followed, dressed in the finest Greek styles. One was a dark-skinned Nubian. The other looked Greek, with regal bearing and older than the youthful African girl.

Crowds in the theater were going wild over the show, it being as fine as any play—perhaps better. Women in the ladies' section were all standing, craning their necks to see. Senators behind Marcus and Canidius were declaring their disgust at such a "ridiculous and lewd spectacle of wealth."

As far as Marcus Antonius was concerned, no wealth could possibly be lewd. He was so immersed in watching the company that it was several moments before he realized the procession was headed straight in his direction.

What was she doing? Was Cleopatra intending to sit in Caesar's chair? Where else would she go? Did she not realize that men and women sat separately during plays? Or was she making a statement? If so, what a declaration!

Curious citizens kept surging forward to gawk, promptly pushed back by the queen's bodyguards. Soon the litter neared Caesar's seat of honor.

The first person to part the silk curtains was a young boy with shoulder-length hair, fine and dark. For his tender age, he was regal in his bearing, as were his robes. Purple silk with spun-gold embroidery flowed to his ankles. On his head was a thin band of gold with a small vulture fanning its wings above his brow. Beneath, a startlingly hawk-like nose protruded—a familial trait Marcus remembered. This had to be Cleopatra's surviving younger brother, Ptolemy. The older one who had contested her for the throne and had Pompeius beheaded had drowned during the Alexandrian war.

As Ptolemy the younger hesitated, staring at the spectators as they all watched him, the queen herself emerged.

Cleopatra wore a flowing Greek chiton of soft white silk. Orange-and-purple embroidered flowers danced around the hem and bodice of her garments. Pearls adorned her neck, ears, and even the sandals she wore. Tiny braids tightened her lustrous, dark hair back snugly, gathering it all neatly to create a round, melon-styled coif. Interwoven between each intricate plait was a simple white diadem ribbon, knotted at the back of her neck and cascading down her back. Her presence had a regal serenity Marcus couldn't deny. Exactly as he remembered, Cleopatra bore a maturity beyond her years.

The enormous crowd watched, dumbfounded and completely silent, forgetting that they'd all gathered together for a play. Here was something much more fascinating. Head held high, Cleopatra glided over to claim Caesar's seat on the raised dais among the men.

Marcus could hear a collective gasp from the male audience around him, senators at his back disparaging her in hushed tones.

Ptolemy suddenly swept his hand at the crowd. "Sister, look at them! They're all poor, and they stink!"

"Sit down and be silent, as you promised," Cleopatra replied coolly, her voice sweet but firm.

She had yet to notice Marcus, who was sitting beneath the dais.

The low humming of irritated voices amplified. Wealthy merchants, the group of senators, and several younger sons of the aristocracy were grumbling about Cleopatra's grave mistake—sitting among the men *and* in Caesar's own chair!

Canidius leaned over to Marcus discreetly. "Shouldn't someone tell her this is the men's section? She should go sit with the women."

"Her brother is with her and is very young. Perhaps she feels she needs to chaperone him. Besides, it would be humiliating for her to leave Caesar's chair now," Marcus replied.

"All the gods forbid Calpurnia shows up!"

Marcus nodded. "I agree. However, I've met the queen before, and she's a brilliant young woman. I'm going to greet her and try to make her feel welcome since nobody else is."

Everyone was staring at her in disapproval, muttering among themselves like gossiping matrons at the baths. Surely, Cleopatra noticed, but she bore it with nonchalance. Well, Marcus Antonius would give everybody in Rome something to chat about for the next week!

He stood up and addressed Cleopatra in perfect Greek. "I see the princess has become a queen."

Cleopatra looked down at him from her high seat. Dimples he remembered fondly punctuated a surprised smile, and her golden eyes twinkled. "Marcus Antonius! How pleasing to see you again. Congratulations to you and your wife on the birth of your son."

"You heard, did you? Well then, congratulations on the birth of yours, as well, Majesty," Marcus answered courteously, sweeping her hand into his and kissing it. Was it his imagination, or did he feel her delicate pulse race?

"With Horus's grace, my sweet Caesarion will be great like his father." Elegantly, she removed her hand from his.

"And this must be your youngest brother?" Marcus said.

"Ptolemy!" she called. "I want you to meet one of Caesar's generals, Marcus Antonius."

Ptolemy was too enamored of the crowd and at this moment was studying the tight-knit group of senators all sitting together, none of whom were smiling. "Sister, why do all the powerful men dress the same? If they're so rich, shouldn't they be able to dress in something more than bedsheets?"

Marcus burst out laughing, along with Canidius behind him.

One of Cleopatra's women snatched Ptolemy's arm, forcing him into a seat.

"Forgive him," the queen apologized. "He's spoiled and hasn't been in public overmuch."

"Have you heard from Caesar?" Marcus inquired.

"I received a brief message just days ago. He looks forward to returning."

"Ah, good." Interesting. Was Caesar coming back soon? He changed subjects. "How do you like his Janiculum villa? I've not been there, personally. But I hear it's breathtaking."

"It is. Caesar's artistic tastes mirror my own. His collection of Greek works is small but admirable. The Dying Gaul sculpture in the gardens is especially poignant."

Marcus raised his brow at that remark. "Really? I'd love to see it."

Cleopatra looked pleased. "Then I must have a gathering after Caesar returns. It would be my pleasure."

When Caesar returned. If he'd even want Marcus there. Somehow he needed to reenter his cousin's inner circle.

After the play, Marcus escorted Cleopatra to her litter, then he and Canidius walked next to it as a means to exit. Eventually, he saw Fulvia making her way down the stairs to meet him.

"I see you've become acquainted with the queen," she said with an air of haughtiness.

Marcus looked at her with a raised brow. "Do I detect a hint of suspicion in your voice?"

"She shouldn't have been in the men's section and certainly not in *Caesar's* seat," Fulvia spat, unamused.

Marcus laughed, taking her arm. "Fulvia, I know you well, and had you half the chance Cleopatra did this afternoon, you would have helped yourself to Caesar's seat too."

"Did she beguile you, as she has Caesar?"

"We met when I was in Alexandria—years ago—before she was queen."

"I see."

Marcus glanced back at her. She was looking straight ahead. Venus! Fulvia was jealous.

But Marcus could no longer deny it. Just as he'd first felt it in Alexandria, there was an attraction between him and Cleopatra that was palpable.

And Fulvia knew it.

Marcus rolled onto his back in abandon, laughing at Antyllus, who grabbed his nose, squeezing hard. It was early summer, and news of Caesar's imminent departure from Spain had Rome abuzz, chattering about what life would be like under a new one-man rule.

With a slurpy kiss on both of Antyllus's cheeks, Marcus hoisted himself up, offering the baby to Mother. "I'm going to ride out and meet him," he announced.

"That should validate your loyalty," Fulvia said approvingly from where she sat on a garden bench.

"I agree," Mother seconded, her graying head nodding serenely in the sunlight dappling the peristyle courtyard. "You'll be seen as one of the first to welcome and support him. Just let someone accuse you of plotting assassination after that!"

Marcus knew it couldn't hurt his chances of earning Caesar's good graces again.

Before leaving Rome, he solicited help from Canidius and Tuccius, distributing pamphlets to people in the Forum to remind them of Marcus Antonius's devout allegiance to his cousin Caesar. Each listed acts of his bravery in Gaul, service with Legio XII in Bibracte, et cetera, et cetera. In only four days, the fickle populace was even calling him their "favorite" again.

Indeed, if journeying halfway to Spain meant a possible pardon from Caesar, the ride would be worth it.

Marcus traveled northwest from Rome, taking only Eros. He intended to stay ahead of the sizeable senatorial delegation, also planning to intercept Caesar.

"This is one of the mythical routes of Heracles," Eros remarked as they trotted along the Via Domitia toward Narbo Martius.

"Really? Where did you hear that?"

"Scrolls, Dominus."

"You read too much." Marcus snorted, giving his slave a crooked smile. More and more, he had learned to depend upon the young Greek, trusting him implicitly.

Upon reaching Narbo, they camped for a day or two to await word of Caesar's approach. The place was alive with legionaries left behind to hold the city at Caesar's back. There was a feeling of heightened expectation throughout town, for the soldiers knew their imperator was coming. Brothels were busier than usual, wine flowed, and occasional tavern brawls broke out. Yes, Caesar had kept Narbo secure from renegade Pompeians or parties of Gallic outlaws.

As Eros stoked a cooking fire, Marcus relaxed on a worn animal skin draped over a cart wheel. Occasional hoofbeats and soldiers' laughter filled him to overflowing with contentment. It was excellent being near the activity of legionaries again.

Out of nowhere, a clear voice hailed, "It's been too long since we shared a camp, Antonius!"

Startled, Marcus looked up, then grinned broadly. Before him rode a solitary horseman, travel-worn and wearing dust-covered armor.

"Trebonius! And I was just thinking how wonderful it was to be camping near legionaries again. Where have you been?"

"With Caesar. He sent me on ahead to prepare Narbo's garrison for his arrival." He dismounted, his horse lowering its head wearily and blowing. "Munda was hard-won," he said. "Don't believe anyone telling you otherwise."

Marcus arose to embrace his old friend. "Word in Rome was total victory. Is that not true?"

Trebonius hesitated before answering, tying his reins to a nearby tree. His demeanor certainly didn't match that of a victorious legate. "Yes, the war's over," he muttered in confirmation. "Caesar's *master* of Rome." Bitterness branded his tone.

Picking up his wine, Marcus raised his cup. "Well, I toast his success then!" He took a swig, calling for Eros to bring another cup. Together, he and Trebonius shared the fire, relaxing and stretching their legs as they drank.

Trebonius had aged. Still healthy and fit, his hair was thinning. Age had creased both sides of his mouth, and a pensive seriousness pervaded the easygoing sense of humor Marcus remembered.

"Spain was bloody," he sighed under his breath. "It's tragic how Caesar's 'success' was won against our own brothers."

"War is war." Marcus shrugged, shaking his head. "Caesar is victorious. So let's all live to enjoy the bounty of our imperator's new government."

Draining his wine, Trebonius inhaled sharply. "New it will be. There's already talk of great change coming." Setting his cup aside, he queried, "Tell me something—why do you talk about his 'new government' with such enthusiasm when Caesar chucked you aside like overripe fruit?"

Marcus winced. That stung—Trebonius bringing up his demotion so bluntly. It continued to frustrate him when other men—some far less loyal—remained at Caesar's side or held office in Rome when he didn't. But Marcus had decided. He would reunite with his cousin and win him over again. He wouldn't fail—despite being his own worst enemy more often than he liked to admit. He would regain every bit of the imperium he had lost.

Since Marcus didn't answer his question, Trebonius changed subjects, sharing another piece of news. "Labienus fell. Did you hear?"

"I didn't." Marcus shook his head. "I'll choose to remember him as a great soldier, a true man of war."

Trebonius virtually spat the next words. "Caesar *desecrated* his body."

"How so?"

"He ordered it decapitated."

Raising his brow, Marcus blinked. "Ho! A warning to others, I suppose. Labienus betrayed him, after all."

Trebonius scoffed. "Caesar should've remembered who helped him win Gaul—especially when he forgave so many others. Without Labienus, he would never have become a conqueror."

Personally, Marcus guessed Caesar was relieved the wormy old fig was gone for good.

"You should also know Caesar has a new favorite," Trebonius added.

"Who?"

"Well, there's still Marcus Junius Brutus."

"He's old news." Marcus shrugged. "Well, he's Servilia's son, after all, and Caesar was always sweet on her."

Trebonius tossed his head back laughing. "He won't bother with that old hag when he has that little Egyptian sphinx waiting in Rome to pleasure him!"

This time Marcus didn't join in with Trebonius's laughter. This whole conversation was taking an entirely different turn, and it made him uncomfortable. A balmy breeze fanned the nearby cooking fire as Eros hauled a terra-cotta crock of hot bread from the coals. The boy was listening to every word. Marcus knew it. Choosing his own carefully, he asked, "So who's the new favorite?"

"Gaius Octavian. Strangest sort you'd ever meet. Nothing more than a boy, really. Slight of stature, skinny, and knows absolutely *nothing* about warfare. He was supposed to join Caesar in Spain early on but got caught in a storm and survived a wreck before arriving at the war's end."

"Atia's son . . . " Marcus mused. "I've not seen him since he was an infant."

Trebonius leaned toward him, away from Eros's ears. "Some think he's Caesar's *lover*. They shared a tent in Spain and were always together. Silly boy follows him about like a dog. If I were Caesar, I'd publicly take roadside whores at every stop to clear myself from such scandal. To take an occasional slave boy with discretion is one thing, but piddling with one's own nephew?"

"*Great*-nephew," Marcus corrected.

"Still—appalling!"

Baffled, Marcus asked, "Why are you telling me these things?"

Trebonius glanced about, lowering his voice even more. "Antonius, there are many men—good, reliable Romans—fearful of Caesar."

Marcus frowned, staring into his cup. Had Trebonius taken up Labienus's cause? "What are their concerns?"

"The Senate intends to laud Caesar with accolades. But I say he's only a man and should receive nothing more than any other Roman. And he should march straight into the Curia when he returns to lay down his dictatorship so the Republic might be reinstated."

"Oh, be fair, Trebonius. What's wrong with rewarding victors? Celebrating triumphs is nothing new, and Caesar's not been in Rome long enough to celebrate any of his. Pompeius had that honor, as did others before him, including my own grandfather. And as for the Republic? It's been dead for years. It's time we let it rest in peace."

Trebonius pressed on urgently. "Hear me. Many of us believe Caesar will try to reinstate the monarchy. Who only knows how that despot Cleopatra's influenced him? We intend to *stop* him."

Marcus stared at Trebonius, forcing himself to remain calm. "With force?"

Nervously smiling, Trebonius whispered, "Well, didn't you send an assassin to deal with him yourself?"

Marcus stood up abruptly, shaken and angry. This was the *last* thing he wanted resurrected while trying to curry Caesar's favor. He stepped back, putting space between himself and Trebonius. "That *murderer* was most likely sent by Dolabella to slander and destroy my credibility." Voice escalating, he cried, "I had nothing to do with it! Caesar is my dearest kinsman, and I would never betray him."

Marcus saw that Eros had forgotten all about the bread. Attentive to their argument, his mouth sagged in obvious concern.

Self-conscious and flushed, Trebonius also rose, changing his manner. "Ah, well. Forgive me." Then he extended his hand swiftly. "It's so good to see you again, my friend. I hope I may still call you that?"

Marcus stared down at proffered peace. A new ambiguity was surfacing—more men conspiring to end Caesar's leadership. It meant more unrest.

Still awaiting a response to his proffered arm, Trebonius settled for clasping Marcus's shoulder firmly. "Come, Antonius. We've endured too much together to part unpleasantly."

Still wary, Marcus relented slightly, forcing himself to accept Trebonius's regret.

Then the subject immediately resurfaced as Trebonius whispered softly, "Consider joining us. Stand up for the Republic. You'd make your grandfather proud."

Marcus raised both hands as a barrier, shaking his head. He would not be swayed. "If you really are my friend, never ask me that again. Rome has moved beyond the Republic, and we'll have to wait and see what she becomes. However, I know Caesar well. He'll create something far greater than anyone can conceive. Say no more to me about treachery, for I'll not have it."

Determined to push the shocking thoughts of sedition aside, he struggled to maintain composure and hospitality. "Eros," he called. "Prepare Gaius Trebonius some food."

No, he wouldn't turn his back on this friend, but no longer did he wish to break bread with him either. Without another word, Marcus Antonius retired for the night, leaving Trebonius to eat alone.

CHAPTER XX

CAESAR HAD CHANGED.

The vigorous, physical energy he'd once exuded was fading. He was pale and drawn. Wrinkled skin Marcus had never noticed sagged under his thin neck, and occasionally he rubbed his eyes.

Even his mode of travel was different. Caesar usually preferred to walk or ride at the head of his army to exude authority, so Marcus was shocked to see that he was in a litter. Because of Trebonius, it was no great surprise seeing young Gaius Octavian stepping out first, assisting his great-uncle.

Eager to fulfill his mission, Marcus spurred his horse into a canter to be first in greeting the imperator ahead of the slower-moving senatorial delegation. He dismounted and strode toward Caesar, arms wide and grinning. They embraced.

He whispered in his cousin's ear, "I'm here to congratulate you on your victory, and I pledge my allegiance to your service and cause. Be assured of my loyalty, my friendship, and my support, for all these sentiments are heartfelt."

After releasing Caesar, he started to step back but was relieved when the imperator embraced him again, kissing both sides of his face. "Gratias for this kindness, Antonius. I should not have doubted you."

No, you shouldn't have, Marcus thought, still forcing his warmest smile while clasping Caesar's hand.

And why hadn't Caesar called him to Spain instead of this boy Octavian? By the looks of him, the little turd was probably useless. Unless Trebonius's scandalous rumor was true.

"Ah! Senators, thank you for coming," Caesar called out, stepping past Marcus and heading toward the delegation, one arm high in greeting. Some of them rode mules; others had retinues following richly decorated wagons. Nearly two hundred were in the party, all to meet Caesar, laud him, and court his favor.

Just like me, Marcus thought. Well, he'd humbled himself before, though this time around promised a better outcome—he hoped.

Behind him, Octavian coughed. Marcus turned about. "You must be the baby I once held who sported a bad rash."

"My maladies are nobody's business," the youth quipped in a surprisingly clear, strong voice.

Marcus chuckled and lifted his hands in surrender. "Sorry. I meant no harm." He took a moment to study Octavian, who was gazing toward Caesar with obvious admiration. Whether it was that of a lover, Marcus was skeptical. Like Atia and the rest of that branch of the family, Octavian's eyes were pale blue. And the blotchy skin and light complexion he'd had as a baby had failed to fade as he approached adulthood. "How old are you now?"

"Eighteen," Octavian replied.

He didn't seem interested in conversation, but since there was nothing better to do, Marcus persisted anyway. "How's your swordplay coming? Any close calls in the battle?"

At least Octavian looked his way this time. "I was detained by storms and didn't fight."

Marcus nodded. He remembered Trebonius saying something about that.

Then Octavian added sanctimoniously, "Caesar had to achieve victory without me."

And how in Mars's name did he ever *do that?* Marcus bit his lip to keep from bursting into laughter.

Arrogant little shit!

Obvious disappointment shaded many a senator's face that day when their offers of wine and rest were waved away by Caesar, who was anxious to get moving on to Narbo. But to Marcus's delight, he addressed Octavian, who was still standing near the litter with Marcus. "Go ride with the officers. I'll speak with Antonius alone."

Octavian glanced at Marcus briefly, his pale, staring eyes unreadable, but certainly not friendly.

Caesar's litter was really too small for two grown men, especially of Marcus's and Caesar's stature. Nevertheless, Marcus reclined facing his cousin, legs safely at an angle with one foot sticking out the side.

"How is Fulvia?" Caesar queried, a crooked smile playing on his mouth.

"She bore me a son. Antyllus."

Caesar's eyes widened. "Really? Excellent news! She's a fetching creature. Her offspring should be handsome indeed."

"Are you well?" Marcus probed.

Caesar sighed. "This last battle reminded me of Alesia," he recollected. "Lots of tight fighting, and it took longer to win since the enemy refused to surrender." Waving his hand dismissively, he added, "Pompeius's youngest son, Sextus Pompeius, escaped again, taking to the sea. He's hardly worth pursuing now."

"Rome will restore you," Marcus said hopefully. "You can enjoy triumphs, games, and a certain Egyptian who awaits you."

Caesar snorted good-naturedly. "*That* one owes me much. I restored her kingdom, you know."

Marcus offered an obligatory smile, well aware he'd also lent a hand in securing Cleopatra's fortunes, long before Caesar ever set foot in Egypt. "Well, consider yourself repaid," Marcus assured. "I've heard little Caesarion mirrors you."

Caesar tensed, cocking an eyebrow. Marcus could already sense the conversation turning too personal for his preferences. "She shouldn't have brought the boy, or named him after me," he stated. "He's illegitimate and not a Roman citizen."

Marcus stared at him incredulously. "Seriously, Caesar? You can do whatever you wish. You're the most powerful man in the world."

Caesar seemed thoughtful and spoke cautiously. "I must take care managing change. Many traditionalists remain in the Senate who will not welcome me."

Marcus wondered if he was aware of any conspiracy. "Indeed. I spoke with Gaius Trebonius just last night about that very thing. He says you have many ideas in store."

"That I do. I've a hefty sum of gold in the Temple of Ops for future use in building projects and maintaining loyalty." Caesar smiled. "Rome is an old city and looks that way. It's time she was reborn. How is my new forum progressing?"

"Quite well, actually. The first columns of the Temple of Venus were raised just last month."

"I swore an oath to her, promising a temple upon my victories. Also, our calendar's a disaster. One can hardly tell what month it is, with seasons so out of harmony with any given date. Alexandrians have a scientific model upon which I'll base a new calendar. Its accuracy will be much improved."

"And your triumphs?"

"Ah yes—of course. And games—there will be plenty, marking not only my victories, but the building of my forum. People must see Caesar giving of himself bounteously. And he'll continue to give."

A lull descended in their conversation, the litter rocking lazily.

Caesar broke the silence. "And I've not yet spoken of it publicly, but I intend to invade and take Parthia."

Marcus's eyes lit up. "Parthia? I should like to assist with that."

Caesar promised, "And you shall! I've already given it thought. You'll secure my back in Macedonia with several legions there."

What? Not conquering at Caesar's side? "Surely, you'd need me with you to help with the war itself?"

Caesar waved off his concern. "Actually, I'm thinking of taking Octavian. The boy needs experience . . ."

Octavian!

"But we needn't discuss particulars yet," Caesar went on, "for now I wish to reinstate you. How should I reward your devotion? Tell me."

Marcus was still thunderstruck at the thought of Octavian heading an army, but Caesar's assurance of reinstatement lifted his spirits a bit. Perhaps later he could convince Caesar to take *him* to Parthia rather than the little shit.

As for his reinstatement, Marcus had in mind several things. "Surely, you'll take the consulship for yourself," he began. "Appoint me to the second chair. That way, I'll help you administer Rome as you see fit."

Caesar nodded wholeheartedly. "Yes. We'd work well together. Consider it done. I wish to be generous. What more?"

"My brothers, Gaius and Lucius, should benefit. They've been loyal, both risking much on your behalf."

"How would praetor sound for Gaius? And Lucius can be my tribune."

Marcus laughed inwardly. Gaius as praetor? What an absolute master Caesar was at politics! In that office, his brother would have to fund many of Caesar's games! Old weasel was already figuring on ways to save coin—turning Gaius's honored service into financial gain. Oh, well—it'd be Gaius's coin, not Marcus's. And anyway, planning entertainment was better suited to his brother's talents than anything military. "Agreed," he chuckled. "Gratias, Caesar."

The conversation stilled, but Marcus remained troubled about last night's conversation with Trebonius. Perhaps it was best to tell Caesar what little he knew. He lowered his voice in warning. "Caesar, I've heard troubling things. Gaius Trebonius—"

"He performed poorly in Gaul after Labienus defected and knows it displeased me," Caesar mumbled derisively, head wagging.

"He mentioned a conspiracy forming of which I feel obligated to warn you."

"Against *me*, you mean?"

"Yes."

"I've given clemency to many undeserving men—an act for which you fault me. Yet now they owe me their lives as a result. So I won't fear petty words. They'll be loyal. Watch and see!" He smiled brightly.

Oh, Marcus would watch, all right. For those men would either owe Caesar their lives or be his utmost peril.

Marcus returned to Rome several days ahead of Caesar's winding retinue.

He found the city paralyzed by fear. Apparently, traveling Gauls had showed up in the Forum, causing a stir by announcing that Pompeian renegades had formed a new army and were marching on the city. People panicked. Shops closed and plebs took to the streets, crying and tearing their hair.

It had also turned cold—early autumn's first chilly breath made Marcus long for warmth. He decided to surprise Fulvia, and his blood pulsed, thinking of the lovemaking he'd soon enjoy.

Moonlight poured into a narrow alley leading to the back entrance of his domus. Two doormen in the back of the house hastily arose to greet him. They were the back-door janitors, set to guard against unwanted intruders.

"Welcome home, Dominus," they both murmured as he hastened past.

Marcus was carrying his helmet and, on a whim, put it on. A mischievous idea took hold. He crossed through part of the peristyle courtyard, finding the overlap in the building design leading to his and Fulvia's spacious cubiculum. There was a lovely terrace attached with a low wall. He hefted one leg up at a time. Then he intentionally landed noisily, snickering to himself. She'd certainly hear that.

Face hidden inside his helmet, he reached up quickly to tie his cheek-guards securely before she appeared, covering both his chin and mouth. Just a few short steps around the corner brought him face-to-face with Fulvia, who met him boldly, brandishing a small dagger.

"Who are you?" she demanded.

"A messenger—from your husband, lady." Marcus lifted his voice's pitch. Funny! He could practically see her heart leaping beneath her breasts, despite her courage.

"Why did you come in this way? And where is he?" she asked breathlessly.

He sprang forward and grabbed her shoulders, kissing her full on the mouth before she could scream or utter a gasp. She manipulated the blade, poised dangerously to strike his groin. But his hand was ready and caught her wrist. The weapon clanged noisily to the floor. Fulvia wriggled from his grasp, shoving both hands hard against his bronze cuirass, pounding with both fists until his whisper stilled her. "It's me!"

Instantaneously, her fear morphed into lust, and he felt her softness yield to passion. She dropped her head back and laughed in eager pleasure.

"I'll be consul in the new year."

Fulvia's eyes lit like lamps. "You did it! You and Caesar are reconciled."

It was Marcus's turn to laugh. Then he covered her mouth with his, guiding her toward their sleeping couch.

Each citizen was included in Caesar's triumphs, receiving wine, sausage, and bread at street corner stalls. Thousands celebrated and drank in the Forum Romanum. Swags of roses and late-blooming wildflowers adorned monuments. Temples were scrubbed and cleansed of graffiti, and Suburan fullers and other guildsmen even shut down their businesses to honor the dictator.

The only people not reveling were slaves toiling at the imperator's new forum site. His new temple to Venus Genetrix stood majestically, gleaming in polished marble veneer. Its elevated base alone was half the height of the proposed new Curia building, whose foundation now supported the beginnings of walls. No doubt, Caesar had purposefully designed the temple to dwarf the Senate's building.

Banners hung from scaffolding, splashing color along the Via Sacra, where conquering legions marched throughout the week. Each of Caesar's victories received an entire day of festivities, making these triumphs the longest party in Rome's memory.

Marcus rode in the Gallic triumph. He led Legio XII, which he'd commanded at Bibracte. In front of the marching men, just behind enormous gilt carts bearing Gallic treasure, Legio XII was followed by hundreds of mustached chieftains and warriors in chains.

Meanwhile, Vercingetorix was towed in a rolling cage. After years spent inside the Tullianum, awaiting this day, his life had been nothing but anguish. Long, matted hair framed a face that was imperceptible due to thick blue woad that legionaries had used to cover his pallor. It added to the drama and attempted to hide his gauntness after being imprisoned for so long. Manacles dwarfed his now-frail body, and he sat in one corner of his cart, broken and listless. He was but a wraith of the wild-haired barbarian king he'd been in Gallia Comata. Bits of rotten fruit, chicken bones, and rocks pelted him as the oxen hauled him along.

This was his final journey. Later he'd be strangled, as Lentulus was.

Marcus regretted that. Vercingetorix had been a worthy adversary—worthier than Pompeius, even. What a pity that Caesar's mercy didn't extend to him, as it had Cicero, Brutus, and others. Such was the fate of a defeated foreigner at the hands of Rome.

A few days later, Marcus, Fulvia, and Mother were welcomed by Uncle Hybrida at his home overlooking the Forum. Uncle was thrilled to have been pardoned, and Caesar had even returned his former property to him.

Together, the Antonii gawked at the wealthy display of Egyptian wares in the Alexandrian triumph. Cleopatra's sister, Arsinoe, who had raised arms against Caesar along with her late brother Ptolemy, walked in chains. Arsinoe was quite striking and fiercely courageous. Dressed in a simple long woolen tunic, she held her head high. The plebs honored her nerve. At first, they fell silent, then chanted for Caesar to be merciful to her.

He responded in kind, sparing Arsinoe's life and sending her into exile to far-away Ephesus to take refuge in the Temple of Artemis.

After the triumph, the family reclined on couches overlooking the Forum when Uncle Hybrida ambled out of the house, followed by a bevy of slaves bearing trays of delicacies. "Sweet family, it's time to *feast*!" he exclaimed, beaming.

"I am feasting," Mother laughed. "With my eyes! The city's never been so alive."

Though a mere shadow of the strapping, unpolished man who had once dreamed of military glory, gray-headed Hybrida radiated joy. Marcus had relented and sent Tonia to move in with him and Antonia. Hybrida joyfully embraced his role as grandfather, buying the girl baubles and a kitten. Crowned with the same shining auburn hair as her mother, quiet little Tonia loved her grandfather's dotage. Antonia had put on weight, no longer bothering much with her own appearance. She stayed well out of Marcus's way, not deigning to speak to or even look at Fulvia.

"Perhaps that's what Caesar really is—a Titan," Hybrida suggested with a crooked grin, scooting onto a bench beside them.

"Maybe . . . " Mother pondered. "Look at the size of that new temple. It's as though Titans have moved into Rome. Oh, these lavish games and entertainments sweep me away, it's true. An entire month of the year is renamed 'Julius'? Shouldn't it all please me since I share his gens? Yet I wonder—"

"That it's all too much?" Marcus asked. "That he's being adorned with the trappings of kingship?" It's what a lot of men in the Senate were muttering—though not in awe and wonder.

Fulvia smiled, nodding her head, gazing out at the city. "We owe him much. Many people do." She dropped her head back, laughing aloud, gold and garnet earrings swinging from her ears. One of her hands strayed to Marcus's, grasping it. "What's next, my love? Deification?"

Marcus chuckled. "Actually, there's talk of it. And he'll probably take on permanent dictatorship."

"No!" Mother gasped at him, incredulous. "Anyone granted such honor is bound to suffer hubris."

"Mother, he's done things no man has done since Alexander the Great," Marcus reminded her.

In thoughtful silence, they all gazed down into the Forum; a group of plebs far below were shaking their fists, jumping about in euphoric glee, chanting, "Caesar, Caesar, Caesar!"

Marcus was rather surprised at Mother's reaction. After all, who was he now? Soon he'd be *Consul* Marcus Antonius. Caesar had made it so. Yet it was an unending paradox. Pompeius was defeated and gone, Rome was at peace—the most powerful nation on earth with Caesar at its mighty head.

Then why did he feel such unease?

Marcus paraded down the path to Caesar's Janiculum villa, surrounded by his consular lictors. Up on the villa's terrace, Cleopatra was laughing and holding little Caesarion. Their mirth echoed off the stonework. Snowflakes feathering Rome in white dusted her face and that of her son.

Unused to the cold weather, a warm fur mantle covered most

of her rich Greek-style gown. Gold glittered on her ears. Caesarion playfully reached into the air, snatching at flakes.

Marcus smiled, stopping in his tracks; his lictors followed on cue. He watched her, recalling their first meeting in Alexandria. When he'd met her at fourteen, her most urgent desire in visiting Rome had been to see snow. His heart felt glad to see her having that chance.

It was a glorious day despite the cold. And what a relief *not* having Fulvia here. The woman had a controlling nature that Marcus hadn't noticed prior to their marriage. She wanted to be involved in everything he did, socially, politically, and by Mars—she probably wished she could march with a legion!

Recently, they'd attended two social engagements that included Cleopatra, and both times Fulvia had questioned him suspiciously afterward about the queen. Granted, it really was astounding. In the rare moments he and Cleopatra were together, they always resumed easy conversation as though they'd been friends for millennia. Certainly, Fulvia had sense enough to know he'd never lure the queen from Caesar. Such a dalliance would permanently sever his ties to the dictator.

He assured his wife that her concerns were ridiculous. But he had to admit—Cleopatra was remarkable. Did she really love Caesar? Surely not. He was more than twice her age. Despite Caesar's reputation for womanizing, Marcus couldn't imagine any sort of deep romance between them. Friendship? More likely. Or rather, Cleopatra simply did what was necessary to preserve her kingdom.

He wouldn't fault her there.

Upon entering the villa's magnificent atrium, Marcus found Caesar headed outside to join the queen. The dictator may not have been pleased at first that she'd brought the boy, but he was proud of the little fellow. And Caesarion's presence had spurred lots of talk about who Caesar's heir would be. Legally speaking, he was out of the question. He was foreign-born. Of course, Caesar could easily make provision for him in some other way—even adopt him. Or might he simply change Roman law?

After pondering that, Marcus thought not. There was controversy with everything Caesar did. Oh, Caesarion would rule someday, but it would be in Egypt. Declaring him legitimate now might cause another war since Cicero, Cassius Longinus, and Marcus Brutus would never cater to that.

Truth be told, nothing was any easier since Pompeius's defeat and death. Caesar was master of everything except people's minds.

Tonight hundreds of guests would arrive here at Caesar's Janiculum estate for a party thrown by the queen. But today Marcus was here to honor Caesar's great-nephew, Gaius Octavian.

As soon as winter was done, Octavian would depart for Greece to study. Then, next spring, he remained Caesar's choice to accompany him into Parthia. The very thought made Marcus grind his teeth. It was standard practice for former consuls to become governors of provinces. Marcus's upcoming official status as consul fated him as being the next governor of someplace. Caesar had chosen Macedonia for him. Thus he'd be sitting on the sidelines again instead of accompanying Caesar on what had to be the adventure of a lifetime—the conquest of Parthia.

It rankled him.

As for this afternoon, only a few people were attending Caesar's personal invitation on his great-nephew's behalf. Marcus had been invited without Mother or Fulvia. However, it meant that Fulvia would be asking detailed questions later—questions concerning the queen, of course.

"Even my own family is at war with itself," Caesar had remarked earlier that week. "Atia refuses to come to her own son's party because Cleopatra is hosting it. And I knew not to ask your mother. She's almost as traditional as Atia and far too close to Calpurnia."

The Janiculum villa was Caesar's retreat, a private property he shared with few people aside from his royal mistress. Lamps and braziers warmed the interior on this snowy winter day. Greek art mingled tastefully with Egyptian pieces; elegant furnishings and colorful mosaics offset vivid wall paintings depicting natural history.

Marcus followed the sound of voices and laughter and found himself in a small indoor triclinium painted sumptuously in a Nilotic scene. Brightly lit with high lampstands and warmed by braziers, he could almost imagine being in Egypt again, surrounded by lounging crocodiles and simple fishermen. It had probably been redecorated, in anticipation for Cleopatra's visit.

On the dining couch was the honored guest, Octavian, his sister, Octavia, and another young lady. Marcus joined them, relaxing on the soft upholstery opposite the two women, who were entertaining a kitten with strands of beads.

Marcus studied Octavia. Some men claimed she was one of the most beautiful women in Rome. Strange he'd never noticed her before. She had long sand-colored hair gathered into a loose bun. Pale, flawless skin accompanied rosy cheeks and a sweet, serene smile on an honest, innocent face. Unlike her younger brother, her features were gentle despite those cool, light blue eyes the siblings shared.

Now that he saw them together, Marcus noted that Octavian was shorter than his sister. He had to bite his lip to hide a scornful smile. The boy's sandals were built up with thick soles, elevating his height. Carefully trimmed, wavy reddish-blond hair curled over ears that were altogether too large for his slight frame. Woolen leggings and a long-sleeved tunic warmed him beneath a dark brown toga.

"Salve," Octavia interrupted his thoughts with her kind smile and warm voice. "Let me introduce my friend Scribonia."

Marcus smiled. "It's my pleasure."

Scribonia blushed. "And mine, Consul-elect." She was attractive, but not near as lovely as Octavia.

"Have you begun any preparations for your governance in Macedonia?" Octavian asked.

Of all the things he could ask . . . "It's a year off yet," Marcus reminded him.

"Well, it's your assigned province after your consulship, and I'm sure Caesar will want you knowledgeable about it before taking command there."

Marcus narrowed his eyes slightly at Octavian's imperious tone. Damn, he was irritating! "Remember, I won't take the curule chair until Januarius."

"My husband, Marcellus, visited Macedonia once," Octavia said, saving the moment. "He says it gets terribly cold in the winter—much colder than it does here."

Marcus smiled at her when her brother butted in like a goat. "Places get cold, Sister," he stated, his voice flat and matter-of-fact. "Even desert countries, such as that of our hostess, become frigid at night during winter."

"Have you traveled abroad?" Octavia asked Marcus in genuine curiosity.

He decided he liked this girl. She was polite, direct, and kind, much like Calpurnia, only far more beautiful. "I have. Greece, Syria, Egypt, and of course, Gaul. Gods, it was cold *there*! I remember gulping porridge down as fast as possible some mornings before it froze over!"

Both the young women laughed.

"See, Brother," Octavia tittered, "there's nothing wrong in traveling a bit. Look at Antonius. He's healthy as an ox, so Apollonia will be good for you, I think. And it shouldn't be overly cold there."

"Caesar once sent me to Greece for my education too," Marcus offered. Maybe that would help him find some common ground with Octavian. "If you dislike the notion of going, I did too, at first. But once there, I fell in love with Greek culture."

Octavian lay still on the dining couch, rigid and austere as a Doric column. It was impossible to ascertain what he was thinking beyond those calculating eyes.

"My purpose in Apollonia is not to enjoy a holiday, but to study and prepare myself for the Parthian campaign. Caesar intends to keep me at his side, you know. Me—and my friends."

That stung like a scorpion's barb, and Marcus had nothing to say in return. He was still mortified that this delicate, inexperienced youth and his "friends" had all been chosen over him to share the glory of the Parthian conquest at Caesar's side.

Caesar may have rewarded him with the consulship, but Marcus sensed that the man no longer trusted him as he once did. Still, he forced a smile, unabashedly relishing his next remark. "Parthia lies far in the East. It'll be an exhausting journey for anyone with fragile health."

Octavian didn't hesitate. "Oh, my dear friend Marcus Agrippa is helping me prepare. I intend to be of great service to Uncle."

"*Great*-uncle, you mean," Marcus corrected in a low voice. Sensing a presence nearby, he glanced up.

It was Cleopatra, still holding her son. "Octavian, Caesar and I have something for you. Antonius, come join us too. Octavia and Scribonia may stay since they're so enjoying my cat. I'd never presume to disturb them."

Octavia glanced at the queen appreciatively, then turned her head back to Scribonia as she tossed some beads onto the floor, causing the kitten to leap off her lap in pursuit.

Marcus excused himself, arose, and followed Octavian, Caesar, and Cleopatra down a corridor to a small indoor garden complete with dancing fountains.

On an ebony table rested a small box wrapped in the finest purple silk.

Caesar gestured to the gift. "It's for you, dear boy. Open it!"

Octavian looked first at Caesar and then Cleopatra. His gaze was so serious it was nearly comical. "For me?"

"Yes," Caesar affirmed. "I wanted to give you something before you left, and this token was the queen's idea. It once belonged to her father, Ptolemy Auletes."

"And to his father before him," Cleopatra added, nodding graciously.

Why Marcus was asked here, he had no idea. He watched Octavian untie the fabric, lifting out a small ivory box. Inside was a flawless onyx intaglio ring bearing the image of a sphinx.

"Magnificent," Octavian gasped, mesmerized.

Caesar sat down abruptly on a marble bench behind Cleopatra, looking gray and stiff. "I saw the real sphinx while in Egypt," he reminisced distractedly, one hand rubbing between his eyes. "What a marvel! Octavian, you must visit it one day."

"Egypt? Perhaps I shall go there," Octavian murmured, examining his gift.

"I shall ready one of the finest rooms in the palace for you," Cleopatra promised, smiling warmly. "It shall await your visit." She passed Caesarion off to one of her maids, who quietly left with the child.

"What do you think of the gift?" Caesar asked Marcus, shifting uncomfortably. "Is it worthy of him?"

Worthy of him? "Well—now he must earn it with hard studying and training for the Parthian War, mustn't he?" Irritating little dung-beetle had probably never even lifted a gladius.

Marcus saw Caesar's eyes suddenly widen, his face looking almost crazed. He uttered what sounded like a stifled cough and collapsed sideways onto the ground. Cleopatra whirled about and dropped to his side.

But it was Octavian who moved faster than Marcus thought him capable. He rushed to Caesar's side, roughly shoving the queen away and pulling out a small ivory stick from a tiny bag at his side. He forced it firmly between Caesar's lips.

Visibly quaking, Caesar was rigid as a leather scabbard. A foamy lather oozed on both sides of his mouth where Octavian had forced the utensil in.

"He's divine—" Cleopatra breathed in revered awe. "It's the falling sickness." In wonder, as though worshipping her lover, she caressed Caesar's twitching arms and shoulders as he convulsed.

"How long has this been going on?" Marcus demanded, voice low as he glanced about, relieved to see no slaves lurking in the shadows. "Does it happen often?"

"I first saw it in Spain," Octavian answered. "It happened frequently there, so he kept me near him in case of an attack."

Well, that explained a lot. Octavian's presence wasn't for sex, but to help during one of these onslaughts. Ho! If any of the Optimates caught wind of it . . .

"He collapsed twice in Egypt," Cleopatra recalled. "My physician Olympos says that men with this condition are closest to the gods."

With a gasp and sudden fit of coughing, Caesar finally came to himself, his taut body relaxing. He looked spent, a sheen of cold sweat on his brow. Marcus helped Octavian turn him onto his side, bloody spume dripping from one side of his mouth.

"He's bleeding?" Marcus murmured worriedly.

"He bit his tongue during the seizure," Octavian replied, shaking his head. "I was unable to force the rod in fast enough. It's over now. He just needs to rest."

Caesar remained pale and unable to rise, both hands still shaking.

Marcus stepped in to assist. Carefully, he hoisted Caesar up over his shoulder and followed Cleopatra to her private chamber. Inside was a palatial sleeping couch covered with cushions and dried lavender. As he lowered Caesar across it, Marcus looked hard at both the queen and Octavian, giving voice to what they all were thinking.

"Nobody must find out about this."

CHAPTER XXI

44BC

OUTSIDE POMPEIUS'S THEATER, WHERE THE SENATE STILL met on a regular basis, Caesar grabbed Marcus's arm and leaned in. "Antonius, right after you make your Lupercal run tomorrow, offer me a crown of laurel and let's see what happens."

Marcus frowned. "The Senate will not—"

"Don't you think I know that!" Caesar snapped. "When they refuse, I'll transfer the honor to Jupiter Rex. The plebs love shows of piety. However, I want to know where the people's hearts are."

Since returning from Spain, Marcus had seen more change in Caesar's personality. Power, privilege, and distinctions of every sort had spiraled him into a strange sort of fantasy-like state in which he acted like a king, high priest, or god. Optimates blamed it on Cleopatra's influence, but Marcus knew something they didn't.

It was the falling illness meddling with his brain.

"A crown of laurel?" Fulvia exclaimed when Marcus told her of Caesar's request. "How arrogant. The Optimates will prevent him from accepting kingship."

"Careful. You may underestimate him," Marcus countered. He

figured anything was possible now. "He's the people's champion. Given the right circumstances, he might be crowned king."

Caesar had become notorious for bending and breaking rules since Alesia, traipsing on Roman tradition like a slave stomping grapes. As co-consul, Marcus found himself in the uncomfortable position of abettor. No longer did it matter whether he disagreed with something. As Caesar's fellow consul, he was expected to play the role of supporter.

Tomorrow was Lupercalia.

It was an ancient fertility rite, and its traditions went back so far nobody really knew who had started it. Marcus was one of the selected men who would strip down to nothing but loincloths and run through the streets with a piece of animal hide, whacking women who wanted to become pregnant.

Some Optimates, Cicero included, were outraged that a consul of Rome would be running naked during a public festival.

Good! That meant it was bound to be a memorable day.

Inside a cavern-like grotto overlooking the Circus Maximus, Marcus knelt on the stone floor with a handful of other naked men chosen to run for Lupercalia. Legend held this to be the very cave where a she-wolf suckled Romulus and Remus.

Priests were singing repetitive phrases in some ancient tongue long forgotten to modern ears. Busily skinning each sacrifice, they took turns with the verses in nasal, two-part harmony. It was messy business, blood and entrails littering their work space next to a sizzling altar.

"Marcus Antonius."

Marcus arose.

An approaching priest dipped one hand in a vat containing dog and goat blood, smearing his forehead liberally. For some reason, lost in centuries of tradition, he was expected to laugh aloud at this moment. He let his head fall back and laughed heartily, filling the cave with such infectious jollity that others, including the priests, started grinning and chuckled too.

Little did they know what was coming at the end of the runner's course. For all any of them knew, they might have a new king in Rome today.

One priest handed him a narrow slice of goatskin to cover his loins. Marcus tied it about his waist and between his legs. Bowing his head obediently, he opened his hands. Within moments, slick, warm strips of newly shredded dog and goat hide februa were placed atop his palms. Clumsily, he braided them into a whip to be used on women passing his way. Another priest offered him another silver basin of blood, and he dunked the braided februa into it, letting it soak. After removing it, his hands were red and dripping, as was the februa.

The Lupercal priests headed to the cave entrance, scattering blood as far as they could. One gave the sacred utterance, "Go, anointed ones! Sprinkle Rome's women to make them fertile for the gods' use!"

First out of the cave, Marcus bolted down the narrow path where girls were already waiting, hitching up tunics and exposing bare legs, thighs, and buttocks. Warmth pulsed through his veins despite the chill air, warming him. The sight of comely women baring extremities charged his blood.

Still, he thought ahead to today's plan. He had to find Fulvia . . .

Militarily trained, he ran well ahead of the others. Women and men pressed close about him, screaming. Now at the foot of the Palatine, he entered the Forum. The Lupercal route through Rome would end at the Rostra, where Caesar waited, sitting on a recently bestowed golden throne.

Marcus mindlessly smacked the rump of a plebian girl. She giggled and screeched, rejoining the crowd. He looked ahead, scanning the area. Where was Fulvia? She said she'd be near olive trees next to the new Curia construction.

Bare feet hammering the pavement, sweat beaded Marcus's forehead, spiting the cold. Every single exhale turned to mist in the clear morning air. Prostitutes at a food stall whistled and called as he passed, admiring his lean, powerful body. His muscles were rigid whenever he stopped suddenly or whirled about, lashing out with his februa to switch a hopeful female. Part of the crowd started shouting his name in rhythm, so he lifted his februa, grinning and waving at them in response.

Soon he was jogging the final course down the Via Sacra, well ahead of other participants. Another well-dressed lady, probably a senator's wife by the look of her, lunged out before him, expecting a slap. Without hesitating, he whipped her bare leg.

He continued his course, this time nearing the Curia edifice, panting.

That's when Fulvia materialized as planned, lifting her silken stola so that one long, sleek thigh was visible. Undaunted by his sweaty, blood-smeared face, she reached out, wrapping one arm about his neck, forcing him to meet her in a kiss.

Nearly naked, Marcus couldn't help but feel aroused as her bare leg arced up to wrap around his hip, her hot tongue seeking his. Fulvia was a singular woman, brazenly embracing things most females would never dare. He had to admit his wife was full of sensual surprises. How many men could say that? Plebs in the crowd cheered loudly, welcoming their display as part of the fertility rite. Marcus half felt like backing her against the olive tree and taking her here—in front of the crowd. Ha! What would Rome think of that?

By now, his februa had dried, so he brushed it down her bare leg like a caress. Fulvia laughed, playfully biting his earlobe before pulling away. She snatched the februa from his hand and discreetly replaced it with something else: stiff, smooth bay leaves encircled into a corona.

"Go crown the king," she whispered sarcastically in his ear.

With a deep breath, he turned and strode toward Caesar's dais on the Rostra. Renovations on the old monument had just been completed this week—ones he had sponsored. "Marcus Antonius made this" was chiseled on the marble veneer beneath Caesar's seat.

Looping the corona over his shoulder, he gripped the beak of a captured enemy ship, hoisting himself atop the platform with ease. Next to Caesar, he lifted the corona high, the mob screaming with excitement.

Marcus lifted his other hand to silence the people. As they settled, he moved the corona above Caesar's head. "A crown for a king!" he cried loudly so all could hear, his bare chest heaving from his run.

At first, everyone responded in a fervor, wildly jumping, hooting, and calling. Marcus was beginning to think he really would be crowning Caesar. Presently, however, he noticed movement to his left.

Ah yes. Here they came.

A large delegation of Optimates, including Marcus Junius Brutus and Gaius Cassius, began shouting and waving fists in protest. As obedient as sheep, plebs saw them and gradually fell silent.

The Optimates' ire only made Marcus enjoy the moment more. Why not make a *real* show of it? Brazenly, he lifted the corona again above Caesar's head, tempting Fate. "I ask you, people of Rome!" he thundered. "Should our Caesar wear a crown?" But this time the horde was hesitant and restive. Some people in the back started to boo, joined by the Optimates.

At that, Caesar stood, smiling pleasantly and lifting his hand for silence, ever capable of hiding his inward feelings. "Antonius," he ordered, "let us crown Jupiter Rex, Rome's one and *only* sovereign!"

That pleased everyone, plebs and even Optimate senators cheered. Damn, but Caesar knew how to appease a multitude! Then came the usual chant of "Caesar, Caesar, Caesar . . ."

Marcus leaped from the Rostra, jogging past the Tabularium and heading uphill to the Capitoline, where the great Temple of Jupiter Optimus Maximus stood. As he ran, he held the corona high, its shining waxen leaves shimmering in the sun.

Since Lupercalia, Caesar's actions had been full of great urgency. It was as though he had decided to force himself upon Rome, whether the city was ready for him or not. Immersed in preparations for the Parthian campaign, he erected a gilt likeness of Cleopatra inside his magnificent Temple of Venus Genetrix. Upon its dedication, Gaius Cassius railed about it, demanding Caesar answer for placing a foreign queen in the very heart of Rome. Marcus Junius Brutus also condemned the act, asking the Senate whether Caesar considered himself divine, now that he'd blatantly confirmed that his mistress was.

"It raises eyebrows. He's only asking for trouble by placing her statue inside a temple's holy grounds," Mother reasoned inside the litter after the temple's dedication.

Marcus considered the statue pleasing to the eye but was forced to agree. For years, he had been prepared to embrace Caesar as Rome's sole leader. He thought that, by now, Rome would be ready too. But now uncertainty dogged him. Caesar was full of self-importance and interested in nothing but *his* projects, *his* Parthian campaign, *his* self-glorification . . .

It seemed unreal that in just a few weeks Caesar would head east to Greece. Marcus would remain in Rome until after his term as consul ended. Then he'd sail to Macedonia to assume his proconsulship. Caesar would be there, waiting on him, with Octavian. And they'd wait until all of the grand army was gathered by the next spring. Then they'd depart for Parthia to avenge Crassus and reverse the humiliation Rome had suffered.

And Marcus Antonius would sit in Macedonia—*damn* it all!

Marcus Aemilius Lepidus was magister equitum, the office

Marcus held prior to his demotion. Lepidus was an affable sort, not overly ambitious and capable of working well with men who were.

It turned out that he was an exceptional host as well. Tonight's event was a small dinner party—men only—to discuss an important Senate meeting taking place the next day.

For once, Caesar was in fine spirits. And no wonder! He'd spent the entire afternoon with Cleopatra.

As cups were refilled after dinner, Piso remarked, "Damn, but that Cassius is becoming openly hostile."

Caesar sloshed Falernian around in his cup before sipping and speaking. "He's a typical Optimate—always has been. But I agree he's an enigma. Personally, I was hoping some of Brutus's good manners would rub off on him, but he continues to be blunt, gruff, and set in his ways."

"I'm afraid he's dangerous," Piso warned. "You should consider reinstating your personal guard."

Marcus nodded. "I've already told him that." Only days ago, Caesar had done the unthinkable, dismissing his trusted bodyguards. Did the man have a death wish?

Caesar laughed. "Antonius has pleaded with me to do so. And so has your daughter. But to what end, Piso? Can Caesar not freely walk in Rome among his people? These men are merely exercising their views. Many of them were spared after Pompeius's war, so they owe me allegiance."

Unable to hold back any longer, Marcus exploded in frustration. "But they never *give* it, do they? You insist they're loyal, but their every word is *venomous.* Piso is right. You're inviting disaster upon yourself."

Lepidus interfered, trying to gentle the conversation. "Gentlemen, end the frustration and let's celebrate. Caesar has been assured that tomorrow the Senate is giving him a parting gift before he leaves for Parthia. They're bestowing sovereign powers upon him throughout all of our provinces, excluding only Rome proper."

Silence fell for several moments before Piso rubbed his chin, saying softly, "Then you will be a king? It will be so?"

"Except in Rome," Lepidus reiterated.

"I cannot deny the people if they wish to honor me so," Caesar said proudly.

"Only take care," Marcus heard himself say. "These men we just spoke of—the Brutuses and Cassiuses—aren't likely to throw you a party tomorrow night in honor of the occasion. I happen to know their intentions. We've talked about it before."

"And they are?" Piso inquired, eyebrows raised.

"They want to *kill* him."

Caesar reached out, chuckling and clapping Marcus on the back. "Antonius! Just look at him, friends. This courageous killer of Gauls has become as fretful as a poor widow these last months." When Marcus shook his head, ready to argue, Caesar held up a hand, preventing his protest. "With your powerful physique at my side, who would raise a hand against me?"

Everyone laughed except Marcus.

Outside, a low rumble of distant thunder was the harbinger of an approaching storm.

"You think my concern is funny," Marcus admonished, "but I happen to know these men would smile to see you dead."

Everyone was silent a little too long after that until Lepidus said, "We all have men in our lives who would smile to see ill fortune find us. And yet they hold their peace, as will Brutus and Cassius. Caesar's right. They're simply opining."

Thunder rolled again, closer this time.

Lepidus added, "Listen to that. You know, my father always spurned the belief that thunder heralds approaching doom. He always drank to a peaceful passing—and he was graced with one, dying quietly in his bed. I hope to do the same." He snorted good-naturedly. "It's the best way to go, I think. What about all of you?"

"Change the subject!" someone else called out.

"Indeed," Piso said. "What a morbid direction our evening's taking, Lepidus. And who here has the power to determine how or when death occurs? I only hope my family would be well cared for. Not to mention my library!"

Everyone laughed, Piso raising his cup of wine and grinning before drinking. His literary collection at his expansive villa in Herculaneum was the most impressive one in all Italia.

Marcus felt their eyes on him next. He disliked talking about death. Mother believed it invited bad luck. He doubted that, but why tempt Fate? He shrugged, saying, "I should like to die honorably. Never at the hand of an enemy."

The others raised a toast to that, Caesar muttering, "Well-spoken, Antonius."

"And you, Caesar?" Lepidus asked curiously.

Through the high triclinium windows, lightning flashed, followed by a deafening clap of thunder.

Gaius Julius Caesar stared long and hard into his wine cup before responding, his blue eyes blazing. "How would I want death to come?" he pondered aloud. "Quick and unexpected."

Marcus nodded approval and joined the others as they drank to Caesar's preference for mortality.

> *Calpurnia to Marcus Antonius, Consul:*
>
> *This morning my husband is unwell. Please extend his regrets to the Senate, as he will be unable to attend today's meeting.*

Marcus tossed Calpurnia's note to the floor, then rolled over on his sleeping couch.

During the night, a powerful storm had rocked Rome from one end to the other. Winds were still jiggling the window shutters softly and rhythmically, just enough to induce sleep.

Marcus pulled Fulvia close, snuggling into her warmth to ward off the cool air. If Caesar wasn't going to the Senate, he'd stay home too.

Nearly adrift again, he heard soft footsteps.

"Dominus, a second message has arrived," Eros whispered.

Looking up groggily, he saw the slave clutching a scroll. "From whom?"

"Senator Decimus Brutus Albinus. He says Caesar is attending the session, after all."

Marcus had never much liked Decimus Brutus, who was of no close relation to Marcus Junius Brutus. He'd been another close friend of Clodius and Curio who frequented their brothel back in the old days. And never once had he paid anything to support it. Marcus considered him just another bad memory. But it wasn't until the time of Pompeius's sole consular rule that Decimus transformed into an unpleasant, and outspoken Optimate.

Marcus rubbed sleep from his eyes, considering. Why would Decimus Brutus be intervening to get Caesar *to* the Senate? That sounded suspicious.

Hackles raised, he threw the coverlet off.

"What day is it?" mumbled Fulvia, stretching and turning over.

"The ides of Martius," Marcus replied, yawning. "Eros, get my toga. It seems I must look like a consul today after all."

CHAPTER XXII

MARCUS WALKED TO CAESAR'S DOMUS, FLANKED BY HIS consular lictors. Winter's chill was loath to release Italia, and even while waiting in the crowded atrium, he shoved both hands into the sinuses of his purple-striped toga for warmth.

Once he finally appeared, Caesar elected to take his small sedan chair to Pompeius's theater. Marcus walked behind it, along with his lictors and several important clients of Caesar's.

As the theater came into view, a bearded man scurried out from the press surrounding Caesar's delegation and shouldered toward the dictator's transfer.

Suspicious, Marcus barked, "Stop him!"

Instantly surrounded by rods and axes, the stranger yanked off his hood and raised his hands, yielding. "Please, please—no violence! I am Artemidorus, a teacher of logic. I have an urgent message for Caesar. It's vital that he see it."

Marcus snatched the sealed scroll out of the logician's hands. "What's so important?" he demanded, examining the wax seal.

Artemidorus narrowed rheumy old eyes at Marcus with reservation. "It is for Caesar, not anyone else." Pausing only a moment, his lip trembled slightly before he added, "I beg you, Consul, he must see this *now*. If you are loyal, give it to him!"

Marcus glanced ahead in annoyance; Caesar's retinue was getting farther and farther ahead. His lictors stood to the side, scrutinizing Artemidorus.

Irritating old fool! "Be on your way, and I'll give it to him," Marcus growled under his breath.

With that, he and his lictors moved ahead with long, rapid strides through the crowds. By the time they caught up with Caesar's litter, they had arrived at the grand theater of Pompeius. Marcus carefully passed the scroll through the curtains.

"Probably someone's petition," he said.

"Concerning what?" Caesar demanded. Slaves were arranging a small wooden step onto which he'd dismount.

Marcus shrugged. "I have no idea of the contents. Some Greek logician said it was important. Read it later if you want."

Caesar muttered unpleasantly about being heckled night and day, so Marcus left the scroll in his hands and let it go. He signaled his lictors to wait near the litter and accompanied Caesar up the stairs and into the vestibule. Tight clusters of senators, clients, and foreign delegates made it slow going.

The Curia chamber inside the theater was smaller than the original. Its capacity handled most of Rome's original Senate. However, Caesar had appointed hosts of new senators, their numbers far exceeding the building's space. Hundreds of men's voices reverberated within the chamber.

Just as they progressed into the assembly hall, Marcus felt someone grip his shoulder from behind.

"Antonius."

Turning around, he was face-to-face with Gaius Trebonius.

"Ah, later, my friend," Marcus said. "I'm attending Caesar. After the session, perhaps?"

Trebonius entreated, "Surely you can make time for a brother at arms, Consul. Today you *owe* it to me."

Marcus raised his brow at Trebonius's presumptive tone. "I owe you nothing."

Looking back, he saw Caesar proceeding alone into the Curia chamber. And within heartbeats, the dictator disappeared completely, engulfed in a sea of togate men, attendants, and public slaves bustling about to find seats or deliver last-minute messages before the meeting started.

Ready to follow, Marcus hadn't even turned around before he felt a large, fleshy body behind him. Then another pressed close on his right. Hefty slaves had materialized on every side, as if from nowhere. The one behind him whispered, "Call out and I stick you like a boar."

Meanwhile, Trebonius was pleasantly urging, "Come, join me." He moved closer so Marcus could hear. "Trust me when I say you do owe me a *great* deal today."

"What is this?" Marcus hissed. "Caesar awaits me, and we have pressing business. Call off your thugs!"

Nobody moved, but Marcus felt a sharp blade press between his shoulder blades, the bald man in front sneering, "Not so loud, Consul. My dominus asked you to come politely."

The Curia vestibule had nearly emptied. Most everyone was inside, only stragglers hurrying in, hoping to find room in the back.

Marcus had no choice but to follow Trebonius. As he glanced about desperately, he spied Eros just coming in. As usual, the slave knew to meet his master inside, anticipating Marcus's customary requests for wine or errand-running during meetings. In a flash, their eyes met. Marcus nodded stiffly, his face tense and distressed. He hoped Eros would recognize danger and run for help.

Indeed, alarm dawned on Eros's face, and his eyes widened. The silent message was conveyed.

Marcus was driven into a small, dim shrine to Venus. Once inside, Trebonius's bodyguards retreated, closing and securing the heavy door. Marcus turned back, shouldering it hard, straining, trying to get out. It was no use.

Trebonius alone remained in the room with him.

"Are you mad?" Marcus fumed. "Arming your slaves in the Senate and threatening me? I'm *consul*, Trebonius! This is an outrage!"

"They're not the only ones bearing arms today," he revealed, pulling a pugio from his toga. "Today weapons are . . . necessary."

Marcus's breath caught in his throat. "You're going to kill me?"

Trebonius shook his head. "I have no intention of harming you. That's why you owe me."

"Stop your riddles!" Marcus hissed furiously, all patience gone.

"A host of men demanded your life last night."

"What 'host'?"

Trebonius just leaned against the wall, running one finger gingerly along the blade of his pugio. "The host killing Caesar as I speak. I warned you—tried inviting you to join us. Today we liberate Rome."

Marcus's blood iced in his veins. Clumsy in his toga, he scrambled desperately toward the single stair leading out. It mattered little now just how many bodyguards were outside. He'd tear that door apart by hand to warn Caesar in time!

Trebonius anticipated his response, bounding forward.

Marcus whirled around, grabbing Trebonius's pugio-laden wrist and twisting forcefully. They were much the same size and evenly matched. For a moment, either could have won the struggle. But then Trebonius stepped forward with one leg, gaining an advantage by shoving Marcus backward and pinning him to the door, pugio at his throat.

Overpowered, struggling was futile now. What was worse were the muffled sounds he heard outside. Scuffling, shouting, general panic . . .

Suddenly, the door burst open. Marcus staggered sideways to catch himself. All hope dimmed when one of Trebonius's slaves reported, "Safe now, Dominus."

"Is it done?" Trebonius asked.

"Aye."

"You killed him?" Marcus interrupted, incredulous and looking from one to the other. "Caesar is *dead*?"

"Yes," Trebonius confirmed. "And you owe me and Marcus Brutus your life. We refused to kill you. Cassius and the rest wanted your blood too, but you and I were comrades at arms and you saved my life once. The score's even now."

Abruptly, Trebonius disappeared out the door, brandishing his weapon and joining other voices shouting about liberty.

Stunned, Marcus stared down at his toga, spattered with droplets of blood from where Trebonius had held the pugio to his throat. He could hear his own ragged breathing, and his hands were trembling.

Caesar's luck had run out.

Marcus peered around the doorway. Someone shadowed the entry into the assembly space.

"Eros!"

The slave turned and hurried to him, horror etched on his face. "Are you safe, Dominus?"

Marcus nodded, willing his legs to move. "What happened?"

"I tried to follow you, but Trebonius's slaves guarded the door. Then I ran to the chamber for help. I overheard senators placing bets on how many blows it would take to bring him down! It must have been happening at that very moment! But there were so many people—I couldn't see anything."

Marcus paced to the chamber and stood at the gaping doorway. A few terrified slaves darted out in panic, their masters having already fled.

Far below, just as he'd once seen in one of his nightmares, Caesar's corpse lay in pools of blood on the mosaic floor, a colossal bronze of Pompeius Magnus in full armor towering above the murdered dictator of Rome.

Marcus squeezed his eyes shut in shock. Surely when he

reopened them—but, no. He wasn't dreaming. This was real. Caesar was dead and near his body lay a scroll, vaguely familiar.

"Watch the door," Marcus ordered Eros. Warily glancing about, he descended to the Senate floor, staring down at the bloodied man who had been his counsel for so many years. His scalp crawled as he passed bloody footprints stamped onto the stone floor, retreating from where Caesar lay—those of his fleeing murderers.

What cowards! He wasn't even armed.

Slowly, Marcus leaned down to retrieve the scroll, half-soaked in Caesar's blood. He swallowed bile at the brutality of his cousin's injuries. It was one thing to see gore on a battlefield, but Caesar was family.

Artemidorus's little wax seal was still intact. Snapping it loose with his thumb, Marcus read the clear, precise script, penned by a learned man:

> *Artemidorus, Teacher of Logic, to Gaius Julius Caesar, Dictator:*
>
> *I teach the sons of Decimus Brutus and Gaius Cassius Longinus. Today these men and others plan to murder you during the session.*

Marcus stopped reading. "Dear gods above—the old man was trying to *warn* him!"

Consternation, shame, and remorse all flooded his psyche. He'd carried this warning in his own hands! "Ho—if only I had *opened* it. If only he'd read it!" he exhaled aloud.

A gentle hand steadied him. "Would he have believed a stranger when he never believed you?" Eros had quietly come down. "You were his most loyal friend."

"And Decimus Brutus?" Marcus snarled, looking back at the tablet again. "That bastard convinced Caesar to come this morning, even after Calpurnia excused him. Oh, Decimus will die. I swear upon avenging Mars—someday they'll *all* die for this."

Emotions took hold, tears of revulsion flooding his eyes. Spirit lurching, as though in an earthquake, he vacillated from rage to grief and back again, while he stood, staring down at Caesar's blood-smeared corpse. If only time could be turned backward. Despite the self-absorbed, demanding master Caesar had become of late, how would Rome survive without him?

Marcus Antonius was now the first man in Rome. A cold sweat broke out on his brow as the cold realization of danger descended like a pall.

Breath catching in his throat, he knelt down on one knee, gently taking Caesar's hand and removing his signet ring. Stiff as an automated theatrical machine used to winch a god onto the stage, he clumsily pocketed the ring into his small purse under his toga. It would go to Calpurnia until an heir was named. Marcus's flesh crawled. Caesar's flesh was still warm, as though he was but asleep.

His hand trembled slightly as he reached up to dictator's face and closed his still, staring eyes. Marcus wasn't used to touching the dead, and a chill swept up his spine. Only then did he realize he'd not been breathing since first kneeling at Caesar's side. As though having run a race, he panted several times, croaking out a sob or two and shaking his head in disbelief.

Then years of soldiery checked his somersaulting feelings. Next came resolve. There was no time for grief. Not now.

Family first.

"Eros, go straight to the Palatine. See if Gaius and Lucius made it home. Tell them to assemble an armed escort and take Mother to my domus on the Esquiline. After you see to their safety, go to Calpurnia, then Queen Cleopatra. Tell them who you are and what has happened. Advise them to bolt their doors and remain in their residences until I'm able to secure the army and provide for their protection. Go—*now*!"

"Dominus, you may still be in danger!"

He was right. If Trebonius wasn't lying, only two conspirators had argued for his life. Others could still pose a significant threat if they were about. From the grim looks of Caesar's body, twenty to thirty men had probably participated. Perhaps even more had been indirectly involved.

Bloody butchers!

Eros waited, looking about, his face apprehensive.

"Do as I command." Marcus grimly left things as they were. "I'll see to my own safety."

Together, they ascended the steps, peering outside from the vestibule. Though Marcus didn't see any senator types, curious plebs were starting to near the steps of the building. Women were crying, and the typical mob-like confusion that was Rome on any given day was escalating.

Word had spread quickly.

Marcus stepped back into the shadows, stripping off his toga. "Give me your mantle."

Eros mutely obeyed, pulling his cloak over his head, fibula pin intact.

Marcus hitched up his broad-striped tunic marking him as consul and slipped Eros's garment over his head. Though too small for his large frame, it would do. Fortunately, it included a hood.

"Careful, Dominus," Eros whispered.

With only a wordless nod, Marcus left him, jogging down the stairs away from the crowd. Several older plebians approached, their eyes troubled. They probably only wanted to question him. However, he took no chances, bolting into a run past Caesar's new forum and disappearing into the Subura.

Rome's surviving consul ran for his life.

When Marcus finally made it home, Fulvia, Mother, Gaius, and Lucius were anxiously waiting in the atrium. Lucius immediately poured out his experience during the assassination before he and Gaius fled. "Some of those curs were saying they wanted our blood too, Brother," he insisted.

"It was anarchy," Gaius agreed. "So many men surrounded

Caesar that we never saw actual blood, just the assassins' fever to kill. Like a pack of wolves against one helpless gladiator."

"Is he really dead?" Mother murmured in stunned disbelief.

"Yes," Marcus panted, still winded from running. "Now listen, all of you—I'll be inviting Marcus Lepidus here, and I must take care. Last night I trusted him." Snorting in disgust, he shook his head, incredulous, "Damn! I trusted Trebonius and Decimus this morning! Now I don't even know my supporters from my enemies. Therefore I won't assume Lepidus is loyal until the army's in *my* hands."

They all stared at him in stunned silence.

Marcus continued thinking aloud. "According to Trebonius, most of them did want me dead. Since you're my family, that means all of you could be in danger too. Do *not* leave this domus without my permission. Understood? Gaius, Lucius—see that every entrance, both public and private, is barricaded and guarded, night and day. Hurry!"

"Is the city in a state of war?" Fulvia asked in a hushed voice.

"Until I know for sure, I'll treat it as such."

Marcus Antonius, Consul, to Marcus Aemilius Lepidus, Magister Equitum:

A successful conspiracy was carried out, and Caesar is dead. If you remain loyal to his cause, hurry to my domus so we can strategize on how best to protect the city's interests and ourselves.

Lepidus arrived by midafternoon. Marcus had been wearing ruts in the atrium floor mosaics from pacing.

As the two men embraced, he considered that Lepidus's show of grief appeared genuine.

"Unimaginable!" he cried. "And just after we spoke of death so capriciously last night."

Marcus nodded in agreement, then spoke, still grasping Lepidus by both arms. "We must ally ourselves. But first you must understand something. You may command the army in name, but the legionaries owe you no loyalty. I've been considered Caesar's second since Alesia. The men know me, and they'll follow me. We'll have need of legions to keep the peace. So relinquish your command in my favor."

Lepidus froze, incredulous. "How can you ask such a thing, Antonius!"

"I mean no dishonor." Marcus shifted tactics. Time to dangle a carrot before the donkey. "Look—Caesar recently mentioned how you desired a priesthood to increase your imperium. Transfer command of the army to me, and once we control Rome, I'll see that the Senate appoints you pontifex maximus. I give you my word."

Lepidus stared at him, eyes round. "Caesar's *priesthood*! And here I thought you cared nothing for political ploys."

"I care about restoring order, and I can't do it without your support. Will you agree?"

With one eye twitching slightly, Lepidus hesitated but finally nodded. "Very well," he breathed, accepting Marcus's firm handshake. "But how will I know you'll keep your word?"

"My personal slave, Eros, will document an agreement for us both to seal. It will remain in your keeping. Now stay and dine with us. We've much to discuss."

Transfer accomplished, Marcus's first acts were sending a full cohort to surround Caesar's domus and another to the Janiculum, protecting both Calpurnia and Cleopatra.

During the evening meal, Marcus stood up before Lepidus and his family. Everyone fell silent. In memory of Caesar's shade, he pulled his dark toga of mourning over his head in reverence and sprinkled wine on the floor. Then he closed his eyes momentarily in silence.

Afterward, he addressed them all sternly. "From now on, everything in our lives is subject to politics. You will watch me do and say many things, and sometimes you'll question my actions. However, what I do is for our safety. This household is now in mourning. Fulvia, Mother, whenever you're in public, you both must wear mourning attire and leave your hair long. Gaius, Lucius, Lepidus, we'll cease shaving and appear in public in dark togas, as I am tonight."

"Where did the conspirators go?" Lepidus queried.

"Brutus, Cassius, Trebonius, and others are in sanctuary at the Temple of Jupiter."

Lucius spat, "Take some legionaries up there tonight and put them all out of our misery."

Lepidus nodded in agreement.

"No," Marcus countered, shaking his head. "Their position is strategic. They've taken shelter in a place where it would look ill if we raised arms against them. The Temple of Jupiter Optimus Maximus is Rome's most sacred place. It would be heinous for us to force entry there. A terrible politician I may be, but even I know that much." Frustrated, he chewed his lip for a heartbeat before resuming, "As much as I would love putting them all to the sword, there must be no violence against them. Not *yet*."

"What about mobs?" Mother asked. "I care nothing for these murderers, but certainly their poor families were not all party to their plans. Surely, we must consider their innocent wives and children who are now exposed to the plebs' wrath."

"I rather doubt *Servilia's* innocent," Fulvia opined. "Old bitch probably helped Brutus plan the whole thing. She was so bitter when Caesar spurned her. And there's Portia, Brutus's wife, who's as much an Optimate as he."

Marcus shook his head again. "I disagree, Fulvia. Mother is right. Let's not hold them suspect. I'll send a guard to each of the conspirators' homes, protecting their families. A limited military presence here and there in the city will also help keep order in the streets."

"But, Marcus, how will you pay them?" Gaius blurted. "I happen to know your love of gambling has led to more debt."

"Caesar stored gold in the Temple of Ops," Marcus answered.

"You'd take gold from a *temple*, Antonius?" Lepidus gasped. "Such treasures are tithes! Do you dare anger the gods by robbing them?"

Marcus snorted and responded with a grin. "I'm not that devout. Nor was Caesar. He was practical. By placing coin there, it was relatively safe."

"Poor Calpurnia," Mother breathed. "We must also see to her needs."

Marcus agreed. Besides, Calpurnia held the key to his current need—coin.

Trappings of death darkened Caesar's domus. Still and stark, only one torch lit the entrance where wreaths of pine hung solemnly on the door. House slaves wore black, moving noiselessly in a vacuum of silence. In the center of the atrium, Caesar's corpse lay in state, incense smoldering on every side.

Mother hurried to embrace Calpurnia, who didn't bother hiding her grief. Marcus slowly approached the body of his general and kinsman.

Truthfully, his emotions were at war. Caesar had turned his back on him—his own cousin—at the first suggestion of disloyalty. Though they had reconciled, it was clear there had still been distance between them. And it smarted how Caesar wanted Octavian at his side in Parthia.

He closed his eyes. Once more, disbelief descended in a rush. This morning the corpse lying before him had been alive, conversing with him, breathing the same air, walking at his side.

Now he was no more.

Marcus tugged his toga over his head, yielding to a moment of private emotion. Into his mind flooded distant memories of simpler times—Caesar cantering beside him to Baiae, Caesar across a table from him ordering him to Greece for his own good, Caesar once telling him he was like the son he never had . . .

Marcus reopened his eyes and studied his former commander. White and drained of lifeblood, his face bore a gash from one of his attackers. Another wound grazed his neck. Still wearing his slashed and bloodied toga, it was impossible to gauge the extent of his injuries.

"I wonder which one was fatal?" Calpurnia pondered aloud, joining him next to her husband. "Someone said a knife entered his heart, just here." Tenderly, she placed one hand over Caesar's motionless breast.

"I only wish—if I had been there—"

"Say no more." Calpurnia braided her fingers into his. "They plotted well to force you from his side. You would have fought for him like a lion. At least your life is spared."

Marcus looked down at the hand she held. Taking hers more firmly, he squeezed it. Never was there a more appropriate time than now . . .

"This is yours until the will is read," he whispered. His other hand, busy at his belt, removed Caesar's ring from his purse.

Calpurnia's hand flew to her mouth. "I wondered where it was," she breathed.

"I will ever be your friend. Know that."

"Oh, I do. Might I ask a favor?"

"Anything."

"As consul, you're the most influential member of my husband's side of the family. Will you offer eulogy at his funeral?"

Swallowing hard at the sentiment, he buried his head in her shoulder and sobbed a reply, "Yes. Oh yes. You honor me."

She placed a gentle hand on his head, rocking him like a child. "Your loyalty always deserved more reward."

Marcus straightened and released her, taking hold of himself and focusing on the task at hand. At least Calpurnia recognized his devotion. He swiped wetness from his eyes.

"Now—how might I help Rome in this bleak hour?" she asked.

"You have a steward, a man well-versed in Caesar's financial matters?"

"Faberius? Yes. I'll fetch him."

Presently, a short, efficient-looking slave entered the room. "How might I serve you, Consul?"

"Understandably, Rome is in crisis. I need a hefty sum to pay off Caesar's veterans and enlisted legions to maintain their loyalty."

Faberius glanced nervously at Calpurnia.

Marcus went on, "I know Caesar stored a vast fortune inside the Temple of Ops. He told me about it. Your master would have wanted you to turn it over to me in such an emergency as this."

The slave hesitated.

"As he wills, Faberius," Calpurnia ordered firmly.

Faberius nodded. "But I will need help. Laborers, ox-carts—it is a vast fortune in gold."

"Of course. I'll send trusted officers and servants to meet you there tonight after dark. They'll assist in loading and transferring it."

"Yes, Consul."

"Marcus, perhaps Calpurnia should stay with us until things settle?" Mother suggested.

"You're most welcome," he seconded.

Calpurnia placed a hand upon Caesar's still breast. "I won't leave him here alone. Until his rites, my place is at his side. After that, Father will be taking me to Herculaneum. He wants me away from public life."

"Understood, dearest," Mother assured. "But if you change your mind, send word."

"I've ordered legionaries to surround the domus. You'll be safe." Marcus nodded at Mother, turning to leave.

"Wait, Marcus. Before you go, there's something else you must have." Calpurnia left briefly, hurrying down the corridor and returning with a large leather satchel full of maps and correspondence. "I think most of these things have to do with the

Parthian campaign. But there are other documents that may be important. Take them. Consider them yours."

"Who is the executor of his will?" Marcus asked.

"My father."

"Remind him to make request for it at the House of Vestals. I and my brothers will be happy to serve as witnesses for the reading."

As they rode home in the swaying litter, Mother was too quiet.

"What's wrong?" Marcus asked, breaking the silence.

Mother swallowed hard. "You have much in your hands, my son. Be wise with the power you wield."

"I'm trying to make sound decisions."

Something more was troubling her. He waited for her to speak on her own volition. "You shouldn't take the gold from the temple. It will anger the gods. Nor will housing it in your domus sit well with the people. That will be used against you."

Marcus sighed wearily. "I have soldiers to pay. And believe me when I say their pay will decimate this fortune in no time. It'll not sit long in my domus. Hopefully, once the will is opened, Rome will have more assurance of my position and cease its grumbling."

"Your 'position'?" She leaned toward him, whispering, "Are you expecting to be named his heir?"

Marcus chewed his lip. He did wonder. Legionaries had always expected it, and others too. Everyone in Gaul thought he was Caesar's choice—even Uncle Lucius.

But that was before he'd fallen out of favor.

CHAPTER XXIII

FOR THE NEXT TWO DAYS, ROME'S STREETS WERE EERILY silent, mostly due to martial law imposed by the legions transferred to Marcus's command. Now he needed to venture into murky political waters and entertain the Senate.

Minerva would have to grant him wisdom for this one.

Still unsure of friend versus foe, Marcus played it safe. He called for the assembly to meet at the Temple of Tellus, located right next to his domus.

Just before the meeting, he met with Piso.

"Concerning Caesar's will," Calpurnia's father began in a low tone. "The Vestals delivered it. Apparently, it's new. Caesar changed something this past September, supplanting an earlier version. Let's meet here with your brothers as witnesses. As consul, your presence will be to officiate."

"Understood. Is it still sealed?" Marcus queried.

"Yes. And it shall remain so."

"Good. Your daughter should be there. Also, invite Cicero and others from the Senate you consider worthy. The contents will need to be made public and its reading witnessed by others besides just us. My brothers shouldn't be the only ones, especially since I'm consul."

"Agreed," Piso concurred.

Only the gods knew what Caesar's will had in store.

The Senate's session at the Temple of Tellus was understandably well-attended. In fact, some senators had to stand outside since the temple was one of Rome's oldest and was short on space. Cicero came, along with Philippus, the Antonii brothers, Uncle Lucius, the statesman Aulus Hirtius, Piso, Lepidus, and some of the newer senators Caesar had appointed.

Once assembled, an emotionally charged Philippus requested the floor first. "Brothers, the 'king' is dead. Therefore his mandates and acts stand in question. We cannot allow a tyrant's decisions to stand! If we cast Caesar's decisions aside, the *real* Senate will rise again. The Republic will be saved!"

Amidst confused arguing and cheers, Marcus rose from his curule chair. He lifted his hand, awaiting silence. Once the chamber settled, he began, "I see complications in Philippus's suggestion. Think about it. If we hastily agree that Caesar's decisions, appointments, and laws should be declared null and void, then anyone here holding office no longer does so. Furthermore, anyone here to whom Caesar promised office *next* year would also lose that distinction. Do any of you really want to give up the honors he bestowed upon you?"

Marcus paused, awaiting comments. There was nothing but silence. "I thought not. Furthermore, I move that the office of dictatorship be *abolished*. Never again will it trouble Rome as it has done so these past forty years, first with Sulla and then with Caesar."

When Philippus started objecting, Cicero intervened, "Good Philippus, everyone knows how you grieved over the Senate's shackles under Caesar. However, today I must agree with Antonius. To overturn everything would invite disaster. By eliminating the dictatorship, we have surety that no other Caesars will insinuate themselves."

To Marcus's relief, the Senate wholeheartedly agreed, and Caesar's decisions stood. Furthermore, the title of dictator was struck from Rome's offices. For once, old Chickpea actually played into *his* hands. Next, he'd have to seal peaceful negotiations with the conspirators and lure them off the Capitoline.

Marcus Antonius, Consul, to Marcus Junius Brutus and Gaius Cassius Longinus:

I write on behalf of the Senate. We wish to extend an offer of pardon and meet with you. Please respond with your intent so we might discuss terms.

Marcus Junius Brutus to Marcus Antonius:

Cassius and I require surety of your intentions. We demand a hostage. We will accept none other than your son. Send him to the Capitoline with his nurse, and we will meet as requested.

"Marcus, *no*!" Mother protectively clasped her grandson to her breast. "You're sending your heir to killers as a peace offering, proving senatorial goodwill? Tell me when the Senate has ever been at goodwill with anyone?"

She had a point.

Marcus was as troubled at the conspirators' demand as she was. If only they had accepted his counteroffer. Fulvia offered to accompany Antyllus instead of his nurse. But they refused. They likely knew of Fulvia's brazen nature and didn't want her in their midst.

Marcus counteroffered a final time. He argued that Antyllus

would only go to the Capitoline if Brutus and Cassius took up temporary residence in his and Lepidus's households until everything was resolved. That would get the ringleaders off of the Capitoline and force the rest to behave. And most importantly, it would give Marcus a little peace, knowing that he and Lepidus held Brutus and Cassius as hostages in turn.

They agreed.

Marcus pulled little Antyllus gently from Mother's grasp.

She sobbed. "Think on this—they wanted *you* dead, didn't they? Here would be their chance to destroy your offspring! Don't subject him—"

"Enough!" Marcus barked. "You think I want this? Was it my idea? It's a demonstration of peace—that's all—a show for the populace. They'll have no choice but to treat Antyllus with mercy, for they desperately need the people's approval. Killing the consul's boy right after murdering Caesar wouldn't endear them to anyone. Didn't I say I'd have to do things you'd question? Plebs want peace, so peace we must extend. With Cassius as our houseguest, the others up there will have to be civil."

At least this was the argument he'd rationalized to convince himself of his son's safety.

Marcus cradled Antyllus against his shoulder. Strange how his boy could sleep peacefully in the midst of a quarrel. Emotion getting the best of him, he added, "And if they do harm him, I'll tear those bastards to pieces with my own hands!"

Fulvia came forward and kissed her son's head, running her fingers through his wavy, dark hair that was so like Marcus's. It was true she preferred men's games, but her somber comportment now betrayed a mother's worst fears. "Juno," she whispered, her cheek near her son's head, "hear my prayer. Keep him safe. Hold him dear. This day I pledge to sacrifice ten white cows to you, so protect him, I *beg* you."

To Dis and *Hades* with ten white cows! There was no putting a price on Antyllus's safety.

Marcus led the procession of senators to the foot of the Capitoline, adjacent to the new Curia, which was still under construction. He carried Antyllus, the baby's nurse following behind.

The way was crowded, plebs jostling for position and yelling. Everyone was vocalizing something—whatever solution they thought best: peace, order, vengeance, justice. Marcus's lictors used force several times, keeping people out of his path. When he reached the foot of Rome's highest hill, he found Marcus Junius Brutus, Gaius Cassius, and Gaius Trebonius flanked by other conspirators, all awaiting him.

Brutus was a tall, angular man who kept a pale complexion despite occasional soldiering. Thinning, dark hair arced over his brow, shadowing a lineless face that rarely smiled. Marcus had never liked him much. He was too much the philosopher, like Uncle Lucius.

Gently, Marcus raised Antyllus high so the crowd saw him. A somber silence fell, the plebs seeing the toddler as a sacrifice keeping peace between the two factions. Satisfied that their hearts beat with that of his son, Marcus handed Antyllus over to Brutus, though it was against his very nature. Antyllus didn't comprehend what was happening and began to cry in unfamiliar arms. Marcus's heart lurched, and he clenched his teeth as Brutus promptly passed the child to Trebonius.

"Peace! Peace! Keep peace!" plebs surrounding them thundered.

Marcus glared at Trebonius, thinking, *Ho, here's your peace—but it best not be at the expense of my child's life.*

Trebonius smiled slightly, also holding Antyllus up to the crowd.

Marcus couldn't help himself. He strode over to Trebonius and threatened under his breath, "Harm him and you'll never sleep soundly another day of your life, wondering *when* and *how* I'll kill you."

A heavy lump of emotion settled at the base of his throat when he forced himself to turn his back on his son. With a will of steel, he forced his emotions to calm. Then striding steadily, he climbed the steps of the nearby Temple of Saturn and raised his arms, signaling that he'd speak. As the mob settled, he proclaimed loudly, "Caesar may be dead, but his acts and decrees will stand. In addition, to keep peace in the city, by decree of the Senate and people of Rome, we graciously extend official pardon to Caesar's assassins."

Many people in the crowd jeered, shouting in favor of killing the assassins and ridding Rome of their stench. Others murmured and nodded, unsure of the decision but welcoming peace for as long as it would last.

Descending the stairs, Marcus turned to Brutus again, extending his hand. After clasping it, he embraced several other conspirators, including Cassius and even Decimus Brutus. Oh, there was back-patting and feigned pleasantry. Marcus's false and forced smile was so rigid he feared his face would crack apart like crumbling terra-cotta.

Lepidus made further show of goodwill by loudly reminding the crowds how Brutus would dine and reside in his house, with Cassius residing with the Antonii. And tomorrow, once the Senate met and peace was confirmed, Antyllus would be returned safely.

Father Jupiter, Marcus prayed it would be so!

As afternoon turned to evening, Marcus prepared his household for their morose, humorless houseguest: Cassius.

"It's just another act," he reminded everyone. "I dislike the idea because it dishonors all of us just *having* him here. But remember, by doing this, we ensure Antyllus's safe return."

Fulvia dutifully saw to every detail of the evening's dinner. At first, all went well, if one disregarded awkward pauses in conversation. But then Cassius asserted that Brutus be allowed to speak at Caesar's funeral.

"After all," he reasoned, "you're speaking, are you not, Antonius? To be fair, people should hear from both sides."

Marcus snorted. "It's a funeral, not a Senate meeting."

"Then I'll argue from the standpoint that Brutus was like a son to Caesar."

"Sons don't generally kill their fathers," Lepidus pointed out.

Marcus eyed Cassius. Steely, wiry hair hovered over a prominently long nose. Cassius wasn't overly tall like Brutus, modestly concealing an impressive physique under his toga—that of a hardened soldier. Flinty gray eyes harbored inflexibility.

"He'll speak at the very beginning, then, before the actual rites," Marcus compromised, to a gasp from Mother. Then, unable to help himself, he added, "Though I doubt Calpurnia will appreciate having her husband's murderer participating in the funeral."

The stare Cassius gave him in response could have turned anyone to stone. And things went downhill from there.

Struggling for polite conversation, Gaius changed subjects. "Cassius, weren't you stationed in Syria at the time of Crassus's defeat, saving some of his fleeing army? Tell us about the Parthians."

"A stealthy lot—Parthians," Cassius reflected, still glaring at Marcus and taking a swig from his cup. "Not unlike some in this very room. They all fight best at night, you know. My cavalry managed to take a few of them just across the Syrian border from us. We tossed their bodies into the river."

"Not worth burying, eh?" Lucius said drily.

"Not any more so than—" he stopped, everyone staring straight at him, well aware whose name he nearly spoke. Then Cassius actually had the nerve to tilt his head back and bark in laughter at his error.

Marcus sat erect, eyes piercing a clear challenge. "Speak openly," he growled. "On the ides, you wanted to kill me too, did you not?"

Cassius cocked an eyebrow, peering first at Mother, then at Fulvia. "Ladies, do you *really* care to hear what I wanted to do?"

"Say whatever you wish," Mother replied with cool composure. "We're bound by a promise of peace to dine with you, so we're prepared to tolerate your *intolerable* company."

Marcus grinned, proud of Mother's wit.

Cassius signaled Castor to refill his wine cup. Inhaling deeply, he said, "My suggestion was to have Trebonius and his slaves kill you after they separated you from Caesar. Then we were going to drag both of your corpses through the streets of Rome all the way to the river's edge, place you in sacks with stones, and toss you in where sewage runs out."

Marcus ground his teeth. Face hot with fury, he stood up, ready to either kill Cassius or order him out of the domus.

Fulvia stopped him by standing up too. Firmly, she placed her hand atop his to still his temper and remind him just *who* was at risk. It was she who wound up with the final word. "Speaking of sewage, Cassius, not even our beloved Cloaca Maxima could channel out all the shit we've endured with you tonight!"

Marcus roared with laughter, accompanied by his brothers. Fulvia was more a man than many!

Morning dawned with a rush of activity in preparation for the official reading of Caesar's will. Castor and Eros detained Cassius in the back of the domus, where he wouldn't be seen, especially by Calpurnia or her father.

Marcus busied himself in the atrium, face grizzled with the beginnings of his mourning beard. Impatient, he was directing slaves where to exhibit busts of deceased family members.

"Is this necessary?" Mother asked, entering and seeing what he was doing.

"I want our family to appear more than ready to assume any responsibility. Just in case."

Mother hesitated before she finally spoke. "Marcus, you have achieved honor enough to raise our family out of shame and into merit. I'm as proud as any mother should be and more. Your father's disasters have been more than vindicated, as have Lentulus's. Why not relinquish imperium? Better safe than in an early grave. This game is becoming dangerous."

Marcus stopped and stared at her, stunned. With one hand, he dismissed the two slaves and moved closer to her. "No Roman is ever 'done' achieving power, and you know it."

Mother opened her mouth to reply, but he lifted one hand, stopping her. "By laying down my imperium, I'd look defeated—or incapable. Is that what you want? No. I'm in the arena now. I can't turn back."

Senators began arriving, everyone wearing black. All would serve as witnesses for the reading. Cicero was one of the first through the door, of course. Philippus even came, though he didn't dress to honor the dead. His loathing for Caesar had always been public knowledge, cowardice being his only probable excuse for not joining the conspiracy.

Marcus sat down in his curule chair in front of the impluvium. Fulvia stood just behind, one hand on his shoulder. Mother remained at Calpurnia's side, as her father, Piso, snapped the will's seal and read aloud for everyone to hear.

"Conscript Fathers, members of the gens Julii, guests of honor, and Consul Antonius, hear what words the departed left before Dis claimed him:

> *"I, Gaius Julius Caesar, write this will to testify what persons are appointed to my wealth, estate, and name. My principal heir is Gaius Octavianus, son of my niece Atia. He shall receive three-quarters of my remaining wealth after other disbursements are made as duly directed. He is also to be my adopted son, receiving my name and whatever honor it holds—"*

Marcus froze. Piso was still reading, but he no longer heard. Bright lights orbited before him and his ears thrummed.

Stunned? Yes.

Humiliated? Definitely.

In agreement? *No*!

Gaius Octavianus? That diseased great-nephew who had never even drawn a gladius? What in Mars's name was Caesar *thinking*?

Marcus's eyes swept the room, seeking others' responses—Philippus, Octavian's stepfather, registered horror on his face. Cicero looked puzzled, his slave Tiro whispering in his ear.

Mind racing, Marcus listened to Piso again, considering the other proclaimed heirs as Piso named them. Quintus Pedius—a nobody. But Decimus Brutus Albinus? In Caesar's will? *He was one of the bloody assassins!*

And where was Marcus Antonius?

Nowhere!

He realized his hand was shaking and hoped nobody noticed. Then there was the metallic taste of blood from where he'd chewed his lip until he'd bitten it.

Where was the military hero who helped make Caesar conqueror of Alesia and led undermanned legions to victory at Pharsalus? How had Caesar forgotten what he had risked in bringing troops across the Adriatic in violent storms?

Even common plebs got more! Each free citizen would receive monetary supplement as well as the gift of Caesar's Janiculum properties—their gardens, grounds, and the villa in which Cleopatra presently resided.

But as confounded as Marcus was, there was no time for him to dwell on Caesar's blatant oversight. At sundown, Rome's dictator was scheduled to pass into the underworld, and his oldest remaining blood-relative had agreed to give his spirit its due.

Not that he felt much like doing so now. But he'd promised Calpurnia, and the gods above knew none of this was her fault. Above all, Marcus had to keep calm. Injustice could be hashed out later.

Tonight, in the Forum Romanum, he had the speech of a lifetime to deliver.

Atop the Rostra, Marcus Antonius stood before a silent, solemn throng, prepared to deliver Caesar's eulogy. To one side sat a lidded basket.

Brutus's opening remarks received little acclaim. People were naturally moody and uncertain how to react to the murderer of someone whose funeral they were attending. When Marcus mounted the platform, he moved confidently. If he played this right, he believed his oration would send a charge of excitement bolting through the Forum like lightning.

Caesar's honor guard led the funerary procession into the Forum, accompanied by hundreds of hired mourners and tibicines playing dirges on their double flutes. Legionaries somberly set the bier on the Rostra.

Dressed in a stately black toga, Marcus took his time, circling Caesar's body, gazing down at the remains. Before this morning, he would have wept genuine tears. But now his heart spat upon the corpse for betraying his faithfulness. Whatever did that soft boy Octavian have, to be so honored? And Marcus wondered—had *his* name been in the will before Caesar changed it in Octavian's favor?

But now to focus—every eye was upon him. Every person in Rome knew him to be a staunch Caesarian. He would move forward with his plan to ruin the conspirators, regardless of the bitterness poisoning his spirit. He needed to be every bit the actor Cytheris ever was. And he'd do it. Brutus and Cassius would be running for their lives by the time he finished.

Abruptly, he stopped circling Caesar and raised his hand. Mourners desisted their cries, and musicians ceased their playing.

Assuming character, he shook his head mournfully, asking, "How can it be, good citizens? How is it that I'm giving this eulogy instead of you?" It was a metaphor, but he saw them nodding. Oh, how the plebs had loved Caesar.

"Listen as I read aloud the honors that first the Senate and then you, the people, bestowed upon this man in recognition of his leadership. As I do so, imagine my voice to be yours, not mine."

Gesturing to the body, he recited, "Caesar was revered, the Father of his Country, benefactor, leader." Shaking his head again, he clenched one fist in mock frustration, gesturing to the mangled corpse before him. "Is *this* proof of his many mercies?"

Not a sound. The Forum had never been as hushed.

"Whoever accepted Caesar's clemency went unharmed. He never demanded any honor laid upon him. They were *bestowed* upon him. Good people, by paying homage now, though he be dead, you defend us against any accusation that some made of Rome losing its freedom to a despot."

Marcus waited, letting that sink in. People began calling out their own loyalty to Caesar, and with inward satisfaction, he saw concern scribed upon the faces of Brutus, Cassius, and other conspirators clustered below him among the senators.

Reverently, he pulled his dark toga over his head, pointing toward the Capitoline and Jupiter's temple. In powerful voice, he invoked, "Jupiter Rex, sovereign of my ancestors and other gods, I am prepared to *defend* Caesar. But since my equals here have decided peace is for the best, I can only pray that it is."

Plebs murmured heartfelt affirmation at that, but furious shouts erupted, not only from the conspirators but from other senators as well.

"Unacceptable, Antonius!"

"That's unfair to whom we pledged protection!"

"Recant that—you go too far!"

Marcus smiled at the response. Waving his hands in a gesture of denial, he called out, "Peace! Don't you see that what happened to Caesar was too terrible to have been the work of just any man? It was the work of evil *spirits*! So let's deal with the present, not the past, since our present sits poised on the edge of a gladius. We risk being dragged back into civil war, destroying our city's great families. Let's guide great Caesar to join the dead, singing him the customary dark songs."

What Marcus did next occurred on a whim, his theatrics astonishing even himself.

He lifted his arms as though Caesar were a god. Changing his voice to a sing-song chant, he extolled his kinsman, reciting his many victories and calling to him personally. "You were the only man *ever* to avenge Rome for the violence she suffered three hundred years ago by the savage Gallic people. You set fire to *their* lands, avenging the burning of your country!"

At this, the plebs became frenzied, chanting oaths to Caesar's shade, jumping up and down in unison and lifting hands or balling fists in emotion. Their fervor encouraged Marcus, and in a daring move, he kicked the lid off of the basket at his feet. Inside was Caesar's bloodied toga, and he whipped it out to thousands of gasps. One of his lictors stepped forward on cue, and Marcus took up his fasces, draping the stained garment over the axe. He lifted it high, striding back and forth across the Rostra, displaying it like a banner.

As calls of heartfelt grief and outrage climaxed, Marcus shouted over the din so all could hear, "What would Caesar have thought of this day? He'd say, 'To think I actually *spared* the lives of the very men who *killed* me!'"

Utter chaos erupted.

Someone serendipitously raised up a wax effigy of Caesar, brandishing it and turning it about. On it were twenty-three stab wounds, conveniently complimenting Marcus's dramatics.

Beneath him, the large group of conspirators began to retreat, cloaking themselves, splitting up, scurrying away. Good! For all Marcus cared, they could all cower and run like dogs.

Still holding aloft Caesar's bloody garment, he watched as the crowd took control of the funeral. Calpurnia watched helplessly. One trembling hand covered her mouth in emotion.

Piso hurried forward, grabbing Marcus's arm. "You've stirred them to madness!"

Marcus placed his hand comfortingly upon Piso's, assuring him, "Caesar belonged to the people. To the people let him return. Let them send him on his way."

Several emboldened plebs pulled Caesar's bier off the Rostra, holding it carefully lest he teeter off. Thousands of voices intoned a traditional funerary song as they carried the corpse to an open area a stone's throw east, where plebs were already stacking carts, pieces of wood from market stalls, furniture, pine boughs, and kindling. Together, they created a makeshift funeral pyre. Before long, Caesar's body rested on top, at a precarious angle but stationary. Moments later, the pile was ablaze. Blended with the roar of citizen's chants was the sound of a conflagration's popping and cracking.

Marcus went back to Calpurnia and offered her his arm. She allowed him to guide her to the front of the Rostra.

"See," Marcus assured her gently, squeezing her hand. "They're honoring him—just in their own way."

She trembled, uttering no sound, but nodded bravely. It was a very different yet touching end to what was meant to be a stately procession to the Field of Mars for burial.

Marcus, Calpurnia, and Piso stayed on the Rostra, motionless, watching. Plebs surrounded the blaze, joining hands and lifting them in honor, swaying from side to side. Even Rome's Jewish population processed into the space, toting expensive furniture to add to the conflagration.

They had loved him too.

Sparks and smoke rose high, joining Caesar's spirit as night cloaked Rome as dark as Marcus's own heart.

Gaius Octavian Caesar in Apollonia to Marcus Antonius, Consul in Rome:

Salutations.

I write in deepest grief, accepting my father's appointment as heir and adopted son. I will leave for Rome tomorrow morning. Let us meet soon after my arrival to consider what should be done next to protect our interests.

Whenever an infrequent opportunity arose to see Cleopatra, it lifted Marcus's heart. And how pleasant after these past days to feel a flutter of inward joy.

It was well-known that while in Rome she had received little welcome or acclaim from Caesar's colleagues. Now that he was dead, she had no reason to stay. Spring sailing season had arrived, and the many crates and chests packed and waiting in the villa's atrium clearly declared her intentions.

Upon entering her apartments, Marcus found the queen sitting on a curule chair, crowned with a simple gold diadem. She was dressed for mourning, in a simple dark silk tunic.

The day was warm, breezes light. Winter's chill had finally succumbed to spring's temperance. It was the first time they'd been alone together since that day so long ago in Alexandria at the Isis temple.

"Consul. How kind of you to come. Please sit down. I know we share grief."

"Majesty," Marcus acknowledged courteously, taking the cushioned chair she indicated.

"I'll miss his company," she said simply. "Your eulogy was extraordinary."

She had attended the funeral incognito? "Gratias," he replied, inclining his head.

"What a grand influence you exhibit over your people. Shrewdly done, although I hope the conspirators will be brought to justice."

"You're always capable of reading into motives. Vengeance will be sought someday, I assure you. Already things in the city are too dangerous for Brutus and Cassius. They left Rome last evening, following my oration." Marcus smiled knowingly. "Things were too dangerous for them after that." He paused. "So you were there—at Caesar's funeral?"

She nodded. "I wanted Caesarion to witness it. We were hidden in the crowd."

"It was unforgettable."

"Might I offer you refreshment?" she offered.

"I wish I could," he replied, genuinely disappointed. "Unfortunately, I have many responsibilities to which I must return."

"Of course."

"I'm here for two reasons," he explained. "The first is your safety. Caesar's will is now posted upon the Senate doors. He left this villa and its lands to the people of Rome. Already my guards stationed around these grounds have encountered plebs snooping about. They're naturally curious, wanting to see what was left to them."

"We're nearly packed and shall depart tomorrow at noon."

Marcus nodded. "Understand it's not my intention to force you to leave. My concern is for your safety, and unfortunately Rome is a dangerous place."

"Understood," Cleopatra assured him. "There's little reason for me to remain."

Marcus lowered his voice, genuinely regretful. "Secondly, I feel obligated to inform you that your son was not included in Caesar's will."

Cleopatra inhaled sharply. That had to be a blow—a harsh one. "Not mentioned—at all?" she asked in a small voice.

Marcus shook his head.

"Who was the fortunate recipient, then?"

"Gaius Octavian."

"Ah! That frail, brooding boy Caesar insisted on entertaining and honoring, right here where we sit. The one to whom I even gave my father's onyx ring." She spat out the final words, resentment unfettered.

Marcus added, "He's already written me declaring his intention to accept Caesar's offer. I'm sorry. This must be difficult for you."

Cleopatra stared outside, watching a peacock open its full fan. "Surely, he included you somehow. You were his loyal friend and kinsman. How did you benefit?" She turned back to him, and their eyes met.

Marcus snorted bitterly, his bleak expression her answer.

He arose and she followed, walking over to him. She reached out and tenderly took his hand. "Then we both grieve for more than one reason," she whispered.

He eyed her momentarily. Grieving? No. Neither of them was really grieving.

Damn you, Caesar, Marcus thought. What have you done to us?

CHAPTER XXIV
44-43BC

JEALOUSY AND ENVY WEREN'T TYPICAL EMOTIONS FOR Marcus Antonius.

Until now, that is.

Pent-up resentment had morphed into a most unlikely form: Gaius Julius Caesar Octavian. Thanks to his dear, departed great uncle, that was his new name.

At first, Marcus chided himself. It was foolish despising someone so physically inconsequential, possessing merely a head full of facts. But since returning to Rome from Greece, Octavian was no longer unknown. Caesar's adopted son and heir held loaded dice. Still, what sort of influence could a boy of nineteen years hold over men of senatorial rank? He had no military experience, was too young to officially enter the Senate, and looked wan and unhealthy as ever. Other than a revered name, he possessed nothing.

And today "the boy" was waiting in Marcus's impressive atrium.

Well, let him sit on that bony little ass all day! He could wait until Marcus was good and ready to receive him. And if he sat there long enough, maybe he'd go away.

Yet hours passed, and Octavian remained. Castor hurried into the triclinium for the third time that morning, announcing him again.

Marcus picked at a midmorning repast of fruit. He was trying to be too busy—scanning scrolls originally sent to Caesar from foreign delegations. Then Mother arrived for one of her frequent visits with Antyllus, Fulvia following close behind. They settled at their usual places on the dining couch.

Unsurprisingly, his wife was first to bring up the visitor. Lately, she was becoming more and more adept at annoying him. "Your mother just said Gaius Octavian is in the atrium. And here you are, morosely drinking wine? Not seeing him will only make things worse."

Her voice had an edge that scathed him, along with new auburn locks much too close to Antonia's former hues.

Best to answer her concern directly. "He's trying to replace my imperium with his own. You wouldn't want that to happen any more than I."

He felt both women scrutinizing him and glancing at each other before Mother responded, "Jealousy is an unsightly blemish on your face, Marcus. Remove it at once and go make your peace. Distant though it might be, you share blood with him."

Gods, what a morning!

Doubly irritated now, Marcus's hopes for peace and quiet were dashed. He snatched a husk of warm bread and tore a piece off with his teeth, washing it down with one more swig of honeyed wine.

"Actually, I dislike him too," Mother confessed, carefully placing a giggling Antyllus on the couch before lowering herself onto some cushions. "Think of him as an annoying little bee, buzzing about your flowers. You mustn't get stung, so don't swat at him. Instead, build him a small hive, letting him make honey for *you*."

Fulvia agreed, choosing another analogy more suited to his tastes. "Your mother's right. Best to let him think he drives at least one horse on your chariot, my love."

And so the damnable dilemma named Octavian was going

nowhere. Nor would either woman in Marcus's life hold her peace until he acted. Grumbling, he plunked his wine cup down onto the small serving table and got up.

"And leave your testy temper here with us," Mother sagely warned.

Before knowing the contents of Caesar's will, Marcus had been ready to die avenging his cousin's death. Now he was trapped into playing the role of faithful Caesarion, secretly hating the dead dictator with a boiling umbrage akin to that of a jilted lover. What he really felt like telling this great-nephew-turned-Caesar's son was better left unsaid. Not even when Cassius dined here had he felt such animosity toward a guest.

Octavian rose when Marcus strolled in, meeting his gaze with those cool, aloof blue eyes. Wavy, auburn-colored hair formed two curling pincers in the middle of his forehead. His expertly designed toga was blue, its border embroidered simply but elegantly with gold thread. It contrasted with the homespun, gray woolen tunic showing underneath.

"My apologies for keeping you waiting," Marcus said flippantly.

"There's no need. Though since I'm Caesar now, I wonder—would you have kept my father waiting?"

Marcus bristled, smiling cynically. "Well, since you bear such a great name, why do you need anything from me?"

"Actually, there's a great deal I need from you. You removed a certain treasury from the Temple of Ops, and I'm here to reclaim it."

Marcus chewed his lip. Octavian wouldn't be getting any of that gold. It was gone. "It can't be returned," he stated bluntly. "Caesar's will was yet unopened when I accessed it. The entirety was dispersed to troops, ensuring order in the city."

"Really? Or did you waste it all gambling? Cicero might find that interesting."

Conniving piece of shit! Ah. He was allying with Chickpea, was he? "Cicero knows very well where it went," Marcus stated firmly, punctuating his remark by holding up empty hands. "All of that gold was used in the aftermath of the ides to secure peace in the city. It's gone."

A fleeting spark of menace appeared in Octavian's eyes, but his voice was quiet, controlled, and surprisingly masculine. "You're known for your whoring and gambling, Antonius. Plebs will believe Cicero when he speaks of your overspending and gaming. And soon enough they'll believe whatever I say as well."

Marcus raised his voice before catching himself. "Take your threats elsewhere. You're far too young and inexperienced to immerse yourself in politics above your head. Go home to Atia and Philippus, ask them for a stipend, and return to Greece, *schoolboy*!"

Clasping long, pale fingers, Octavian forced a smile. Even if it had been sincere, he would've looked unpleasant. His teeth were small and yellowish.

"I see you refuse to help Caesar," he said. "Then he'll pursue other ways to see his father's will carried out. But always bear in mind that as long as I breathe, your unwillingness to assist me today will never be forgotten." With that said, Octavian pivoted about and walked straight out of the domus.

If Marcus was bewildered and perturbed with him that day, it couldn't compare to the outrage he experienced two days later when Gaius announced that Octavian was in the Forum, paying plebs their allotment from Caesar out of his own pockets.

"Good, patient people of Rome—I, Gaius Julius Caesar, award to you the promised payment my father decreed for each and every citizen." These were his exact words, recorded by the Senate's secretary. "Though Consul Antonius refuses to return gold willed to me, you'll receive your due—from my own purse."

Then, as spring heated into summer, the little weasel somehow came up with enough coin for extravagant funeral games held in Caesar's memory. Despite agreeing that Octavian was aggravating and politically inconvenient, Fulvia loved public games and begged to attend. Marcus reluctantly accompanied her and had to admit the shows were the best he'd seen since Caesar's spectacles.

As he and Fulvia were leaving on the last night of entertainment, Eros caught his attention.

"Look, Dominus!"

Marcus glanced up. Eros was pointing up at the night sky. Everyone else was captivated too. A bright streak in the heavens shone like a flaming arrow. As the crowds dispersed, they gasped in awe and wonder at the sight. And Octavian, ever the opportunist, climbed high onto the temporary amphitheater's wooden scaffolding so that everyone saw him. "People of Rome," he cried, "behold a phenomenal sight! It's the spirit of my beloved father, Caesar, flying to the gods!"

Amidst the crowd's shouts and whoops of adoring approval and exclamations, Marcus ground his teeth in exasperation. Snatching Fulvia's elbow, he led her toward their litter.

Nightmares rarely occurring since before Pharsalus began again. And that wasn't the only inconvenience. Wonder-boy convinced some of the troublesome legions in Campania to side with him, using hefty bribes of five hundred denarii for each common legionary, donated to him by Cicero and his ilk. Old Chickpea remained silent about the business, even though the recruiting was illegal. After all, Octavian held no public office. Nor had he received senatorial sanction to recruit.

Next, Marcus was visited by a legionary delegation of centurions. "Consul, we're here to voice concerns about you and young Caesar."

Marcus hated hearing them call Octavian that. His popular "gifts" to the plebs had almost everyone referring to him as "Caesar" or "young Caesar" now.

Swallowing his annoyance, Marcus forced himself to listen. A different centurion requested, "Our men need both you and young Caesar to give us a gesture of your goodwill toward one another."

"You never appear together," explained a third with furrowed brows. "Everyone fears you hate each other. We in the legions want peace between you."

Neither Marcus or Octavian had a choice.

In full consular pomp, surrounded by his lictors bearing their fasces, Marcus Antonius met Octavian atop the Capitoline, before the Temple of Jupiter, in a public show of unity. Representatives from various legions were present, as was an assembly from the Senate. An ox was sacrificed in Jupiter Optimus Maximus's honor, jointly paid for by Marcus and Octavian.

"Young Caesar's" hand-clasp was limp, cold, and clammy. In other words, anything but sincere. Marcus was wary, trying to determine what this boy with nothing but a name was thinking.

Only now Octavian *did* have something more than just a name. He had senatorial support, Cicero, his cronies, *and* legions backing him—illegal or not.

Marcus Antonius, Consul, to the Conscript Fathers of the Senate and People of Rome:

I've always maintained that great Caesar's appointments made prior to the ides of Martius be honored. However, something troubles me. While most of his murderers fled to Greece, shamed, dishonored, and forced to leave, one remains far too near. That man is Decimus Brutus, one of the top conspirators, yet a man Caesar honored in his will. This traitor to our now Divine Caesar controls the very volatile province of Gaul, which Caesar himself conquered.

What if Marcus Brutus and Cassius persuade him to join with the Gauls to turn on Rome? It would be disastrous. Make no mistake, for those same two men are busy in Greece, turning over rocks to gain support against us here. Should Decimus Brutus be trusted to govern such an important and strategic post so near us? I say not. In fact, I urge you to reconsider him entirely.

Allow me to present myself as a far worthier

candidate for the province of Gaul. Decimus Brutus may go in my stead to Macedonia, which was my original assignment. I'm sending my own brother Gaius Antonius over ahead of time to prepare for his arrival. This will ensure that his governance is true to Rome and not that of Brutus and Cassius.

Marcus and Gaius galloped their horses neck to neck, racing thunderously down the Via Appia.

Marcus leaned forward, spurring the animal hard and edging ahead of his brother. White lather flecked both horses' necks, and their hooves spewed dust. It was a hot day in the new month of Julius.

Marcus decided to accompany Gaius as far as Three Taverns. Absence from Rome was a welcome relief from the burdens of the past months.

With a snort from his mount, he reined in, waiting for his brother to catch up. Gaius was no soldier, but he was loyal, and Marcus was desperate for loyalty of late. What could it hurt giving him a mission requiring mostly reporting and communication?

Breathless and smiling broadly, Gaius exclaimed, "I concede! Only you can make losing fun, Marcus!"

Marcus grinned as they plodded along, letting the horses rest.

Gaius became thoughtful. "You seem happy enough with Fulvia," he observed, loosening his reins and stretching his legs.

"Do I?"

"She's a fetching woman and has given you a son. What more do you want?"

"I want her hair brown again," Marcus said, smirking.

Gaius laughed, the sound reverberating off an especially large tomb to their left. "Why complain? Let her be the fashionable lady she is."

Marcus shook his head. "Reminds me too much of Antonia."

"Ah. Painful memories?" When Marcus didn't answer, Gaius pressed on. "Aside from her red hair, do you love her?"

Marcus looked at Gaius sharply. "Must you ask?"

"I think the two of you are a fine match."

Marcus sighed, considering an answer. "I'm sure Fulvia loves me. She'd probably die for me."

"And you for her?"

Marcus looked away sadly, staring at a passing mule-cart laden with melons. "Gaius, something in me died after losing Fadia. It's like—like I can't allow myself to love anymore." He shrugged, unable to express himself.

Gaius reached over and placed a hand on his arm. "Do you want to?"

Marcus blinked at the question, actually surprised to hear himself answer softly, "Yes."

Gaius smiled. "Then you shall. There's some woman out there who'd match you perfectly. Once you find her and the timing's right, you could take her as a lover. And when things settle and I return, Mother wants me married too!"

Marcus nodded. "I agree. You've waited a lot longer than I. Consider yourself fortunate!"

"Well, you're the oldest and Father's heir. It's only right for you to pave the way."

"Then I'll be on the lookout for a suitable match," Marcus assured him. "Meanwhile, you're my eyes and ears in Macedonia. Legionary spies loyal to me in Greece have gathered evidence that Brutus and Cassius are recruiting. Any information you can provide about their activity will help."

They entered an area full of comforting shade trees and rode in silence for a time. Then Gaius spoke, "Do you think Decimus will obey a senatorial recall?"

Marcus scowled. "First I have to *get* the senatorial recall. But he'd better. I already planted spies among his troops, ready to alert me to what he does upon receiving my orders. A Macedonian proconsulship would end my imperium in Rome. We Antonii have regained much honor, and I won't see it trampled on by an inexperienced boy. So if the Senate refuses to reassign me to Gaul, I suppose I'll have to force the matter. Caesar's little prodigy has already cemented an alliance with Chickpea. This morning I learned he's heading to Campania to try winning more of those hard-assed legions there."

"So much for your mutual sacrifice of peace to Pater Jupiter," Gaius snorted.

Marcus set his jaw. Cicero would do his best to prevent Decimus's recall. He wanted Marcus Antonius out of the way. Of that, he was certain.

"Gaius, when you reach Macedonia, keep a few cohorts but send the rest of the legions to Brundisium, where I can meet them and take command. Their added numbers will deter Octavian's efforts and perhaps dissuade Decimus from crossing me. If an underage youth can illegally raise and lead troops, then what's wrong with me illegally booting one of Caesar's conspirators out of Gaul if I must?"

Gaius nodded. "I'll send all I can to you. These days, whoever has the biggest army wins, no?"

"Only Mars knows how Octavian has managed to gain this much influence, but there it is," Marcus grumbled, shaking his head and swatting at a fly. "He constantly advertises his divine descent from Caesar at every opportunity. And now, after all of my peacekeeping efforts, the legions love him for vowing revenge on Brutus and Cassius. Soldiers question why I haven't been more active in resisting them myself. And can you please explain to me where he comes up with all his coin? He's not Caesar—he's King Midas!"

Gaius laughed, then silence descended again, the rhythmic tread of their horses' hooves the only sound.

"I'm sure that little diatribe Cicero just wrote has further fired your temper too," Gaius finally ventured.

Marcus screwed up his face at the thought of Cicero and spat to the side of the road. "It's said he's working on a whole series of speeches to insult and humiliate me."

"Then I stand corrected. Whoever has the biggest armies *and* most poisonous words wins."

"Just send those legions back, Brother. We *must* keep building our military influence, or we won't survive. Strange, you know. Fifteen years ago, I cared very little if I ever gained political power. Now here I am, fighting to keep something I never thought I wanted." Marcus shook his head at the irony.

Ahead were three modest ramshackle buildings, comprising the small Three Taverns complex. Halting his horse and dismounting, Marcus led the way to a water trough. Leaving their animals to drink, they stood, Gaius dipping his hands in and rinsing his face. "I'll sacrifice for you," he promised, water running off his chin, dribbling back into the basin. "I know you hate Octavian, but remember who has the most experience—and the most brothers!"

They both chuckled, and Gaius clapped Marcus on the back. It was true—Gaius could always make him smile. "Soon I'll have more sons," Marcus commented. "Fulvia's with child again. Between you, me, Lucius, Antyllus, and the new one coming, we should be able to give Octavian a good ass-whipping one of these days."

In laughter, the Antonii brothers lovingly embraced.

"Fortuna bless you, Marcus," Gaius murmured. "The way you and Fulvia are going, our recruiting will merely consist of arming your sons. Now find me a lusty wife with enormous breasts, and once I return, Mother will have her wedding."

Marcus hugged him once more, kissing Gaius's cheek and patting his back. Who knew when they'd see one another again? "Let's hope so. You're a good brother, Gaius Antonius. Now send me those legions, and may the gods keep you safe."

Marcus lounged on the grass next to Antyllus and a pile of scrolls, working on an assault plan should he be forced to oust

Decimus Brutus without the Senate's endorsement. As days passed, that possibility looked more and more likely. More opposition to his proposal had risen from the Senate than he'd bargained for. He decided that if they didn't change their minds by month's end, he'd head north and take command forcefully.

Sitting nearby on a bench in the warm, late-summer sun, Mother picked Antyllus up and rested his head in her lap.

It was then that Fulvia interrupted them, marching over and exclaiming, "Marcus, listen to the latest."

"Let me guess," Marcus mused. "Cicero again?"

"Yes! In his latest *Philippic*, he claims you'll come to an early end like Clodius and Curio, just because of being married to *me*! As though their deaths were *my* fault?"

Marcus snickered. "He's trying a new angle." He looked back down, eyes anchored to the map of Gaul he was studying. Carefully, he traced lines along possible routes leading north to Mutina, Decimus Brutus's stronghold in Cisalpine Gaul.

"He's poisoning the Senate against you," she cried loudly, vying for his attention. She let the papyrus dangle near his face, jabbing at it with her finger. "Here, he accuses *you* of causing the war with Pompeius—saying you were Rome's Helen of Troy! He goes too far. Swear to me he'll die for this!"

Mother tilted her head back, giggling, "What a way with words that man has. *Helen of Troy?*"

"Actually, I already read that one," Marcus sighed. "He also insists I was one of Caesar's assassins and supports Octavian by accusing me of stealing that gold from the Temple of Ops."

"And here," Fulvia went on, "he says you slept with Curio!"

Still not raising his head, Marcus replied sternly, "That, I refuse to discuss."

"I always knew you'd never hear the end of it," Mother muttered under her breath.

"Cicero has a loose tongue, spewing deceit like a cobra spits venom," Marcus stated evenly. Finally, he looked up, jaw set and eyes alight with hatred. "Mother, did you know while he was railing at me in one of his speeches, he mentioned my 'children with Fadia'?"

"The slave girl?" Fulvia interjected, raising her eyebrows. "I thought the one child you sired on her was lost."

"Exactly!" Marcus said. "That's my point. Mostly, the man writes outright lies or twisted truths. Even though it infuriates me, sometimes he actually amuses me with his absurdities."

"Absurdities to *us*," Mother said pointedly. "Unfortunately, with it coming from Cicero, people believe what he says."

Antyllus squirmed and squealed, so Mother placed him on the grass, letting him play with a leather ball.

Fulvia suggested, "You should write some dreadful things about Cicero. Undoubtedly, you harbor a wealth of spiteful words to counter his. Begin with his executing men without trial."

Marcus shook his head. "It's not worth the trouble. I've consular duties and am on the brink of war to take Gaul from Decimus Brutus."

"Whatever does Cicero really know about us Antonii anyway?" Mother mused. "How often has he been in your presence or mine? I tell you, the gods will judge him someday for attacking us so."

"Why wait on the gods' ill timing?" Fulvia hissed in a poisonous voice. "Kill him *now*, Marcus! Caesar went about forgiving all his enemies, and we know where that got him. You have legionaries at your beck and call. *Do it!*"

Mother looked aghast. "You are not my daughter with those words! Cicero murdered my husband, but as much as I despise him, I wouldn't murder him."

Mother had no idea how brutish Fulvia could be. This was only the tip of a very long spear. Marcus studied Fulvia with a cautious gaze, choosing his words carefully. "I agree he must die for the many disgraces he's caused us," he answered. "But invading his domus with men at arms would be disastrous. Nor could I stroll into the Senate with a knife and stab him as did Caesar's assassins. I can't risk more disfavor. Not now."

Fulvia pursed her lips in frustration and knelt down in front of him. "Then promise me—at your first opportunity, he must *die*!"

Mother suggested a different tactic. "Or you could reconcile with him again. At least that way the slander would stop and he'd be the aggressor."

Fulvia stiffened in outrage. "*No!* No reconciliation, Mother!" she ranted. "He has insulted Marcus publicly to the point of no return."

Mother had shied away from Fulvia's outburst, drawing Antyllus closer to her. Marcus set his papyrus aside and reached for her hand to steady her. "Mother, I've waited a very long time to deal with Cicero. I've never forgotten what he did to Lentulus and those other poor men without a fair trial. He's been our enemy since my youth, assaulting us with grief, injustice, and now his unbearable tongue." He looked at his wife. "Fulvia, when the right time presents itself—I assure you my vengeance will be swift and final. That much I promise."

Fulvia grinned with a ferocity that raised Marcus's hackles. Anger consuming her, she twisted and wrenched the papyrus scroll containing Cicero's attacks until it tore in half. Throwing it to the ground, she used one foot to grind it into the lawn. "The very hand writing these insults will be cut *off*!" she cried.

"Fulvia, contain yourself!" Mother gasped. Antyllus didn't understand his mother's rage and began to whimper.

Marcus stood up and lifted his son into his arms. "Yes, someday Cicero will go to the gods at my order." Gently, he jiggled the baby, bringing a smile back to Antyllus's face. "And as for cutting off his hand, Fulvia's actually on to something there. It would serve as a warning to anyone else daring to humiliate this family."

Eyes shining with rage, Fulvia held her head high. She moved over to Marcus, kissing him hungrily, her tongue weaving between his teeth.

But her lustful moment was short-lived. Marcus broke away, sauntering back into the domus, his son in his arms. As he entered the cool atrium, he sat down on the edge of the fountain. Antyllus giggled, trying to grab at the falling water with chubby hands.

Marcus watched his son enjoy himself while he considered the enigma that was his wife. Oh, Fulvia exhibited loyalty and love, to be sure. But her overzealous, fixated nature was often far from endearing.

CHAPTER XXV

GAIUS ANTONIUS IN MACEDONIA TO HIS brother Consul Marcus Antonius in Rome:

The Macedonian legions are on their way to Brundisium. Hopefully, Neptune will grant them a speedy crossing from Greece. I've kept four cohorts here. Brutus and Cassius continue recruiting. It's said they're heading steadily east. I hope they don't enter Macedonia.

Keep me apprised of the situation in Italia.

To avoid argument, Marcus let Fulvia accompany him to claim the Macedonians. She begged to come, and was still in the early stages of pregnancy. Her physician assured him that she'd be safe to travel.

It was new and unconventional, bringing a woman on a military mission. Usually, only prostitutes lived among legions, and then only on the outer edges of fortifications. Not to mention that some legionaries believed having a woman in camp was bad luck.

But when did Marcus Antonius ever adhere to convention?

It was nearly ten days' march to Brundisium, so as he rode, he had plenty to ponder. First and foremost was Gaius's brief message. If Brutus and Cassius were soliciting that far eastward, would they discover his brother more or less undefended in Macedonia. Marcus worried that he'd erred, sending Gaius into unanticipated danger.

His other food for thought was Fulvia. What did she really mean to him? Some days he really thought he loved her. But where was the overpowering emotion that could reduce him to tears or drive him nearly mad with passion? Or had Fadia been merely a frantic infatuation of youthful desire?

No. Their love had been genuine. The void left at her death was worse than any wound. Perhaps these days in Brundisium with Fulvia would trigger an answer, one way or another. He'd been honest with Gaius. Marcus wanted love again.

Ah . . . Fulvia. Her forceful and manipulating nature was bothersome, regardless of her intentions. She was a willful woman and had a habit of getting what she wanted. Yet she had one incredibly redeeming trait: devotion.

Before leaving Rome, he sternly reminded her, "No meddling in legionary affairs. This will be my business, not yours."

Once encamped in Brundisium, Marcus and Fulvia were about to retire for the night when young Gnaeus Tuccius requested permission to enter the praetorium. He was along to negotiate and act as liaison between Marcus and the legionary commanders, allowing Canidius to remain in Rome to look after Antonian interests along with Lucius.

Tuccius bore unwelcome news. "Sir, legionaries here have convinced their superiors to demand more coin for their loyalty. Octavian has been courting their support by courier."

Marcus rubbed his eyes. "Competing for my legions now, is he? Well, I don't play his game. Soldiers under my command are professionals. They'll be paid once they've *earned* their keep. Give each man an extra ration of salt tomorrow along with my word of honor that they'll be treated fairly, just as Caesar Imperator always treated them."

"Greedy *pigs*!" Fulvia spat, causing Tuccius to glance at her and cock his eyebrow. "Are we made of gold?"

Marcus ignored her, noting the apprehension on Tuccius's face. Wearily, he sat down and sighed, "Out with it, Tuccius. What did they demand?"

"They're holding out until they hear directly from you. They reminded me how Octavian promised his men five hundred denarii each. His grand offers are the talk of the camp."

The next morning Marcus climbed up on the platform during assembly, ready to address his troops. Usually, whenever he appeared before his men they cheered and chanted his name. Today their silence unsettled him. When he spoke, they offered no acclaim or acknowledgement. Immediately following, even centurions came forward demanding bribes for loyalty. Many of them also voiced disapproval that he'd not yet avenged Caesar's death.

Marcus forced himself to swallow angry oaths. In as controlled a voice as possible, he reminded them, "It seems you lower yourselves to demands other than just the honor of fighting for Rome." He shook his head in disappointment. There was no response; the men stared at him, stone-faced. "I'll honor your request *this once*," he conceded, "extending an extra one hundred denarii per man. As for seeking vengeance for Caesar, the time's not right."

The men considered his words, talking among themselves, until a cheeky centurion had the audacity to speak up. "Consul, you offer us far less than young Caesar. I could head north right now with my cohort and pledge him my services. If he promised his men five hundred denarii, then we expect that or more from you."

Enough was enough! "I have *clearly* stated my offer," he warned angrily. "Do you really think Octavian will pay you what he says he will when I can't? Don't insult me by demanding more!

Remember, I've been at this game longer than that boy. And you all know the punishment for desertion. Don't be foolish!"

Abruptly ending the meeting, he stalked back to the praetorium. Rankers and centurions alike stepped aside, grumbling and eyeing him with dark stares.

"*Five hundred* per man!" he exclaimed to Fulvia and Tuccius over dinner. "Not even Crassus could have afforded that. It'll empty my coffers just to give them the extra hundred each."

"Many have accepted," Tuccius spoke calmly, "but you must expect to lose some. There was violence in the ranks after you left."

"Decimate them," Fulvia suggested with a shrug, popping a nut into her mouth and continuing while chewing. "These men have made a mockery of you with their unrealistic demands. They deserve harsh punishment."

Decimation? Oh, Marcus hated that thought. Certainly, the killing of every tenth man would strike fear into the ranks, but it could also stir up more mutiny.

Accompanied by a number of hand-picked guards, he toured camp that night, speaking to some of the men personally. Far too many legionaries were in dissent, something he'd rarely seen while serving with Caesar. He and Tuccius had to break up four fights! These legions had been far from Rome—in Macedonia—for so long they had become unruly and unpredictable.

It had to stop.

Late that night in the praetorium, he paced worriedly.

"Remember, some are committed to us, sir," Tuccius reminded, trying to stay positive. "It'll be those holdouts who will be treacherous if things continue to escalate. And loyal men will be endangered, not to mention ourselves."

Marcus turned on him sharply. "I came here to take command, and I won't back down! Even if only *half* the Macedonians join me, I'll still be better off than when we came. Those others—they need a lesson in authority."

"Decimation," Fulvia whispered again.

Marcus was tiring of her interruptions, but sadly, she was

probably right. "Tuccius, go enlist help from the officers who are loyal. Find out who the ringleaders are and arrest them. We'll execute them in the morning. In addition, any unit refusing to accept my offer and join our ranks peaceably will face decimation. Hopefully that'll frighten loyalty into them. I'll reward any officers with coin whose cohorts peacefully take my oath."

Marcus tossed and turned all night.

Decimation was a terrible business. It was the most extreme punishment Roman generals used to maintain control over disorderly troops, and up until now he'd never had to use it. Every ten men drew lots, the losers facing death by bludgeoning at the hands of their own comrades.

It turned out that an entire cohort refused to comply. Things were grave, and now he faced the unavoidable. Sickened, he ordered the men to draw lots.

In dawn's gray shadows, he resignedly sat atop his horse, head throbbing, not from wine, but from stress and lack of sleep. A long string of condemned legionaries and centurions knelt naked before him with their hands bound. Oh, how he hated this—well-trained men being beaten to death at his command . . .

One condemned centurion shuffled forward clumsily, sinking down before him and begging for mercy, tears of terror and remorse streaming down his battle-hardened face. Marcus set his jaw, ignoring his pleas, wishing he was anywhere but here. This man would die like the others.

Tuccius loudly read their sentence while thousands of men looked on. This would be a public example, hopefully discouraging other foolishness.

Morning's soft sunlight was interrupted with shouts, screams, moaning, the thuds of cudgels, lashes, and stones striking human flesh. It was surreal, a sickening scene. In the middle of all this slaughter, a sudden movement to the side caught Marcus's attention. He dropped his jaw in shock.

Surely, this was another nightmare! Weren't these executions appalling enough without *this*?

It was Fulvia, accompanied by a bevy of her slaves, arriving by litter.

Shocked beyond belief that she'd even desire to witness this, Marcus was infuriated that she'd come in the middle of the executions—and in such rich finery. As though she were headed to the theater to see a play.

Soldiers turned away from watching their dying comrades to see their general's wife in all her jewels and bright silks step out of her litter to watch the show. Even more outrageous was just how close to the violence she stood. Craning her neck for a better view, Fulvia was closer to the dying men than Marcus.

When one soldier took his turn at clubbing a condemned man from his contubernium, the club struck the victim's skull, splattering blood and brain matter straight onto Fulvia's cheek. Unaware that human gore now painted her face, she looked out self-importantly over the proceedings, as though she belonged there.

Teeth clenched in rage, Marcus felt ill enough to vomit. He had long been desensitized to slaughter; that was not the issue here. It was the fact that Fulvia's unwomanly behavior was humiliating him and bound to haunt him for the rest of his life—just like the Curio scandal. Once the last condemned soldier was proclaimed dead, Marcus whipped his horse's head about.

"Your wife, sir," Tuccius whispered discreetly, gesturing to Fulvia.

"*Damn* my wife!" Marcus hissed through set teeth, spurring his horse so hard the animal snorted and pawed at the air before bolting off.

When Fulvia returned to the praetorium, Marcus was waiting. Snatching a cloth, he flung it at her hard. "Wipe your face, *bitch*! One of my men's brains is smeared all over your cheek!"

Struck by the cloth as much as catching it, she dabbed at her face tentatively, unprepared for such a hostile reception and unaware she was wearing an executed man's body fluids. Inadvertently, she smeared the soldier's blood all the way down her neck, only noticing after three or four swipes. "Very well, there's blood on my face. But why are you so angry?"

Marcus glared at her, incredulous. "I don't believe you. Are you not a woman? Why would you want to watch a decimation? How could you shame me so, coming out to watch my men die as though it were some gladiator spectacle? You're my *wife*! A highborn woman of Rome! You had no business there *whatsoever*!"

Fulvia looked genuinely stunned. "I—I came to support *you.* I knew you hated to kill those men, regardless of their disloyalty. I attend the games back home. What's the difference? Blood is blood, is it not? Why should it matter who it comes from, slave or free? And why should I not offer you support since I'm here?"

"It's not the same!" Marcus shouted, enraged. "Never, *ever* confuse military executions with games, Fulvia. Gladiators are nothing but slaves and criminals used for entertainment or funerary expiations. Military executions end the lives of freeborn citizen legionaries. *Never* do I take such action lightly, sentencing soldiers to punishment or death. By wearing that man's blood on your face, along with all your wealth and finery, you cheapened my actions and his death. You *humiliated* me in front of my army!"

Livid, he left her, shaken and blood-smeared. Behind him, the tent flap snapped shut over her pleading voice.

"Husband, forgive me. *I love you!*"

Marcus practically heard her heart break. Ah, well. At least he had the answer he sought regarding his feelings for Fulvia. Never would she accompany him again—anywhere. And *never* would he love her.

Marcus left camp, riding off alone to a nearby village and carousing at a local brothel, getting splendidly drunk. Tuccius came looking for him the next morning, but Marcus stayed on for several more days. When he finally sobered up, he made a crucial decision.

He was going to bypass Rome altogether, head straight to Mutina, and confront Decimus Brutus.

Fulvia *and* the Senate be damned!

Proconsul Marcus Antonius in Mutina to his Mother, Julia Antonia, in Rome:

Salve. If this letter finds you well, then I am well.

Spring is slowly coming to the north, and Decimus Brutus refuses to surrender. Therefore I've completed siege works surrounding Mutina. I assume Cicero will try to destroy any of my remaining senatorial credibility, so keep me informed of what takes place.

Once, you encouraged me to set out on a political career. Well, I have achieved the status of consul. Outwardly, I will fight for the Caesarian cause, avenging your cousin. But inwardly, my spirit fights for us—for the Antonii—as I have absolutely no reason to respect old-fashioned Republican traditions which I have never seen to succeed.

Fulvia Bambula in Rome to her husband, Marcus Antonius, in Mutina:

Dearest husband, we yearn for your victory as Cicero continues spreading deceit. He has slandered you for your priestly duties last season in the Lupercalia and even calls on the revered spirit of your grandfather to chastise your 'flagrant abuse of military power.' Does he not see that he backs you against a wall with his poisonous tongue? I swear to Juno I shall have it cut out! I know you think me bloodthirsty or unwomanly, but I only wish I could prove my sincere love for you.

Be forewarned that Cicero is sending relief to Decimus Brutus. Take care, for the new Consuls Aulus

> *Hirtius and Gaius Vibius Pansa are leading an army to his aid.*

Not even at Pharsalus had Marcus seen such an impasse in battle.

The Senate had retaliated against him, sending three sets of forces to aid Decimus Brutus. Vibius Pansa, an experienced military man, Aulus Hirtius, and Octavian all headed north to confront the Antonian army.

At first, Marcus stayed put, merely maintaining his siege works. Scouts located Hirtius and Octavian's camp, nearby and just north of the Via Aemilia. Marcus kept them busy, sending in skirmishes to see to it that nobody in Octavian and Hirtius's camp got much sleep. Then cavalry scouts from farther down the road galloped in with news that Vibius Pansa was riding to their relief with three legions.

Marcus called for a consilium. He gathered his centurions along with Lucius, Tuccius, and a few tribunes, crowding around a map of the area.

"Here's what I propose. Scouts say the territory around this village called Forum Gallorum is marshy and hard to traverse. I say we surprise Pansa with infantry along the road and hit him with everything we've got."

"But our cavalry is one of our best offenses, and they'd be useless in the marsh," Tuccius pointed out.

"Oh, we'll use them. Just farther down the road where the ground is better for horse. They'll wait until Pansa's engaged and attack his flanks."

"It'll be a fairly even fight," Lucius observed.

Marcus smiled grimly. "Pansa has men who deserted me down in Brundisium—men from the Macedonian legions who should have honored my orders, but didn't. Once our boys find out that they are in the ranks, they'll be itching for blood and games."

"Who will lead, sir?" This from Tuccius.

"I will. I want you and Lucius to remain here with a careful eye on Octavian and Hirtius. I'm taking our best men—veterans and men from the Macedonians who are still pissed at their former brothers in arms for betraying me. Send word immediately if there's movement from their camp. Understood?"

Marcus left late in the day, eagerly leading a crack contingent of cavalry and what loyal Macedonian legions he had to give Pansa a true Antonian welcome. Just as he thought, the legionaries were thrilled at the thought of repaying their former comrades for their treachery in Brundisium.

Equipped for a surprise attack, the cavalry bound their horses' hooves with leather or cloth to mute sound as much as possible. Legionaries fighting around the marshes decorated their helmets with branches, boughs, and grasses to blend into the swampy environs. They moved at a whisper, passing through the village amidst hovels, stables, behind wells and walls, invisible as air.

Darkness was their shield.

Forum Gallorum's terrified townsfolk retreated into the woods, fearful of the coming slaughter.

As planned, Marcus sent his cavalry on ahead. Pansa's line would be long, and he'd have his more experienced veterans in front.

Perhaps Pansa's men saw glints of Antonian armor or helmets upon approaching, for as they passed through the village, his vanguard hesitated. Quickly, Marcus dropped his hand and a flaming arrow whizzed into the air—signaling attack.

Surrounded by bogs, Pansa's front line panicked, many of his men springing sideways into the marsh instead of holding ground on the road. Marcus smiled grimly. By quitting the road, they met his legionaries hiding in the quagmire surrounding it.

It was a slogging, messy struggle in close quarters—like Pharsalus. Pansa's front lines barely had time to draw gladii. Antonian centurions swapped their lines effortlessly despite the soft ground. Pulse rushing, Marcus watched from where he commanded just amid a line of trees in the village. His horse quivered beneath him, starting at the sounds of screaming men and clashing blades, both sides foundering in muck.

Damn! That center of Pansa's persisted in tight formation, though the consul obviously struggled to send relief to his front. Overall, confusion combined with legionaries bound on vengeance against one another blocked the road with an immoveable wall of hostile bodies.

Night's black sheath made it difficult to discern what was happening. Casualties mounted on both sides. Legionary slaves and medics struggled to pull wounded and dead out of the way. Marcus yelled encouragement to his infantry in the bogs. "Hold your lines! Hold this road! Stand firm!"

Centurions on both sides were sounding whistles for opposing front lines to change again and again. Officers could be heard scolding soldiers for prematurely changing guard when the nearby calls were confused with those from opposing ranks. As was always the case with night fighting, it was often impossible to distinguish friend from foe. Marcus was still hopeful at the outcome, but right now it was impossible to tell who was really winning.

When several hours of fighting had passed, a tribune with the cavalry rode in. "Their left is caving, and rumor has it Pansa's wounded!"

It was true. Before long, Marcus saw the enemy falling back and turning to run. Pansa's more seasoned troops had either fallen or fled. Men toward the rear were panicking. Breathlessly, Marcus shouted, "Chase those newer recruits. You'll know who they are. They'll be the ones pissing themselves at the sight of your blades. Go!"

Victory! How sweet was her taste!

Marcus's weary men loosely assembled on the road, happily composing soldier songs about Pansa's defeat and humiliation. Together they ambled along in predawn darkness, arm in arm, faces covered in blood and mud. Some swigged posca, passing wineskins from man to man.

Fortunately, there had been no desperate message from Mutina concerning Octavian and Hirtius. Buoyed by his men's sense of fun and pleased with their success, Marcus rode among them, composing a few verses of his own to their cadences, sharing their raw humor, and even swinging off his horse to march at their sides.

If only it could have lasted . . .

Victory! How fickle her disposition!

Within a few miles of camp, a single rider barreled toward them, weaving his horse through the disorganized, celebrating legionaries. Marcus disengaged from his revels to receive the horseman, a separate darkness from night's gloom turning his mood.

"Sir! It's Aulus Hirtius and Octavian! They're in full battle array in front of our camp at Mutina!"

Gods—this meant they'd have to face them head-on just to enter camp again. Well, at least Lucius and Tuccius got a messenger out. Better to know it now . . .

Marcus shouted to a tubicin and a nearby centurion, ordering formation. As the trumpet blared, nearby soldiers stared at him in wide-eyed shock. Everyone was in utter confusion, and Marcus bitterly regretted his men's loose array. Many of them were too drunk by now to even respond appropriately.

Strung out along the roadway for several miles and with many of them full of wine, there was no way they could take on a fresh army. Marcus cursed himself for allowing his men a reprieve. Had they remained organized, they would've had a fair chance despite fatigue and low numbers.

Not now.

"Back to formation!" he shouted repeatedly. Nervous and snorting, his horse circled as he fumbled at its girth, tightening his saddle to remount. A legionary stepped up and snatched his horse by the bridle, stilling the animal. As he heaved himself up by the saddle horn, Marcus wished this was merely another of his nightmares.

Soldiers were still gawking at him in bewilderment, and a

few even looked at one another and laughed, still swigging from their skins. But centurions were yelling and had started striking stubborn, drunken slackers.

Relieved to see reorganization beginning, Marcus whipped his horse's head back toward Mutina and commanded his infantry forward.

All odds were against him now.

Hirtius's army was fresh and strong, all formed up and ready to fight in front of the Antonian fortifications. Marcus scanned the walls his men had built months ago. Its main entrance was blocked and swarming with enemy legionaries. There was nothing for it except to force their way through. He ordered centurions to switch ranks frequently and maintain order as more men caught up with their disordered units.

It sickened him as the fight unfolded. His tenacious Macedonian legionaries he had acquired at Brundisium, who had courageously won the victory over Pansa during the night, were first to fall. Within an hour of engaging, Antonian units were disintegrating. Marcus saw terrified men bolting through the night back toward the marshes.

After an hour or so, he ordered his cavalry to ride wide. Ever proud of his horse, Marcus watched them carve open a passage for his men to pass into camp. Once inside the walls, they might be able to counterattack Hirtius, using men from inside the fortifications. But what took place was far from success, aside for the fact that their camp was still in a fine defensive order.

Hirtius's men were deadly quick to follow, and compared to this grisly bloodbath of desperation, last night's bout now felt like a pleasant jaunt through the countryside. Marcus barely made it to his praetorium before Tuccius burst in, warning that Hirtius's troops had broken through and were marching straight down the cardo toward them.

Slamming his fist onto a portable desk, Marcus snapped, "I want my personal guard *surrounding* this praetorium. If we lose this camp, the siege is over and the rest of our men will be theirs. We'll be corpses! Lucius, you and Tuccius lead a fresh cohort straight at them. *Now!* I'll follow with whoever's left in my cavalry."

Wordlessly, his brother and Tuccius hastened to follow orders.

Hirtius's men reached Marcus's personal guard in no time. These were men Marcus had hand selected to serve as praetorium sentries whenever he slept. Amidst curses, shouts, and mortal screams of agony, his heart hammered as he watched Hirtius riding hard toward several guards already engaged in combat.

"It's Hirtius! Take him *down*!" Marcus screamed.

Two personal guardsmen heard him and reacted. Both men ran forward in the parade ground's space, launching their javelins in perfect form. Both spears slammed Hirtius square in the back. He was probably dead before hitting the ground.

Relieved and breathless, Marcus remounted, leading his cavalry onward and leaving his praetorium behind. It would take tight, dangerous fighting to force the enemy back outside their walls, but it had to be done. Many Antonian legionaries were still outside the fortifications somewhere. Perhaps with Hirtius dead he could turn things around.

Then Fortuna threw her dice again.

Octavian, of all people, materialized with a sizeable unit, just as Lucius's infantry sent the rest of Hirtius's cohort running for their lives back outside the fort. Somehow Caesar's heir had heard about Hirtius's death and managed to slip into camp, to retrieve the body. Under cover from his bodyguards, he hauled Hirtius back to his horse. After Octavian remounted, several of the men helped, lifting Hirtius's body up and placing it in front of the youth.

Marcus had to admit that Octavian's actions were noble. But he made a mistake. He signaled his men to retreat back outside the Antonian wall. What was he thinking? He could have won the day.

And now? A loss? Stalemate? All Marcus knew for certain was that last night's triumph had been snatched from his grasp.

A consilium was called.

Marcus chewed his lip, pacing from one side of the tent to the other. Despite a lack of sleep, he was alert and energized. Eros brought in wine, but Marcus countered him. "No. No wine. Take that entire amphora and use it to cleanse our wounded."

There were far too many.

Lucius reported to Marcus in the middle of the tent, breathing hard and reaching out to embrace his elder brother. Like Gaius, his experience in the field was limited, but he had more of a stomach for war. "Will Octavian return?" he asked worriedly.

Marcus nodded, thoughtfully answering his brother. "Oh yes. I still can't understand why he retreated. He had us. Tuccius, what've we got?"

Tuccius blinked wearily, scanning a large vellum scroll. "Half our men are dead. Our legions were already undermanned, so we have no real fighting force left."

"But we held this camp," Lucius snarled. "And Decimus Brutus is low on provisions. He must be starving, or he would've joined in the fight. Soon he'll have to surrender."

Marcus shook his head. "No, we aren't holding Mutina with so few men, especially when Octavian will return. And if I left one of you behind while I went to summon relief, you'd be dangerously exposed. I won't do that."

"What about heading north?" Tuccius queried.

Really, that was their only option.

Marcus nodded. "This summer I sent Canidius up to Lepidus in Gaul with additional units. One of Caesar's old generals, Ventidius Bassus is also nearby. He's always been loyal."

Tuccius mused, "If we get up there and they all pledge allegiance to you, then our forces would be stronger than *anything* the Senate sends."

"But the mountains will be cold, Brother," Lucius warned. "Can we even make it—what with the wounded and so few provisions?"

Marcus clapped him on the shoulder. With a plan unfolding, he was eager to get moving. "It won't be easy, but we'll have to. And

Lepidus won't be pleased when I take the reins of leadership from him a second time."

"When do we break camp?" asked Lucius. "Right now, everyone's exhausted."

"We won't leave yet. Wounded men are still stranded in those marshes. At daybreak, every available centurion and cavalryman are to return there to seek out any wounded. Some of this was my own damned fault," he muttered. "We were *fools* not to be in formation after defeating Pansa." Marcus shook his head, furious with himself.

Mule carts and cavalrymen rescued countless injured men in the marshes, and despite low rations and terrible loss, morale was bouncing back. Marcus spent most of his time visiting the wounded, kneeling at their sides and clasping their hands. He needed to instill as much trust and hope into their spirits as possible. The journey north would be difficult. Then spies sent to Octavian's camp returned. They were organizing, preparing for another attack.

It was time to march.

While soldiers were breaking camp, Eros entered the praetorium with a shaving bowl. "No," Marcus refused. "I won't shave until I've mourned my men who have died. And if we survive this and combine forces with Lepidus, I'm going to honor those two men who killed Hirtius."

"How, Dominus?"

"I've been thinking about it for the past several days. I'm going to make it a great honor to be in my personal guard. I'll triple their pay and give them a name." He chuckled to himself and then added, "Yes—I'll call them praetorian guards."

As smoke from their burning siege works and fortifications blackened the skies, a lone courier galloped into camp bearing a letter from Rome. Eros brought it to Marcus as he and Lucius were busily packing personal belongings.

"From your Mother, Dominus."

Julia Antonia in Rome to her son Proconsul Marcus Antonius in Mutina:

Beloved Marcus, my fervent prayer is for your safety. Now sit down and prepare yourself, for I have much news.

Brutus and Cassius are building a massive army in the East. Undoubtedly, they intend to use this force to return to Rome and reinstate themselves in the Senate. While passing through Macedonia, Brutus arrested Gaius and is holding him prisoner. Piso overheard Cicero talking in the Senate. He intends to recommend that Gaius be executed! I've written to Brutus myself pleading for mercy on his behalf.

Now I must tell you about affairs in the Senate.

Cicero has bestowed a fabricated title of propraetor upon Octavian in absentia. All of this just to ratify his illegal recruiting. Then he proposed to declare you an enemy of the state due to your "unprecedented siege upon an elected official."

We knew that if Cicero succeeded, it would only be a matter of time before someone betrayed you. So Fulvia formed a daring plan. She and I dressed the whole household in mourning. Every slave, your wife, Antyllus, and I walked straight to the Senate on the day Cicero was about to exact measures against you. Fulvia carried Antyllus, and she and I climbed to the top of the Rostra, our slaves lining the front of the platform, each one unified with us. Plebs were outraged when they heard what Cicero was about to do, and as a result his plan failed.

Now with a heavy heart, I must report that your Uncle Lucius Julius has joined the Optimate cause.

I cannot understand him, my son. He fought loyally for Caesar, and I had hopes that you and he would reconcile someday. Cicero has published too much poison, and your uncle is tainted by it.

Therefore I applaud your plan to kill Cicero. His insults to our gens are unending. Now he calls you "Spartacus"! How dare he compare you to a lowborn slave who was an enemy of Rome!

Yesterday, I learned that your former friend Gaius Trebonius has died. Dolabella was on his way to Syria to take up his proconsulship there. On his way, he encountered Trebonius and had him murdered. Shortly thereafter, Cassius heard about the incident and hunted Dolabella down, killing him in turn.

Fulvia sends her love. I know you are estranged, but I tell you, there has never been a more valiant supporter seeing to your interests here in Rome. You have her undying devotion and support, Marcus. She is near her time, and I pray you will reunite with her once you're home again.

May Mars shield you and Minerva grant you wisdom.

CHAPTER XXVI

43-42BC

HIGH IN SOUTHERN GAUL'S LOFTIEST ELEVATIONS, conditions remained icy and frigid. It was a terrible time of year to be in a mountain pass.

Marcus had driven his men hard these past weeks since leaving Mutina, striving for a quick pace to stay ahead of any pursuit. But now the terrain was slick—slowing them. Cavalrymen led the ascent through the mountains. With the horses plowing through deeper snows, the infantry had an easier time.

Unforgiving winds whipped up snow flurries, stinging the faces of legionaries in the Alaudae, Legio V. "The Larks," as they were nicknamed, no longer resembled swift birds. Their wings had been clipped at Mutina. Other legionaries from the bedraggled VII, VIII, and IX followed behind. At least their ranks were gaining some reinforcements along the way. Marcus wasn't ashamed or too proud to grant slaves freedom if they joined him. Nor did he hesitate, under the circumstances, to commandeer sons of farmers and men from a few villages they passed. Veterans would train the new men once they were out of the mountains. Extra numbers might give them better chances despite the work involved to train them into real soldiers.

Food was scarce, and everyone supplemented meager rations with wild berries, nuts, and vermin culled in the lower elevations. Cavalrymen often sacrificed their own porridge to their horses.

Today Marcus was riding alongside Publius Ventidius Bassus, a former legate of Caesar. Marcus hadn't known him well during the Gallic War, but he knew he was loyal to Caesar's memory. He had joined Marcus's battered forces without question. In front rode their guide, a native Gallic warrior Ventidius trusted.

Ventidius's grizzled face bore more hair than his balding head. He had joined Marcus's example, growing a beard to mourn men lost at Forum Gallorum and Mutina.

"Let's hope they hold out," Marcus voiced, worried. He looked back, surveying the circuitous line behind him.

Hoarse and speaking through cracked lips, Ventidius asked, "I know you sent your brother Lucius ahead with scouts to locate Lepidus. But what if he proves less than welcoming? A legate of his—Plancus—promised the Senate that 'Antonius won't be a problem for long.'"

Smiling grimly, Marcus assured him, "You joined me, didn't you? So will Lepidus. His military experience is minimal, and he knows it. What's more, his men do too. They'll prefer fighting for me." At this point, he had to be confident and hope for the best.

This tactical retreat was the biggest gamble of Marcus's career. Since leaving Mutina, they'd encountered nothing but suffering, misery, and strain. As a result of tearing into raw mice or fowl, many men fell ill. Legionary physicians urged them to cook whatever meat they scavenged, but with fuel running short above the tree line in these higher altitudes, that was impossible. Also, the wounded slowed progress. Many died from exposure or festering wounds. But since their present course was too rocky for carts, slaves and faithful comrades ported them on stretchers.

Marcus's concerns didn't just end with the conditions and needs of his army. After receiving Mother's letter, he worried about his family. Were they out of harm's way? Had Fulvia had the baby yet? Would Brutus be receptive to Mother's pleas and spare Gaius? And what was happening in Rome?

Riding for ten days through bitterly cold and inhospitable passes, the tide turned as they descended into lower country. Marcus ordered a halt and dismounted as several horsemen approached at a rapid trot. One rider pressed ahead of the others.

"Marcus, it's me—Lucius!"

Gods, what relief! Marcus leaped down, both men engulfing one another in a hug. "What news?" he asked, his voice betraying desperation.

"Three days ago, we ran into Lepidus's sentries down on the lower passes," Lucius explained breathlessly. "When they learned who I was, they granted us passage. We've been camping on the opposite side of a river from their army, and they've let us be. Lepidus hasn't responded to my inquests, but Canidius did. He told me to encourage you to come on."

Well, well. Antonius might remain a problem for Octavian and his Senate a bit longer.

Late in the day, they entered a large glen surrounded by sparse trees along the narrow River Argenteus. Just on the opposite bank was Marcus Aemilius Lepidus's enormous, fortified encampment.

After setting up their own camp, centurions assembled the men into formation before a sweeping hillside. Marcus used the natural acoustics, ordering officers to relay his words back to everyone in the rear.

"Just across the river is my friend Marcus Aemilius Lepidus. Word is the Senate ordered him to destroy me, but my hope is that he joins us instead. Given time, I hope to be Caesar's avenger, and together we'll sniff out Brutus and Cassius, for their reckoning is due."

Even with starvation and fatigue, a heartening cheer followed Marcus's words. Gods, was it ever time for *something* inspiring. Lifting a hand to silence them, he continued, "Tonight we're not fortifying camp. Many of you have brothers, cousins, and friends among Lepidus's army. Go to them. Tell them Marcus Antonius will welcome them into his ranks, and once reinforced, we'll show Rome I'm no traitor! After all, we need men willing to stand against Caesar's murderers!"

That was a powerful lure, and Marcus was encouraged by another roar of approval. Oh, they were exhausted, but their spirits were vigorous.

Indeed, legionaries craved revenge for Caesar. Regardless of Marcus's feelings of betrayal, he continued to play the role of Caesar's loyal second. Repressing his emotions in the last year, the bitterness of omission from the will was a hot coal in his core, spurring him on to do whatever was necessary to bring glory to the Antonii. Strange and sad, but there it was. His loyalty to Rome itself had been shaken through his betrayal from both Caesar and the Senate.

That night he, Lucius, and Ventidius shared a simple meal of salted porridge together in the praetorium. Afterward, they sat quietly sipping their last stores of posca and relaxing for the first time since Mutina.

Presently, a sentry announced an exhausted courier.

The man's clothing was travel-worn and his face chapped red from wind and weather. "Dominus Antonius," he breathed. "It took me weeks to find you." He knelt at Marcus's feet, offering two sealed tablets, both bearing the wax image of Anton, his ancestor and purported link to Hercules. Studying him a moment longer, Marcus recognized him as one of Fulvia's slaves.

"What is it?" Lucius inquired. "Who's it from?"

Signaling Eros to see to the courier's needs, Marcus stood up, carrying the tablets to a nearby lamp for more light. With a flip of his thumb, he snapped the first seal, recognizing the bold yet feminine scrawl. "This first one's from Fulvia," he answered, holding his breath. Though indifferent to her now, she was still his wife, and politically steadfast. Oh, how he hoped his family was safe. "Looks like the second is from Mother."

"News from Rome, then?" Ventidius probed. They were all eager for the latest.

Hurriedly skimming Fulvia's tablet, Marcus snorted bitterly. "They finally declared me an enemy of the state, after all. But it seems old Titus Pomponius Atticus is an old friend of Fulvia's family. He offered Mother and Fulvia safe haven in one of his houses outside the city. That's where they're staying. Atticus is a good man despite being Cicero's friend." He read a few phrases further before exclaiming, "And I'm a father again! Lucius, you have another nephew!"

Lucius threw his head back to laugh in joy, the sound seeming foreign after all their hardship. "Oh, we needed good news! What's his name?"

"Actually, that was a matter of contention before we left Rome. Mother won. I wanted another Gaius, but she suggested a Julian praenomen to reflect continued loyalty to Caesar. I finally agreed. He's Iullus Antonius. It should make for good politics. Octavian may hate admitting it, but we share Caesar's blood, he and I, whether he likes it or not."

Lucius shook his head regretfully. "Caesar should have named you heir, Marcus."

"That ship has sailed. I must move forward."

"And we're with you," Lucius promised, glancing at Ventidius for support. "Always know that."

Ventidius raised his cup in agreement. "Indeed."

"Gratias. You remind me how fortunate I am," Marcus sighed, pausing to read more of Fulvia's letter until coming to another point of interest, which he immediately shared aloud. "Ah well, Octavian got himself approved by the Senate as Caesar's son. Wherever does that boy get his mettle? Says he seized the entire state treasury to pay his legions and named *himself* consul, all behind old Chickpea's back!"

"Really?" Lucius responded in amazement. "I wonder what a break with Cicero means for him—as well as us? But consul? Surely, his age made him ineligible."

"Cicero probably uttered those very words." Ventidius grinned grimly and rubbed tired, reddened eyes.

Marcus nodded, swallowing some wine before continuing. "Brutus and Cassius think leaving me alive was their fatal mistake, but what they may not realize is that they opened a Pandora's Box called 'Octavian,' making everybody's lives miserable."

Nodding in agreement, Lucius asked, "Any other news?"

Marcus blew his cheeks out, reading again, "Little pissant's certainly been busy. He's convinced the Senate into passing a law decreeing death sentences for Caesar's murderers and for Sextus Pompeius, who aids them."

"Pompeius?" Ventidius raised bushy eyebrows in surprise. "Who'd ever think that pup would have amounted to anything with just a few ships left to him?"

Marcus nodded, nose still in Fulvia's letter. "Seems he's made a name for himself, pirating for the Optimate cause."

"Let's hope his ambitions stop there," Ventidius sighed, shaking his head.

Marcus changed the subject. "Well, now that night has fallen, we need to walk about camp and encourage fraternization. Presently, Sextus Pompeius is less of a problem than attaining Lepidus's army."

For several days, the two encampments maintained their positions. Sentries on Marcus's side of the river were instructed to alert their officers should Lepidus make any threatening moves. However, with legionaries mingling and shouting to one another on both sides of the river, there was more a spirit of merriment in the air than anything else. When Marcus heard that several of his cohorts received grain gifts from soldiers in Lepidus's camp, he thought it was time to risk all.

"Surely, you wish to shave now, Dominus." Eros wasn't asking. He was stating, staring at his master with a raised brow.

Marcus reached up, stroking his wind-burned face, then broke into a radiant smile. "Actually, no. Do I look frighteningly wild and unkempt?"

Eros didn't reply. The answer was in his eyes.

"Good! I want everyone in Lepidus's camp to see that I've suffered along with my men. They must see our situation as dire. Remember the night we escaped Pompeius through the sewers? Caesar made Gaius and me an example before his legions, all battered and filthy from swimming in shit. Men respond to that sort of thing."

"Lepidus won't be pleased to give up command again. Especially if he promised the Senate to destroy you," Eros pointed out.

"Let me start educating you on the Senate. First of all, what a man *says* to them and how he actually feels are two different things entirely. This is a risk I must take for us all. True, no man feels pleased watching his soldiers leave for a new general. And here I am, putting him through it a second time. But he's reasonable and not as ambitious as I."

Eros cinched the lacings of Marcus's cuirass tighter. He'd lost weight again during their journey of hardships. "I'll wear my armillae, but no gladius," he ordered. "They must know from the start that I come in peace."

"I fear for you, Dominus," Eros whispered.

Marcus turned about to face him. Eros held up his paludamentum—his cloak of high command. He shook his head. "No. I have to go for a little swim to reach the other side, so that'll only weigh me down. Now—how do I look?"

"Hairy, unarmed, and like a man who needs a bigger army," Eros answered.

Marcus grinned at him, ready for the adventure. "Good. Then it's time for me to cross *my* Rubicon.

And cross it, he did.

Marcus walked straight into the river in front of legionaries on both sides, every soldier cheering him on. Clinching his jaw at the icy water, he swore silently against the numbing cold. Two more steps plunged him in over his head, his cuirass weighting him down. For a panicky moment, he struggled against the depth, current, and armor, then resurfaced using powerful kicks to stay afloat. For a time, he was forced to swim downstream before crossing over to climb ashore.

Fraternizing legionaries from his army and Lepidus's had followed him as he was tugged downstream. As he pulled himself out of the water, soldiers descended upon him in droves. Several offered their own cloaks to dry and warm him. Chilled to the bone, he embraced as many as he could, shivering but laughing, slapping backs genially and responding to their excited greetings. Lepidus's men buoyed him on every side, leading him to the main gate of their camp.

The wooden doors opened as a uniformed officer stepped out.

"Canidius!" Marcus exclaimed in relief, hurrying forward to embrace his friend.

"Gods, Antonius, what a sight you are! And you're freezing cold!" Canidius laughed, shaking his head. "After what I heard about Mutina, I was afraid you were lost."

"Me? It takes more than one pitfall to bring me down," Marcus responded grinning, slapping his friend on the back.

Canidius lowered his voice. "Plancus, another of Lepidus's staff, and others heard from the Senate two weeks ago. They ordered Decimus to pursue you and finish you off and sent the same order to us. Cicero ordered sixty days of thanksgiving to celebrate your annihilation."

That caused Marcus to pause in shock. His lighthearted joy at the welcome to Lepidus's camp faded.

Cicero *again*—and he was leading Rome in celebrating his obliteration?

Marcus came to his senses, seeing Lepidus approaching from the gate. "What about him?" he asked Canidius, nodding toward Lepidus. "Will he join me or kill me?"

His friend snorted. "He knows the sentiments of his men. He'd better join you!"

Marcus nodded, leaving Canidius and striding boldly toward Lepidus, arms outstretched. "My friend—and I hope my ally!"

"Yes, Antonius." Lepidus nodded, also embracing him in welcome, though he was stiffer and not as warm as Canidius. Marcus symbolically kissed him on both cheeks in friendship as soldiers from both sides cheered. Lepidus responded courteously but dispassionately. It was enough for now. Men on both sides of the river were banging shields and shouting in chorus, applauding the transfer of power.

Marcus Antonius was now supreme commander of not only Lepidus's seven legions, but those of his other general, Lucius Munatius Plancus, whose men demanded to join the "great Marcus Antonius."

Twenty-three legions! Not a bad reaping, especially considering he hadn't even drawn a sword since Mutina.

Sitting in the praetorium with his four new legates, Marcus prepared to deal the first of his blows to the Optimates.

"After hearing how the Senate has finally declared Caesar's assassins outlaws, I'd like to put an end to Decimus Brutus."

"Then you'd best hurry," Plancus said. Marcus decided he genuinely liked this large, affable man. "If I were in Decimus's boots, I would've already packed up and run."

"I agree," Canidius said. "He may already be safely away. Could we get help from someone who could intercept him?"

"The Gauls," Ventidius asserted. "I have connections with chieftains who disliked his appointment and were ready to join you in your siege."

Marcus nodded. "Good. Ventidius, I'll leave that to you and offer a purse for whichever chieftain finishes him."

Marcus chewed his lip a moment, then spoke again. "Friends, it's time the Senate knows our strength." He paused, staring down at the Persian carpet beneath his feet. It was as stained and dirty as his own hands would soon become. "I can't and won't make Caesar's mistake. At every opportunity, I must deal with my opposition. My enemies in Rome, as well as Caesar's assassins demanded my lifeblood, and now they'll find I'm not so easily finished. I'm sending a courier to Rome, letting them know we're heading their way. Now understand I have no intention of marching on the city, but they don't know that. Once they hear of our numbers, Cicero and Octavian will be spatting over who offers us peace first!"

CHAPTER XXVII

DECIMUS BRUTUS WAS PROMPTLY LOCATED AND KILLED BY Ventidius's band of Gallic warriors. The entire camp celebrated as the Antonian army took their sweet time during the next months, journeying south toward Italia. Wounded men were healing and newer recruits were on their way to the completion of training. Marcus's army was strengthening.

Then near Italia's border, a lone courier sought Marcus out, bearing a letter from Gaius:

> *Gaius Antonius in Macedonia to his brother Marcus Antonius:*
>
> *Dearest Brother, Marcus Junius Brutus has extended every kindness and comfort during my house arrest. However, today he informed me that I must die in retaliation for Decimus Brutus's murder. Members of the Senate, led by Cicero, have persuaded him to execute me.*
>
> *Brutus has assured me he'll arrange my burial here in Macedonia and pay for the rites. Know that you have always been the best of brothers. I will write*

Mother to tell her farewell.

Pray for my passage to the dark land. I wish to die with honor.

Marcus could barely speak, but managed, "Canidius, we're entrenching here."

"We don't know where the nearest water source—"

"Doesn't matter." Marcus left his friend abruptly, riding off. Under some trees, he clumsily dismounted, sinking against his horse. Emotion crippling him, he sobbed like a child, burying his head in the animal's warm flank.

No—*no*!

Eros found him, and Marcus felt his slave's gentle hand on his shoulder, patiently offering silent comfort. He managed only two words, "Find Lucius."

Within the hour, Lucius reported to the praetorium's privacy. There, the two remaining brothers Antonii embraced for a long time, weeping. There were no words for the hurt and anger Marcus felt inside.

Ever since Caesar's will had gone public, he had sought a well-defined personal reason to hunt Brutus and Cassius down—one besides the legions' vengeful demands over the assassination. Hadn't Brutus, along with Trebonius, preserved his life on the ides of Martius? But now things were drastically changed. Now Marcus looked forward to raising his gladius against Marcus Brutus and Gaius Cassius Longinus. His mourning beard for Gaius would remain until both assassins were dead. Their downfalls would be his offering to Gaius's shade.

As he grieved with Lucius, Marcus was furious with himself. The day he sent Gaius to Macedonia, he had never imagined that Brutus and Cassius would ever venture that far northeast. He had been so wrong. So *tragically* wrong.

Gaius's death shook him mightily, as no other had since Fadia's. For several days, Marcus sank into a despair he'd never experienced before. It was a deep, fathomless gloom that held him in grief and anguish like a vise. He couldn't function. He couldn't make decisions. After several nights of overwhelming sorrow and inactivity, Lucius finally brought in a legionary physician to tend him.

"It's severe melancholia," the physician diagnosed.

A full week passed before Marcus could shake off his dark shroud enough to break camp and lead his army steadily southeast. By this time, several missives had been sent to the Senate informing them that the "renegade Marcus Antonius" now had a mighty force at his disposal.

Lepidus, Plancus, and Ventidius Bassus were proving to be a loyal staff. Together they reorganized the huge, combined force, and now their army was content and battle-ready. And Marcus rewarded the two sentries who had killed Hirtius with the honor of being his first praetorian guards. In addition, he selected more soldiers to fill additional praetorian positions, based upon valor and commendation from higher ranking staff. Now he had a trusted detachment just to protect his person. In this day and age, it was a much-needed assurance.

When the Senate's message finally arrived, it was written by someone they knew Marcus would trust: Calpurnius Piso.

> *Calpurnius Piso in Rome to Marcus Antonius in Gaul:*
>
> *Peace and health to you. On behalf of the Senate and Consul Gaius Octavian Caesar, I write to propose a negotiation. We could meet near the River Lavinius near Bononia . . .*

Consul? How was this happening?

Marcus lay awake all night, pondering Piso's letter. He detested Octavian, but if they joined forces, they'd be a respectable match for Brutus and Cassius. And perhaps by driving a wedge between Octavian and Cicero, attacks on his person and name might be prevented.

Once his intention to accept was known, Lepidus wasted no

time in demanding partnership in the coming negotiations, as well as a title of equal standing to whatever Marcus hoped to gain. Argument about this matter would be dangerous, so Marcus agreed. Really, he owed Lepidus a great deal. The man had peacefully relinquished command twice in his favor.

In his own mind, Marcus formed a plan he hoped would diminish Cicero's influence and elevate himself and Lepidus into a position comparable to Octavian's new imperium.

Caesar, Pompeius, and Crassus had formed a triumvirate. Why not Marcus, Lepidus, and Octavian?

Bononia spurned late autumn, remaining sun-drenched and balmy.

On a small island in the middle of the River Lavinius, Marcus Antonius and Marcus Aemilius Lepidus sat under a brightly painted pavilion. Its awning flapped in a stiff breeze as the two men awaited the day's momentous meeting.

Sadly, the pleasant weather was wasted on Marcus. Lost in thought, he recalled the last time he'd seen Gaius. After racing their horses and discussing love and marriage, his brother had been loyal unto death, sending him the Macedonian legions and keeping only a remnant to protect his own interests.

Marcus tormented himself. Again, the death of someone he loved had been caused by his own selfish motives. Perhaps he should have gone ahead with the original plan to govern Macedonia. Less blood would have been shed, and his brother would still be alive.

But he wouldn't have the army he had now.

Eros tried comforting him. "Only the gods know what could have been, Dominus. He might have died anyway. Who are we to change Fate?"

Such wisdom from a slave.

Still, in this game of power, Marcus wondered what—or *who*—

the gods would demand as his next sacrifice?

Marcus swatted a fly and paced to the riverbank, impatiently chewing his lip. On his side of the river was the encampment of his fifty thousand men. He'd ordered them into formation along the bank, showing off his full strength. Octavian needed to see how soldiers of Rome answered to him.

Though bargaining with Caesar's heir sickened Marcus to the point of actual nausea, the notion of peace was music to legionary ears. He forced a grin, casting sorrow aside, and lifted an arm to his men in recognition. They responded heartily, cheering, waving gladii and pila.

Something stirred behind him. Marcus turned.

Lepidus had risen, nodding toward the opposing riverbank, where Octavian's camp now lay. "Here they come."

A flotilla of rowboats steadily made way toward the island. First, Marcus saw Calpurnius Piso. Calpurnia's father stood tall in the prow of the closest boat, smiling and lifting one hand in greeting. Though aging, he was still an authoritative man who maintained strong senatorial sway.

Behind him was Octavian. Skin pale and untouched by the elements, he sat rigid, the autumn breeze ruffling his unruly red-blond hair. If he and Marcus didn't hate one another, they'd likely share grief. Octavian's mother, Atia, had unexpectedly died in the past year, and Octavian still wore a mourning beard—though not as full and handsome as Marcus's. Regardless of his lack of facial hair, there was a natural distinction in his bearing. Maybe he got *that* much from Caesar.

Octavian's personal guard accompanied him in the other boats following. One condition to the meeting had been an equal number of bodyguards present on both sides. Marcus's praetorians stood silently, visible on both sides of the pavilion.

Piso lifted the hem of his toga, stepping out of the craft as it smoothly skidded ashore. "Salve, Antonius!" he called. "I bring greetings from your wife and mother. They continue mourning your brother's recent death."

Marcus embraced Piso, the older man patting his back affectionately. The dark loss of Gaius, still so new, washed over him again. He bit his lip and squeezed his eyes shut to avoid tears. Octavian would *not* see him weep.

Discreetly, he whispered to Piso, "How's my mother?"

Marcus felt Piso's sympathetic hand squeeze his shoulder. "Deeply wounded. But your recent good fortune has cheered her."

During this exchange, Octavian was quitting the boat, making his way over in full consular garb. Folds of his elegant, striped toga hung over his left arm. Without hesitating, he extended his right hand to Marcus, who shrewdly noted Caesar's signet ring on his middle finger. On the other hand, he wore the gift from Cleopatra. Octavian looked more mature despite his overly prominent ears that still stuck out too far.

"Greetings, in memory of my father," he said. "Allow me to convey my condolences, also. I'm told your brother died honorably."

Fewer words would be wisest, Marcus thought as he clasped his rival's arm. "And it saddened me to learn of your mother's death. She was a kind lady."

Legions on both sides of the river erupted into cheers. Marcus used the moment to his advantage, taking another step forward and placing his arm around Octavian's shoulders, the two men walking from one side of the little island to the other together, waving at their men. Afterward, Piso and Octavian exchanged curt words with Lepidus, Octavian eyeing him circumspectly. Then at last, they all made their way to the shaded pavilion, Eros materializing to water wine and serve it.

Marcus took a deep drink as Piso began.

"On behalf of the Senate and people of Rome, we're here to propose a truce and negotiate a joint agreement. I insist all proceedings remain civil, for the good of the Republic."

Or whatever was left of it!

Marcus nodded. "Of course, Piso." Then he proposed a toast, lifting his cup again. "May we drink and be of the same mind on many things today."

Octavian nodded courteously, as did Lepidus. Together, all four men drank, then got to business.

Setting his cup aside, Octavian began. "Since becoming consul, I've sworn an oath in my father's memory to bring his assassins to justice. Antonius, now that Decimus Brutus is dead, there's no reason for us to quarrel. Think how imminent the downfall of Brutus and Cassius would be by combining our forces and resources. It would also send a strong message to that pirate Sextus Pompeius, who's been raiding Italia's coasts."

Marcus took another gulp of wine, warning, "My support will only be granted if your terms are *acceptable*." With one hand, he gestured toward Lepidus, adding, "And to start with, you must equally allow my friend and ally Lepidus into our decision-making."

Octavian raised a critical eyebrow, indicating three was a crowd. The glance he gave Lepidus was cold and mistrustful. Marcus smiled to himself, pleased to have taken consul-boy by surprise. He used this as momentum. "I propose the formation of another triumvirate, like that of Caesar, Crassus, and Pompeius. We'd share joint rule between us for say—the next five years?"

"And what sort of authority would you and Lepidus hold?" Octavian asked.

Marcus snorted. "Same as you. We'd expect full consular power."

"It's only fair," Lepidus concurred, nodding.

"Is it indeed?" Octavian snapped. Recovering, he graced Lepidus with one of his insincere smiles that looked *nearly* genuine. Marcus knew better.

"Actually," Octavian mused, "I think if we utilize three-man rule, it needs to be with complete auctoritas, without senatorial control."

Piso interjected, "The conscript fathers will surely object to such power."

Octavian shrugged. "They'd also object to another civil war, Piso. Such administration would be virtually the same as when my father ruled as dictator, and as Antonius just said, it would only be for a limited restorative period. Not for life."

That settled Piso for the time-being, but he looked anxious.

Knowing he needed assurance, Marcus suggested, "The Senate would expect a full disclosure of our plans. That should include an outline for a full-scale campaign against Brutus and Cassius. It would serve as a means to sell ourselves to the people and our legions."

"Which of us would carry the campaign to Greece?" asked Lepidus.

"Me," Marcus stated immediately. "I'm the only one with enough experience to run a campaign this large."

Octavian seized the opportunity, smugly taunting, "Perhaps, but that skill failed you at Mutina."

Marcus stiffened at the insult, but Piso sternly intervened before he could speak, his words directed to Octavian. "Be civil, young Caesar. Say nothing you'll regret."

Octavian nodded slightly at Piso before readdressing Marcus. "I stand corrected, Antonius. By all means, you shall go. You fought at my father's side, and I'm sure he'd expect you to avenge him. However, I shall accompany you. Since we now have a *third* party," he emphasized, nodding toward Lepidus, "let him remain in Rome to watch our backs."

Marcus leaned back in his chair, shaking his head doggedly. "It'll take more than Lepidus to watch our backs in Rome."

"I agree," Lepidus managed. "All three of us harbor enemies there. I should think I would be in the most dangerous territory of all. Greece will seem tame to you without the Senate hounding you like Cerberus turned rabid."

Octavian nodded. "Then let's address that problem. But first, there's one thing I require."

Marcus tilted his head back, uncertain. Octavian was ever a surprise.

"My father must be deified."

Lepidus chuckled. "The Senate has toyed with that for some time, even when Caesar was alive."

"Why is this so important now?" Marcus inquired. "Couldn't it wait until after the campaign? You could return to Rome triumphant over his assassins, demanding Caesar be made a god."

Stubbornly, Octavian shook his head. "If I die in Greece, I've no guarantee either of you would carry out my wishes in this matter. So I'll see it done first and foremost. It's my condition. I mean to honor him with every fiber of my being. I'll also propose a temple built for his worship in the Forum built upon the very spot where the crowd cremated him. Disagree, and this meeting is ended."

Piso squirmed. "I see nothing unseemly with this—unconventional request if it promises continued peace. Deifying Caesar isn't a new idea. Under the circumstances, it'll easily pass."

"I accept," Lepidus agreed with a simple shrug. "Caesar was a great man. What's wrong with allowing the plebs to worship his memory? Just don't go demanding it of the rest of us, who saw him as an ordinary mortal."

Marcus hesitated.

There was something about this he didn't like, though he couldn't quite put his finger on it. He recalled that night at the theater, when the shooting star raced across the heavens, and how Octavian seized the moment for personal gain, shouting to the crowd how his father was going to the gods, or some such nonsense. Somehow this deification would work the same way—to further his cause. Caesar's "godhead" would merely be the vehicle. Problem was, there was no way to know exactly *how* he'd use it. Devious little—

"Antonius? Do you agree?"

Lepidus's voice returned him from his thoughts. Before the meeting started, Marcus knew he'd have to endure compromises. All of the others were watching him, awaiting his approval.

"Very well. I agree," he sighed in concession, giving Caesar's heir his darkest stare.

Octavian smiled brightly, rubbing his hands together and preparing for the next topic. "Excellent. We hasten slowly, then. Antonius, why not seal our commitments in trust we could both share? What about a marriage pact of some sort to cement our ties? I've no wife yet."

Marcus chuckled. What woman in her right mind would want to marry this little creature! However, someone did come to mind, may Venus help her. "My stepdaughter, Clodius's girl, is almost old enough," he offered.

Octavian's light blue eyes widened slightly in surprise. "Excellent!" he agreed, nodding and extending his hand to clasp Marcus's.

Now that poor Clodia's fate was sealed, Octavian skipped ahead to the most daunting topic of all. "With that agreed upon, we must determine a means by which we can adequately raise funds for such a huge military endeavor. Between us, we need to transport and feed one hundred thousand men."

Staggering, but true.

"Optimate Senators have all been bled dry already," reminded Piso, lifting both hands in emphasis.

He was right, Marcus knew. Those cupboards were bare.

"I think it's been over a hundred years since Rome's taxes were increased," Lepidus ventured.

Octavian added with emphasis, "Then let's raise them to squeeze out what we must. Beating Brutus and Cassius won't be financially rewarding."

"Heavy taxation may bleed a few extra pieces of silver out of the plebs, but it won't yield enough," Piso warned, a worried expression etched on his proud face.

"What about our women?" Lepidus suggested.

Marcus stared at his colleague, cocking an eyebrow in amusement. "You'd bleed taxes out of your own wife, Lepidus?"

"If we taxed their jewelry, we'd profit from it," he said. "Think of all the gold dripping from our ladies' ears and necks."

Actually, it wasn't a bad idea.

"And there's always the way Sulla cleaned house," Octavian whispered softly. "He achieved financial gain *and* removed his opposition all at once."

"Proscriptions?" Lepidus's voice trembled. "Public lists of those who have betrayed any of us?"

"Mostly of those who are rich enough to *pay up*," Marcus corrected.

"By the gods, no!" Piso gasped. "Too many families are still scarred with that horror. It's out of the question!"

Octavian shook his head. "Actually, Piso, it's the only way we'll gain what we need and have everyone's unquestionable obedience."

Lepidus grudgingly admitted, "Caesar's genius was only eclipsed by one flaw—he left his enemies alive. Now they're *our* enemies."

"And it will maintain peace in Rome while we're on campaign," Octavian pointed out, leaning back. "Your thoughts, Antonius?"

Marcus cocked an eyebrow at Piso, who looked positively panicked. "Well, I'd be lying if I said I hadn't thought of it. But only as a last resort."

"And that's exactly where we stand," Octavian argued impatiently. "It's the only recourse to meet our needs."

"*If* I agreed to such bloodletting," Marcus said carefully, "it'll involve men only—no women or children must be harmed. Is that understood?"

Octavian sniffed. "Suit yourself, but if we included women, their jewels and finery would be ours without any taxes. And by including children, think on this! Extended family would even step forward with bribes just to protect them. We'd be showered in silver!"

Evil, bloody little bastard. He'd purposefully end the lives of *children*?

"No *women*," Marcus repeated flatly. "And no *children*." His words were clear and stern. "Proscribing someone is black enough as it is."

Piso sat in shock, shaking his head. "I shouldn't have come," he murmured. "This is monstrous! To declare men's lives as forfeit and open the way for mercenaries to destroy families just because they're wealthy or against you? And each of you will pay out of your own purses the men who slay them?"

Marcus looked at him defiantly, raising his voice. "Remember, Piso. Most of the men I'm thinking of made your daughter a widow and intended to kill me too. You and I both know that those men who wielded the daggers didn't act alone. And others were in on the plot but just didn't participate. If we're after the conspirators, then they're guilty too." Turning to Octavian, he reached for a wax tablet and stylus. "I have some of Caesar's old records that Calpurnia entrusted to me. They contain numerous names of Optimate supporters who countered him. Most aren't even noble. Just merchants or wealthy freedmen."

"I've already created similar lists in preparation for this day," Octavian said. "We'll compare notes."

He'd prepared lists in advance? Dis of the dead, what a fiend! "Well, then," Marcus deliberated, "since you cast Cicero off like a discarded olive pit, let's start with him. My family's waited a long time for this moment."

At that, Octavian sat back, mulishly crossing his arms. "No. Cicero supported me when you did not. I won't hand him over cheaply."

Piso was aghast, his mouth dropping open, staring at Octavian in horror. He exploded, "But you *would* hand him over at a price?"

"Of *course*, he would!" Marcus spat. "Tell me what it is, boy."

Octavian froze, his cool blue eyes filled with such hatred that it sent an unexpected chill down Marcus's spine. Leaning in closely, he hissed, "Understand something, Antonius. Whatever peacemaking takes place on this island will never replace the memory of being forced to wait for hours in your atrium while you drank yourself into courage enough to face me."

Marcus smacked his fist down onto the table with such force wine sloshed out of their cups.

Just as he stood to respond angrily, Piso got up too, intervening again. "Peace! Both of you. Bury your hatred and move forward. Gods, I hate to see men condemned, but if this be your price for harmony, begin your grim list."

Keeping his voice low, Marcus repeated his demand to Octavian. "Name your price. Cicero is *mine*."

Octavian tilted his head back, considering an answer. "My price? What shall it be? Ah! I know—Lucius Julius Caesar."

Piso groaned, shaking his head wearily.

Lepidus looked desperately between Marcus and Octavian, eyes bulging. "What? Antonius, he demands your own *uncle*!"

"Don't do it," Piso was pleading, his head wagging pathetically. "It will finish your mother's heartbreak."

Marcus's mind raced, ignoring them both, focusing on Octavian. "Why him?"

Octavian presented him with another false smile. "My reasons are personal."

Marcus shifted uneasily, wondering if Octavian knew of the enmity between him and Uncle Lucius. And Piso was right. If he agreed to the trade, would Mother ever forgive him? Especially now that Gaius was dead? And yet he'd betrayed the Antonii again by recently switching his allegiance.

Unless—perhaps he could warn Mother and save Uncle Lucius's life. She could take him in under her own roof if Marcus let her know—and she'd be more forgiving. And *maybe* Uncle would have a memorable little lesson on just how helpless Lentulus felt before he died.

For a fleeting moment, Marcus was nineteen again, desperately facing his uncle down, surrounded by vengeful, anti-Catilinarian senators. Squeezing his eyes shut a moment, he still saw Uncle's haughty demeanor, cruelly refusing to plead mercy on Lentulus's behalf.

Marcus swallowed hard, staring Octavian down. "It's a high price," he said haltingly. "However, I agree to the trade."

Octavian accepted his hand, clasping it. "What tremendous progress we're making," he exclaimed.

Feeling less than pleased at bloodying his hands, Marcus kept one thought in the forefront. Cicero would die, and at long last, Lentulus would be avenged!

CHAPTER XXVIII

MARCUS ANTONIUS IN BONONIA TO HIS Mother, Julia Antonia, in Rome:

I write this in haste, for time is of the essence. To pay for our coming war with Brutus and Cassius and to secure Rome in our absence, we must resort to proscriptions. I demanded Cicero's life first and foremost. However, Octavian struck a hard bargain, demanding Uncle Lucius's life in return for Cicero's. I'll do what I can to have him exonerated. But in the meantime, take him into your domus. He mustn't leave, as someone is sure to hunt him down.

Indeed, I know you're angry with me. However, this was the only way I could ensure Cicero's execution. Forgive me, Mother. Power is poison. And I've swallowed enough now to be called ruthless.

Marcus's return to Rome was anything but joyous.

Morning crowds in the Forum stood in hushed silence, reading lists of men that he, Octavian, and Lepidus had condemned. Each day new names were added and tacked to the Rostra. Most bystanders were educated slaves, sent by their masters to see whose names were there. Whenever one read their master's name, the reaction was the same—sheer panic.

Another breed of creatures was also loitering in the Forum and scanning the lists on a daily basis. They were the cold-blooded opportunists, unfazed at killing for a handful of denarii. They took careful note of each name, deciding exactly who to hunt down. To earn their reward, they only needed proof of the victim's death—usually a head or hand bearing a signet ring would suffice.

The whole business was bloody, awful, and sickening. Marcus had never wanted to be feared, and now he was. It was respect he wanted, something the Senate was loath to bestow.

Only one death during the monstrous days of proscriptions did he eagerly await.

Cicero's.

Last he'd heard, the aging statesman had fled to one of his properties in the south. It would only be a matter of time. Marcus had dispatched several centurions to do the task. This way it would be official, military, and execution-like. It wouldn't do for Chickpea to die at the point of some random mercenary's dagger.

Today Marcus entered the peristyle courtyard of the old Antonii domus on the Palatine, where Mother still lived. His heavy crimson-bordered toga swished around his ankles. He bore good news and looked forward to spreading joy instead of trepidation. At the very least, this visit was bound to be memorable.

Uncle Lucius had lived under Mother's roof ever since Marcus's letter had reached her. It went without saying that he didn't dare leave, afraid someone was waiting outside the domus with a sharpened pugio. Hopefully, this meeting between the three of them would offer some reconciliation.

During this morning's Senate session, Marcus had managed to repeal most of Lepidus's women's tax law and then had Uncle

Lucius officially pardoned. Ha! Octavian hadn't seen that one coming! Marcus had to stifle laughter during the meeting as his enemy's flashing blue eyes fired wrath at him.

Mother was with Uncle Lucius in the triclinium, taking wine and cheese together.

"Salve, Mother, Uncle."

Uncle Lucius Julius immediately arose, his jaw set grimly. Mother sat up but said nothing.

"Have you come to kill me, Nephew?" Uncle demanded.

"No. I have good news. This morning I had you pardoned. I suggest you wait a few days before leaving. In fact, once word is out, I'll send an armed escort home with you, just to be safe."

Marcus walked to the other side of the dining couch to kiss Mother, who stiffened but allowed him the privilege.

"I hope you're not expecting eternal *gratitude*," Uncle Lucius spat. "Sometimes I think I should have died instead of seeing my beloved Rome running with the blood of her greatest citizens."

Marcus raised his eyebrows, "Greatest citizens?"

"Stop it, Lucius!" Mother exploded, prompting Marcus to look her way in surprise.

"Stop this nonsense and remember of what I've reminded you every day you've been here. When have you ever really shown any kindness to Marcus? And yet here he is, granting you clemency. He's one of the three most powerful men in Rome now, like it or not, and he's come here to hand you the wings of freedom. Yet you still speak to him contemptuously!"

"Gratias, Mother," Marcus responded, impressed. "I had no idea you were on my side."

"Silence!" she snapped at him with the authority and icy abruptness of a field commander. "As for you—you had no right to trade your own uncle like a gaming piece! Two weeks ago, armed legionaries came to my door. I knew they were hunting him down. Your uncle—your *own blood*—was forced to hide in the slave quarters while I faced them. I opened the door only to come face-to-face with a centurion, flanked by a full contubernium—stalking my brother as though he were an animal! I swore to them that before they entered my domus, they'd have to strike the womb that birthed their general! How *could* you, Marcus? Have you lost sight of everything decent?"

"Proscribing him wasn't my idea. Octavian demanded it, and it was the only way for me to get to Cicero."

At that, Uncle Lucius's face reddened with fury. He paced toward Marcus threateningly. "You're saying Cicero's *death* was more important to you than my life?"

Marcus stiffened at his tone, quipping back, "As much as Lentulus's death was more important than your sister's happiness—*yes*!"

Mother sprang up, moving between them. "Please!" she gasped. "No more of this." She sighed. "Lucius, you and I weren't at the meeting in Bononia, so we'll never know what really happened. But Marcus has used his influence to pardon you. For that, at least, thank him. After all, today he did for you what you *refused* to do for Lentulus."

Why, indeed he had.

But then she rounded on him. "By Juno's grace, I tried my best to raise you in a good and upright home. Our times are so violent you don't always know who your enemies are, that's true. But Marcus, swear to me, never, *ever* condemn family again. Swear it by oath to me *now*!"

She was starting to weep tears of hurt and suffering, and Marcus's gloating swiftly melted into compassion. Uncle Lucius was right, after all. He was guilty of wanting Cicero dead more than he wanted his uncle alive.

He reached for her, entwining his fingers with hers. Then tenderly, he encompassed her into his arms and she broke down. Eyes closing, he crooned, "Shh, it's over. He's safe."

"And you'll be going to fight again. Must I lose all of my sons to civil war?"

Marcus kissed the top of her head, promising, "I'll never, ever raise my hand against our own blood again, Mother. I swear by Hercules my ancestor." Then he was holding her again and wondering just how far that grace would extend in the family tree. Surely distant cousins, like Octavian, could be excluded.

Mother pulled herself together. She reached over, taking her brother's hand and placing it into Marcus's. "Please say something kind to one another. End this hatred once and for all."

Something *kind*? Oh, that was pushing it. Marcus pursed his lips, but she gave him a determined, motherly look—not altogether affectionate either.

"Very well. Uncle, from this day forward, I will do my utmost to show you my good nature and give you the same respect I owe my own brother."

As he spoke, Marcus noticed for the first time that Uncle Lucius looked frail. His frame was slighter and bonier than it used to be, though his voice was still strong. "I accept your sentiments, Marcus. And I too will do my best to show you regard. We are family. I suppose I should've given you more thought when you were younger and impressionable. Forgive me that."

It was outlandish hearing such words from him. Was he really sincere?

But that day Marcus sat down anyway, joining Mother and Uncle Lucius for the rest of the afternoon, retelling family stories and avoiding mention of Lentulus or the proscriptions.

Deep within, he hoped it wouldn't be his last meal with them.

Cicero was dead!

One of Marcus's centurions, a certain Herennius, had finally caught up with him. Cicero instructed the officer to "kill him properly," then bared his neck in a similar gesture used by gladiators to receive a deathblow.

At last. This battle had been very personal. Though Marcus had never been religious, the first thing he did was visit the small atrium shrine among his ancestors' wax death masks. Head covered in piety, he murmured aloud, "The blood of Marcus Tullius Cicero is offered as tribute to the shades of my father, Marcus Antonius Creticus, and especially in memory of Publius Lentulus Sura, my stepfather. It has taken a long, long time, and for that I beg pardon. But at last your shades may rest knowing that both your reputations and your blood have been avenged."

Now there was only one more person for whom he sought vengeance. By defeating Brutus and Cassius, he would justify Gaius's spilled blood. And Caesar's—though that only mattered politically now.

Later that afternoon, Marcus received news that ruined the rest of his day. He was in his tablinum, preparing instructions for the Brundisium garrison in preparation for the army's departure to Greece, when in walked Eros. And he wasn't smiling.

"What is it?"

"I must speak with you, Dominus. You need to hear what has happened today in the Forum from me before hearing it elsewhere."

Marcus pushed away the papyrus on which he'd been working and sat back in his chair. "I'm listening."

"Domina Fulvia paid her respects to Cicero's severed head and hands today."

Whenever the state demanded an execution of a highborn citizen, his head was usually displayed in the Forum on a pilum. Many of the proscribed victims' remains were down in front of the Rostra, including Cicero's, his head on a pilum, one hand nailed to the platform. Marcus Tullius Cicero would never speak against the Antonii again.

Marcus shrugged. "It's no surprise to hear she was there. She was as pleased as I to hear he was executed."

"Oh, I'd say she was more pleased than you. She has acted shamefully, Dominus."

Marcus frowned. What had she done now? "Go on."

"Domina had her slaves bring her litter up very close to Cicero's head and hands. She was unfazed at the smell and conditions of the other men's remains. As soon as she was recognized, plebs gathered to watch. She turned toward the crowd and cried, 'How proud Cicero was of the words he spoke against my husband. But look where he is now! This tongue will never insult Marcus Antonius again!'"

"There's nothing wrong with that. Fulvia will be Fulvia," Marcus said with a knowing smile.

"It's what she did afterward," Eros warned.

Marcus frowned, gesturing for Eros to continue.

"First, she removed her palla and hairpins. Then she grasped one of the pins like a dagger, jabbing it into Cicero's tongue again and again. Dominus, she stabbed at it in such a frenzy that his tongue became a contorted, punctured piece of meat."

Marcus went numb, horrified. "And the mob? What did they do?"

"She was so absorbed in her act she didn't notice them all falling silent and sullen. One of her slaves finally hurried up, stilling her hand. He said, 'Lady it's best you go home now.'" For a few moments, Marcus sat frozen. Here he was, a hardened soldier, and for once in his life his stomach rocked and he felt nauseated at the thought Fulvia's actions.

She'd gone too far this time.

That night, when he was more composed, Marcus flung open the door to Fulvia's cubiculum. The noise startled little Iullus, who awakened and began to cry. A nurse sleeping at the foot of Fulvia's sleeping couch scurried over to pick up the child.

"Out," Marcus ordered her. He entered the room masterfully, like he used to in the past when he hungered for her body. Only tonight sex was the last thing on his mind.

However, Fulvia misinterpreted his intent. Slowly and enticingly, she lowered the silk of her shift until the orbs of both breasts were exposed. Closing her eyes, she arched her chest toward him and lay back, spreading her legs. "It's been too long," she moaned.

When he didn't respond, she opened her eyes.

Marcus reached over to a chest and picked up a wool blanket, tossing it atop her nakedness. "Wasn't my example of Chickpea enough to satisfy you? What in the name of the gods were you thinking? Tearing pins out of your hair and stabbing at his tongue like some demon from Hades!"

She rose to her feet, shaking her head and taking a tentative step toward him. "Oh, Marcus. It's never my intention to anger you. It seems I can do nothing right. Please—come to me. I'll prove my love and loyalty as a woman should, making you forget—" She reached for his crotch, but he countered her, batting her hand away and shoving her hard back onto the bed.

"Pleasure yourself." He shook his head miserably. "I have no intention of ever touching you again. As if my own actions with these proscriptions haven't been vile enough, leave it to my overly ambitious wife to *eclipse* me!"

She raised her voice, scrambling to the edge of the sleeping couch and desperately crying out to him, "Everything I've done has been for you! I've given you sons, and I stood with you during those decimations in support! As for today, I merely reminded everyone how poisonously Cicero spoke against you and how deeply it offended us!"

"Can you not see? There was nothing wrong in what you *said*! But skewering his tongue like meat and desecrating the dead in public—in front of crowds in the Forum? No. I'll be the one facing repercussions from that." Turning on his heel, he left her alone in the dark chamber.

Marcus Antonius was done with Fulvia Bambula!

CHAPTER XXIX

42-41BC

QUEEN CLEOPATRA PHILOPATOR OF EGYPT, ISIS Incarnate, to Marcus Antonius, Triumvir:

This message is to inform you that Gaius Cassius Longinus sent envoys to my court demanding military support. I refused him but may soon face his wrath if I don't respond favorably. Please know that I've deployed shiploads of reinforcements and supplies to you.

You should also be aware that Brutus and Cassius have made overtures to the Parthians for aid and will be receiving gold from them and several thousand archers.

I refuse to serve the murderers of Caesar, and I remain your loyal ally.

In getting to Greece, the triumviral fleet wove its way through a blockade of enemy ships commanded by Cassius's crack admiral, Ahenobarbus. Somehow they managed to land safely near Dyrrhachium with their entire army intact. After such close scrapes in his crossing during the war with Pompeius, Marcus was beyond relieved. But his enthusiasm was short-lived.

Octavian promptly fell ill.

Yet "Divi Filius"—"the son of the god"—insisted he would participate in the battle. Yes, now he was inferring that he possessed godhead by relation to Caesar. Aha! *This* was how he used Caesar's deification to his advantage.

Marcus finally confronted him on day three. "This war won't be won by sitting here on our asses waiting for you to feel better," he snapped. "I'm leaving tomorrow with twelve legions. Follow with the rest once you're up to it."

As planned, he departed the next day, his army practically flying to the environs of Philippi, where Brutus and Cassius waited.

Within days, watchtowers were erected around camp, and Marcus climbed atop the easternmost one, surveying the landscape.

Stately and serene, Phillip of Macedon's city of Philippi lay in the morning light, barely two or three miles away to the east. Even from here, one could see the town's glorious theater carved into the acropolis hillside with a naked eye. Behind his triumviral camp, cooking fires from farmers' huts wafted upward wraithlike, sending gray plumes into the still air.

Below him, legionaries were still digging ditches and finishing barricades and walls with excavated dirt and timber they'd harvested while traveling eastward. They had worked night and day, and spirits were high.

Their general's, however, were not. Marcus rubbed weary, dry eyes. His camp was in a terrible location.

Brutus and Cassius had claimed the high ground. Flanked by rocky promontories on both sides, they had safe cover, controlling the port of Neopolis farther east along the Via Egnatia, which bisected Greece's girth as snugly as a centurion's belt.

In contrast, Marcus's camp was just south of the roadway on a low floodplain next to a huge marsh separating farmers' fields from the rest of Philippi. Most of the surrounding area was a rugged, unforgiving landscape; formidable enough to travel upon, much less on which to wage war.

And another damned marsh!

In sour temper, he eyed the direction of the closest enemy battlements to his own—Cassius's—and chewed his lip. Marcus's original hope was to place himself closer to the conspirators' camps, making it awkward for them to position their men in battle array. That plan fizzled when Cassius attacked Marcus's advance guard, forcing him back.

In hindsight, Marcus realized how foolhardy he'd been to press onward without Octavian and their army's full strength. If the conspirators opted to attack him now with their full forces, it could be disastrous. This would have been the ideal time for Cleopatra's forces to have shown up. But they didn't. For ten days, the opposing forces stared one another down, and that damned Octavian still hadn't arrived!

And then a crafty, strategic move presented itself. Marcus seized upon the opportunity.

Under cover of night, he sent a patrol of soldiers and engineers into the marsh with orders to outflank and cut off Cassius's supply route along the Via Egnatia. Tall, plumed, reedy plant growth was so thick and high that it dwarfed his men. They'd have to be stealthy as they cut their way through the thick, jungle-like marsh unnoticed. For over a week, work seemed to proceed as planned.

For Marcus, it was frustrating.

It was impossible to oversee anything from his position. He used the time to train and prepare reinforcements he'd send in to replace the trailblazing team once they hit the Via Egnatia just east of Cassius's fortifications. What a shame he wouldn't get to see the look on the conspirator's face when he learned his supply route had been intercepted!

Another frustration were the barriers preventing him from taking a wide survey of their surroundings. Marcus considered the many times he'd ridden around battlefields at Pharsalus or Alesia.

Here at Philippi, he couldn't ride northeast even two miles before encountering the steep grade of Brutus's knoll. Immediately to the south were the marshy conditions, and lastly, to the southeast was the city itself, yet another barrier.

Philippi's acropolis was especially high, crowning the tallest point in the region. As time passed, it occurred to Marcus that perhaps Cassius had made a mistake in not choosing to use that lofty height to his advantage. It would have led to a lengthy siege. The Philippians didn't know how lucky they were to have escaped that.

Scouts came and went, Marcus constantly sifting through information. One report was promising. It indicated possible weaknesses in Cassius's walls. Two scouts claimed to have gotten within a stone's throw of them. Built to look imposing, they mostly consisted of wattle and loose stone.

Around the time Marcus was considering ways to either ram or scale Cassius's higher ground, Octavian suddenly arrived. Sentries reported he was traveling by litter, borne by his soldiers and still sick, which made Marcus scoff. He scribbled hasty orders, designating the younger man's army to join his to the north of the Via Egnatia, directly opposite Brutus. Now the conspirators would face them at full strength.

A day or so after his arrival came discouraging news. Cassius's men had discovered Marcus's tunneling scheme, and Caesar's assassin had retaliated by starting construction on a barricade of his own through the marsh, cutting off the Antonian moles from their own camp.

Marcus climbed back up the same tower as usual, pondering his next move to try and extricate his soldiers from their entrapment. As he stood there scrutinizing the marsh, a muddied, breathless scout ambled up.

"Sir, Cassius's boys are just ahead in the tall rushes, by way of the city," he reported.

"Are you sure it's not our own men who are trapped?"

"It's the enemy, sir. I heard them bragging how they'd be

earning Cassius's gold in less than a day if they finished their work."

Marcus frowned. The men he'd sent out to try and cut Cassius off would be without food and water before long, if they weren't already. It was time for a diversion to enable his entrapped men to either join in the fracas or get to safety. Perhaps an engagement might even draw Cassius out of his encampment. Turning to the scout, Marcus ordered, "Sound for assembly! We're going to attack those bastards and save our men!"

Marcus sent hasty word to Octavian, wasting no time in setting his forces upon Cassius's legionaries, who were just finishing their countering earthworks. Using several cohorts, he led the raid himself, his powerful horse heaving through the soft, swampy ground, muck spraying every direction.

Men on both sides screamed and shouted, desperately trying to arrange themselves into formation while contending with the pesky plant growth that was as tall as Amazons and preventing them from fighting in any normal, organized manner. Marcus finally caught a glimpse of some of the unfortunates who had been building his causeway. They were worn and desperate, having had little food, water, or rest. Yet he was heartened. They were joining in, pitching a surprisingly aggressive fight.

Disengaging and riding back for a better view, he discovered a new concern. Dust was rising from Brutus's camp up on the higher ground. Gods, was he was coming out to aid Cassius? Now they'd all measure Octavian's worth. At the least, he'd arm his battlements and send missiles down on them while they passed.

His own fight was turning into a standoff. He sent in reserves and personally cut down two of Cassius's legionaries himself by doggedly breaking through the lines, encouraging his men forward.

But whatever was happening behind him was becoming more worrisome than his own skirmish. Where was Octavian? Didn't he see Brutus's men on the move?

Handing over command to his primus pilus, Marcus rode back a short distance, unsure of what to think. If Octavian's camp fired missiles at Brutus's soldiers, they'd either scamper like rabbits or charge headlong toward the marsh to relieve Cassius's boys.

One of Marcus's praetorians hailed him, pointing at new arrivals from Cassius's camp. It was Cassius himself.

Well, Marcus Antonius knew what he was going to do while he had the chance! Sending orders back to camp, he waited breathlessly as an entire legion streamed out, marching straight toward the steep, rocky mount of Cassius's fortifications.

By now, Marcus's troops in the bog were gaining the upper hand as Cassius's contingent struggled, barely holding ground. Their combat became sloppier and more desperate despite their general's arrival.

With Cassius came more infantry. Was he too late? There was still plenty of fighting left down here, especially with fresh men on both sides. Centurion whistles sounded amid clangs of parried blows, grunting, and loud cursing. Things looked promising, so Marcus decided to leave a primus pilus centurion in command and lead the charge up to Cassius's camp.

Mud-covered and barely recognizable, he galloped out of the swamp and cantered uphill, leading the climb. All around, men were panting and cursing. His own horse blew and groaned, slowing to a walk and straining uphill, drenched in sweaty lather. Up the steep incline, they steadily gained ground. Marcus paused, looking down toward the marsh. Good. Cassius was plenty occupied with the skirmish below.

As men filed past, he barked, "Don't let your little asses get tired! Show Caesar's killers how *real* Romans fight! Ram that wall!"

The scouts' assessments were accurate. Only three or four ladders appeared on the other side, for the small, light battering ram they'd ported up took no time to crunch through Cassius's portals. Legionaries formed shield walls as they stormed the gaping hole. Fortunately, only a brief surge of missiles rained down. Once a second section of wall caved, enemy soldiers fled for their lives.

Inside, Marcus's men went a little mad. He ordered centurions to hurry ahead to set guards over any war chests discovered inside the praetorium. But legionaries were wildly plundering whatever they could elsewhere, raping camp prostitutes and female camp-followers unfortunate enough to still be there. One contubernium celebrated when they located and captured all of the wheat in Cassius's grain stores. Another detachment overturned four heavily stocked wagons full of oil, which subsequently caught fire in the middle of the foolishness. Marcus ordered two tribunes to single out the men involved in that wasteful fiasco. It was outrageously unacceptable having edible or usable provisions destroyed.

Marcus reined in, surveying the destruction. Black smoke from the burning oil churned upward from the scene. The only prisoners were a handful of slaves and the women and camp-followers. Cassius's praetorium had partially collapsed, and Marcus's praetorian guards were posting themselves around it while searching for the war chest.

Marcus swung down from his horse, feeling confident. But just like at Forum Gallorum, the feeling didn't last long. Hoofbeats signaled the arrival of a breathless staff officer he vaguely recognized as one of Octavian's. Whipping his horse mercilessly up the steep grade, the man hung on like a scared cat as his animal jumped, clearing the remains of the wall.

"Triumvir Antonius! Brutus has broken into our camp, and we're without a general, sir. Caesar has disappeared!"

"Disappeared?"

"Yes, sir. We fear he's dead!"

Marcus's eyes widened at that. Was there any such luck?

Together, he and Octavian's man climbed up Cassius's ramparts overlooking their camps. Marcus expected a spectacular view of the entire battlefield. However, what greeted them was more confusion. Clearly, the Antonian legionaries were in control of the marsh fight. Marcus saw mule-carts hauling his injured men back to camp and some of the less wounded limping back on their own.

But it was the scene beyond, around Octavian's camp, that caused his jaw to drop in horror.

Instead of entering the marsh to aid Cassius, Brutus's troops had attacked Octavian's walls. Thousands of soldiers were churning up a cloud of dirt, marring the view of the triumviral encampment. Occasionally, legionaries on both sides could be seen running in and out of the confusion, resembling termites scrambling through burning timber.

Marcus stiffened and balled his fists, furious. Whirling about, he called to a centurion. "Go back to camp and organize a march on the double to relieve Octavian. Launch a counterattack on Brutus's men. I'll be there as soon as I can!" To another centurion standing below, he called, "I'll leave you three cohorts here to round up the enemy and find the war chest. Sound an assembly for the rest to form up. We're heading back down there!"

It took the rest of the day to ward off Brutus's sacking. Fortunately, legionaries left in the Antonian encampment had acted quickly, sending out reinforcements. Roughly eight thousand of Brutus's men fell. But Marcus was sickened, for by nightfall he learned that nearly double that number was lost in his and Octavian's combined army—most being from Octavian's camp.

Desperate for something positive to happen, Marcus grimly hoped it would be the discovery of Octavian's corpse.

Late the following afternoon, the weather changed. Weeks of dry, dusty conditions ended abruptly with heavy rains. Despite the mud, cries of wounded men, and lack of leadership in Octavian's camp, Marcus received astounding news.

One of the scouts who had ridden east toward the coast and Neopolis returned. He swept into Marcus's praetorium, full of excitement. "We intercepted a group of Cassius's soldiers fleeing toward the coast. Cassius is dead. His men have sailed to the island of Thassos with his body. It's expected Brutus will join them there to bury him."

Marcus rose from his desk, hardly believing his ears. "You're certain?"

The scout nodded. "They told us where some of Cassius's staff officers were, and we hunted them down. Apparently, he got false reports that Octavian had overrun Brutus's camp and the day was lost for them. Cassius had one of his slaves kill him."

Marcus sat down heavily, stunned at Fortuna's capricious turn. Stroking his full mourning beard thoughtfully, he was, for once, grateful for the confusion of war. Cassius dead and Octavian missing! Fortuna be praised!

After the rains, it turned cold. A heavy frost transformed Philippi's plain into fields of spun silver. Marcus stood in his usual place atop the tower, staring out over the ramparts, this time at Brutus's camp. When a wind whipped up, he drew his paludamentum around his shoulders tighter, warding off the frigid air.

Brutus's fort was alive like a hornets' nest. Hundreds of Cassius's men had joined his ranks. Sounds of hammering and sawing drifted across the plains. The conspirator was probably enlarging his defenses and digging in for a long siege. Within an hour, more of Brutus's scheme materialized when a scout reported a large contingent of legionaries leaving his camp to begin work on a new line of barricades, heading perpendicular to the marshes.

No, he certainly wasn't giving up.

It didn't bode well. Provisions taken from Cassius's camp wouldn't last long, and the triumvirs were short on grain. They'd be lucky if food stores lasted a week with all the mouths needing bread.

A sentry interrupted his thoughts. "Triumvir Antonius, you have a visitor."

Marcus shifted his gaze to Cassius's ruined camp, where the oil fires were still smoking after two days. "I have a tribunal this morning," he replied.

"Sir, it's Triumvir Octavian Caesar. He's returned."

Well, *piss* on Fortuna, then!

"He was in the marsh, sir," the soldier explained. "He's ill and says he hasn't eaten since he left camp."

And *why* did he leave camp? He was no better than a deserter.

Following the sentry back to the praetorium, Marcus whipped his tent flap back to find Eros standing solicitously over Caesar's heir. The young man rested in Marcus's chair, drinking warmed wine and wrapped in a clean woolen blanket.

Eros met Marcus's eyes cautiously.

Octavian heard him enter and set his wine aside, standing up stiffly to greet him. "Forgive my intrusion, Antonius. After I warm myself sufficiently, I'll return to my camp and direct repairs. But I wanted to come here first to hear what happened."

Marcus ignored his words. "Where in Jupiter's name have you been?" he demanded. "I hear your men even searched for you in the latrines!" From the corner of his eye, he saw Eros raise a hand to his mouth, coughing to disguise laughter. He didn't bother hiding his own smirk.

"The attack occurred so suddenly," Octavian parried. "I had no time to prepare. Brutus's army caught us all by surprise. And my physician insisted I was in no condition to fight."

Marcus cocked his eyebrow. "A surprise attack? Really? You're telling me sentries in your towers were deaf and blind to an army gathering outside their camp day before yesterday, kicking up a dust cloud as high as Mt. Vesuvius? Well, just so you're aware, your absence cost our army sixteen *thousand* lives—most of which were from *your* camp! I know you've hardly ever lifted a gladius, but I assume you're aware of what usually happens to legionaries if *they* desert?"

Marcus felt completely justified in berating the boy. He lifted his arms as Eros unlaced his cuirass. Granted, Octavian's face did look pale, but didn't it always? Dark shadows under his eyes alluded to lack of sleep. But more illness? Pah! His only malady was cowardice.

"I—I was persuaded to seek temporary shelter," he stammered.

"I had a prophetic dream warning me to leave camp." He swallowed hard, genuinely flustered and avoiding eye contact. "Hopefully, Venus will now see fit to restore my health so I can properly avenge Father."

"So where exactly did you go? Where were you hiding?"

Octavian raised his head finally, his eyes meeting Marcus's, those cold, blue chips of ice immoveable and full of loathing. "I wasn't *hiding*," he hissed, gripping both sides of the chair with white knuckles. "I took *refuge* in the marshes. Nobody would find me there. I'd be able to survive!"

In the marshes? Right. If only he'd run straight into Cassius's men. He would've shit himself!

"Well, while you were busy preserving your life in the mud," Marcus informed him, "I defeated Cassius. And because of some miscommunication, he committed suicide, thinking it was Brutus's camp in flames and not yours." Accepting wine from Eros, he raised his cup. "So here's to marshes and mistakes. When they turn out like this, I'll even toast sick, fainthearted heirs of Caesar!"

Grinning broadly, he lifted his cup in Octavian's direction and took a mouthful of wine.

Publius Canidius Crassus to Marcus Antonius, Triumvir:

I must report a serious setback.

We have lost two legions and a large number of supply ships under the command of Gnaeus Domitius Calvinus. Calvinus's flagship survived, but Brutus's admiral, Ahenobarbus, completely annihilated the rest, most of the men drowning in deep seas.

I risked patrolling parts of the beaches in enemy territory looking for anything that may have washed up, but there were no survivors or supplies found.

However, scouts have reported prisoners taken along beaches controlled by Brutus.

As always, I await your orders.

In the three weeks since Cassius's defeat and death, Marcus insisted he and Octavian follow Brutus's every move as he continued excavating. His earthworks and barricades moved gradually south, even passing Philippi's southern gates. Marcus kept his men in hot pursuit, pressuring his every effort by their mere presence. Octavian even forced himself out of his cot and spent half-days astride a horse. He suggested moving his camp below Marcus's to stay in line with Brutus. Marcus wholeheartedly approved, relieved to be rid of his bothersome presence.

Every day the triumvirs formed their men up in broad array, but Brutus's advantage was high ground, and he refused the bait. Unlike Cassius's walls, scouts assured Marcus that Brutus's battlements were well-built and problematic to approach.

Another problem was that, like Pompeius before him, Brutus owned the seas. He intercepted every grain-bearing ship Rome sent, further depleting triumviral food stores.

Marcus and Octavian swore their officers to silence about the recent losses of Calvinus and his supplies. It would be bad enough for morale if their own men heard of it. But it could be worse should Brutus's army learn they had any sort of advantage—which they did.

Marcus kept hoping Cleopatra's promised shipment of supplies would finally arrive. However, he heard nothing more from Egypt.

Things were becoming dire.

Four days earlier, legionaries had gulped down the last of the grain from Cassius's camp despite strict rationing. Soon everyone would be a lot thinner. The next step was choosing which pack animals to slaughter.

Marcus sat up late with Octavian and their quartermasters,

running down lists of stock in the highest supply. Orders were dispatched for cavalrymen to scavenge farmhouses west of Philippi and other villages farther afield for any meat or grain. But nobody harbored hopes of anything substantial showing up. Brutus and Cassius had stripped the area of nourishment before the triumviral army ever arrived. Locals were already facing deprivation and hardship.

Yet the only expected parts of war were the odd and *un*expected things that happened.

Eros awakened Marcus well before dawn just days later with astonishing news. "Dominus, Brutus is forming a line!"

Marcus hastened up the ramparts to see for himself.

Brutus's entire army stood on Philippi field, less than a half mile from camp. Looking farther into the distance, he smiled wryly, seeing a good number of townspeople from Philippi gathering in the seats of the theater to watch the show. Nodding at the audience, he exclaimed to Eros, "Well, let's not disappoint them. If it's drama they want, I'll give them a show they'll never forget!"

This was his opportunity to end the war—once and for all.

As Eros dressed him for battle, Marcus pondered aloud, "Why is he engaging? He has every reason to stall while we starve down here."

"Only the gods know," Eros murmured, securing a leather buckle that supported Marcus's gladius.

"Maybe it's his men," Marcus mused. "They might be demanding action, sick of being pent-up in that fort and knowing they lost the better of their two generals." Marcus had learned one lesson in the past decade with his experiences in civil war: Romans fighting Romans was costly, bloody, and stress-provoking.

As he watched his lines form up, remorse touched him briefly. In a matter of moments, cousins would slay one another, brothers would face-off, and many would never return home. To be sure, it was troubling. Yet, this was where Marcus Antonius felt most at ease—on the battlefield. Today he would end this. Today would be *his.*

Brutus attacked first.

Marcus and the triumviral army held their ground under a forceful, unforgiving assault. Front lines fluctuated on both sides, buckling and then recovering. Just like at Pharsalus, tight fighting turned into pushing, shoving, and stabbing matches. Infantrymen morphed into boxers, using shields to smash faces and skulls. Mingled with sweat were smells of steaming feces from the disemboweled. Blood sprayed from man to man in the lines due to the unimaginably tight space. For the first grueling hours, nobody knew the outcome.

During some of the worst, concentrated fighting, Marcus rode halfway up a rise to observe the field. Somebody would tire, and he didn't want it to be his men—especially with fresh cavalry yet unused.

As he watched, an idea formed.

In a ruse, he sent his cavalry out, making it look as though their intent was to outflank the enemy's left wing. Marcus was well-known for using cavalry in this manner, and as he'd hoped, Brutus and his generals recognized the classic Antonian maneuver and reacted immediately. Brutus turned his left wing to counter the horsemen.

Perfect!

Marcus wasted no time, calling for a tubicin to sound off, recalling his horse. Instantly, the cavalry turned tail, charging back while he sent his infantry hard into Brutus's middle, embedding themselves deeply and infiltrating the line's center.

Never one to sit on the sidelines, he chose that moment to charge in himself, whipping his horse toward the legionaries bearing the brunt of Brutus's holdouts.

"Forward, *now*! Don't stop! Break them!" His voice was gravelly from yelling, lost in the pounding of leather-embossed wood striking helmets and ear-splitting screams of pain and rage all around him.

Thankfully, the deception worked. His own men now surrounded him as Brutus's center caved. Most of the enemy turned tail, running.

Marcus rode on, leading a surging pursuit, when his horse suddenly dropped hard from under him. Completely unexpected, the sharp jolt passed clear through his saddle. A shattered pilum, buried as a trap in Brutus's territory, had impaled and gutted the animal. It fell sideways, kicking and twisting in a mass of blood and intestines.

Head over heels, Marcus tumbled and scrambled back up, hauling his leg free of the beast's weight. Smeared with horse blood and offal, he was relieved to find himself virtually unscathed.

His infantry was streaming by, most of them looking his way in concern or curiosity at his misfortune. Still in shock to find himself unhorsed, he blinked—heart hammering in his throat. Gods, he hoped his fall wouldn't sap his men's spirits or cause their superstitious natures to conjure dismal portents. Spitting blood on the ground from a broken lip, he motioned them forward with his arm, roaring, "Stop staring! Move your asses on to win this war!"

Several men saluted him at that, following their centurions, who bellowed similar orders.

Before him, his poor horse was suffering. It thrashed in agony with noisy squeals and snorts. Kneeling down, he held the animal's neck gently but firmly with his left hand, trying to calm it. With his right, he deftly slid his gladius over its throat to end the torture.

Tuccius cantered up. "You all right?" The man was ever at his elbow these days. He was a good soldier and had proven his worth these past months.

"I'm fine, but I need a horse!"

Moments later, Marcus was riding again, though Tuccius had terrible taste in mounts. His horse was inferior to a drover's mule.

When starving men fought, their intensity scorched like fire because, when men were hungry, there were no barriers powerful enough to keep them at bay.

Marcus sent orders for Octavian to secure their camps against skirmishers while he hunted Brutus down. As he galloped by to catch up with his men, legionaries cheered and waved. After several miles, he called for another fresh horse and continued on with his cavalry in the direction of the fleeing army, followed by slower-moving infantry.

By sunset, they came up empty and claimed a ridge near surrounding forests, ensnaring a perimeter of land where reports had pinpointed Brutus's whereabouts. Plenty of his injured were captured en route, and the fallen littered a well-trampled path. Mysteriously, Brutus hadn't run east, but had instead doubled back, as though intending to return to his original camp.

Back at Marcus's side on another horse, Tuccius asked, "The men want to know if we can risk fires?"

Marcus sighed wearily. "No. Tell them to sleep together and keep their swords drawn. I'll join the watches myself. We want our exact location kept quiet, for we don't know exactly what numbers Brutus still has."

That night Marcus sat among his infantrymen, who had trailed in after the cavalry. He listened and laughed at their bawdy stories, telling a few of his own. Air up here in the hill country was crisp and cold. Everyone shared cloaks while sitting under the inky sky, lustily voicing desires for warm women.

Early in the predawn darkness, scouts rode into the makeshift camp. "Antonius, sir! We have Brutus!"

Though half-asleep, the words brought Marcus upright. He rose stiffly from sitting against Tuccius's back for support. As the men watched, he threaded his way through the crowd of soldiers. They all stepped aside, revealing two battle-weary men straddling horses with their hands tightly bound. One wore a magnificent breastplate bearing Brutus's crest of Pegasus with outstretched wings. A bloody wound on his leg was draining, and his helmet kept his face shadowed in the darkness. The second man wore no helmet and was easier to discern. Scant chestnut hair hung limply over a homely, pockmarked face. Wounded as well, his forearm bore a messy gash.

"Marcus Junius Brutus?" Striding forward, Marcus addressed the first man uncertainly, cocking his head, hoping to recognize something familiar. When he received no immediate response, he barked at a cavalryman riding next to the captive, "Untie them."

Reaching over with a pugio, the cavalryman sliced through the ropes around first one and then the other prisoner's wrists. Slowly, the first stranger reached up, removing his helmet. He was not Brutus, but a much younger man with a frank and courageous face. He nodded silently at Marcus in solemn acknowledgement, causing a noisy stir among the Antonians.

Tuccius immediately piped up with the obvious, "That's not Brutus!"

The rest of the men grumbled reproachfully, one cavalryman butting Brutus's imposter hard in the gut with the end of his javelin, doubling him over in the saddle, gasping. The second prisoner grimaced, wincing when someone smacked his jaw with a sharp stone, drawing more blood.

"He's a liar, he is!" accused another cavalryman. "He should die for his treachery!"

Many men began to nod and shout in agreement.

No, Marcus wasn't having this. Enough blood had been spilled. He lifted his hand in warning for the others to be silent. "Silence! All of you!" And to the prisoners, he changed his tone, becoming gentler. "Who are you?"

"Triumvir Antonius, sir—I'm Lucilius, one of Brutus's staff officers," the pretender answered above a few muttered curses. Drawing himself up courageously, he shouted over them loudly, "And wouldn't any of you do the same for your general so he could escape if the Fates damned you?"

Marcus smiled, impressed. "I certainly hope they would," he replied.

"And this is Quintus Dellius," Lucilius introduced the pock-marked man.

Dellius spoke up self-importantly, "I was a diplomat for Gaius Cassius. I only recently joined Brutus's camp."

"Where's Brutus?" Marcus demanded, ignoring Dellius. "How many legions are with him?"

"We left him northeast of here, probably ten miles back," Lucilius answered. "He still has four legions."

Marcus stroked his beard thoughtfully. "Hmmm—four *undermanned* legions, right?"

Lucilius shook his head assuredly. "You won't take him alive."

Marcus breathed in deeply. After Cassius's suicide, he rather doubted it. "Well then, you've saved me the awkwardness of facing him in defeat. I recognize honor when I see it."

Quintus Dellius settled somewhat at Marcus's words. "Will you spare our lives for our courage, then, Triumvir? I hear you're a fairer man than that young upstart calling himself Caesar. We're both officers. Can't you find a use for us?"

"They can dig our latrines to shit in!" one infantryman called in the darkness, and everyone laughed except Lucilius and Dellius.

Marcus stepped toward them, shaking his head. "Dismount," he ordered. That Dellius had big balls—or at least he *thought* he did.

Two legionaries scurried forward, holding the heads of the horses as Brutus's men slid down.

"Come here, both of you," Marcus said.

Dellius wasted no time. Marcus embraced him in a hug worthy of friendship. Releasing him, he kissed him on each cheek. "You came to me an enemy. Stay as my friend and join my staff."

Swallowing hard, Lucilius also limped forward—painfully, due to his wound—and received the same merciful treatment. "What of Brutus?" he asked.

"If he allowed you to act as his decoy, he knows his life is forfeit. He was just buying time for the inevitable. You could've lost your lives, but I offer them back to you now if you join me."

Gesturing at Dellius and Lucilius, Marcus spoke loud enough

for the others to hear, "These men are tired and need food. And their wounds need tending. Who will treat them courteously? They're my friends now. Will they be yours?"

At that, several legionaries shuffled forward, offering Lucilius and Dellius what comforts they had: watered posca and bits of dried fruit. Another man cut off the hem of his tunic, offering to bandage Lucilius's leg.

As the morning wore on, several cohorts of infantry arrived in the company of Canidius, who had just led his units in from the coast. Then, a little later in the day, scouts discovered Brutus's body, slain by his own hand. Not yet stiff, he had probably still been alive when Lucilius and Dellius joined Marcus.

Silence descended as the killer of both Caesar and Gaius Antonius arrived at their makeshift camp, draped across the back of a cavalry horse. Two legionaries lifted it, laying it out for Marcus to see.

Without a word, he bent one knee to close Brutus's half-open eyes. The unsmiling mouth remained somber in the humorless expression the conspirator always wore. Marcus considered him. He'd been a stoic, an idealist, and probably the only one of the conspirators really acting on personal convictions. All the others, including Cassius, just coveted power.

Truly, if he were a lesser man, he'd hack off Brutus's head right now and treat him the same as Gaius. But Gaius had said in his letter that Brutus had treated him well. Right here and now was a rare opportunity to show character on the field, and Gaius would have encouraged him in that. Today Marcus Antonius was victorious. He would show his fallen enemy respect.

He arose, unlatching fibulae on each of his shoulders that clasped his long, heavy paludamentum to his cuirass. For several moments, he stood, holding his cloak and gazing down at the man who had murdered his cousin and ordered his brother's death. When he chose his words, he spoke loudly, as he had at Caesar's funeral, willing that every man present should hear. "Now your shade must make peace with Caesar," he cried.

With a swift motion, he unfurled his paludamentum, draping it over Brutus's body. Then he turned his back and walked away.

The steadily growing crowd of cavalry and legionaries stepped back, making way for their general. Someone began a rhythmic thudding on a shield, leading the rest of the army to join in, as a chant of triumph sounded that Marcus had always dreamt of hearing:

"Imperator! Imperator! Imperator!"

It was the highest acclamation of praise a Roman could receive. It had been Pompeius's title and then Caesar's.

Now it was his.

Canidius and Tuccius both saluted him smartly as the chorus swelled. Stopping before them, he turned slowly, tapping his heart in appreciation and nodding in acknowledgement.

Then Canidius led out a tall, splendid bay horse. Calling loudly above the accolades, he announced, "Antonius, some cavalrymen discovered this fellow among Brutus's fallen staff officers yesterday. He has quite a story. He once belonged to Dolabella. One of Cassius's officers claimed he lost it to one of Brutus's men while gambling. With that history, such a magnificent horse should go to Philippi's champion."

Marcus grinned. The animal really was handsome; a dark bay similar to the beloved horse his friend Eumenius had given him years ago, that had been lost at Alesia. "Gratias! I need a new horse!" he exclaimed, circling the animal appraisingly. The men had already saddled it with Marcus's own livery.

He sprang up, swinging on amid cheers.

"Back to camp?" Canidius asked.

Marcus nodded in reply.

The chorus continued, men still banging shields with gladii, cavalrymen thumping their breastplates in a noisy, repetitious salute, falling in behind him as he spurred his new horse into a canter.

"Imperator, Imperator, Imperator!"

Marcus Antonius rode upon the very moment of this glory.

This was a time for which he'd longed and for which he'd trained—for which he'd been afraid would never come. At long last, he claimed a major victory—achieving glory and prestige for the domus Antonii. This was for his father, for Lentulus, and for Gaius.

Ever since Marcus had seen the crowd of people gathering in Philippi's theater two days past, watching the battle play itself out, he had been drawn there for reasons he couldn't explain.

Today he came alone—except for his praetorians—riding his new bay through throngs of people. Some wanted to greet him, kiss his dusty military boots, and praise him for ending the war. Others looked afraid. Even worse were the gaunt, starving farm families whose food stores had been commandeered by either his men or the conspirators'. At Philippi's gates, magistrates welcomed him formally, thanking him for sparing their city from pillage.

Shortly afterward, he processed through the town, but Marcus ordered the entourage to stop in front of the theater. While everyone else waited, he entered alone, climbing the radial-shaped stairs to the top of the upper diazoma, the highest section. Here he had a lofty view of the battlefield. Rugged countryside surrounded Philippi proper—city of Philip of Macedon, father of Alexander the Great.

His eyes swept the city center, taking in its arched gates and the agora. Now commerce could begin again. The Via Egnatia had reopened to trade. From here to Neapolis on the Aegean coast, all territory now lay in the hands of the triumvirs.

Marcus intended on gifting Philippi ample coin for reparations from the war, as well as some of the grain stores he'd captured from Brutus. People here were desperate—especially for food. Then Canidius had mentioned that the aqueduct in Neapolis needed work. He'd fund that too. Let the people know that Imperator Antonius was generous. Where Brutus and Cassius had strained every coin from the poorest villages, he would be lenient and give as much as possible to counter the recent burden of war.

Indeed, from Marcus's eagle's nest view, atrocities from the battle were visible. Between the theater and evening's crimson-splashed sunset, he beheld the heartrending tragedy of triumph. Legionary cremations were still taking place on a large parcel of farmland beyond the marshes. Already an enormous mound had risen where thousands of Roman soldiers would be entombed for posterity in an earthen tumulus that might rival the height of Philippi's acropolis.

Marcus's nightmares of late resonated with the din of iron on iron, the strength and courage it had taken to beat back Brutus's army, and how sharp was the blade of civil war. That last reality haunted his heart more than any other.

After facing-off on the field and hacking one another to pieces, these same dead men from both sides were now being sent to Elysium together as brothers. Many a mother, father, sister, and son would grieve as word trickled into Rome of how more of her bravest men had died—again in a war *between* Romans.

Marcus's eyes were drawn to the flaming funerary pyres. It was as though he could see the very spirits of his men and Brutus's rising toward the skies. Was it physical fatigue or the enormity of emotion he'd carried these past several days? Or were his eyes really seeing smoke billow into forms and faces of Romans rising into the encroaching night.

There! For the briefest moment—a plumed helmet—a hand reaching out. And was that an eagle rising like a phoenix through the sparks?

He blinked his wet eyes, full of guilt as he watched their spirits ascend.

Because of this, he felt he owed it to his men, his family, and every pleb in Rome to *try* to work with Octavian. But how? They held nothing but contempt for one another. The triumvirate of Caesar, Crassus, and Pompeius had worked, but only for a time and under different circumstances.

And Marcus was different from all of those men—especially Caesar.

Marcus Antonius didn't possess a calm, collected demeanor, but passion. Nor did he have his late cousin's patience. His gifts were energy and charisma. And two days ago, his talent on the battlefield had been put to the test and proven. Caesar should have seen this. He should have seen proof that Marcus belonged on the field, not in the Senate. The childhood dream he once had of being the world's greatest soldier had come true.

But how would it be used now?

Why not let it be dedicated solely to the East? Marcus could be the one to invest in making it politically sound again. Yes! He could revive Caesar's battle cry against the Parthian Empire to regain Crassus's lost eagles. *He* could be the one to lead that campaign to victory. And what of the unrest in these eastern provinces that had challenged the Senate and many a proconsul's patience? He could unify them and perhaps create client kingdoms to follow his lead—that of a Roman—to instigate peace. Such a new work could kindle something unheard of in Rome's history—a unity of East and West, forging an empire similar to what Alexander the Great had envisioned.

These achievements could be accomplished in the East—*without* Octavian or even Lepidus at his side. Marcus Antonius would claim the East and find his way.

As the sun sank beyond view, its shining light replaced by that of burning corpses, it was difficult to see past the mountain of death that civil war had wrought. Marcus turned away from the grim glow on the horizon.

No, he had no wish for godhead—not like Caesar or Octavian.

Instead, Marcus Antonius Imperator would become a legend.

AUTHOR'S NOTES

I ALWAYS FEEL COMPELLED TO GIVE THANKS TO THE MANY people who stood behind me as this book was born. First on my list is a woman I never had the joy of actually meeting face-to-face, though we became one another's proofreaders in the early stages of my work. Sadly, Mary Dove passed away before she ever got to see her own book published, much less mine. Mary, this one's for *you*!

I have a bevy of fabulous readers who have already given this pony a ride: Sarah, Mercedes, Marian, Troy, Elizabeth, and Sharon. Thank you so much.

For the many edits, patience, ideas, and willingness to reread whatever I send her, a hearty "thanks" to my editor-extraordinaire, Jenny Q. It's an honor to use your eyes! Jenny's gifts exceed the grammatical, and I owe her and Historical Editorial a great deal for the consistent excellence in cover design as well.

Cathy Helms of Avalon Graphics and Tamian Woods of Beyond Design International are two exceedingly talented graphic designers who have tackled my mapmaking with gusto. And I simply couldn't get the job done without Roseanna White's knack for elegant detail in formatting. Ladies, your gifts are appreciated.

Lastly, there are several people who have guided me and inspired me through Italy, Greece, and beyond to introduce me to Marcus's world and offer me hope while journeying through the mires of authorship. For her expertise in Rome, *grazie* to Silvia Prosperi and her company, A Friend in Rome. Silvia has always been there to help and gave me some real guidance and mapping of where the Cloaca Maxima's access was near the Basilica Aemilia. My gentle guide, Ioanni Kiourtsoglou escorted me through Philippi's ancient city and battlefield, as well as his home town of Kavala (ancient Neopolis). Thank you for giving me the inspiration for *Second in Command*'s final pages and for informing me about the possible mass grave containing soldiers from the battle. Standing atop that theater, looking out over the battlefield where my characters fought, starved, and won is a life experience I'll *never* forget!

NYT bestselling author Margaret George continues to be an encouragement and has taken such a mentoring role in the overall backing and interest in my work. Her sound suggestions, proactive support, sense of humor, and heart for Antony's story continue to motivate me.

Second in Command was a much different book to write than *Son of Rome*. For the reader, I expect it'll have a much different feel. Probably the main factor is that there's a lot more information on Antony's life from ancient sources during this period and throughout the rest of his life.

We know that he went to Gaul around the time of Caesar's second Britannia invasion. It isn't known whether or not he actually accompanied Caesar. However, had he done so it would certainly have been as an untried officer. Trebonius was there and had an active role, as he's mentioned more than several times in Caesar's written account. Since Antony and Trebonius did form a friendship and occupied a tent together in Gaul, I thought it would be appropriate to include him in Britannia. The battle where the Tribune Durus is killed actually occurred, as did the skirmish in the woods with Trebonius and his men. Caesar speaks in fascinating detail regarding the Britannia invasion, and you may read about it and the Gallic conquest further in his *Gallic Wars.*

Publius Clodius was indeed just as divisive as he's portrayed. The scene in the Forum Romanum where Antony chases him, sword in hand, actually occurred, along with the scandal regarding Fulvia, and Antony's spontaneous ruse about his becoming Cicero's "noble and gallant friend." Marc Antony learned from both Clodius and Curio exactly how to incite a mob, and I might add, he learned from the *masters.*

When Caesar was declared an enemy of the state, accounts record how Antony and his company snuck out of Rome in a cart, dressed as slaves. Despite it being the "official story" from ancient sources, I had problems believing it. Pompeius would surely have had every point of entry/exit under surveillance. As shrewd as Marc Antony could be, I wondered if he may have escaped a different way. My late friend Mary Dove suggested an escape through the sewers, much like Victor Hugo used in the famous scene with Jean Valjean and Marius in *Les Misérables.* I loved the idea and have used it in this story. To me, it makes perfect sense. Besides, I can just imagine Antony pulling off something like that!

Stefan G. Chrissanthos wrote a scholarly article suggesting that the mutiny of 47 BC was far more serious than ancient writers reported. It appeared in *The Journal of Roman Studies* and was entitled: *Caesar and the Mutiny of 47 BC.* Caesar was rarely negligent; however, in this scenario, I found no evidence of him giving Antony any financial support either before or during the crisis. Antony has always been harshly criticized by scholars for his lack of control over the Campanian legions in this uprising. I suppose we'll never know for certain, but I tried to grant him a little exoneration here.

The passing of time in general and the calendar year in the 1st century BC is challenging to relate to a reader when writing a novel set in these ancient times. In Antony's day, the calendar was so terribly flawed that seasonal weather didn't even reflect the designated time of year in which it should have been taking place.

Though Julius Caesar is certainly a controversial figure in history, he was also a Renaissance man. While in Egypt with Cleopatra, she introduced him to the Egyptian calendar, and prior to his assassination, he made it the official calendar of Rome. In fact, the Gregorian calendar we use today was based upon Caesar's model.

In the aftermath of Caesar's assassination, there was certainly chaos in Rome. However, Antony did a phenomenal job of holding the city's peace together, contrary to what some recent television series have portrayed. He worked tirelessly and must have gotten very little sleep during that time, and he received little or no reward for it! It is difficult to ascertain the accuracy of Appian of Alexandria's account of Antony's oration at Caesar's funeral. However, I used his account and paraphrased it, trying to lend to it as much accuracy as possible.

Little Antyllus really was used as a hostage in those uncertain days, although we don't know exactly how long he was kept at Jupiter's Temple or who (if anyone) accompanied him. What I decided to omit, due to the enormous cast of characters (all with confusing names), was that Lepidus's son was also used as a hostage at the same time. I have done my best to keep the rest of the Ides' aftermath as historically exact as possible.

The time frame my story enters toward the end of this book is known as the "Imperatorial Period," when imperators (great generals) like Caesar and Antony were ruling—more so than the broken Senate.

Rome didn't have any sort of "police force" for public safety until the Augustan Age. Shortly after Caesar's death, there was such concern for personal safety that both Antony and Octavian recruited personal bodyguards in mass quantities. Somewhere and somehow during that time, the term "praetorian" began to stick—undoubtedly because these select men guarded their generals' praetoriums. The *Oxford Classical Dictionary* indicates that Augustus was using multiple cohorts of praetorians by 27 BC, and that the term "praetorian" was utilized by that time. As Rome entered the Imperial Age, praetorian guards were always the ones involved in the protection of the emperor. And as was the case of Claudius and Caligula (and others), they were the literal *making* and *breaking* of emperors too.

It is difficult for us today, with modern political correctness conflicting with Judeo-Christian values, to truly understand the psyche of a typical ancient Roman. There simply was no sanctity of life in their culture. Men of high standing didn't much bother with concealing extra-marital affairs. It wasn't until the Augustan Age that an attempt was made to make adultery a heinous offense, and that mindset just never "took" in Roman society. Romans did have their own virtues. They included honor, influence, dignity, and political/martial power. These were the mainstays of their way of thinking.

Many people today simply proclaim Julius Caesar to have been genocidal in his conquest of Gaul. Indeed, an excellent case could be made for just that. On the other hand, one must also consider the ruthlessness it took for Vercingetorix to send the hapless Mandubii into the "no-man's zone" to die. Antony, Octavian, and Lepidus used the notoriously violent method of proscription—the condemning of men for money—to advance their agenda and take full control of the Senate. Ruthless? Cruel? In some cases, horrific? Absolutely.

But for them, *in their day*, it worked.

Patricia Southern's excellent biography on Antony explains that men of his generation never got to see the Roman Republic work properly. I think her case is extremely insightful of the troubled and sometimes ferocious methods by which law and order was executed during the final years of Rome's Republic. I might add that such cold-bloodedness would continue into the Imperial age as well. In studying the ancient world's rulers for this trilogy, I've determined that to survive back then, you *had* to be ruthless.

Now that two of my books in the trilogy are complete, that only leaves one more. And for most readers, I know they're looking forward to reading about one of history's greatest love stories—one that has influenced Shakespeare, film, and television.

Make no mistake, that story will be there, in its entirety, but in my best efforts, it will be honestly written and delivered.

Read on!

ALSO BY BROOK ALLEN

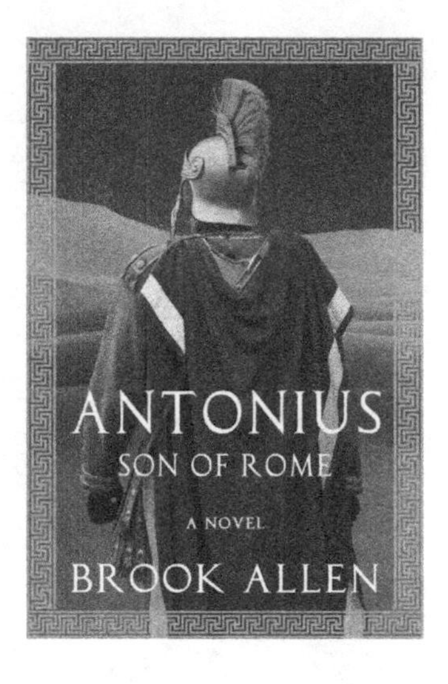

Antonius: Son of Rome

After young Marcus Antonius's father dies in disgrace, he yearns to restore his family's honor during the final days of Rome's dying Republic. Marcus is rugged, handsome, and owns abundant military talent, but upon entering manhood, he falls prey to the excesses of a violent society. His whoring, gambling, and drinking eventually reap dire consequences. Through a series of personal tragedies, Marcus must come into his own through blood, blades, and death. Once he finally earns a military commission, he faces an uphill battle to earn the respect and admiration of soldiers, proconsuls, and kings. Desperate to redeem his name and carve a legacy for himself, he refuses to let warring rebels, scheming politicians, or even an alluring young Egyptian princess stand in his way.

CPSIA information can be obtained
at www.ICGtesting.com
Printed in the USA
LVHW091208090520
655280LV00001B/11